jor 4/15/04
JP

NORA ROBERTS

"Keep your world, Kadra, Demon Slayer. Or come with me."
He beckoned with a voice seductive as a caress. "I will give
you the Demon Kiss. I will make you my queen and plant my
young inside you. We will rule this new world together."

"You want to kiss me? To join with me?"

"We are well matched. Together we will have power beyond all imagining."

"Come, then." She all but purred it. "Come embrace me."

P9-BZG-771

Titles in the Once Upon series

ONCE UPON A KISS
ONCE UPON A ROSE
ONCE UPON A DREAM
ONCE UPON A STAR
ONCE UPON A CASTLE

Once Upon A Kiss

NORA ROBERTS
JILL GREGORY
RUTH RYAN LANGAN
MARIANNE WILLMAN

JOVE BOOKS, NEW YORK

This is a work of fiction. Names, characters, places, and incidents either are the product of the authors' imagination or are used fictitiously, and any resemblance to actual persons, living or dead, business establishments, events, or locales is entirely coincidental.

ONCE UPON A KISS

A Jove Book / published by arrangement with the authors

PRINTING HISTORY
Jove edition / October 2002

Collection copyright © 2002 by Penguin Putnam Inc.
"A World Apart" copyright © 2002 by Nora Roberts
"Impossible" copyright © 2002 by Jan Greenberg
"Sealed with a Kiss" copyright © 2002 by Ruth Ryan Langan
"Kiss Me, Kate" copyright © 2002 by Marianne Willman
Cover art and design by Tony Greco and Associates

All rights reserved.
This book, or parts thereof, may not be reproduced in any form without permission. For information address: The Berkley Publishing Group, a division of Penguin Putnam Inc.,
375 Hudson Street, New York, New York 10014.

Visit our website at
www.penguinputnam.com

ISBN: 0-515-13386-8

A JOVE BOOK®
Jove Books are published by The Berkley Publishing Group,
a division of Penguin Putnam Inc.,
375 Hudson Street, New York, New York 10014.
JOVE and the "J" design
are trademarks belonging to Penguin Putnam Inc.

PRINTED IN THE UNITED STATES OF AMERICA

10 9 8 7 6 5 4 3 2 1

CONTENTS

A WORLD APART   1
  Nora Roberts

IMPOSSIBLE   95
  Jill Gregory

SEALED WITH A KISS   207
  Ruth Ryan Langan

KISS ME, KATE   275
  Marianne Willman

A WORLD APART

Nora Roberts

1

IN THE SWELTERING jungle, under the blood-red sun, Kadra hunted. Her steps were silent, her eyes—green as the trio of stones that encrusted the hilt of her sword—were alert, watchful, merciless.

For four days and four nights she had tracked her prey, over the Stone Mountains, beyond the Singing River, and into the verdant heat of the Land of Tulle.

What she stalked rarely ventured to these borders, and she herself had never traveled so far in the south of A'Dair.

There were villages here, small enclaves of lesser hunters, settlements of farmers and weavers with their young and their animals. The young were as much food to what she hunted as the cattle and mounts were.

She trod on the mad red flowers that were strewn on the path, ignored the sly silver slide of a snake down the trunk of a tree. She saw, sensed, scented both, but they were of no interest to her.

The Bok demons were her only interest now, and destroying them her only goal.

It was what she had been born for.

Other scents came to her—the beasts, large and small, that inhabited the jungle, and the thick, wet fragrance of vine and blossom. The blood—no longer fresh—of one that had been caught and consumed by what she hunted.

She passed a great fall of water that raged over the cliffs to pound its drumbeat into the river below. Though she had never walked upon this ground, this she knew by its light and music as a sacred place. One that no demon could enter. So she stopped to drink of its purifying waters, to fill her water bag for the journey yet to come.

And poured drops from her hand to the ground in thanks to the powers of life.

Beyond the falls, the busier scents of people—sweat, flesh, cooking, springwater from a village well—reached her keen senses.

It was her duty to protect them, and her fate that none among them could ever be her companion, her friend, her lifemate. These were truths she had never questioned.

At last she caught the overripe stench that was Bok.

The sword streaked out of its sheath, a bright battle sound as she pivoted on the heels of her soft leather boots. The dagger, its point a diamond in the sun, flipped from its wrist mount to her hand.

The dark blue claws of the Bok that had leaped from a branch overhead whizzed past her face, missing their mark. She set into a fighting stance and waited for his next charge.

It looked oddly normal. Other than those lethal retractable claws, the scent, the needle-sharp fangs that snapped out when the lips were peeled back for battle, the Bok looked no different from the people they devoured at every opportunity.

This one was small for his species, no more than six feet, which put him on a level with her. He was naked but for the thin skin of his traveling armor. Except for claws and teeth, he was unarmed. The vicious gouges across his chest and arms were stained from his pale green blood. And told her he had run afoul of his companions and had been forced out of the pack.

A distraction for her, she imagined, and didn't intend to spend much time dispatching him.

"They sacrificed you," she said as she circled. "What was your crime?"

He only hissed, flicking his long tongue through those sharp teeth. She taunted him with a happy grin, muscles ready. Above all else, she lived for combat.

When he leaped, she spun her sword up, down, and severed his head with one smooth stroke. Though the ease of the job was a bit of a disappointment, she grunted in satisfaction as the green blood sizzled and smoked. And the body of the Bok melted away to nothing but an ugly smear on the ground.

"Not much of a challenge," she muttered and sheathed her sword. "Still, the day is young, so there is hope for better."

Her hand was still on the hilt when she heard the scream.

She ran, her dark hair flying behind her, the band of her rank that encircled her head glinting like vengeance. When she burst into the small clearing with its tidy line of huts, she saw that the single Bok had been but a brief distraction, delaying her just long enough.

Bodies of animals and a few men who had tried to defend their homes lay torn and bleeding on the ground. Others were running in panic, some holding their young clutched to them as they scattered. And she knew they would be hunted down and rent to pieces if a single demon escaped her duty.

Sorrow for the dead and the thrill of upcoming battle warred inside her.

Three of the Bok were crouched in the dirt, still feeding. Their eyes glowed red, their vicious teeth snapped as she charged. They sprang, mad enough with blood to choose fight over flight.

She cleaved the arm from one, leaped into a flying kick to knock another out of her way as she plunged her ready dagger into the heart of the third.

"I am Kadra," she shouted, "Slayer of Demons. Guardian of the red sun."

"You are too late," the remaining Bok hissed at her.

"You are outnumbered. Our king will tear out your heart, and we will share in the feast."

"Today you go hungry."

He was faster than the others, and fueled by his grisly meal. This, she knew, would be an opponent more worthy of her skill.

He chose not his claws but the long hooked blade he drew from the sheath at his side.

Steel rang to steel as the screams and the stench rose around her. She knew there were at least three others and she knew now that the demon king, the one called Sorak, was among them.

His death was her life's work.

The Bok fought well with his sickle sword, and swiped out with those blue claws. She felt the pain, an absent annoyance, as they dug furrows over her bare shoulder. Instead of retreating, she pushed into the attack, into the flashing blue and silver to run him through with a fierce thrust.

"I am Kadra," she murmured as the Bok smoked to the ground. "I am your death."

She wheeled to aim her weapon and her gaze on the demon king and the three warriors that flanked him outside the open doorway of a hut.

At last, she thought. Praise the powers of life, at last.

"I am your death, Sorak," she said. "As I was death for Clud, your father. On this day, in this hour, I will rid my world of you."

"Keep your world." The king of demons, regal in his red tunic and bands of gold, lifted a small, clear globe. "I go to another. There I will conquer and feed. There I will rule."

His handsome face was sheened with sweat and blood. His dark hair coiled, sleek and twisted, like snakes over his elegant shoulders. Then he bared his teeth, and the illusion of rough beauty vanished into horror.

"Where I go, the food is plentiful. There, I will be a god. Keep your world, Kadra, Demon Slayer. Or come with me." He beckoned with a voice seductive as a caress. "I will give you the Demon Kiss. I will make you my queen and plant my young inside you. We will rule this new world together."

"You want to kiss me? To join with me?"

"You have shed the blood of my sire. I have drunk the blood of a slayer. We are well matched. Together we will have power beyond all imagining."

His three warriors were armed. And a demon king's strength knew no equal among his kind. Four against one, Kadra thought with a leap of her heart. It would be her greatest battle.

"Come, then." She all but purred it. "Come embrace me."

She pursed her own lips, then charged.

To her shock, the demon swirled his cloak, and with his warriors, vanished in a sudden flash of light.

"Where . . . how?" She spun in a circle, sword raised, dagger ready, and her blood still singing a war song. She could smell them, a lingering stench. It was all that was left of them.

Women were weeping. Children wailing. And she had failed. Three Bok, and their hellborn king, had escaped her. Their eyes had met, and yet Sorak had defeated her without landing a blow.

"You have not lost them yet."

Kadra looked toward the hut where a woman stood in the doorway. She was pale and beautiful, her hair a midnight rain, her face like something carved from delicate glass. But her eyes, green as Kadra's own, were ancient, and in them it seemed worlds could live.

In them, Kadra saw pain.

"Lady," she said respectfully as she stepped toward her. "You are injured."

"I will heal. I know my fate, and it is not time for me to pass."

"Call the healer," Kadra told her. "I must hunt."

"Yes, you must hunt. Come inside, I will show you how."

Now Kadra's eyebrows raised. The woman was beautiful, true, and there was an air of magic about her. But she was still only a female.

"I'm a demon slayer. Hunting is what I know."

"In this world," the woman agreed. "But not in the one where you must go. The demon king has stolen one of the keys. But there are others."

She swayed, and Kadra leaped forward, cursing, to catch her. Frail bones, she thought. Such delicate bones would shatter easily.

"Why did they let you live?" Kadra demanded as she helped the woman inside.

"It is not in their power to destroy me. To harm, but not to vanquish. I did not know they were coming." She shook her head as she lowered herself into a chair by a hearth left cold in the heat of day. "My own complacency blinded me to them. But not to you." She smiled then, and those eyes were brilliant. "Not to you, Kadra, Slayer of Demons. I've waited for you."

"Why?"

"You call me lady, and once I was. Once I was a young girl of rank who took a brave warrior into her heart, and gave him her body in love. He was killed in the Battle of the Singing River.

"It was a great battle against the Bok and the demon tribes who joined them." Impressed, Kadra tilted her head. She had been weaned on battle stories, and this was the greatest of all. "Many were destroyed on all sides. Many brave warriors perished, as did three slayers. The numbers of Bok were halved, but still Clud escaped and since increased those numbers again to plague our world.

"I watched the battle in my fire, and in the moment my love was struck down, in that moment of grief, I bore a girl child. She who was born to take up a sword as her father had done. She who would be more than those who made her. You are she. You are my blood and flesh and bone. I am she who bore you. I am your mother."

Kadra retreated one step. Where there had been pity was now anger. "I have no mother."

"You know I speak true. You have vision enough to see."

She felt the truth like a burn in the heart, but wanted only to deny it. "Humans who are not slayers keep their young. They tend and guard and protect them even at the risk of death."

"So it should be." The woman's voice thickened with regret. "I could not keep you with me. My duty was here, holding the keys, and yours was your training. I could not give you a mother's comfort, a mother's care, or a father's pride. Parting with you was another death for me."

"I need no mother," Kadra said flatly. "Nor father. I am a slayer."

"Yes. This is your fate, and even I could not turn your life's wheel away from it. As I cannot turn it now from where you must go, from what you must do."

"I must hunt."

"And you will. Our world and another are at stake. I could not keep you then," she stated. "I cannot keep you now. Though I have never let you go."

Kadra shook her head. She was accustomed to physical pain, but not to this hurt inside the heart. "The one who bore me was a warrior, as I am. She died at demon claws when I was but a child."

"Your foster mother. A good and brave warrior. At her side you learned what you needed to learn. When she was taken from you, you learned more. Now, you will learn the rest. I am Rhee."

"Rhee." Kadra, fearless in battle, went pale. "Rhee is a legend, a sorceress of unspeakable power. She is closed in a crystal mountain, of her own making, and will free herself when the world has need."

"Stories and tales, with only some truths." For the first time, Rhee's lips curved in a smile lovely in humor. "The green of Tulle is my home. No mountain of glass. You have my magic in you, and it is you who must free herself. There is great need. In this world, and the other."

"What other?" Kadra snapped. "This *is* the world. The only world."

"There are more, countless others. The world from which the demons sprang. Worlds of fire, worlds of ice. And a world not so different from this—yet so different. Sorak has gone to this world, through the portal opened by the glass key. He has gone to plunder and kill, to gather power until he is immortal. He wants your blood, wants your death to avenge his father. More, even more, he wants the power he believes he will gain by making you his mate."

"He will not have me, in this world or any. He would have slain his own father in time if I had not destroyed Clud before him."

"You see the truth. This is vision."

"This is sense."

"Whatever you choose to name it," Rhee said with a wave of her hand. "But a king cannot rule without vanquishing his most feared foe. Or changing her. He will not rest until you are destroyed by death or by his kiss. He goes through the portal to begin his own hunt. With every death from demon hands in that place, another here will die. This is the balance. This is the price."

"You speak in riddles. I will fetch the healer before I hunt."

"If you turn away," Rhee said as Kadra got to her feet, "if you choose the wrong path, all is lost. The world you know, the one you need to know. There is more than one key." Rhee breathed raggedly as her pain grew, took another clear globe from the folds of her skirt. "And more than one mirror."

She waved a hand toward the empty hearth. Fire, bright as gold, leaped into the cold shadow.

In it, Kadra saw another jungle. One of silver and black. Mountains . . . No, structures of great height—surely they could not be huts—rivers of black and white that had no current. Over them great armies of people marched. Over them battalions of animals on four round legs raced.

"What is this place?"

"A great village. They call it a city. A place where people live and work, where they eat and sleep. Where they live and die. This is called New York, and it is there you'll find them. The demons you must stop, and the man who will help you."

Though fascinated, and just a bit frightened of the images in the flames, Kadra smirked. "I need no man in battle."

"So you have been taught," Rhee said with a smile. "Perhaps you needed to believe you needed no one, no man, to become what you have become. Now you will become more. To do so, you will need this man. He is called Doyle, Harper Doyle."

"What good is a harper to a warrior?" Kadra demanded. "A fine warrior he'll make with his song and story as sword and shield."

"He is what you need. You will fail without him. Even with him there is great risk."

"Why should I believe any of this? Any witch might conjure pictures in a fire. Any woman might spin a tale as easily as thread."

"The stone in your crown of rank, those in your sword, I gave to you. For strength, for clear vision, for valor, and last, for love. They were my tears when I gave you to your fate. In my eyes you see your own. In your heart, you see the truth. Now we must prepare."

Kadra set her hand on the hilt of her sword. "I am prepared."

With a heavy sigh, Rhee got to her feet. She walked to a wooden cupboard, took out a metal box. "Take this." She offered a bag of stones. "Where you go," she explained, "they have great value."

Kadra looked into the bag of shining stones. "Then where I go is a very foolish place."

"In some ways. In others, fantastic." Rhee's expression was soft. "You have much to see. I will give you what knowledge I can, but there are limits. Even for me." She held out her hands, gripped Kadra's before Kadra could draw back.

"The rest," she said, and glinting tears scored down her cheeks, "is up to you, and the man called Doyle."

A great roar, like rushing water over cliffs, filled Kadra's head. In it were words, a hundred thousand words, spoken in countless tongues. A pressure, as a boulder laid on her heart, filled her chest.

The light was blinding.

"Valor and strength you have, my child. Use them on this journey wild. But open yourself to vision, to love, before it's too late. Gather them close and face your fate. Would I could keep you safe with me," she murmured, and her lips brushed a kiss over Kadra's. "But once again I set you free."

The world whirled and spun. The air sucked her in, tumbled her, then spat her rudely out.

2

Sᴘʀᴀᴡʟᴇᴅ ɪɴ ʙᴇᴅ, plagued by the mother of all hangovers, the man called Doyle let out a surprised and pained grunt when a half-naked woman dropped on top of him.

He saw eyes of intense and burning green. Eyes, he thought blearily, that he'd been dreaming of moments before he'd awakened with a head the size of Nebraska.

There was an instant of recognition, a strange and intimate knowledge, and with it a bone-deep longing. Then there was nothing but shock.

He had time to blink, a split second to admire what he was certain was a very creative hallucination, before the very sharp and very real point of a dagger pressed against his carotid artery.

"I am Kadra," the mostly naked and well-armed hallucination stated in a throaty voice as oddly familiar as her eyes. "Slayer of Demons."

"Okay, that's really interesting." If he'd been drunk and stupid enough the night before to bring a crazy woman back to his apartment, and couldn't even remember heating up the sheets with her, he deserved to get his throat cut.

But it really wasn't the way he wanted to start the day.

"Would you mind getting that pig-sticker away from my jugular? You're spoiling a perfectly good hangover."

Frowning, she sniffed at him, then used her free hand to pull up his top lip and study his teeth. Satisfied, she drew back the dagger, slid it handily into its wrist sheath.

"You are not a demon. You may live."

"Appreciate it." Going with instinct rather than sanity, Harper shoved her, snatched at the dagger. The next thing he knew, she'd executed a neat back flip off the bed, landed on her feet beside it. With a very big sword raised over her head.

"You win." He tossed the dagger aside, held up both hands.

"You yield?"

"Damn right. Why don't you put that thing down before somebody—especially me—gets hurt? Then we can go call the nice people at the asylum. They'll come pick you up and take you for a little ride."

Disgusted that she'd landed on a coward, she shook her head. But she lowered the sword. "Are you the harper called Doyle?"

"I'm Harper Doyle."

"We have to hunt."

"Sure, no problem." Smiling at her, he eased toward the far side of the bed. Whatever that feeling had been when he'd first looked into her eyes, he was sure now he hadn't been drunk enough, hadn't been stupid enough to bring her home with him. "Just let me get my hunting gear and we'll be off."

Using his body to block her view, he slid open the drawer in the nightstand and drew out his Glock. "Now, put that goddamn sword down, Xena."

"I am Kadra," she corrected and studied the object in his hand. "This is a gun." The name, the purpose of it were floating in her head, in the maze of knowledge Rhee had given her. The fascination for it, this new weapon, made her yearn. "I would like to have one."

She looked at him, studying his face for the first time,

and found herself shocked that it brought her another kind of yearning.

"I was sent to you," she told him.

"Fine, we'll get to that. But right now, put the sword down," he repeated. "I'd really hate to spoil my record and shoot a woman."

It was more comfortable to study the gun, and her feelings for an interesting weapon. "The missile goes through flesh and bone. It can be very efficient." She nodded, sent her sword home. "Perhaps you are a warrior. We will talk."

"Oh, yeah," Harper agreed. "We're going to have a very nice chat."

His head felt as if someone had spent the night attempting a lobotomy with a dull, rusty blade. He could accept that. In a bemused celebration of his thirtieth birthday—how could he be thirty when he'd been eighteen two minutes ago—he'd consumed a tanker truck of alcohol. He'd been entitled to get plastered with a couple of pals. He was entitled to the hangover.

Having a woman—a gorgeous green-eyed Amazon who filled out her black leather bikini in a way that gratified every young boy's comic book fantasies—leap on him out of nowhere was a really nice plus. Just the sort of happy birthday surprise a man who'd reached the point of no return on the path to adulthood could appreciate.

But having that erotic armful hold a knife to his throat wasn't part of the acceptable package.

And where the hell *had* she come from? he wondered as she stood there eyeing his gun. There was nothing but simple curiosity and avid interest on that sharp-boned siren's face.

Had he been so drunk he'd forgotten to lock his door? It was a possibility—a remote one, but a possibility. But she'd called him by name. No way she was from the neighborhood. He was a trained observer, and even if he'd been a myopic accountant rather than a private investigator he would have noticed a six-foot brunette with legs that went to eternity.

"Jake." The solution trickled through his suffering brain. Though he relaxed a little, he held the gun steady. "Jake put you up to this, didn't he? Some weird-ass birthday surprise. Jake's who sent you."

"I am sent by Rhee, the sorceress. How is it that a harper has such a weapon? Have you killed many demons?"

"Look, it's too early in the morning for Dungeons and Dragons. Show's over, sister."

"I am not your sister," she began as he eased out of bed. Then her eyebrows shot up. He was naked, but that neither surprised nor shocked her. Her instant and elemental attraction did.

He was taller than she by nearly a full hand, broader in the chest and shoulders, with fine, sleek muscles.

Reevaluating, she pursed her lips. His hair was the deep brown of oak bark, and though unkempt by sleep, it created a good frame for a strong face. His eyes were the bold blue of the marsh bells, his nose slightly crooked, which told her it had weathered a break. His mouth was firm, as was his jaw. Though his skin was pale, like a scholar's who closeted himself with scrolls, she began to see possibilities.

"You have a fine build for a harper," she told him.

"Yeah?" Amused now, though still cautious, he reached for the jeans he'd peeled off the night before. "How much did Jake pay you for the gig?"

"I know no Jake. I do not take payment for slaying. It is my destiny. Do you require payment?"

"Depends." How the hell was he going to get into his jeans and hold the gun at the same time?

"The knowledge was given me that these have value in your world." She tugged the bag of stones from her belt, tossed them on the bed. "Take what you need, then dress. We must begin the hunt."

"Look, I appreciate a joke as much as the next guy. But I'm naked and hungover, and it irritates me to wake up with a knife to my throat. I want coffee, a barrel of aspirin, and a shower."

"Very well. If you will not hunt, show me how to use your weapon."

"You're a piece of work." He gestured toward the bedroom door with the Glock. "Out. Back to Central Casting, or Amazons R Us, or wherever the hell—"

She moved so fast that all he saw was a blur of limbs and leather and flying hair. She leaped, executed a handspring off the bed, and some part of her—boot, elbow, fist—connected with his jaw.

An entire galaxy of stars exploded in his head. By the time they novaed and died, he was flat on his back, with her standing astride him turning the Glock over in her hands.

"It has good weight," she said conversationally. "How is the missile . . ." She trailed off when with a twitch of her finger she fired. Her eyes widened with something like lust when through the open bathroom door, she saw the corner of his vanity sheared off.

"It is faster than an arrow," she commented, very pleased.

Not Jake, he corrected. Jake might have a weird sense of the ridiculous, but his old college friend wouldn't have sent him a lunatic who liked to play with guns. "Who the hell are you?"

"I am Kadra." She nearly sighed with the repetition—perhaps the harper was loose in the brains. With some sympathy she offered a hand to help him up. "Slayer of Demons. I have come to hunt, to fulfill my destiny. Though it does not please either of us, you are obliged to assist."

"Give me the gun, Kadra."

"It is a good weapon."

"Yeah, it's a good weapon. It belongs to me."

Her lips moved into a pout, then her face brightened again. "I will fight you for it."

"I'm at a disadvantage at the moment." He got to his feet, very slowly, kept his voice mild and easy. "You know, naked, hungover."

"Hung over what?"

"Maybe we could fight later, after we clear up a few points."

"Very well. I will give you the weapon, and you will give me your word that you will help me hunt the Bok."

"Helping people's what I do." Maybe she was in trouble, he thought. Not that he intended to get involved, but he could at least listen before he called the guys in the white coats. "Is that why you're here?" Gently, he nudged her gun hand aside so he wouldn't end up with a bullet in the belly. "You need help?"

"I am a stranger here, and require a guide." She reached out, squeezed his biceps. "You are strong. But slow." With no little regret, she returned the Glock. "Can you make more of the gun?"

"Maybe." She'd threatened him with a knife, with a sword. She'd knocked him on his ass and disarmed him.

Damn if he didn't respect her for it.

In any case, she'd made his first morning as a thirty-year-old man interesting. He hadn't become a PI because he liked the boring.

Added to that, there was something . . . something about her that pulled at him. Her looks were enough to knock a man flat. But it wasn't that—or not only that. You couldn't find the answers, he reminded himself, unless you asked the questions.

"I'm going to put my pants on," he told her. "I want you to step back and keep your hands away from that sword."

She stepped back. "I have no wish to harm you, or any of your people. You have my word as a slayer."

"Good to know." When she was at a safe distance, he tugged on his jeans, then snugged the gun in the waistband. "Now, I'm going to make coffee, and we'll talk about all this."

"Coffee. This is a stimulant consumed in liquid form."

"There you go. In the kitchen," he added, gesturing toward the door.

She strode out ahead of him. Whatever shape he might have been in, Harper thought, however baffled he might be, a man who didn't admire and appreciate that view was a sorry specimen.

Still, he glanced at the front door of his apartment as he passed. It was locked, bolted, chained.

So she'd locked up after she'd come in, he decided. He looked back to see her stop and gape out the living room window. Like a kid might, he mused, at her first eyeful of Disneyland.

So high, she thought in wonder. She had never been in

a hut where the ground was so far below and so many people swarmed beneath. Their costumes were strange to her, strange and fascinating. But fascination turned to awe when she watched a cab zip to the curb, saw the woman leap out.

"She rose out of the belly of the yellow beast! How is this done?"

"You pay the fare, they let you out. Where the hell are you from?"

"I am from A'Dair. In my world, we have no beasts with round legs. I don't—wait." She closed her eyes, searched through the knowledge Rhee had given her. "Cars!" Those brilliant eyes opened again, smiled into his. "They are machines called cars and are for transportation. That is wonderful."

"Try to find one in the rain. Honey—"

"Yes, I would like honey, and bread. I am hungry."

"Right." He shook his head. "Coffee. Coffee first, then all questions can be faced. Come with me. I want you where I can see you."

She followed him into his tiny galley kitchen. While he measured coffee, she ran her fingers over the surface of the counter, over the refrigerator and stove. "So much magic," she said softly. "You must have great wealth."

"Yeah, rolling in it." He made a reasonable living, Harper thought. But he was what you could call between active cases at the moment. Maybe he could hold off on the guys in the white coats, see if she needed an investigator, and had enough to pay his retainer. "Jake didn't send you, did he?"

"I do not know this Jake." She peered at the side of the toaster, delighted with her own odd reflection. "I know no one in this world, save you."

"How did you get here, to my place?"

"Through the portal. It is . . ." She straightened, trying to decipher the knowledge, then to express it. "There are many dimensions. Yours and mine are two. The Bok stole a key and have entered yours. I have another." She drew the clear globe out of her pouch. "So I have followed. To hunt, to kill so that our worlds will be safe. You are to help me in this quest."

Poor kid, he thought. She was definitely a few fries short of a Happy Meal. "You can't just kill people in this world. They lock you up for that."

"You have no slayers to fight against evil here?"

He dragged a hand through his hair, then rooted out some Extra-Strength Excedrin. Isn't that what his father had done? And what he himself had wanted to do as long as he could remember? To go after the bad guys, on his own terms?

"Yeah, I guess we do."

The woman was definitely in some sort of jam, even if it came out of her own oddball imagination. He would just keep her calm, ask some questions, see if he could dig out the problem. When he'd done what he could, he would make a few calls and have her taken someplace where she could get some help.

It would be the first good deed of his new decade.

"So, you come from another dimension, and you're here to hunt down some demons."

"The king of demons and three of his warriors have entered your world. They will need to feed. First, they will hunt for animals, the easy kill, to gather strength. Where are your farms?"

"We're a little short on farms on Second Avenue. So what do you do back in—where was it?"

"A'Dair."

He could run a search on the name on his computer, see if he could pinpoint where she'd come from. She didn't have a discernible accent, but the cadence, the rhythm of her speech sure as hell didn't say New York.

"What do you do back in A'Dair besides slay demons?"

"This is my purpose. I was born a slayer, trained, educated. It is what I do."

"Friends, family?"

"I have no family. She who raised me was killed by a tribe of Bok."

Mother killed, he thought. Trauma, role playing. "I'm sorry."

"She was a fine warrior. Clud, sire of Sorak, took her life, and I have taken his. So there is balance. I have learned that she who bore me was another. Rhee, the sorceress. Her blood is in me. I think I am here, able to be here, because of that blood." She sniffed the air. "This is coffee?"

"That's right."

"It has a good scent."

He poured two mugs, offered one. She sniffed again, sipped, then frowned. "Bitter, but good."

To his surprise, she downed the entire mug in one swallow, then swiped a hand over her mouth. "I like this coffee. Dress now, Harper Doyle."

"How do you know my name?"

"It was told to me. We will hunt the Bok together."

"Sure. We'll get to that in a little while."

Her eyes narrowed. "You don't believe. You think I'm loose in the brain. You waste my time with too many questions when we should act."

"Part of what I do in my little world is ask questions. Nobody's calling you a liar here. Why shouldn't I believe you're a demon slayer from an alternate universe? I'm always getting clients from other dimensions."

She paced up and down the narrow room to work out the logic. He was mocking her, and this was not proper. Lesser warriors were not permitted to show a slayer disrespect.

Yet, she admired him for it even as she found his demeanor frustrating.

This was his world, Kadra reminded herself, one of wonders far beyond her ken. So her world would be beyond his. If she were in his place, she would not believe without proof.

"You must be shown. I cannot blame you for doubt. You would be weak and foolish if you didn't question, and the weak and foolish would be of no use to me."

"Darling, keep up that sweet talk and you'll turn my head."

She didn't have to understand the words to recognize the sarcasm dripping from them. A little impatient, a little intrigued, she held one hand up, and the other, with the globe in its palm, out.

"My blood is of the sorceress and the warrior. My blood is the blood of the slayer. I hold the power of the key."

She drew her mind down to the globe, drew the power of the globe into her mind.

Harper's kitchen wall dissolved as though it were a painting left out in the rain. Through it, he saw not the apartment next door but a thick, green jungle, a curving white ribbon, and a sky the color of pale blood under a fierce red sun.

"Holy shit," he managed before he was sucked into it.

3

THE HEAT WAS enormous, a drenching, dripping wall of steaming water. It was a shock, even after the jolt of pain, the blast of blinding light. Even so, his bones felt frozen under his skin as he stared out at the tangle of towering green.

New York was gone, it seemed. And so was he.

Not a hangover, he thought, but some sort of psychotic event brought on, no doubt, by too much liquor and too many loose women.

As he watched, dumbfounded, a snake with a body as thick as his thigh slithered off into the high, damp grass.

"We can stay only a short time," Kadra told him, and her voice was dim, tinny, light-years away. "This is the west jungle of A'Dair, near the coast of the Great Sea. This is my world, which exists beyond yours. And the knowledge says, in balance with it."

"I've been drugged."

"This is not so." Annoyed now, she clamped her hands over his arms. "You can see, you can hear and feel. My world is as real as yours, and as much in peril."

"Alternate universe." The words felt foolish on his tongue. "That's pure science fiction."

"Is your world so perfect, so important, that you believe it stands alone in the vastness of time and space? Harper Doyle, can you have lived and still believe you are alone? My heart." She pressed his hand to her breast. "It beats as yours. I am, as you are."

How could he dismiss what he saw with his own eyes. What he felt, touched—and somehow knew. Just, he thought, as he had somehow known her the instant their eyes had met. "Why?"

She nearly smiled. "Why not?"

"I recognized you," he managed. "I pushed that aside, clicked back into what made sense so I could deny it. But I recognized you, somehow, the minute I saw you."

"Yes." She kept her hand on his a moment longer. It felt right there, like a link. "It was the same for me. This is not something I understand, but only feel. I do not know the meaning."

And in some secret chamber of her warrior's heart, she feared the meaning.

"I'm standing here sweating in a jungle in some Twilight Zone, and it doesn't feel half as strange as it should. It doesn't feel half as strange as what's going on inside me, about you."

"You begin to believe."

"I'm beginning to something. I'm going to need a little time to process all the—"

She whirled, the sword streaking into her hand like a lightning bolt. A creature, no more than three feet high, with snapping teeth in both its mouths, shot out of the brush and leaped for Harper's throat.

Despite the shock of it, his instincts were quick. His hand whipped down for his gun. It hadn't cleared the waistband of his jeans before Kadra's sword sliced through both heads with one massive stroke. There was a fountaining gush of vile green liquid that stank like sulfur.

Heads and body thunked, a grisly trio, onto the ground, then began to smoke.

"Loki demon," Kadra said as the three pieces melted away. "Small pests that usually travel in packs of three." She lifted her head, sniffed. "To your left. You will need your weapon," she added, and pivoted to her right as another of the creatures jumped through a curtain of vine.

Instinct had his finger on the trigger, and if that finger trembled a bit, he wasn't ashamed. He heard the slice of her sword through air just as the last—please, God—of the miniature monsters charged him.

He shot it between the eyes—all four of them.

"Christ. Jesus. Christ."

"This is good aim." Giving Harper a congratulatory slap on the back, she nodded over the smoking heads. "This is a fine weapon," she added, sending his Glock an avaricious glance. "When we go back to your world, you will provide me with one. It lacks the beauty of the sword, but it makes an enjoyable noise."

"Their blood's green," Harper said in a careful voice. "They have two heads and green blood. And now, how about that, they're just melting away like the Wicked Witch of the West."

"All demons bleed green, though only the Loki and the mutant strain of the Ploon are two-headed. On death, the blood smokes and the body . . . melts is not inaccurate," she decided. "You have witches in the west of your world who die like demons?"

When he only stared at her, she shrugged. "We have witches as well, and most of them the powers of life have instilled with good. My home is east," she continued. "Beyond the Stone Mountains, in the Shadowed Valley. It is beautiful, and the fields are rich. There is no time to show you."

"This is real." He took one long, deep breath and swallowed it all at once.

"Our time here is short. There is a clearing, and a village in it. Rhee lives there. We will go."

Since she set off in a punishing jog, he had no choice but to follow. "Slow it down, Wonder Woman. I'm barefoot here."

She tossed a scowl over her shoulder, but modified her

pace. "You drank excessive spirits last night. I can smell them on you. Now you are sluggish."

"Alert enough to kill a two-headed demon."

She let out a snort. "A child with a training bow could do the same. Lokis are stupid."

As they ran down the narrow, beaten path, a flock of birds flushed out of the trees and into that odd red sky. He staggered to a halt. Each was its own rainbow—a bleeding, blending meld of pinks and blues and golds. And the song they sent up was like the trill of flutes.

"Dregos," she told him. "Their gift is their song, as they are poor eating. Stringy." She slowed to a trot as they came to the clearing.

He saw houses, small and tidy, most with colorful gardens in the front. People dressed in long, thin robes harvested out of them what looked to be massive blue carrots, tomatoes the size of melons, and long, yellow beans spotted with green flecks.

There were men, women, children, and each stopped work or play and bowed as Kadra came into view.

"Greetings, Demon Slayer," some called out.

She acknowledged this with what Harper supposed was a kind of salute by laying her fist on her heart as she walked.

Those long legs ate up the ground toward a small house with a lush garden and an open front door. She had to duck her head to enter.

Inside, a young girl stood by what he assumed was a cookstove. She stirred an iron pot and looked up at them with quiet blue eyes.

"Hail to Kadra, Slayer of Demons."

"We come to speak with Rhee."

"She sleeps," the girl said and continued to stir. "She suffered a demon bite during the attack."

"She did not say." Kadra moved quickly, shoving open a door. Within, Rhee lay pale and still on a bed. The emotions that churned in her were mixed and confusing, and through them came one clear thought.

Mother. Will I lose yet another mother before my own end? "Is it the sleep of change?"

"No. She was not kissed, only bitten beneath the shoulder as she tried to guard the keys. Nor was it a mortal bite, though she had pain and there was sickness. More than necessary, as she did not see to the wound quickly."

"She . . . spent too much time with me."

"Not too much, only what was needed."

"Your mother?" Harper looked through the doorway at the woman on the bed, and laid a hand on Kadra's shoulder. "Can we get her to a doctor?"

"I am Mav the healer," the young girl told him. "I tend to her. I have drained the poison, given her the cure. She must sleep until her body regains strength. She said you would come, Kadra, with the one from the other world. You are to eat."

Mav ladled out some of the thick broth from the pot. "And to wash in the falls. In this way, you will take some of this place with you into the next. You must be gone within the hour."

"Do you want to sit with her awhile," Harper began. "Take some time with her?"

His hand caressed her shoulder, a gesture of comfort she had known rarely in her life. "There is no time." Kadra turned away from the doorway.

"She's your mother."

"She bore me. She set me on this path. Now I can only follow it."

She sat down at the table where Mav had put the bowls and a round loaf of golden bread. There was a squat pitcher of honey and another of water as white and sparkling as snow.

Because he was tired, hungry, and confused, Harper sat. This is real, he thought again as he sampled the first taste of the rich, spiced broth. It wasn't a dream, a hallucination. He hadn't just lost his mind.

Kadra tore off a hunk of bread, poured honey over it, and ate with a concentrated focus that told Harper she wasn't concerned with taste, only with fuel.

"Do you have family?" she asked Mav between bites.

"I have two brothers, younger. My mother who weaves.

My father was a healer as well. Sorak, king of demons, killed him this morning."

"I was not quick enough." Grief thickened Kadra's voice. "And your mother is a widow."

"He would have killed us all, but you came. He fears you."

"He has cause. I regret that death touched you."

"He came for Rhee, for the key. Her powers are not as strong as they were, and he made demons from wizards so he might track her. She explained to me while I tended her so I might tell you."

Mav folded her hands and spoke as if reciting a story learned by heart. "The other, the world beyond with yellow sun and blue sky, is full of so much life, and most who live there have closed themselves off from the magic. They will not understand, they will not believe, and so the Bok will slaughter them. Flesh, passion. Innocence and evil. Sorak craves this, and the power he will gain from it. The power to destroy you."

"He will die there." Kadra drank the tankard of spring-water quickly. "This is my vow, on your father's blood." She pulled out her dagger, sliced a shallow gash across her palm, and let her blood drip onto the table. "And on mine."

"It will comfort my mother to know it. But there should be no more bloodshed here." Mav reached in her pocket, took out a white cloth, and deftly wrapped it around Kadra's hand. "You must wash in the falls, for cleansing, then go."

When Kadra got to her feet, Harper sighed and got to his. "Thanks for the food."

Mav blushed, cast down her gaze. "It is little to give the Slayer and the savior. Blessings on you both."

Harper took one last glance at her. Kid couldn't be more than ten, he thought, then ducked out the doorway.

He had to double his pace to catch up with Kadra. "Look, just slow down a minute. I'm trying to keep up here, in more ways than one. I don't usually spend my mornings visiting alternate dimensions and killing loco demons."

"Loki."

"Whatever. So far you've jumped me, held a knife to my

throat, threatened me with a sword, punched me in the face, and sucked me through some . . . wormhole in my kitchen. And all this on one lousy cup of coffee. This isn't your average first date."

"You do not have the knowledge, so you require explanations." She moved through the jungle at a brisk pace, eyes tracking, ears pricked. "I understand this."

"Beautiful. Then give them to me."

"We will cleanse in the falls, return to your world, hunt down the Bok and kill them."

He considered himself a reasonable guy, a man with an open mind, an active sense of adventure and curiosity. But enough was enough. He grabbed her arm, yanked her around to face him. "That's what you call an explanation? Listen, sister, if that's the best you can do, this is where we part ways. Send me back where I come from and we'll just put this all down to too much beer and fried food."

"I am not your sister."

He stared at her, at the faint irritation that clouded her glorious face. Helpless, he began to laugh. It rolled out of him, pumping up from the belly so that he had to bend over, brace his hands on his thighs as she cocked her head and studied him with a mixture of amusement, puzzlement, and impatience.

"I'm losing it," he managed. "Losing what's left of my mind." Even as he sucked in a breath, a spider the size of a Chihuahua pranced between his feet on stiltlike legs and gibbered at him. Harper yelped, whipping out his gun as he stumbled back.

But Kadra merely booted the enormous insect off the path. "That species is not poisonous," she informed him.

"Good, great, fine! It just swallows a man whole."

Kadra shook her head, then loped down the path. Keeping his gun handy, Harper followed.

Red sun, he mused as he looked up at the sky. Like, well, Krypton. If he followed comic book logic, didn't that mean that he, from a planet with a yellow sun, had superpowers here.

Concentrating, he took a little jump, then another. On the third, Kadra looked back at him, her face a study in baffled frustration. "This is not the time for dancing."

"I wasn't dancing I was just . . ." Seeing if I could fly, he thought, amazed at himself. "Nothing. Nothing at all."

He heard the roar like a highballing train. It grew, swelled, pounded on his eardrums as he jogged after her. She swung around a curve on the path, and he looked up.

In front of them, white water plunged from a height of two hundred feet or more. It screamed over the cliff, dived in a thundering wall, then pounded into the surface of a white river.

Flowers, some unrecognizable, some as simple as daisies, teemed along its banks. There, with the wild grass and wildflowers, with the sunlight spilling in rosy streaks through the canopy of trees, a unicorn lazily grazed.

"My God." The hand still holding the gun fell to his side. The mythical beast raised its regal white head and stared at Harper out of eyes so blue and clear they might have been glass. Then it went back to cropping the grass.

The beauty of it, the sheer wonder, wiped his temper away. Now I've seen it all, he thought. Nothing will ever surprise me again.

He realized the fallacy of that a second later when he glanced back at Kadra.

She'd stripped. The black leather lay piled on the bank, her sword, her dagger crossed over it. She'd pulled off her boots, her wrist sheaths, and was even now reaching up to lift the circlet from her hair.

She was, Harper thought, more mythical, more wondrous that the white-horned creature. Her body was curved and sleek, the color of the fresh honey she had poured over the breakfast bread. Her dark hair, arrow straight, rained over her shoulders, down her back, lay tauntingly over one magnificent breast.

His body tightened, his mouth went dry. For one blissful moment, he lost the power of speech.

"This is a sacred place," she began as she laid her circlet on her crossed blades. "No demon can cross its borders. Take off your clothing, put down your weapon. You may take no cloth or metal into the falls."

So saying, she dived.

It was a picture he knew would remain etched in his mind forever.

"Things are looking up," he decided, and peeling off his jeans, he jumped in after her.

The water was cool, sluicing the sweat from his body in one glorious swipe. When he surfaced, he felt the last nasty dregs of the morning's hangover sink to the bottom of the river. In fact, he realized as he struck out after Kadra and the falls, he didn't just feel clearheaded, didn't just feel good. He felt charged, energized.

She waited for him at the foot of the falls, treading the churning water lazily. Her eyes were impossibly green, impossibly brilliant.

"What's in this water?" he shouted.

"Cleansing properties. It washes away negative energies."

"I'll say."

She laughed, did a quick surface dive that gave him a brief and wonderful flash of her butt. Then she rose again, a vision of black and gold, under the pounding spill of the water. She climbed nimbly onto a plateau of rock, stretched her arms wide to the sides, and let the water beat over her.

He lost his breath, and despite the cool relief of the water, his blood ran hot. He hoisted himself up in front of her, laid his hands on her hips. Her eyes opened again, and her eyebrow quirked.

"You're the most magnificent thing I've ever seen. In any dimension."

"I have a good build," she said easily. "It's made for fighting." She bent her right arm, flexed her biceps.

"I bet it holds its own in other sports."

Though she couldn't ignore the trip of her own heart, or the quick click of response in her belly, she only smiled. "I enjoy sporting, when there's time for such things. You're very handsome, Harper Doyle, and I have a yearning for you that is stronger than any I have known before."

"Do you think you could pick one of my two names and stick with it?" Since she didn't seem to object, he slid his hands around her thighs, then over her silky butt.

"Harper is your title."

"No, it's my name. My first name." He really had to get a taste of that lush, frowning mouth. But as he dipped his head, she laid a restraining hand on his chest.

"I do not understand. Are you the harper called Doyle?"

"I'm Harper Doyle, and before this turns into a comedy routine, Doyle is my family name. Harper is the name my parents gave me when I was born. That's how it works in my world. I'm not *a* harper," he added as the light began to dawn. "I'm not, what, like a minstrel? Jesus. I'm a PI."

"A pee-eye? What is this?"

"Investigator. Private investigator. I . . . solve puzzles," he decided.

"Ah! You are a seeker. This is better. A seeker is more useful on a hunt than a harper."

"Now that we've worked that out, why don't we go back to me being handsome." He drew her closer so that her breasts—cool, wet, firm—brushed his chest. His mouth was an inch from hers when he went flying.

He landed clumsily, swallowing water on his own curse. She was still on the rocks when he came up and swiped the hair out of his eyes. She was grinning. "You made a good splash. It is time to go."

She dived, struck out for the bank. Oh, he was handsome, she thought as she hoisted herself out. Very handsome, and with a clever look in his eyes that made her want to join her body to his.

Something about him was making pricks on her heart, as if trying to find the weakness, the point of entry.

He would be a strong lover, she knew. And it had been a long time since she had desired one. If time and fate allowed, they would have each other.

But first, there was the hunt.

By the time he pulled himself onto the bank put on his jeans, she was strapping on her sword. He didn't bother to think, just went with the moment. And tackled her.

She let out a surprised little grunt and studied his face with some approval. "I misjudged. You do have speed."

"Yeah, right, it'll help on the hunt. But right now . . ."

He lowered his head, all but tasting that beautiful mouth. And once more he went flying. But this time it was through the portal. The blast of light, and sharp, shocking pain.

He landed hard, with Kadra once more on top, on his kitchen floor. "Damn it!" He banged his head sharply on the base cabinet, felt the unmistakable shape of his gun dig into his bare back. "Give me some warning next time. A damn signal or something."

"You have your mind too much on sporting." She gave his shoulder a pat, then levered off him. Sniffed the air. "We will have more coffee, and plan the hunt."

"Okay, Sheena, let's reevaluate," he said as he got up.

"I am Kadra—"

"Shut up." He slapped the gun down on the kitchen counter while her mouth dropped open.

"You would speak so to a slayer?"

"Yeah, I'd speak so to anybody who busts uninvited into my house and keeps giving me orders. You want my help, you want my cooperation? Then you can just stop telling me what to do and start asking."

She was silent for a moment. She had a ready temper, something even her intense training hadn't completely tamed. To lose it now, she told herself, would be gratifying, but a sinful waste of time. Instead, she measured Harper, then nodded with sudden understanding. "Ah. You're talking with your man-thing. This is a common ailment in my world as well."

"This isn't my dick talking." Or at least, he'd be damned if he'd admit it. "I want answers. The way I see it, you're looking to hire me. That's fine. You want me to help you track down these . . . things. That's what I do. I find things, solve problems. That's my job. I work my way. Let's get that part straight."

"You are a seeker, and you require payment. Very well." Though she thought less of him for it, she wouldn't begrudge him his fee. "Come with me." She started out, turned when she saw him standing firm. "If you will," she added.

"Better," he muttered, and followed her into the bedroom, where she scooped up the leather pouch she'd tossed on the bed earlier.

"Is this enough?"

He caught the bag when she flipped it to him. Curious, he opened it. And poured a storm of gems onto the bed. "Holy Mother of God!"

"I am told these have value here. Is this so?" Intrigued, she stepped over to poke a finger into the pool of diamonds, rubies, emeralds. "They are common stones in my world. Pretty," she admitted. "Attractive for adornments. Will they satisfy your needs?"

"Satisfy my needs," he grumbled. "Yeah, they're pretty satisfactory."

He could retire. Move to Tahiti and live like a king. Hell, he could *buy* Tahiti and live like a god. For one outrageous moment, he saw himself living in a white palace by the crystal blue water, surrounded by gorgeous, scantily clad women eager to do his bidding. Drinking champagne by the gallons. Frolicking on white sand beaches with those same women—not clad at all now.

Master of all he surveyed.

Then his conscience kicked in, a small annoyance he'd never been able to shake. On the heels of conscience nipped the lowering admission that the fantasy he'd just outlined would bore him brainless in a week.

He picked a single diamond, comforting himself that it was worth more than he would earn in a decade.

"This'll cover it."

"That is all you require?"

"Put the rest away, before I change my mind." For lack of a better option, he stuffed the stone into his pocket. "Now, we're going to sit down. You're going to explain this whole demon deal to me, and I'll figure out our first move."

"They are out in your world. We have to hunt."

"My world," Harper agreed. "My turf. I don't go after anything until I know the score." He walked to his dresser, opened a drawer, and pulled out a T-shirt. "Normally I don't meet clients at home," he said as he pulled the shirt on. "But we'll make an exception. Living room." He headed out, took a legal pad from a desk drawer, then plopped down on the sofa.

However fantastic the client, however strange the case,

he was going to approach it as he would any other. He made a few notes, then jerked his chin at a chair when she continued to stand. "Sit down. Bok demon, right? Is that B-O-K? Never mind. How many?"

"They were four. Sorak, demon king, and three warriors."

"Description?"

She sprawled in a chair, all legs and attitude. He looked more scholar than warrior now, working with his odd scroll and quill. Though she had never found scholar appealing before, this aspect of him was attractive to her as well.

He has brains as well as muscle, she thought. Intellect as well as brawn.

"Description," Harper repeated. "What do they look like?"

"They are deceptively human in appearance, and so often walk among people without detection. They are handsome, as you are. Though you have eyes blue as the marsh bell, and your hair is cropped short. Those who are foolish enough to be influenced by such things as beauty are easy victims."

"We've established that you're nobody's victim, baby. Be more specific."

She huffed. "They have good height, like you, but their build is less. It is more . . . slender. Hair and eyes are dark, black as a dead moon except in feeding or in attack, where they glow red."

"Glowing red eyes," he noted. "I'd say that's a fairly distinguishing mark."

"Sorak's hair curls." She demonstrated by waving a finger. "And is well groomed. He is vain."

"They outfitted like you?"

It took her a moment, then she glanced down at her hunting clothes. "No. They wear a kind of armor, black again, close to the body, and over this Sorak wears the tunic and cloak of his rank."

"Even in New York, body armor and tunics should stand out. Maybe there's something on the news." He picked up the remote and flipped on the television.

Kadra leaped up as if he'd set her chair on fire. Even

before her feet were planted, her sword was out, raised high above her head in preparation for a downward thrust.

"Hold it, hold it, hold it!" He jumped and, as he might have done to save a beloved child, threw himself between the blade and his TV. "I don't give a rat's ass about what you did to the bathroom sink, but put one scratch on my TV and you're going down."

Her heart pounded in her chest, and her muscles quivered. "What is this sorcery?"

"It's not magic, it's ESPN." He hissed out a breath, then moved in to clamp his hands over hers on the hilt of the sword. She tipped her head back so their eyes, their mouths, lined up.

"It's television, which is arguably the national religion of my country. An entertainment device," he said more calmly. "A kind of communication. We have programs— ah, like plays, I guess, that tell us what's happening in the world, even when it's happening far away."

She drew a breath, slowly lowered the sword while she stared at the picture box where the machines called cars ran swiftly around a circle. "How is this done?"

"Something about airwaves, transmissions, cameras, stuff. Hell, I don't know. You turn the thing on, pick a channel. This is a race. You get that?"

"Yes, a contest of speed. I have won many races."

"With those legs, baby, I'll just bet you have. Okay, I'm turning on the news now so we can see if there are any reports on your demons. So relax."

"How can you use a thing when you have no knowledge of its workings?"

"Same way I can use a computer. And don't ask. I thought you said you knew about this world."

"I was given knowledge, but I cannot learn it all at once." It embarrassed her not to know, so she went back to sprawling in the chair, giving the television quick, suspicious glances.

"All right, we'll take it in stages. Just don't attack any more of my household appliances." He sat again, flipped the channel to the all-news station, then picked up his pad.

"Back to your demons. Distinguishing marks? You know, like two heads, for instance?"

Feeling foolish, she sulked. He had nearly slain a spider with the weapon known as gun, but she had not made *him* feel loose in the brain. "They are Bok, not Loki."

"What makes them stand out? How do you recognize them?" Even as she threw up her hands, he tapped his pencil. "And don't say they are Bok. Draw me a picture."

Taking him literally, she reared up, snatched the pencil and pad. In fast, surprisingly deft strokes, she sketched a figure of a man with long, curled hair, a strong, rawboned face and large, dark eyes.

"That's good. But it's going to be tough to pick him out of the millions of other tall, slim, dark-haired guys in New York. Doesn't shout out demon to me. How do you recognize them—as a species, let's say."

"A slayer is born for this. But others might do so by their stench. They have a scent." She struggled for a moment in her attempt to describe it. "Between the ripe and the rot. You would not mistake it."

"Okay, they stink. Now we're getting somewhere. Anything else?"

"Teeth. Two rows, long, thin, sharp. Claws, which they show or conceal at will. Thick, blue, curved like talons. And when they are wounded, their blood is green. Now we hunt."

"Just settle down," he said mildly. He listened to the news reports with half an ear. The usual mayhem and gossip, but no frantic bulletins about man-eating demons on the loose in New York.

"Why are they here?" he asked her. "Why leave one world for another?"

"Sorak is greedy, and his hunger is great. For flesh, but also for power. There are more of you in this place than on our world. And you are unaware. They can move among you without fear of the slayer. They will feed, gluttonously. First on animals, for quick strength, then on humans. Those that he and his warriors do not consume, he will change so he can build a vast army. They will overtake the world you know and make it theirs."

"Whoa, back up. Change? What do you mean by change?"

"He will turn selected humans into demons, into slaves and warriors and concubines."

"You're telling me he can make people into things? Like, what, vampires?"

"I do not know this word. Explain."

"Never mind." Harper pushed himself to his feet to pace. For reasons he couldn't explain, the idea of having human beings turned into monsters was more disturbing than having them served up as demon meals. "How do they do it? How are people changed?"

"The Demon Kiss. Mouth against mouth. Tongue, teeth, lips. A bite, to draw blood, to mix it. Then the demon draws in the human essence, breathes his own into his prey. They are changed, and are compelled to hunt, to feed. They remember nothing of their humanity. This is worse than death."

"Yeah." The thought sickened him. "Yeah, it's worse. No way this son of a bitch is going to turn my town into his personal breeding ground." When he faced her, his face was set, and the warrior gleam in his eye gave Kadra her first real hope. "Animals, you said. Cats, dogs, what?"

"These are pets." She closed her eyes and searched the knowledge. "Such small prey would not please them. This would do only if the hunger was impossible. They prefer the flesh of the unicorn above all."

"Unicorns don't spend a lot of time grazing in New York. Horses?"

"Yes, horses, cows, goats. But there are no farms, you said. In the wild, they feed often on the lion or the ape."

"Lions, tigers, and bears? The zoo. We'll start there. As soon as we figure out how to outfit you so you blend in a little better with the general population."

Frowning, she looked down at herself. "I don't resemble the other females in your world?"

He scanned the breasts barely constrained by black leather, the long, lean torso, the swatch of leather over curvy hips. And those endless legs encased in boots. Not to mention a two-and-a-half-foot sword.

"I couldn't begin to tell you. Let's see what I can put together."

When she came out of his bedroom fifteen minutes later, he decided she did more to sell a pair of Levi's than a million-dollar ad campaign. And the old denim shirt had never looked better.

"Baby, you are a picture."

She studied herself in his mirror, and agreed. "It is tolerable hunting gear." Testing it, she executed several quick deep-knee bends that had Harper's blood pressure rising. "It will do." So saying, she picked up her sword.

"You can't walk around outside with that thing."

She glanced up, smirked. "So, do I slay demons with bad thoughts?"

"Aha, sarcasm. I like it. I've got something. Hold on." He went to the closet, shoved through it and came out with a long black coat. "A little warm for May, but we can't be picky."

"Why do people in your world cover up so much flesh?"

"I ask myself that question every day." He took another long look at her. Maybe, just maybe, if he'd been able to design his own ideal woman, he'd have come close to the reality of her. "You going to wear the little crown?"

Her hand went to the gold on top of her head. "This is the circle of my rank."

"You want to blend in?" He lifted the circlet off, set it aside. "Put on the coat and let's see."

Scowling, she dragged the coat on, turned to him. "You're still going to turn heads and star in a lot of male fantasies tonight, but you'll do."

Satisfied, he pulled on a battered bomber jacket, hitched it over his gun.

"I want one."

He noted her look at his Glock. "Yeah, I know. But I don't have one to spare." He slid on sunglasses, grabbed his keys. "Let's go."

"Why do you cover your eyes?"

"Styling, baby. I've got a pair for you in my car." He stopped at the elevator, pushed the Down button. "Try not to talk to anybody. If we have to have a conversation, let me handle it."

She started to object, but the wall opened. "A portal? Where does it lead?"

"It's an elevator. It goes up, it goes down. A kind of transportation."

"A box," she nodded as she stepped in with him. "That moves." Her grin spread when she felt the shift. "This is clever. Your world is very interesting."

The doors opened on three, and a woman and small boy got on.

"The elevator," Kadra said politely. "Goes up and goes down."

The woman slid an arm around the boy and drew him close to her side.

"Didn't I tell you to keep quiet?" Harper hissed when they reached the lobby and the woman hustled her son away.

"I spoke with good manners, and made no threat to her or her young."

"Just stick close," he ordered, and took her hand firmly in his.

When they stepped outside, he thought it was a good thing he had a grip on her. She froze in place, her head swiveling right and left. "What a world this is," she breathed. "Blue sky, great huts, so many people. So many scents. There." She pointed to a sidewalk vendor. "This is food."

"Later." He pulled her along the sidewalk. "My car's in a garage a couple blocks over."

"The ground is made of stone."

He had to jerk her up when she bent over to tap a fist on the sidewalk. "Concrete. Men make it and pour it over the ground."

"Why? Is the ground poisonous?"

"No. It's just easier."

"How can it be easier? The ground was already there." She stopped again, mouth agape as an ambulance whizzed by, sirens screaming, lights flashing. "Is it a war?"

"No, it's transportation. For the sick or the wounded."

She digested this and other wonders on the two-block hike. The shops with their goods locked behind glass, the crowds of people in a hurry, the clatter and din of the machines that ran on the wide stone road.

"This is a noisy world," she commented. "I like it. What are these trees?" she asked, knocking a fist on a telephone pole.

"I'll explain later. Just say nothing."

Harper strolled into the garage with a death grip on Kadra's hand. He flipped a salute to the attendant, who was passing the time with a magazine. But one look at Kadra had the attendant gaping.

"Oooh, baby! That is *fine*."

"Why am I called baby here?" she demanded as he whipped into the stairway. "I am not new young."

"It's an expression. Endearment or insult, depending on your point of view." On the second level, he crossed the lines of cars and stopped at his beloved '68 Mustang. He unlocked it, opened the passenger door. "Climb in."

She sniffed first, caught the scent of leather and approved. She was already fiddling with dials and jiggling the gearshift when he got behind the wheel. "Don't touch." He slapped her hand away. She kicked her elbow under his jaw. "Cut it out." Shoving her arm down, he reached for her seat belt. "You need to strap in. It's the law of the land."

When he bent to buckle her up, he saw that she was still miffed. "You sure push my buttons," he muttered.

"This is an expression?"

"Yeah. It means—"

"I do not need an explanation. You are aroused by me."

"And then some." He trailed his fingers over her cheek. Then he opened the glove compartment and tossed a pair of wraparound shades in her lap. "I guess we have to go kick some demon butt before we deal with our buttons."

4

SHE HAD A great deal to think about.

She was primarily a physical creature. When she was hungry, she ate. When she was tired, she slept. And all of her life, her purpose, above all others, had been to hunt.

It was a sacred trust, a sacred gift. She could laugh and weep, desire and dislike, dream and act. But over it all, through every cell in her body was the purpose.

She had been born, raised and trained for it.

But no slayer lived long if she didn't use her brain as well as her might.

Even with the wonder of her first car ride, the thrill of seeing the structures and the people, hearing the blasts of horns, of music, of voices, her mind still chipped away at the puzzle.

She had been sent to this place, and to this man. So their destinies were joined. She would protect him and his people with her life.

He was a seeker, and deserved respect. But as a slayer she ranked highest, save for the sorcerer. And if Rhee had spoken true, she had that in her blood as well.

The man had no right to usurp her authority. He would have to be put in his place for it.

But he was correct. This was his world, and his knowledge of it exceeded hers. If he was to be her guide, then she must follow. However much it rankled.

She desired him, which both pleased and irritated her. Pleased because he was strong and handsome, amusing and intelligent—and he desired her in turn. Irritated because she was unused to experiencing a desire this keen without the time and means to act upon it.

And she was not prepared for what was tangled in and woven through that desire. Lust was appetite, which could be easily sated. But this longing fluttering inside her, like a wild bird fighting to be free, was stronger, stranger than any need of the flesh.

It distracted her, and she could not afford to be distracted. If the Bok escaped her, this world, and her world, were doomed.

"So, how'd you get into the slayer business?"

She turned her head, and even with the dark glasses, Harper felt the heat of her gaze. "It was a gift, given me at my creation. It is woven in my blood, in my bone."

"Let's put it this way. You didn't pop out of the womb with a broadsword in your hand and a little dagger clenched in your teeth."

"I was trained." She liked watching the lights turn colors. She'd processed their purpose herself because she was tired of asking questions. "To track, to hunt, in weaponry. To fight, to build my body, my mind, my spirit."

"How about your parents?"

"I know no father. It is the way of slayers."

"All slayers are women?"

"We are female, birthed by females, raised, trained, and tested."

"What do the guys do? The men."

"Males hunt, farm, become warriors, scholars, seekers like yourself." She shrugged. "Whatever path is open to them. Some, in protecting their land, their families, in battle or in defense of self, kill demons. But they are not slayers."

"Are there more like you back home?"

"There were ten, now there are nine. Four weeks past, Sorak killed one of us. A trap. He drank the blood of a slayer. That is how he had the power, the strength, to elude me, to get this far. She was Laris. She was my friend."

"I'm sorry." Harper closed a hand over hers. "He'll pay for it."

The gesture, the simple warmth and connection, moved her. "There is no payment rich enough. His death will have to do." She looked over quickly when he lifted her hand to his mouth, brushed his lips over her knuckles.

"A custom," he said, reading her shock. "Like an expression. Comfort, affection, seduction. Whatever fits."

Her lips curved. "In my world you would be thrashed for taking such a liberty with a slayer."

"We're in my world now, baby."

"And here the sky is different, and the ground. The customs. I enjoy many of the new things in this place. The drink called coffee, the elevator, and the car. I have not decided if I like the box called television or all your expressions, but I enjoy the sensation of your mouth on my skin."

He parked the car, turned off the ignition. "You got a man back home? A lover?"

"No."

"You're going to have one here." He climbed out, skirted the hood, and opened her door. "We'll walk for a while," he told her and took her hand again. "Stay close."

She let him lead. It gave her the opportunity to observe and absorb, to identify scents. Food came to her again— sweet, spiced, tart. Her stomach tightened in hunger. Perhaps traveling through the portal sharpened the appetites, she thought. If that were true for the Bok, they would already have fed at least once.

She caught the scent of animal among the human. Great cats, reptile, fowl, and more she couldn't identify. And then she saw them, exotic beasts, prowling or dozing in enclosures while people strolled past or stopped to stare.

It gave her a pang at the most elemental level. "It is not right to lock them up. They are not born for this."

"Maybe it's not," he agreed. He hadn't come to the zoo since childhood because it invariably made him sad. "I can't say I care for it either."

"This is a cruel thing you do here. This is a sorry place, this zoo. Is this what you teach your young?" she demanded, gesturing to a little girl being wheeled in a stroller by her parents. "That one species can be locked away for the amusement of another?"

"I don't know how to explain it to you. Civilization has encroached. There isn't as much room as there once was. In captivity, they're safe, I guess, and tended. They can't be hunted or taken as trophies."

"They are not free," was all she said, and turned away.

"Okay, maybe this was a bad idea. It's depressing, and the place is jammed. I wasn't thinking about it being Sunday. It doesn't seem like the time and place for a demon snack. Maybe we should try the animal shelter—dogs and cats. Or hit the stables."

She held up a hand, bared her teeth. "Bok," was all she said.

She was on the scent and ran like the wind. People scrambled out of her way, and those who caught a glimpse of the sword under her coat scrambled faster and farther.

It was a challenge to keep up with her under normal circumstances, but with the obstacle course of people, children, benches, and trash receptacles in the zoo, Harper's lungs were burning by the time he caught up.

"Slow down," he snapped. "You mow down innocent bystanders, we'll get arrested before we get where you want to go. And I can't begin to tell you how much fun the cops will have with your demon story."

"There!" She pointed to a building, seconds before a stream of people rushed out. Screaming.

She drew her sword as she raced through the doorway.

Whatever Harper had expected, it hadn't been this, this stench of blood and death, of fear and rot. In the cages, monkeys were wild. Screeching, screaming, leaping desperately from branch to branch.

He saw the blood and gore on the floor, tracked it with his eyes, and found—to his horror—a man, no, a demon, feeding savagely on a body. A human body.

When the demon lifted his head, his teeth, his eyes glistened red.

It all happened in seconds. The shock, the disgust, the fury. All of those vicious sensations burst through him as Harper drew his gun. And something hideous pounced on his back.

Claws dug into his shoulders, gouged as the thing that attacked him let out a predatory howl. He spun, ramming back into the wall. His gun flew out of his hand and slid across the floor. Cursing, he battered the thing against the wall as his own blood spilled hot down his back. He felt the rough edge of a tongue slide through it, slurp hideously.

Revolted, he flew back with his elbow, aiming high for the throat, hammered down with his heel on the instep of a booted foot hard enough to hear bone snap.

There was a shriek, inhuman. Harper jabbed behind him with his fingers where he hoped to find eyes.

Now it screamed, and the claws released.

He saw what it was now, as he spun around. The face of a man, the eyes of a monster. It came for him, and Harper sprang into the fight.

It was limping from the bones he'd crushed, but it was still fast. Lightning fast. Harper whirled, and the thing hurtled past him. When it turned to charge again, he met its face with a flying kick.

Kadra fought her own demons, swinging her sword to block the slice of a curved blade, evading the swipe of claws as she carefully retreated. She gauged Harper's position by sound. She couldn't risk even a glance behind her. Out of the corner of her eye, she saw Sorak, behind the bars, grinning, grinning as he feasted and watched the battle.

Kadra flipped her dagger out of its sheath, managed to turn enough to judge Harper's distance and position. She feinted, thrust, then leaped to cleave the demon's sword arm from his body.

"Harper Doyle!" She shouted, then heaved him her sword as she snatched the sickle blade from the air to battle the next demon.

They fought back-to-back now, Harper wielding the sword, she slicing with the dagger and blade. Green blood mixed with red.

Still, she saw, Sorak watched.

"I will have you," he called out. "I will have your blood. I will have your body. I will have your mind."

"I am Kadra!" she almost sang it as she thrust through slicing claws and pinned the point of the dagger in the demon warrior's throat. "I am your death." She spun, prepared to leap into the other battle. And watched Harper's sword cleave his opponent's belly.

Through the smoke curling from the demon dead, she scooped the Glock up on the fly as she rushed to where Sorak fed and gloated. She saw only the quick flash of his teeth, the taunting swirl of his cloak as he bolted toward an open door on the side of the cage.

She fired, the explosions of sound roaring through the building. Even so, she could hear the demon's laughter. She vaulted over the safety rail, closed her hands on the bars of the cage where beasts lay slaughtered, and battered at the steel.

"Come on." Riding on adrenaline and pain, Harper wrenched her around. He shot the sword back into her sheath, snatched his gun and holstered it. "Put this away. Now," he snapped, handing her the dagger. "We're getting out, fast. There's no possible explanation for what just happened here, so we're not going to make one. Move!"

She ran with him, through the building, out the rear. He tugged the coat over her sword, wrapped an arm around her shoulders, and tried to look as normal as a couple could who had just battled a pack of demons.

"Keep it slow. Cops are already heading in." He heard the sirens, the shouts. They turned away from the noise and kept walking. How long had they been inside? he wondered. It had seemed like hours. But now he realized it had been only minutes.

"Can you track it?" Harper asked her.

Alone, on her world, the answer would have been yes. But here, with the crowds of people, the scents and sights so unfamiliar to her senses, she was unsure.

"He will go to ground now. He knew. He knew I would come here. Sorak has more knowledge than I thought. Now he has fed, he has amused himself. He will rest and wait. He will not feed again in the daylight."

"Just as well. The place is going to be crawling with cops. Since we're covered with blood, and armed, we wouldn't get very far."

And he had a bad feeling that a lot of the blood was his own. He wouldn't be any good to Kadra in the next round if he was light-headed and shocky. First things first, he thought as he concentrated on staying upright. Get bandaged up, get steady. Then think.

"We'll hunt the bastard down and kill him with his belly full."

It was difficult to turn away from the hunt. But she had seen the demon attack him from the rear and knew he was wounded. She would not leave him behind.

"He has disguised his scent with the animals, and the humans. He will take time for me to find his lair." She steadied him when he swayed against her, and the hand she pressed to his shoulder came away smeared with his blood.

"How bad is your wound?"

"I don't know. Bad enough. Fucking claws. Went right through the leather. I've only had this jacket five, six years."

She turned her head to look at the gouges and was relieved to see the demon had torn more cloth than flesh. "It is not so bad. It was a good battle," she said with sudden cheer. "You fight well."

"Three out of four. It's just the one now."

"He will make more."

The horror of that seized Harper's belly. "We have to stop him."

"We will do what must be done. Now we go back to your hut. Your wounds must be tended. We will rest, eat, think. We will be ready for the night."

Her unerring sense of direction took them back to his car. "Can I sit on the side with the wheel now?"

"No, you can't sit on the side with the wheel now. Or

ever." Hurting, exhausted, he jabbed the key into the lock, wrenched open the door.

"Are all so selfish with their possessions here?"

"A man's car is his castle," Harper stated, and limped around to take the wheel. "Are you hurt?" he remembered to ask.

"No, I am unharmed." Realizing he might take this as a criticism of his skill, she took his hand as he had taken hers. "But I am a slayer."

"Kiss ass."

She cocked her head. The battle had lifted her mood. "This is another expression?"

He had to laugh, had to hiss in pain. On a combination of both, he started the car. "Yeah, baby, but it's one I wouldn't mind you taking literally."

5

THOUGH SHEER WILL kept Harper conscious, he was in considerable pain and woozy from the loss of blood by the time he pulled back into his slot at the garage. Kadra's idea of how to deal with the problem was to carry him.

He had just enough strength left to stop her from slinging him over her shoulder. And just enough wit to realize she could have pulled it off.

"No." Since his limbs had gone watery on him, he warded her off with a scowl. "I'm not being carried across the Lower East Side by a woman."

"This is foolish. You're injured. I am not."

"Yeah, yeah, keep rubbing it in. Just give me a hand."

When she frowned and held one out, he shook his head. "You're a literal creature." He slid an arm around her waist, let her take some of his weight. "Walk and talk," he told her. "Tell me more about this change."

"After the kiss of change, the victim falls into a trance— a sleep that is not a sleep, for one day. During the sleep, the demon blood mixes with the human's. The human becomes what has poisoned him, with the demon's instincts, his habits. His appetites."

Since Harper's breathing was ragged, she tightened her grip and shortened her stride. "When the human wakes he is demon, though some wake before the change is complete and are demi-demons. In either stage, the one who has changed is bound to the one who changed him."

"Is there a cure?"

"Death," she said flatly, and shifted her grip on him as they stepped outside. He was pale, she noted. And his breath was only more labored. It would have been easier to carry him.

But she understood a warrior's pride.

"Your hut is only a short journey. We will go at your pace."

"Just keep talking." His shoulder was going numb, and that worried him. "I need to focus."

"Why did you become a seeker?"

"I like to find things out. Without a PI license, it's called nosiness. With one, it's called a profession. Insurance fraud, missing persons, some skip tracing. I try to stay out of the marital arena. It's just humiliating for all parties to stand outside a motel room with a camera."

She didn't know what he was talking about, but she liked his voice. Despite his wounds, or perhaps because of them, there was grit in it. "Are you a successful seeker?"

"I get by." He looked around but couldn't quite pinpoint where they were. The sounds of traffic, the busy music of the city, sounded dim. She was the only thing clear to him now—the supporting strength of her arm, the firm curves of her body, the scent of the sacred waterfall that lingered in her hair.

It was as if both their worlds had receded and they themselves were all that was left.

"What must you get by?"

"Hmm?" He turned his head. He'd been right, he thought, there really was nothing but her. "I mean I do all right. I do regular legwork for a lawyer. Jake, the one I thought had hired you. He's got a sick sense of humor. That's why I love him."

He staggered at the curb, tried to orient himself when she steadied him. "It is this way." She turned the corner, glanced up and down the street. "Where is the well? You require water."

"Doesn't work that way here." But she was right about one thing. His thirst was vicious. He nodded toward a sidewalk vendor. "There."

With her arm banded around his waist, Kadra watched Harper exchange several small disks for a bottle. He fought the top off, drank deep.

"You must pay for water? Does it have magical properties?" She took it, drank. "Nothing but water," she said with some amazement. "The merchant is a robber. I will go back and speak to him."

"No. No." Despite the dizziness, Harper laughed. "It's just one of the acceptable lunacies of our little world. When water comes out of the tap, it's free. Sort of. When it comes out of a bottle, you pay on the spot."

She pondered this as they came to the intersection. She'd watched the way the people, the cars, the lights worked together. When the metal tree ordered the waiting group to walk, everyone hurried, often sliding and swooping between cars that jammed together and faced other metal trees with lights of amber, emerald, and ruby.

Everyone in the village played along.

She felt Harper sag, and pinched his waist ruthlessly to snap him back. "We have only . . ." She flipped back to his earlier term for the section of road. "One more block."

"Okay, okay." He could feel sweat running a clammy line down his back. His vision was going in and out. "Let's talk about me. I'm thirty. As of yesterday. Unmarried. Came close a couple years ago, but I came to my senses."

"Had the woman bewitched you?"

"No." He had to smile at the term. "You could say that was the problem: she *didn't* bewitch me. This is a huge disappointment to my parents, who want grandchildren. As I'm an only child, I'm their one shot at it."

"Is it not possible in this place to make young without a lifemate? Can you not select a breeding partner for this purpose?"

"Yeah, you could, and a lot of people do. I guess I'm more of a traditionalist in that one area. If I have kids, I want them to have the package. You like kids?"

"I am fond of young. They have innocence and potential, and a special kind of beauty. In time I will select a breeding partner so that I may make life. It is a great honor to make life."

"I'm with you on that." Nearly there, he told himself. Please, God, we're nearly there. "Anyway, my parents live in New Jersey. Another world."

"Was Old Jersey destroyed?"

"Ah . . . no." His head was spinning now. Concentrate, he ordered himself. Just put one foot in front of the other. "Geography and world history lessons later. Let's stick with personal revelations. I didn't want to tie on my dad's cop's shoes, so I veered off into private investigation. I apprenticed with a big, slick firm uptown, but I didn't like the suit and tie brigade. Went out on my own about five years ago. I'm good at what I do."

"It's wasteful to be bad at what you do."

"You know, my dad would lap you right up. He'd like you," Harper explained, breathlessly now. "He was a good cop. Retired three years ago. He'd go for your sense of order."

He fumbled out his keys as they approached his building's entrance. She wanted to ask him why everything had to be locked, like a treasure box, but his face was dead white now.

She dragged him to the elevator, puzzled out the buttons. They had come down, so now they would go up. It pleased her enormously when the doors opened.

"Four," he managed. "Push four. If we have to call 911, I'm going to leave it to you to explain that I've been clawed by a Bok demon."

Ignoring him, and regretting that she couldn't fully appreciate the ride this time, she dragged him out when the doors opened again. She took the keys from him, selected the proper one, and unlocked his door.

"You don't miss a trick, do you? You'd make a damn good PI."

She merely booted the door closed behind them, then bending, lifted him onto her shoulder.

"Honey." His voice slurred. "This is so sudden."

She laid him facedown on the bed, peeled off his ruined jacket, then tore away what was left of his shirt.

His breath hissed through his teeth at the bright burn of pain. "Can you be a little more rough, Nurse Ratched? I live for pain."

"Quiet now." The wounds were deeper than she'd thought. Four ugly grooves and one jagged puncture. The blood that had started to clot flowed freely again. "This must first be cleansed. How do I fetch water?"

"Tap. Bathroom tap. The sink. Damn it. The white bowl—ah, the taller one," he added as he got an image of her scooping water out of his toilet. "Turn the handle."

She found the bathing room, and the sink. And was delighted when water gushed out. She soaked a towel and carried it sopping wet into the bedroom. She felt his body shudder when she laid it over his back.

He fought well, she thought again as she cleaned the wounds. And was stalwart in his pain. He had more than the strength of a warrior; he had the heart of one too. She remembered how his hand had whipped up and closed around the hilt of the sword she'd tossed him.

A good team, she decided. She'd never found a partner she could admire, respect, and desire.

She retrieved her supply bag, reached in for the vial of healing powder that all warriors carried. Her fingers brushed over the cloth Mav had wrapped around her hand.

Lips pursed, Kadra studied her own unmarked palm. Perhaps some of the healer's powers were still in the cloth. Quickly, she made a paste from powder and water.

"This will sting," she told him. "I'm sorry for it."

"Sting" was a mild word for the blaze that erupted under his skin when she spread the medication over his wounds. His hands fisted in the spread, his body jerked in protest.

"Only a moment," she murmured, wrenched by his pain. "It eats any infection."

"Does it chew through flesh while it's at it?" He spit the words out through gritted teeth.

"No, but it feels that way. It is no shame to scream."

"I'll keep that in mind." But he swore instead, softly, steadily, viciously, and earned more of the slayer's respect.

When the paste began to turn from sickly yellow to white, she breathed a sigh of relief. The infection was dying. Over the smeared wounds, she lay the thin healing cloth.

"If there is any magic in my blood," she whispered, "let it help him. Sleep now, Harper the valiant." She brushed her fingers through his hair. "Sleep and heal."

He dreamed, strange, colorful dreams. Battles and blood. Storms and swords. Kadra, with her war cry echoing through dark, dank tunnels. The king of demons feasting on flesh in the shadows.

And he himself delivering the killing blow that sent green blood gushing.

In dreams he knew her body, the feel of those luscious curves under his hand, the taste of her skin, the sound of her moan. He saw her rising over him, warrior, goddess, woman.

He felt, real as life, the warm press of her lips on his.

And woke aching for her.

He sat up, instinctively reaching for the back of his shoulder. He found nothing, no wound, no break in the skin, no scar.

Had it all been a dream after all? One wild booze-induced dream starring the most magnificent woman ever created?

The idea that she was only in his mind depressed him brutally. What were a few Bok demons between friends, he thought as he pushed himself out of bed, when you had a Kadra in your life?

Was the only woman who'd ever stirred him on every level just a product of his imagination? Of wishful thinking? If he could only fall in love in dreams, why the hell did he have to wake up?

Back to reality, Doyle, he told himself, then took a step toward the bedroom door and nearly tripped over his leather jacket.

He scooped it up, fingers rushing over the battered material. Nothing, nothing in his life had ever delighted him more than seeing those bloodstained rips.

He tossed it aside and bolted for the door.

She'd changed back into her own clothes. And was sitting cross-legged on the floor, her nose all but pressed to the television screen, where the Yankees were taking on the Tigers.

"I like this battle," she said without turning around. "The warriors in the white are beating the warriors in the gray by three runs. They are better with the clubs."

"Girl of my dreams," Harper said aloud. "She likes baseball."

"There were other images in the box." And each had startled and fascinated. "But this is my favorite."

"Okay, that does it. We have to get married."

She turned then, smiled at him. His color was back, and that relieved her. His eyes were clear, and held more than recovered health. The lust in them aroused her. "You healed well."

"I healed just dandy."

"I hunted among your stores," she told him. "You have little, but I like this food and drink." She gestured toward the bag of sour-cream-and-onion potato chips and the bottle of Coors.

"You're perfect. It's just a little scary."

"We must eat. Fighting requires fuel."

"Yeah, we'll eat. We'll order some pizza."

He looked hungry as well, she noted. But not for food. She rose smoothly. Her blood was already warm for him. "I'm pleased you are well."

"Yeah. I'm feeling real healthy just now. You can tell me how you managed that later."

"You do not wish to talk at this time." She nodded, stepped toward him. Then she circled around him to check his shoulder—and to admire his form. When she stopped face-to-face again, her eyes were level with his. "Do you wish to join your body to mine?"

He blinked once, slow as an owl. "Is that a trick question?"

"You have desire for me."

Charmed, perplexed, he dipped his hands in his pockets. "Is that all it takes?"

"No." She was never as sure of herself as a female as she was as a slayer. But this time, with him, she felt sure. "But I have desire for you as well. It is a heat in my belly, a burn in my blood. I want to join with you."

"I wanted you before I even met you," he told her.

"This is like a poem." And softened her under the skin. "You are well named. I cannot speak as cleverly, so I will say we have time for this and for food before we hunt again. And that our minds and bodies will be stronger for appeasing both appetites."

On those long, tantalizing legs, she walked past him into the bedroom.

Worlds, he thought as he followed her, were about to collide.

"Whoa. Wait. Hold on." She'd already stripped off her top, and was pulling off her boots. "What's the rush?"

She looked up, a crease between her brows. "Are you ready to sport?"

"Yeah. But we could take a minute to . . ." He stared at her, golden skin, naked breasts. "What am I saying?" He scooped her off her feet and made her laugh by tossing her on the bed.

She rolled, came up on her haunches. Saliva pooled in his mouth as she grinned at him. "You have energy. Good. Strip," she ordered. "We will wrestle first."

"You wanna wrestle?" He unbuttoned his jeans.

"It is stimulating," she began, then lowered her gaze. "You seem to be very stimulated already. I admire your body, baby." It pleased her to use one of his terms of affection. "I want to touch it."

"Are you sure you're not a dream, brought on by one too many bourbons and bumps?"

"I am real." Watching him, she stroked her hands over her breasts, cupped them. "Touch me."

When he came forward, reached, she rolled away laughing. And crooked her finger at him.

He dived.

She obviously took her wrestling seriously—he was pinned in under five seconds. "Two out of three," he said and put himself in the game.

They tumbled over the bed, hands gripping, sliding, legs scissoring. Bodies straining. He wasn't sure if he pinned her by skill or because she'd allowed it. He didn't give a damn. Not when she was sprawled under him, her hair spread out, her eyes hot and green.

"Let's call it a draw," he suggested, lowering his head.

Her hand shot out, wedged between them. "There can be no mouth on mouth. This is not permitted."

"Kisses are illegal in your world?"

"A kiss is a gift." Now it was she who was breathless, from the press of his body, from the knowledge that his lips were nearly upon hers. "One given in promise between those who mate."

"I had mating in mind."

"No, joining. Joining is . . . sport. Mating is for life."

He wanted that mouth, as much as he wanted to breathe. And he wanted her to give it to him. "In this world a kiss is a sign of trust, affection, love, friendship. All manner of things. When a man and a woman join here, a kiss is a part of the union. A pleasurable part. You've never kissed a man?"

"I've made no promise to a man with my lips."

Make one to me, he thought. "Let me show you the way it's done in my world." He brushed his lips over her cheek. "Let me have your mouth, Kadra."

The hand separating them began to tremble. "I can take no lifemate." She felt his breath on her lips, warm, seductive. "It is not permitted for a slayer in my world."

"This is here. This is now." He closed his hand over the one she still held to his heart. "Let me be the first. Let me be the only."

She could have resisted. She had the strength, and though she could feel it melting, she still had the will. But his lips were so lovely, so soft against her skin. The glide of them was like all the promises that could never be given.

And her own lips yearned.

His world, she thought as she yielded. She was in his world now.

Their lips met, silkily. And her breath rushed out in shock at the sensation. The intimacy, the sweet flavor, the smooth slide of tongue against tongue were more potent than any brew she had ever sipped.

With one drink, she was drunk on him.

"Again," she demanded, and dragged him down by the hair until mouth ravaged mouth.

He had thought a kiss a simple thing, just another part of the mating dance. But with her he was whirled into the glory of it. He sank deep into her, and deeper still, until the taste of her was a craving in his belly.

I've waited for you, she thought, bowing her body to his—a body that ached for his hands. How could I have waited for you when I didn't know you existed? How could I have needed you when you were never there?

But when his hands moved over her, she knew it was true. All the passion that was in her blood, all the passion newly discovered, she gave to him.

She was a fantasy come to life. All curves and sleek skin. Urgent hands and avid mouth. She raged beneath him, demanding more even as he gave. She was a feast who commanded him to feed.

Now when they wrestled, their breath was ragged and their skin damp. The mouth that had conquered hers rushed everywhere, tasted all of her.

When she crested, it was like a wave rising up inside her, spilling out on a throaty cry and pouring into him.

She rose above him, as she had in dreams. Woman, warrior, lover. She took him into her, closed around him, and throwing her head back, rode.

Joined, he thought dimly as his blood pounded. Everything inside him was joined with her.

He reared up, banding his arms around her, fusing his mouth to hers as they took each other over the brink.

6

No JOINING HAD ever been so intense or so pleasurable. None had caused her to feel this mysterious sensation that was beyond the physical. Nor to find herself both conquered and victorious.

Bards spoke of such unions, but she had never believed the words were more than romantic delusion.

And they were joined still, she realized. Wrapped tight, fused like two links in one chain. This was more than sport, she thought. She didn't wish it to end.

She rubbed her lips together, experimenting. His taste was still there—his flesh, yes—but it was more. His mouth, the intimacy of the kiss that had been like . . . feeding each other. She hadn't known such matters could have such heat, and yet be tender.

She had never known tenderness, nor had she believed she required it.

Small wonder that in the world she knew, a mouth kiss was reserved for lifemates and was part of the sacred vows that stretched for all time.

If he lived in her world, or she in his, could there have been a lifetime between them?

Thinking it brought such a pang, such a wrench of longing. She was a slayer, she reminded herself, and he a seeker. They could walk the same path only until their battle was won. Then they, like their worlds, would stand apart.

But until their time was ended, she could have what she could take.

"I like the kissing," she said, sliding her hands into his hair as she eased back to see his face. "I would like to do more if there's an opportunity to join again."

"Kissing isn't just for joining." Still lost in her, still steeped in the first heady brew of love, he brushed his lips across hers.

"What else? Teach me."

At the idea of tutoring her, his pulse kicked again. "At times like this, after making love—"

"Making love." Following his lead, she leaned in to rub her lips over his. "I like this expression."

"Sometimes, after, while a couple is still tuned to each other, they kiss to show how much pleasure they were given. It might be long and lazy, like this."

He drew her in again on a slow, gentle glide that brought a purr of approval to her throat. Soft, so soft, deep without demand. Sweet as a maiden's dream.

"Yes," she sighed. "Again."

"Wait. Sometimes, when passions have been roused and people are still caught in that last edge of the storm of them, the tone of the kiss reflects that. Like this."

He caught her to him, close and hard, and his mouth was like a fever on hers. Now she groaned and wrapped around him like rope. He felt the thrill of her on his skin, in his blood, down to the pit of his stomach.

"You make me want." Her voice was thick now, and her heart galloped as if she'd raced to the pinnacle of the Stone Mountains. "In ways I have never wanted."

"You make me need." He held her now, just held her. "In ways I've never needed. What are we going to do about this, Kadra?"

She shook her head. "What must be done is all that can be done."

"Things have changed. Things are different now."

If only they could be, she thought. With him, a joy she hadn't known was locked inside her could be free. "What I feel for you fills me, and empties me. I've never known this with another." Still, she made herself draw back from him. "The fate of two worlds is in our hands. We can't take each other and lose them."

"We'll save them. And then—"

"Don't talk of 'and then.' " She touched her fingers to his lips. "Whatever fate holds for us, we have now. It's a gift to be treasured, not to be questioned."

"I want a life with you."

She smiled, but there was sorrow in her eyes. "Some lifetimes have to be lived in a day."

He wasn't going to accept that. He was good at solving puzzles, Harper thought. He'd find a way to solve this one. He also knew when he was banging against a head as hard as his own. There were times for force, and times for strategy.

"Having a warrior goddess drop on me out of another dimension, visiting an alternate reality, fighting demons, making love. It's been a pretty full day so far." He tangled his fingers in her hair. "What's next on the schedule?"

Strength, Kadra thought, wasn't only a matter of muscle. It was a matter of courage. They would both be valiant enough to accept destiny. "We must hunt Sorak, but we will need food and planning time. He's the mightiest of his kind, and the most sly."

"Okay, we'll order that pizza and fuel up while we figure out our plan of attack."

Nodding, and grateful he hadn't pressed where she was now vulnerable, she rolled off the bed. "What is this pizza?"

No pizza on A'Dair, he thought. Score one for Earth. "It's, ah, a kind of pie. Round, usually," he said as he allowed himself the pleasure of watching her slip on the brief bottom half of her hunting costume.

"You're magnificent, Kadra. 'Beautiful' is too ordinary,

too simple a word," he added when she stared at him. "Do men on A'Dair tell you that you take their breath away, that looking at you is like being struck blind by a force of beauty so strong it's painful?"

His words made her weak, as if she'd slain a thousand demons in one day. "Men do not speak so to slayers."

He rose. "I do."

"You are different." So wonderfully different. "When I hear the words from you, they make me feel proud. And shy. I have never been shy," she added, baffled. "It pleases me that you find me attractive to look at."

"Do you think that's all I meant? You are very attractive. You're right off the charts in that area. But then you add the courage, the brains, the compassion I saw in you when Mav told you of her father's death, the active curiosity, the sense of fun, the heart of a warrior. You're unique to any world, and I'm dazzled by you."

"No one has ever . . ." Her throat burned. "I need time to find the words to give back to you that are as fine and rich."

He took her hands, lifted them to his lips. "They were free. They don't require any trade or payment."

"Like a gift?"

"Exactly."

"Thank you."

He dressed, switched the TV to the news in case there were any updates. He started to call in the pizza order. Then he remembered it wasn't just his taste that had to be satisfied this time. "Okay, pizza can come with a variety of options. Meat, vegetables—stuff like onions, mushrooms, peppers, sausage, pepperoni. It's an endless parade. I usually get it pretty loaded. Is there anything you don't eat?"

"I don't care for the meat of the grubhog."

He let out a quick, huffing laugh. "Check. Hold the grubhog."

He called in the order—explained to her what a phone was—then went into the kitchen for a couple of beers. "It'll take about twenty minutes. Let's figure out what step we take next over a beer."

"I like the beer," she told him.

"Just one more reason we're perfect for each other." He tapped his bottle to hers. "So." He dropped down on the couch, stretched out. "You said Sorak would have a lair. What sort of digs would he look for? What's his habit in living arrangements?"

"Demons live belowground." She crossed her feet at the ankles, then lowered herself in one smooth move to the floor. "They like the dark after feeding. They will burrow, dig tunnels so they may travel under the ground."

She picked up the portable phone he'd set down and began to play with it.

"In the east, Laris and I once tracked a demon pack to a great lair, with many tunnels through the rock and dirt, with many chambers for stores and sleep and treasures. We slew the pack and destroyed the lair with fire. It was Clud's palace, and there I destroyed the king of demons. But Sorak, then prince, was not there. When he heard of this, he vowed to kill the slayers who had killed his sire, and to build a great new kingdom in a place where no slayer could defeat him. I have this."

She flipped back her hair to show him a thin hooked scar at the base of her neck. "Only a demon king can leave his mark on a slayer. This is Clud's. The last swipe of his claws before my sword took his heart."

"Impressive." Harper pulled down his shirt to expose the line of puckered skin on his shoulder. "Skip trace, with a bad attitude and a switchblade."

She nodded. "How did you kill him?"

"It doesn't work that way here—ideally. I kicked his ass, then turned him over to the cops and collected my fee. The authorities," he explained. "We put bad guys—our demons—in jail. In cages, like at the zoo today."

"Ah." She considered that, and found it just. Captivity was a living death. "Is the demon who broke your nose also in his cage?"

"Sucker punch," Harper told her, running his hand down the uneven line of his nose. "Yeah, he's doing a stretch. Pissant grifter going around snuggling up to rich women, then ripping them off, copping their jewelry, draining their bank accounts. Prick."

Kadra angled her head. "I like the way you speak. I find it arousing to listen to your stories."

"Oh, yeah?" He slid down onto the floor beside her, walked his fingers up her boot to her thigh. "I've got a million of them."

"Sporting must wait."

"I like your face. I find it arousing to look at your face." He touched it, just a skim of fingertips over her cheek. "When I was sleeping, I dreamed of making love with you. Then it happened, just the way I'd dreamed it."

"This is vision."

"Maybe." He thought of the blood and the battle, of the dark and the smoke. "One thing, before we get back on track. I've always liked working alone; that's why I went out on my own. I've liked living alone, which is why I've screwed up any potentially serious relationship with a woman. I never wanted a partner, until you."

She lifted a hand to his cheek in turn. A kind of joining, she realized, with only a touch. "I have been alone. It is the way of slayers. I never wished it otherwise, until you. They will write songs about you in my world. The great warrior from beyond A'Dair."

And when she listened to them by the fire, she thought, she would be alone again.

She let her hand drop away, then took a deep drink of her beer. "I tracked Sorak across my world and killed many of his warriors. He has sired no young, and with his death, the power of the Bok will be diminished. I thought he meant to build a lair in some far-off place, a fortress of great defense. But in my world. I did not know he meant to come to this place, to build his kingdom in yours."

"We won't give him the chance. You said he would burrow underground."

"Yes. The Bok require the cool dark when they rest."

"I've got an idea where he might've gone. The subway. We have a system of tunnels under the city, for transportation. The sewers are another option," Harper considered, "but I don't know why anyone, even a demon, would want to set up housekeeping in the sewers if he had any other choices. The trick will be pinpointing the right sector."

"What creatures of your world travel this subway, this underground route?"

"The variety is endless. Just people, of all walks. It's a crowded city. It's another reasonably efficient and inexpensive way to get around it."

He spent the next few minutes explaining the idea and basic workings of the subway system.

"This is clever. You have an innovative and interesting culture. I would like to have more time to study it."

"Stick around, take all the time you want." He rose when his buzzer sounded. He went to the intercom by the front door, verified the pizza delivery, and buzzed the entrance door open.

"You keep a servant in that small box?"

"No." Amused when she came over to peer at it, he explained its function, then opened his door to the delivery boy's knock, paid him, and sent him on his way.

"Was that your servant?"

"No. I gave my servants this century off. He works for the place that makes the food. It's his job to bring it to people when they call on the phone. Hungry?"

"Yes." She sniffed. "It smells very good."

He set the pizza box on the coffee table. "I'll get some napkins—we'll need them—then you can see if it tastes as good as it smells."

When he came back she was sitting on the floor, the lid of the box open, poking a finger at the crust. "It is very colorful. Is this a staple of your people's diet?"

"It's a staple of mine." He lifted a slice, flicked strings of cheese with his finger. "You just pick it up with your hands and go for it." He demonstrated with an enthusiastic bite.

Following suit, Kadra brought a slice to her lips. She bit through pepperoni, through pepper, through onion into cheese and spicy sauce, down to the thin, yeasty crust.

The sound she made, Harper thought, was very like one she'd made during sex.

"I like this pie called pizza," she stated, and bit in again. "It is good food," she added, her mouth full.

"Baby, this is the perfect food."

"It goes well with the beer. It's like a celebration to have kissing and joining, then pizza and beer."

He knew it was ridiculous, but his heart simply melted. "I'm crazy about you, Kadra. I'm a goddamn mental patient."

"This is an expression?"

"It means I'm in love with you. I go thirty years without a scratch, and in less than a day I'm fatally wounded."

"Don't speak of death, even as an expression. Not before battle." She reached out, closed her hand tight over his. "It is bad luck. When it is done . . . When it is done, Harper, we will talk more of feelings."

"All right, we'll table it—if I have your word that when it's done you let me make my pitch."

Baffled, she frowned at him over what was left of her first slice. "Like in the battle of baseball?"

"Not exactly. That you'll let me tell you the way it could be for us."

"When it is done, you will make your pitch. Now tell me more of the subway."

"Hold on." He switched his attention to the televised news bulletin.

The reporter spoke of the attack at the zoo, the murder of the guard and the mutilation of several animals. Witness reports were confused and conflicting, ranging from the claim of an attack by a dozen armed men to one by a pack of wild animals.

"They don't know what they're up against," Harper said quietly as the newscaster reported that the police were investigating the incident and that the zoo would remain closed until further notice. "They don't have a clue. I call them with the truth, I'm just another loony."

"It is for us," Kadra told him. "Rhee has said that we would fight this battle together. He must be destroyed here or driven back where he belongs. There must be balance again."

"Here." Harper rolled his shoulder where a demon had dug its claws. "We finish it here. New York style."

Kadra pondered the images on the television, the moving paintings of the zoo. "This subway. Does it go near the place where they keep the animals? Where we battled today?"

"There are possibilities."

"Sorak would like a lair near prey. It will be dark soon," she said with a long look at the sky through the window. "Then we hunt."

7

SHE BALKED AT changing her hunting gear for jeans a second time, claiming they restricted her. He let it pass, figuring the long coat would cloak most of her . . . attributes.

The thing about New York, Harper thought, as they passed a guy with shoulder-length white hair, two nose rings, and a black leather jumpsuit, was there was always someone dressed weirder than you were.

He wore his ripped jacket, for sentimental reasons. And for the practical one that if he was going up against a demon again, there was no point to sacrificing another garment to the long blue claws.

He had his Glock in a shoulder holster, a backup .38 in an ankle holster, a combat knife sheathed at his back, and a switchblade in his left boot.

He'd have preferred an Uzi, but what he had on hand would have to do.

"I like my work," he told Kadra. "And I like to think it makes a difference to some of the people who come to me with problems." He paused to take a good look at his neighborhood—his city—his world. "But this heading out to save the planet stuff brings on a real high."

"You were born for it." When he glanced over at her, she shrugged. "This is what I believe. We are born for a purpose. How we live, how we treat others who live with us forms our spirit and determines if we will fulfill that purpose or fail. We were meant to face this night together. Meant for it from the moment we were created."

"I like that. And I'll take it one step further. We were meant for each other, too."

Meant to love each other, she thought, and to live alone in two different worlds. Her life had been filled with sacrifices, but none would bring the sorrow of the one she had yet to make.

Harper led Kadra down into the station for the train heading uptown. She would have vaulted over the turnstile if he hadn't blocked her.

"You have to use a token, then you walk through."

"These are very flimsy barricades," she pointed out as she bumped through. "Even a child could get over them."

"Yeah, well, it's . . . tradition."

"Like a ritual," she decided, satisfied. She heard the roar, felt the floor vibrate. "The earth trembles." She was prepared to drag him to safety when he grabbed her hand.

"It's just a train coming in." Still holding her hand, he pulled her onto the platform, where she studied the other waiting passengers.

It was a huge cave, strongly lit. She had never seen so much life, so much motion and magic in one place. "Your people have so many colors of skin. It's beautiful. You are blessed to have such richness of person, such variety." When she glanced back at him, she saw he was smiling at her in an odd way. "What is it?"

"Nothing." He leaned toward her, and to her utter shock, kissed her mouth.

"We cannot join here," she said in a hissing whisper. "It is a private activity."

"It wasn't that kind of a kiss. Remember, there are all kinds."

"I thought you were pretending."

"Is that a polite word for lying? On this side of the portal, people kiss all the time. Lovers, friends, relatives. Complete strangers."

She snorted. "Now I will say you are lying."

"Locking lips is practically a global pastime. And this one'll get you: people pay a fee to sit in a big, darkened room as a group and watch other people's images on a screen—a larger version of the TV, where you saw baseball. One of the things those images often do is kiss."

"I think you are a harper after all, because you tell fantastic tales with great ease and skill."

"Nothing in those knowledge banks about movies?"

She frowned, but tipped her head and searched through. When her eyes widened, lit with delight, he knew she'd hit on it.

"Movies." She tested the word. "I would like to see one."

"It's a date." He heard the rumble of the approaching uptown train. They had another date to keep first.

She liked the train that flew under the earth. She liked the way people crowded inside, bumping together as they clung to metal straps. There were colorful drawings to study and read. Some spoke of magical liquid that gifted the user with shiny, sexy hair. Another advised her to practice safe sex. There was a wall map provided for lost travelers, and yet another picture that boasted its elixir could transform the skin to make it sexually attractive to others.

Kadra leaned close to Harper's ear. "Is sex the religion of your world?"

"Ah . . . you could say a lot of people worship it. Why are you whispering?"

"No one is speaking. Is conversation permitted?"

"Sure. It's just that most of these people don't know each other. They're strangers, so they don't have anything to say."

Kadra considered it, and finding it reasonable, she tapped the shoulder of the woman standing beside her. "I am Kadra, Slayer of Demons. My companion in this dimension is Harper Doyle. Together we hunt Sorak."

The sound Harper made was somewhere between a laugh

and a moan. "Rehearsing," he said with what he hoped was a nonthreatening smile. "New play. Way, *way* off Broadway. Honey," Harper said to Kadra as the woman edged as far away as the press of bodies would allow, "maybe you should just talk to me."

"Making introductions is courteous."

"Yeah, well, you start chatting about demons, it tends to weird people out."

The train stopped. People poured off, people poured on. Kadra scowled and planted her feet. "As you said, how can they defend against Sorak if they are unaware of him?"

"I've thought about that. Thought about going to the cops. The National Guard." Frustrated, he dragged a hand through his hair. "Nobody's going to believe us, and the time we'd waste trying to convince them we're not candidates for a padded cell would only give Sorak more of an advantage."

"You said there were demons in this world, that you put them in cages."

"There are plenty of them. But they're a different type than you're used to fighting. They're not another species, they're us. People come in a variety pack, Kadra. Most of them are good—at the core, they're good. But a lot of them aren't. So they prey on their own kind."

"To prey on your own kind is the greatest sin. You hunt these demons. Who else hunts them?"

"Ideally? The law. It just doesn't always work out. It'll take more than a subway ride for me to explain it to you. I don't always understand it myself."

"There is good and there is evil. The good must always fight the evil as the strong must always protect the weak. This is nothing that can change by walking through a portal."

He linked his hand with hers. Her vision was so clear, he thought. And her spirit so pure. "I love you," he murmured. "I love everything about you."

The warmth poured into her, flooding her belly, overflowing her heart. "You only know one day of me."

"Time doesn't mean a damn." The train jerked to a halt at the next station. "We'll be getting off soon. Whatever happens tonight, I need you to believe what I'm telling you now. I love you. My world was incomplete until you came into it."

"I believe what you say." It felt strange and right to press her lips to his. "My heart is joined to yours."

But what she didn't say, what she couldn't bear to say, was that her world would be forever incomplete when she left him.

"You're thinking that when this is over, we won't be able to be together." He put his hand on her cheek now, kept his gaze steady on hers. "That I'll have to stay in this world, and you'll have to go back to yours."

"There is only one thing that should be occupying our minds now. That is Sorak."

"When we get off this train, we'll worry about Sorak. Right now, it's you and me."

"You have a very domineering nature. I find it strangely appealing."

"Same goes. When this is over, Kadra, we'll find a way. That's what people do when they love each other. They find a way."

She thought of the globe in her pouch. The key that was hers only until the battle was done. The weight of it dragged on her heart like a stone. "And when there is no way to be found?"

"Then they make one. Whatever I have to do to make it work, I'll do. But I won't lose you."

"I can't stay in your world, Harper. I am a slayer, bound by blood, by oath, and by honor to protect my people."

"Then I'll go with you."

Stunned, she stared at him. "You would give up your world, the wonders of it, for me? For mine?"

"For us. I'll do whatever has to be done to have a life with you."

Tears swam into her eyes. She would never have shed one for pain, but one spilled down her cheek now. For love. "It is not possible. It would never be permitted."

"Who the hell's in charge? We'll have ourselves a sit-down."

She managed a wobbly smile. "It would take more than

a subway ride to explain it to you. There are balances, Harper, that must be carefully held. I am here to right a wrong, and am given entrance by the power of Rhee's magic. When I have done what I've been sent here to do, I'll have no choice but to return. You will have no choice but to stay."

"We'll just see about that. Here's our stop."

"You are angry."

"No, this isn't my angry face. This is my if-I-can-fight-demons-I-can-sure-as-hell-fight-the-cosmos face." He gave her hand a squeeze. "Trust me."

She trusted no one more. If she had been permitted to take a lifemate, it would have been Harper Doyle. His strength, his honesty, his courage had stolen her heart. She would miss, for the rest of her life, his strange humor, his bravery, his skilled mouth.

When they had defeated Sorak, she would go quickly and spare them both the pain of leaving. And now she would treasure the time they had left as companions. She would relish the great deed they were fated to accomplish together.

The first order of business, Harper thought, was to get down on the tracks and into the tunnels while avoiding detection by the subway cops. He explained the problem to Kadra as they moved down the platform away from the bulk of the waiting commuters.

"Very well," she said, and solved the dilemma by jumping down on the tracks.

"Or we could do it that way," he grumbled. He flashed his ID in the direction of a couple of gawking businessmen. "Transit inspectors."

Hoping they subscribed to the New York credo of minding their own business, he jumped. "Move fast." He took her arm. "Stay out of the light. Once we're into the tunnels our main goal is to avoid being smeared on the tracks by an oncoming train. Then there's the third-rail factor. See that?" He pointed. "Whatever you do, don't step on that, don't touch it. It'll fry you like a trout."

He pulled his penlight from his pocket as they followed the track into the tunnel. "There are some areas in the system where homeless people set up housekeeping."

"If they have a house to keep, they cannot be homeless."

"We'll save the tutorial on society's disenfranchised for later. Some of the people who manage to live down here are mentally unstable. Some are just desperate. What we're looking for, I figure, are the maintenance areas. Off the main tracks, where there's room to establish a lair."

"There is no scent of people or demon here."

"Let me know when that changes." He felt the vibration, saw the first flicker of light in the dark. "Train. Let's move."

He doubled his pace toward the recess of an access door, and pulling her up with him, he plastered himself to the door. "Think thin," he advised.

He held on as the roar of the train blasted the air, gritted his teeth as the air pummeled them. Through the train's lighted windows, faces and bodies of its passengers blurred by.

"It is more exciting to be outside the box as it flies by than to be inside it."

He looked over at Kadra as the last car whizzed past. "One of these days you'll have to tell me what you do for entertainment back in A'Dair. I have a feeling I'll be riveted."

He tried to keep a map in his head as they wound through the labyrinth. Twice more they were forced to leap for a narrow shelter as a train sped past. But it was Kadra who swung toward a side tunnel.

"Here. Sorak has been this way."

Harper caught no scent in the stale air other than the grease and metal of machines. "Can you tell how long ago?"

"Some hours past, but fresh enough to track."

She moved carefully, knowing the dangers of an underground ruled by a demon. She kept her voice low as they began to hunt. "The Bok sees as well in the dark as in the light. Perhaps better. He will fight more fiercely for his lair than he would even for food."

"In other words, that skirmish we had this morning was just a preview of coming attractions."

She thought she was beginning to understand his odd expressions, so nodded. "Tonight, it is to the death."

She whirled, coat billowing, as she laid a hand on the hilt of her sword. Though he had heard no sound, the beam of Harper's light picked out a shadow in the dark. He'd nearly drawn his gun when he recognized the uniform.

"Transit cop." He said it under his breath to Kadra. "Let me handle this. Hey, Officer. Riley and Tripp from the *Post*. We're cleared to do a feature on—"

He broke off as the figure took one shambling step toward him and his stiletto-like teeth gleamed in the narrow beam of light.

The teeth parted, row after monstrous row. The hands, tipped with bluing claws, lifted. But the eyes—the eyes were still painfully human.

"Help me. Please, God, help me." And with a sound trapped between a sob and a howl, he leaped.

Kadra's dagger shot through the air and into his throat with an ugly sound of steel piercing flesh. The blood that trickled out of the wound was a thin reddish green.

"The change was not complete with this one," Kadra stated.

"He was still human." Furious, Harper dropped to his knees and tried to find a pulse. "Goddamn it, he was still a human being. He was a fucking cop. You killed him without a thought."

"He was neither human nor demon, but trapped between. I ended his life to save yours."

"Is that all there is?" Harper's head whipped around, and his gaze burned into hers. "Life or death? He asked for help."

"I gave him the only help I could. Do you think it gives me pleasure? With his death, one of my people dies. That is the balance." She crouched, pulled his dagger free. "That is the price."

"We could have gotten him to the hospital. A blood transfusion, something."

"That is fantasy!" She shot her dagger home. "He was dead the instant Sorak kissed him." She gestured toward the body as it began to smoke. "Infected with demon blood.

There was nothing to be done for him, in your world or in mine. If Sorak has found one human to change, he has changed others."

She glanced toward the dark maw of tunnel. She would rather face it, even if her own death waited inside, than the hot accusation in his eyes. "If you are unable to do what must be done, go back now. I will go on alone."

"He asked for help. He was scared. I saw the fear." Now all Harper could see was a blackened skeleton. "And he never had a chance." Sickened, Harper got to his feet. "We'll finish it together."

"This is the way. I smell blood, some still fresh." She walked deeper into the tunnel.

8

THEY MOVED IN the dark, guided by the thin beam of Harper's penlight and Kadra's instincts. And they moved in silence.

She had killed a man—and to Harper the charred remains they had left behind in the tunnel were still a man. She had done so with the same cold efficiency she had used to destroy the hideous little two-headed monster in A'Dair.

In the zoo he'd found her brutal focus fascinating, admirable. Even sexy. But there they had fought beasts— savage and hungry and alien despite their form.

This had been a man. How could she be so certain that his lunge forward had been an attack instead of a plea?

"You said it takes time for the transformation," Harper began.

"In my world." She snapped the words out. "I can't know—no one can know—how the change happens in yours. No demon has ever traveled from my world to yours until now. In A'Dair, the demon carries his victim off, into a lair. For twelve hours the human sleeps, a changing sleep that is like death. Only during this period is there any hope of being saved, and even that hope is small. Once the demon wakes, it is too late. The change is irreversible even if he is not complete. He is demon. And he feeds."

"If there's a different time frame here, maybe there's a different structure to the change."

"He waked. He walked. He would have fed on you if he had not been stopped. The blood was already mixed, Harper. His death was a mercy. What was still human inside knew."

She hadn't known love could be painful. She hadn't known that when your heart lay open to another it could be so easily wounded. But hers was, and the hurt ran down to the bone: he had looked at her as if she were the monster.

She didn't want to speak of it. She wished to push it aside and do only what she had come to do. But the ache in her heart was a distraction.

"Every human death is a death inside me." She spoke quietly, without looking at him. "I cannot save them all. I would give my life if that would make it otherwise."

"I know that." But they both heard the doubt in his voice.

The pain of it sliced through her, made her careless, made her vulnerable to what leaped at her out of the dark.

It was snarling, teeth snapping. Its claws swiped, scoring her neck as she whirled to block.

It was old and female. And it was mad. It skittered back, impossibly fast, like a spider, into the shadows. Kadra freed her sword and, going by scent and sound, struck out.

It cackled. That was the only way to describe the sound it made as it attacked Kadra from behind.

Harper's bullet caught it in midair. Blood gushed, that awful hue of mixed red and green, as it thudded to the ground, arms and legs drumming.

An old woman, Harper thought as he stared into the crazed and dying face. One of the pitiful who so often slipped through society's fingers and into its bowels.

She was old enough to be his grandmother.

"You did not kill her." Kadra crouched beside him. "You did not end her life, and you must not take the weight of it. Sorak killed her, and you ended her torment. You slayed the monster. The woman was already dead."

"Do you get used to it?"

She hesitated, nearly lied. But when he lifted his head and looked into her eyes, she gave him the truth. "Yes. You must, or how could you pick up your sword day after day? But there is regret, Harper. There is sorrow for what is lost. The demon has no regret, no sorrow. No joy or passion, no love. I think when they feed on us, they hope to consume what it is that makes us human. Our heart, our soul. But they cannot. All they can take and transform is the body. The heart and soul live on in another place. And that place is locked to them."

"So Sorak's come here. Maybe he thinks he'll have better luck eating souls in this dimension."

"Perhaps."

The woman was all but ashes when Harper looked at Kadra again. "I'm sorry about before. I didn't want to believe it could happen, that we could be used this way. It was easier to blame you for stopping it than Sorak for starting it."

"There will be more."

"And we'll both stop it." He reached out, touched a fingertip to the claw marks on her neck. "You're hurt."

"Scratches, because I was careless. I won't be a second time."

"Neither will I." Not with the battle, he thought, and not with her. He took her hand as they got to their feet. "Let's find this bastard, and welcome him to New York."

Harper kept his Glock in one hand, the knife in the other. The tunnel curved, and a dim light glowed at the end of it. He heard the rumble of a train behind them, but ahead there was silence.

He could see signs of human habitation now. Broken glass, an empty pint bottle that had held cheap whiskey. Food wrappers, an old tennis shoe with the toe ripped out.

"His lair." Gesturing with her chin, Kadra slid her sword out of its sheath. "He is not alone."

"Well, why don't we join the party?" He turned the knife in his hand. "We've brought our host some nice gifts."

She stripped off the coat, flung it aside. "He will not be pleased to see us."

The tunnel widened. There was more debris from the life that had chosen to spread underground. Spoiled food, battered boxes that might have served as shelter. A headless doll. And as they drew closer to the light, a splatter of blood against the dingy wall.

The first three came out in a mad rush, all claws and teeth. Harper fired, sweeping his aim left to right. There was a stench of something not human as one threw the wounded at Harper, then came in like a missile beneath the body. Its teeth fixed in his calf as he sliced upward with the knife.

The teeth continued to grip his leg like a vice even as the thing began to smoke. He cursed, kicked, and felt both cloth and flesh tear as the demi-demon struck the tunnel wall.

He spun clear to see that Kadra had already killed the third, and a fourth that had tried to use the cover of their attack for one of his own.

She wasn't even winded.

"That was too easy," she commented.

"Yeah." He limped over, gritting his teeth against the burning pain of the bite. "That was a real breeze."

"He toys with us." Now she pulled out the healing cloth. "He insults us. Bind your wound."

He knelt, quickly tied the cloth around his bleeding leg. "And just how is sending four advance men with really nasty teeth an insult?"

"He knew we would destroy them. Four, not fully changed, are child's play."

"Yeah." Grimly he tightened the knot on the cloth. "I'm feeling real childlike at the moment."

"He wants us in there. Wants to watch the battle. The smell of blood feeds him almost as much as the taste."

"Okay." He tested his weight on the injured leg. It would have to hold. "Let's go give his majesty a real five-star meal."

She drew her dagger, checked the balance of both blades, then nodded. "For your world and for mine. To the death."

"Let's make that Sorak's death."

They charged.

Kadra caught a blur of movement above, and went into a roll that sent the demon flying over her head. She ran him through with one thrust, pulled her sword out clean before his body hit the ground. Using her hips, she reared up, shot her boots into the next attacker's face. And was on her feet, hacking and whirling.

She heard gunshots and, pivoting, saw Harper slay two demi-demons on his left and set to meet another on his right with his blade.

She spun clear, slicing with her sword, and positioned herself so they fought back-to-back.

"Sorak is close!" she shouted. "I smell him."

"Yeah." Sweat dripped into Harper's eyes and was ignored. "So do I."

He shot a bony, bald demi-demon who still wore a torn and faded New York Mets T-shirt. As the demon smoked and died at his feet, Harper scanned the tunnel.

He couldn't think about who they had been, he told himself, only what they had become.

"I don't see any more of them."

Still back-to-back, they circled. "Sorak!" Kadra shouted. "Come and meet your fate."

As if on cue, light flashed into the tunnel. Through the glare of it, three demons charged.

"He's used the portal. He's brought more through."

Harper fired, and when the Glock clicked on empty, he used it as a club. His leg screamed as he sprang off it to launch himself into a roundhouse kick. The demon barely staggered, shoving Harper so that his wounded leg buckled. He skidded over the floor, and lost his breath and the gun when the demon landed on him.

For the second time, he felt the bite of claws. Screaming in rage, he plunged the knife into the demon's throat, snarled like an animal himself when the thick green spewed onto his hands and face.

When he crawled out, covered with blood, he saw Kadra fighting both of the remaining demons.

Her blades flashed like lightning. She blocked the sickle

sword that one of them swung at her, then plunged her dagger into his belly while she hacked her blade through the second demon.

"Next time," Harper said as he limped toward her, "I get the two-on-one."

Winded, she nodded. "Next time."

The smoking blood hazed the air. She peered through it, pointed her sword at Sorak. His claws and face were smeared with the blood of the body that lay at his feet.

He had fed, and fed again, she realized, and would have the strength of ten.

Still, her stance was cocky, her voice a sneer. "You should have brought an army, demon king. We would have littered this place with your dead."

"I brought better than an army." Sorak reached back and hefted a small girl by the scruff of her neck. She let out a sobbing squeal as her little legs kicked in the air, two full feet off the ground.

Leering, Sorak skimmed his teeth over her throat. "The young are so sweet to the taste. How much for her life?"

Kadra lowered her blade. Though her hand was steady, her heart stumbled in her chest. "Will you bargain your life with a human child's? Is not a king worth more?"

"I was not speaking to you, Kadra, Slayer of Demons." Sorak lifted his other hand, and the gun.

Subway cop, Harper thought on a jolt of panic. Sorak had taken the gun from the transit cop, and he had been too angry to notice the empty holster.

On an oath, Harper shoved Kadra aside as Sorak fired. As she fell, blood streaming from her temple, the sword clattered to the ground.

"No. Goddamn it, no!" Harper fell to his knees, gathering her up, checking quickly for a pulse.

"I was born for her death." Sorak shook the child until she began to wail. "Tell me, Harper Doyle, were you born for death?"

She was alive, he told himself. And slayers healed quickly. He would do whatever he could to give her that time, and to save an innocent child from death. Or worse.

He got to his feet, the knife gripped in his hand. "For yours. I was born for yours."

"Approach me and . . ." Sorak ran a blue claw teasingly down the girl's round cheek as her wails became the mewling sounds of a trapped animal. "I tear her to pieces. How much for the child, Harper Doyle? How much are the young worth in this world?"

Her eyes were blue, Harper noted. Glassy as a doll's now, filled with shock. "How much do you want?"

"You will do. Your life for her life. I would enjoy taking what is the slayer's and making it mine. Throw down your blade, or the child dies now."

"And Kadra?"

Through the stinking smoke Harper saw the gleam of jagged teeth. "Do you think your life is worth both of theirs?" Sorak stepped forward, and Harper could see blood coming from wounds of the claws sliding down the girl's white neck. "I could kill you where you stand with this weapon. But it would be . . . unsporting. Make the bargain, or watch while I give her my kiss."

There was no bargaining with monsters. Even knowing that, Harper could see no choice. "Set her down, let her go. A knife isn't much good against a gun. You're smart enough to know that. In this world, using a kid as a shield is a sign of a coward. I thought you were a king."

"I am more than king here. I am god." Carelessly, he tossed the girl on the floor, then drew out the globe. The portal burst open. "Run, little human child. Run quickly, or I will take you after all."

She ran, weeping. The portal snapped shut behind her.

"And now." Grinning, Sorak streaked forward in a move so fast that Harper had no chance to evade or defend. Using the back of his hand, Sorak struck Harper in the face with a blow so vicious that it threw Harper back against the wall. The knife spurted out of his hand like wet soap.

With the wall bracing him, Harper slid to the ground.

"You are mine now. A warrior slave in my army, in this world. I will rule here."

"Fry in hell," Harper choked out as those claws closed over his throat. In his mind, he called out to Kadra to wake, to save herself from the horror that was coming.

"Soon you will see what it is to be as I am. To lose those weaknesses that make you human." Sorak leaned close, his mouth only a fetid breath away from Harper's, his gleaming teeth bared. "I will give you the slayer when you wake, and we will feed on her together."

He knew pain, agony beyond imagining as that mouth, those teeth closed over him. The shock of it ripped through his system, tore at his sanity as those keen blue claws tore through flesh until he felt his own heart prepare to burst.

The hand that had been fighting to reach the gun in his boot convulsed, dropped limply to the ground.

He had visions of fire and smoke, of blood and brutal death. Torment and anguish. With them came a lethargy that weighed his limbs down like molten lead.

Through the smoke, through the pain, he heard Kadra scream his name.

His trembling fingers closed over the gun. His numb arm moved, slowly, slowly, in exquisite pain to bring it between their bodies. Without being fully aware of where the muzzle was pointed, he fired.

9

WHEN KADRA CAME to, her vision was smeared with blood and pain. Her body knew a thousand stings and aches from the battle. Her ears still rang from it.

And her first thought as she pushed to her knees was: Harper.

The air was clogged with smoke and stink from the blood of a dozen demons and demi-demons. She remembered the child and her heart jerked. Burying her pain, she picked up her sword, gripped it in both hands.

The sound she heard now, slicing through the filthy air, was one of greed, one of bitter glory. Whirling, she swung the sword high over her head.

She saw, huddled by the dripping wall, Sorak, his regal cape unstained as he gifted the bleeding Harper with his evil kiss.

Fear, rage, horror gushed through her and poured out in a single urgent cry that was Harper's name.

She ran, screaming still, the point of her blade pointing toward the ceiling, where it caught the dim light and glinted like vengeance.

The gunshot was a small sound, a muffled crack like the rap of a fist on wood. Sorak's body jerked, and his head lifted with a kind of baffled shock. He pressed a hand to his belly where his blood spilled between his slender blue-tipped fingers.

"I am king of the Bok." Sorak watched in confusion as his own blood poured. "I am god here. I cannot be destroyed by human means."

"Wanna bet?" With what little strength he had left, Harper fired again. "You lose," he managed before his head slumped.

Kadra leaped between them as Sorak collapsed. She whipped her sword down, the point at its heart. "He has killed you. Harper the warrior has sent you to hell."

"And I have made him mine." His grin spread. "And you, Kadra, Slayer of Demons, must destroy what you love or be destroyed by it. I have won."

"He will never be yours. That is my vow." With all of her strength, she rammed the sword home. Leaving it buried in Sorak's body and in the stone beneath, she dropped to her knees beside Harper.

There was blood, his own and Sorak's, on his face. The healing cloth around his wounded leg had soaked through. His eyes were already going dim.

But they met Kadra's now with something like triumph. "He's done."

"Yes." The slayer's fingers shook as she brushed Harper's hair from his face. "He is finished."

"Mission accomplished, huh? The kid." He closed his eyes on a wave of agony, a flood of impossible fatigue. "The kid got back through the portal."

"You traded your life for hers." For mine, she thought. And for mine.

"She couldn't've been more than two. I couldn't stand there and let him . . . Christ." He had to gather strength just to breathe. "Your head's bleeding."

"It's only—"

"A scratch. Yeah, yeah. Got a few of my own." He bore down, fought to clear his vision so he could see her better. "Baby, I'm pretty messed up here."

"I will get you to a healer."

"Kadra." He wanted to take her hand, but couldn't lift his arm. "Bastard kissed me. It works faster here, the change. We can't be sure how fast."

"You will not change. You will *not*." Tears ran down her cheeks unchecked. "I will take you back, through the portal. To Rhee, the sorceress."

"I'm going under. I can feel it." He was cold, cold to the bone. Losing, he knew, the warmth of his own humanity. "We can't take the chance. You know what you have to do."

"No." She gripped his face with desperate hands. "No."

"I dropped the gun. Get it for me, let me do it myself."

"No." She pressed his face to her breast and rocked. "No, no, no."

The smell of her flesh brought comfort, but under it, creeping under it, was an ugly, alien hunger that horrified him. "Don't let me change. If you love me, end it. Let me die human." He pressed his lips to her heart. "I love you. Let that be the last thing we both remember from this. I love you."

He went limp. Panic filled her, a wild weeping as she shook him, slapped him, called to him. But he was in the changing sleep, a kind of living death, and could not be reached.

"No. You will not take him." She leaped up, whirled to where Sorak had died. All that was left was her sword, still in the stone, and the globe the demon king had stolen. She scooped up the globe, then with a piercing battle cry, wrenched her sword free.

Tears streamed down her stony face as she dropped down beside Harper again, wrapped her arms around him.

But when the portal opened and the light burst over them, it took them to a world she had never seen.

The room was white. Through a wall of glass were trees of crimson and sapphire against a pale gold sky. Framed by it, robed in white, stood Rhee.

"Help him." Kadra laid Harper between them, stretched out her arms in pleading. "Save him."

"I cannot."

"You have power."

"So do we all. Child—"

"Do not call me child." Furious, primed for battle, Kadra leaped to her feet. "Some are saved from the changing sleep through sorcery. I have heard the tales."

"It is beyond my means to save him."

"You say we share blood, but you refuse the one thing I have ever asked of you. You sent me to him."

"Not I, but destiny."

"Destiny," Kadra spat out. "Who weaves a destiny that asks a man to fight what is not his war, to risk his life in a battle not his own? This he did. He fought with me, and for me. He destroyed the Bok king when I failed. He laid down his life for a child who was not his own. And for this courage, for this valor, he is repaid by becoming what he fought against. Who asks such a sacrifice?"

"There are no answers to the questions you ask. What did he bring to you, what was your gift to him?"

"Love."

"Then there is a way. Courage and strength," Rhee said as she stepped forward. "Vision and love. With these there is a way for you, only you, to save him."

"How? Whatever it is, I will do. A quest, a battle? Tell me, and it is done."

"A kiss."

"A kiss?"

"A gift of breath, of life and love. If your love is true, if it is pure, one to the other, the power of that kiss, of the love in it, will overcome the evil of the demon's."

"Can it be so simple?"

"Nothing ever is," Rhee said with a smile. "You must be cleansed first. I will help you, and tell you the rest."

"There is no time." Her heart lurched as she gestured to Harper. His fingernails were a pale blue. "He is already changing."

"Time stops here. That I can give you. He will remain as he is while we prepare."

"There is choice," Rhee said while Kadra bathed. "There is great risk."

"I am a warrior," Kadra replied.

"You must be woman and warrior now."

"So I bathe in scented oils, wash my hair with jasmine blossoms. I have no patience for such matters."

"Rituals." Rhee's lips curved as she held out a thick white towel. "Do you not sharpen your sword before battle? This is not so different. Not all warriors are female, daughter, but all females should be warriors. He will need all you are if he is to survive this."

"If I fail, may he stay here? Sleep, as he is sleeping now?"

Gently, Rhee touched Kadra's hair. "Would you wish that for him? An eternity of nothing?"

"I cannot let him change. It was the last thing he asked of me, to take his life so he might end it as a man."

"And will you?"

"I will not let him die a beast. I will not fail him. If I use my sword to end it, I will never lift it again."

This, Rhee thought, was what I wished for you. Beyond valor and might, beyond battle cries and quests, a love so deep it is a drowning pool.

"These are choices that only you can make. There is one more. The magic that passed from my blood to yours is strong. But more potent is the magic you found in your own heart. Trust it."

Rhee closed her hands around her daughter's arms. Arms, she thought now, that had learned to lift a sword and to embrace a man who was her equal. "Give yourself to it without hesitation. If you waver, if you doubt and still do this thing, he may live. You may not."

Rhee offered a long white robe. "Wear this."

"Strange garb for battling life and death." Kadra put it on, belted it. "If my love isn't strong enough, I die."

Rhee folded her hands because they longed to reach out, to touch, to soothe. "Yes. I gave you to your fate once before. And my arms ached from emptiness. I watched you, in my way, as you grew, as you became. And I was proud. But my arms were empty. Now, I give you once more to your fate."

"Did you love the man who was my father?"

"With everything I am. And yet I could not save him. I could only watch while he was taken from me. He would have been proud, as I am, of the life we made together in you."

"Mother," Kadra said when Rhee turned to the arched opening. And she stepped forward, let herself be gathered close. Let herself hold.

"You found kindness," Rhee murmured. "And forgiveness. They will make you stronger." She held tight one moment more, just one moment more. "Be strong, my daughter. It is time."

She led Kadra back into the white room. Now Harper lay on a bed that was draped with thin white curtains. A garden of white flowers surrounded it. Dozens of slender, milky tapers added a quiet light.

He wore a white shirt and trousers. His face, while deathly pale, was unmarked.

Kadra parted the bed curtains. "His wounds."

"This much I could do. His flesh is healed, as yours is."

"He is beautiful. He is . . ." My life, she thought. "I have only known him a day, yet he has changed me forever."

"You changed each other. And that change will be stronger than the one Sorak put inside him. You must believe it."

"A sword is not enough." Kadra glanced over. "Is this my lesson?"

"You have always had more than a sword. Sorak is dead. Together you have accomplished this great feat, and both our worlds are safe. For this gift, each of you is granted passage into both worlds. As you choose."

"How can this be? The balance—"

"Love makes its own balance." Rhee walked to a table where each of the globes stood on a small pedestal. One emerald, one ruby.

"The emerald is your stone, and its key opens the portal to the world you knew. The ruby is his, and its key opens to his world. I must leave you. What you do now is between only you two. I will always be with you. Kadra, Slayer of Demons, your fate is again in your own hands."

Rhee held up her arms and vanished.

"This I must do without sword or dagger." Still, she took her circlet from the table, placed it on her scented hair. "But I am what I am. And all I am is yours, Harper Doyle."

She stepped to the bed, placed a hand on his cold cheek. The words were inside her, as if they, too, had been sleeping. "I love you with heart, with soul, with body. In all worlds, in all times. Come back to me."

And bending, she laid her lips on his.

Love and life, she thought as she breathed both into his mouth. Life and love. Strong as a stallion, pure as a dove. She drew the poison in, gave him her breath. Gift of heart and soul take now from me, and from the Demon Kiss be free.

Pain vibrated through her, but she kept her lips warm and gentle on his. Dizzy, she braced a hand beside his head, and gave.

I would die for you, she thought. I would live for you.

When his mouth moved under hers, when he stirred, she slid bonelessly to her knees beside the bed.

Outside, the sky deepened, gleamed gold, and the jeweled trees shimmered.

Harper dreamed of swimming, fighting through a black and churning sea that was swallowing him whole. He broke through its icy void, searching for her, battling the greedy waves that sucked him back.

Until he slid into a warm white river, floated there. And woke speaking her name.

She lifted her head, and felt no shame at the tears as she gripped his hand. "Yes. Yes, yes." She pressed his hand to her cheek, kissed it, then taking his hand, she laughed in relief at the healthy color in his skin and nails. "Baby," she said, relishing the term, "I am with you."

He saw only white, the gauzy draperies, the glow of candles through them, the richness of the flowers. Then he saw her as she rose up beside him and again laid her lips on his.

"If this is hell," he said aloud, "it's not so bad."

"You are not dead. You live. You are unchanged."

He sat up, amazed at the energy running through him, the absolute freedom from pain. "How?"

"Love was enough."

"Works for me. Where are we? What did you do?"

"We're in yet another dimension. Rhee the sorceress . . . my mother, brought us. She healed us."

"And what, exorcised the demon?"

"That was for me. A kiss waked you, and brought you back whole."

"Like Sleeping Beauty? You're kidding."

She leaned back. "You look displeased."

"Well, Jesus, it's embarrassing." He scooped his hair back, slid off the bed.

"You would rather die, with pride?" Though part of her understood the sentiment perfectly well, it still rankled. She who had never believed in romance had found the event desperately romantic. The kind of moment the bards write of. "You are ungrateful and stupid."

"Stupid, maybe. Ungrateful, definitely not. But if it's all the same to you, let's just keep this one portion of the experience completely to ourselves."

She jerked a shoulder, lifted her chin. And made him smile. "You saved my life, and you made me a man. Thank you."

Now she sniffed. "You are a brave warrior and did not deserve the fate Sorak intended for you."

"There you go. My ego's nearly back to normal now. And can I just say you look gorgeous. Incredible. In fact, there's an expression in my world about how you look right now. It goes something like, wow."

"Ritual foolishness," she replied, flipping a hand at the robe.

"I love the way you look. I love you, Kadra."

She sighed. "I know. If the love between us was not strong and true, you would not have waked so I could be annoyed with you." She looked away from him, deliberately, when he came to her, when he wrapped his arms tight around her.

So he kissed her cheek, kissed her temple where a bullet had grazed. "I thought I had lost you, and that was worse than thinking I'd lost myself."

Yielding, she turned her lips to his. "Harper Doyle."

"Kadra, Slayer of Demons."

She eased back, her eyes solemn despite the humor in his. "Do you wish me to be your lifemate and bear your young?"

"You bet I do."

"This is what I wish as well. This is not a traditional path for a slayer."

He lifted a hand to skim a finger over her circlet of rank. "We'll make new traditions. Stay with me, Kadra. Be with me. We'll stay here, wherever this is. It doesn't matter."

"This is not our place." She stepped back, gestured to the two globes. "The one on the emerald stand opens to my world. The ruby to yours. I believed that to keep the balance we must each go back, must each remain in the world where we came from. But, I have vision."

She looked back at him. "My mother is a sorceress, and her blood is my blood. I see what I once refused to see. I have magic inside me. I must practice with this as I once practiced with a sword. Until I am skilled."

"Slayer and sorceress. I get a two-for-one."

"There can be no balance when love is denied and refused. We are meant, so we will be."

"Choose," he told her. "I'll live in any world, as long as it's with you."

She picked up the bag that held their things, tossed it to him. She lifted her sword. And, crossing to the table, she lifted the globe that rested on a ruby stand.

"The Bok have lost their king, and the slayers who are my sisters will rout them, and continue the fight against all demons. But there are battles to be fought in your world, demons of a different kind to be vanquished. I wish to fight with you there."

"Partners, then." He took her hand, kissed it. "We make a hell of a team."

"And I like the pie called pizza, and the beer. And even more than these, the kissing."

"Baby, we were made for each other."

He swung her into his arms, crushed his lips to hers. When the portal opened, and the light washed in, they leaped into it together.

And went home.

IMPOSSIBLE

❧

Jill Gregory

With love and "kisses" to Larry and to Rachel,
and to my favorite magical ladies,
Nora, Marianne, and Ruth.

Prologue

A GOLDEN MOON rose over the Cliffs of Murgullen as Cyrus the Sorcerer stood in a patch of moonlight and frowned down at his three young protégés, huddling in their cloaks upon the damp grass. Their faces shone pale and hopeful in the shimmering light.

"Each of you," he said in a thin, disgusted tone, "has *failed*. Failed abominably. Not one of you, not a single one"—Cyrus's voice boomed out and the sea tossing fitfully below began to churn—"has received a passing grade upon this, your final and most important test."

Young wizard-in-training Barnaby threw his long, thin body backward with a groan, sprawling upon the earth in abject frustration. Red-haired Ophelia covered her freckled face with her hands and gave a great quivering sigh. Elwas, whose father was a quarter elf, and whose great-grandmother had been a sorceress of some repute, banged his fist on the ground. His pointed ears twitched as he glared at his mentor.

"With all due respect, sir, that is not our fault, but yours.

That exam you gave us was impossible. The things you asked us to do—no wizard can do such things. It goes beyond what we've been taught."

"He's right, sir." Barnaby pushed himself up to a sitting position. His narrow, handsome face was even paler than usual, and he struggled to keep his voice calm. "We don't mean any disrespect, but if you'd asked us to perform something reasonable for our exam, like changing an oaf into a prince, or concocting a healing potion for boils, or making grass grow in the dead of winter, rather than something quite impossible—"

"Enough!" Cyrus fixed him with a quelling glance. "What I asked of each of you was nothing more than to apply yourselves, to incorporate all that you have learned in several areas of our craft, plus a touch of imagination, ingenuity, and intelligence. Being a wizard is not merely about charms and tricks—only fools believe that. One needs creativity to make real magic!"

"But, sir." Ophelia swallowed hard as she gazed up at the imposing figure of the sorcerer in his pointed hat, with his tangled gray beard and flowing robes the color of the mist swirling at his feet. "You wanted us to end the feud between King Vort of Marlbury and Duke Tynon of Bordmoor. Everyone knows that their noble families have been fighting one another for a hundred years!"

"And what does that have to do with anything?" Cyrus shot a cold glare at her.

"Well, it's just . . . impossible!" she sputtered. "How are we to end such a deep and long-standing feud?"

"Especially since wizards—good wizards, anyway—are not allowed to tamper with the minds or hearts of humans," Elwas pointed out. "You taught us that yourself, sir!"

"And for a century the royal family of Marlbury and the llachland dukes of Bordmoor have despised each other, hated each other, killed each other—"

"Precisely," Cyrus snapped. "And that is why this was a challenging but certainly not impossible test of your powers. The fact that each of you failed does not reflect upon the challenge, it reflects upon your own abilities. Obviously none of you is ready to advance to the next level of your training."

"Sir, we are ready. We are proficient in every area. But this . . . this is impossible!"

"So you say." Cyrus's displeasure was clear in the downward curve of his lips.

"No wizard or sorceress could meet this challenge!" Barnaby burst out. "Why, even you, sir, could not stop a feud like this. There is simply no way—"

"Is there not?" Now Cyrus's voice had become silken. But it was edged in ice. He looked at each of his pupils in turn, and there was thinly veiled impatience in his countenance. "There is a way to meet this challenge. There is *always* a way. Would I have presented it to you otherwise? I think not."

The three shrank a little beneath the glitter of his eyes. Cyrus noted the confusion, despair, and frustration on each face. He fought his own disappointment and reminded himself that teaching required patience. His students truly had no notion how to proceed. Each of the three before him had great potential and shining talent, but clearly they were not ready to advance. He sighed.

"Ending this feud is by no means impossible." He spoke in a more level tone. "Any wizard with skill, experience, and a drop of imagination can accomplish it." He cleared his throat, then lifted his arms, so that the flowing robes blew in the sudden wild gust of the wind.

Cyrus closed his eyes. "Watch." His arms lifted still higher, above his head, as if reaching, reaching toward the stars. "And . . ." He shouted over the rising rush of the wind. It grew to a low roar. The students grabbed at the earth as they were nearly blown over the side of the cliff.

"*Learn!*"

1

Two Days Later

THE VISION WOKE her in the blackest hour of night.

Erinn lurched up in her bed in the high-ceilinged chamber, staring without recognition at the crimson silk bed-hangings, which blew softly in the breeze. For one terrifying moment she didn't recognize anything around her, not the satin coverlet upon her bed, or the gilded bench before the flickering hearthfire, or the twin bronze chests near the foot of the bed.

Golden moonlight glimmered across the room, but she saw only the man, the man in her vision. He filled her mind. His face was lean, dark, so incredibly handsome that she could scarcely breathe—handsome in spite of the scar slashing down the left side of his jaw—or perhaps because of it. It added to the aura of strength and toughness and danger that clung to him, real as armor. His hair was dark as the night sky, his body strong. His eyes . . . they pierced hers, bluer than the Sea of Azul. So blue they hurt. Then the scent of musk touched her, whisked past her even as the vision faded into blackness, and the man's face, which had so forcefully and completely filled her mind, vanished like mist.

And her own bedchamber returned, cool and flowing with moonlight. Erinn drew a deep breath, trembling still, and swung her legs over the side of the bed.

She was shivering, but not from the chill night air. From the vision. The man.

"Who is he?" she muttered to herself, as she hastily dressed, yanking on a dark-green woolen gown, fumbling in the darkness.

"My lady?" She heard Tira, her lady-in-waiting, stir in the antechamber.

She called out softly, "No, Tira, stay abed. There is nothing I want."

"Very well, then, my lady," the sleepy voice murmured, and the bedcoverings rustled once more.

Erinn waited a moment before snatching up her fur-trimmed crimson cloak and tossing it around her shoulders. Quietly, she eased open the chamber door and edged out into the stone corridor.

The castle was asleep, and only dimly lit by tapers, as she made her way silently down a curving staircase, through a long hallway, and then outside, bypassing the great hall and the kitchen in favor of a side door that led to the courtyard.

Her mind was roiling as she made her way to the gardens, where tiny spring buds were just beginning to sprout upon the peach and apple trees and delicate flowers nestled just beneath the earth. Moonlight spilled upon the smooth stone bench, and there was little wind—yet still, the night was cold. Early spring in Marlbury was like that—but in another fortnight everything would be abloom and the nights would become soft, soft as a lover's kiss, she thought—and then gave her head a tiny shake.

And what would you know about a lover's kiss? she asked herself silently, hugging her arms around her body as she huddled on the bench and watched the swimming stars above. She'd never had a lover; in fact, she'd only been kissed twice. Her ever-vigilant brothers had seen to that. Though Cadur and Braden amused themselves with every unmarried wench in the kingdom, they felt no one was good enough for their little sister, and no matter how much Erinn complained to her father about their constant interference whenever a young knight or noble tried to engage her in conversation, Cadur and Braden did just as they pleased.

They insisted that when the time came they would find her a suitable husband. In the meantime, they took turns planting themselves beside her at every ball and feast, glowering watchfully at any male guest who dared speak to her. Once, though, Sir Rudyan had followed her after a round of dancing, and stolen a kiss just outside the great hall. He'd been drunk, though, and the kiss had been rough and wet and unpleasant—not to mention that it had gone on far too long. She hadn't enjoyed it in the least. That had been quite disappointing, for she'd always dreamed about her first kiss and how wonderful it would be.

There had been one more after that. This time, it was the charming fair-haired son of the duke of Chalmers, a young man her father had often told her would make a good match for her. He had paid quite a bit of attention to her when they'd met at a feast in Amelonia, and even Cadur and Braden had kept their distance, at her father's instructions, though they hadn't looked pleased about it. And young Stirling of Chalmers had drawn her into an antechamber in the midst of the festivities, placed his hands upon her shoulders, and kissed her—but it had been a dry, unexciting peck, quick and cautious and over in a twinkling. And even though he'd smiled at her as if quite pleased with himself, Erinn had needed to force herself to smile back. She'd felt nothing—nothing but a pang of disappointment. In its own way, the second kiss had been as much a failure as the first.

Failure.

Erinn was beginning to wonder if that was to be her destiny in life—failure at every goal to which she aspired.

Apparently, she wasn't very good at kissing, and she was even less successful at her one supposed talent—magic.

She scowled into the darkness as she leaned back on the bench. The cool air whistled around her, and the castle loomed overhead, tall and strong and gleaming in the moonlight. *Her* castle, her home. She loved it, loved her father and her brothers, and worried constantly about them. They had been at war all their lives with the savage llachlanders across the border, ruled by the duke of Bordmoor. For one hundred years, Marlbury's soldiers had been forced to fight battle after battle to keep their lands and homes safe from the marauding llachlanders.

No one knew how it had all begun—they only knew that the various dukes of Bordmoor had been their enemies for as long as anyone could remember, that Bordmoor despised the Royal House of Marlbury with a fury and passion that left no room for negotiation or treaty.

Battle after battle brought blood, death, grief, and barely enough victory to keep the enemy at bay. So far, they'd not been able to destroy the keep of Bordmoor and bring down the savage duke who ruled that wild land.

If I were any kind of a real witch, like Mama, I could help them, Erinn thought, pain slicing through her. As the wind quickened, catching at her pale gold hair, she lifted her hood and snuggled deeper into the warmth of the garment. But the chill inside her didn't go away.

Her mother had been a powerful witch, a seer with marvelous abilities. She had many times foreseen visions of the llachlanders' battle plans and had been able to warn of impending attacks—even to see where the enemy lay hidden. Once she had caused a great fire to impede a thousand soldiers lying in ambush for the knights of Marlbury, led by her husband, King Vort. During her lifetime, King Vort's army had sustained fewer casualties than ever before. But since her death, things had gone badly for Erinn's father and his troops. King Vort had lost not only his beloved wife but also a source of powerful aid to his kingdom. Tynon, the newest duke of Bordmoor, had won more victories in the past few years than his late accursed father ever had, and there was nothing Erinn could do about it. Marlbury was suffering, the battles were growing increasingly fierce, and the outcomes were rarely in Marlbury's favor.

Tynon was gaining ground.

Erinn only wished she had turned out to be half the witch her mother had been.

Somehow or other, the powers had not been strong in her. Oh, she could do some simple spells and charms, and sometimes, if she concentrated hard enough, she could even move objects with her thoughts, though they traveled slowly and she sometimes had difficulty controlling them once they were in motion. *A most unreliable talent in that department,* she reflected glumly. Her healing powers were modest as well, and she did have visions on occasion, but they had never proved useful and were rarely clear.

Except for this one tonight. It was different from any of the others. More vivid, more immediate, as if the man, the man with the dark, silky hair and the fire-blue eyes, was right there in her chamber, in her mind, in her very soul. . . .

Who was he, and why had his image come to her?

"It doesn't matter," she muttered to the empty garden as the wind whistled around her. None of her visions ever mattered.

Of course, no one knew that. Thanks to her father and brothers, everyone in the kingdom—indeed, in all the lands from the Hills of Davenall to the Sea of Azul—thought that she was every bit as powerful as her mother had been. That had been Braden's idea. He'd convinced their father and Cadur that no one need know about Erinn's "shortcomings," as he so tactfully put it.

Least of all the llachlanders. The people of Marlbury had for years been emboldened and reassured by the notion of a powerful witch acting on their behalf, and it stood to reason that the enemy was to some extent kept uneasy and off balance knowing that they had a foe who could not be defeated by sword or arrow.

It was good policy, Braden had reasoned, to keep the enemy believing that Erinn was a force of strong magic, a witch to be reckoned with.

Thus it was that every victory was attributed to a vision by Princess Erinn—or to a spell she had cast that had somehow hindered the enemy. Her powers were legendary throughout the land, and she'd heard tales that the llach-landers used her name to frighten young children into immediate obedience. She was feared and respected, held in awe and reverence.

And none of it is deserved, she thought dejectedly as she huddled on the bench. She was nothing but a weak and hapless pretender.

And she hated it. But there was no use arguing with her father, much less with Braden and Cadur. They thought they knew best about everything.

The only thing that saved her from total despondency over her inability to be of use was the time she spent helping to care for the widows and orphans of Marlbury. Her father had allowed her to oversee the welfare of families who had lost fathers or sons in service to the king during the border wars. It was Erinn who visited their homes, who sent wagonloads of food or firewood or woolens and blankets to those in need, and who brought smiles to the faces of even the poorest child with stories and songs and treats baked in the castle ovens.

Her efforts on their behalf filled her days, and at night she studied her book of spells. She knew every spell backward and forward—for all the good it did her.

None of them ever worked—at least not the way they were supposed to.

"Erinn!" Her elder brother's voice shook her out of her reverie. "By all the stars in heaven, what are you doing out here at this time of night? Why aren't you in bed?"

Braden's chin jutted out as he strode across the garden and frowned down at her.

"Stop scowling at me, Brade. I couldn't sleep. And—" She suddenly fixed her vibrant green eyes on his strong figure and studied him with interest. "I could ask you the same question. Where have you been?"

"To the inn, visiting a certain . . . friend of mine," he answered impatiently. "Not that I have to account to you, little one."

"And neither do I have to account to you," she retorted, but she was smiling as she said it. At twenty-eight, Braden was three years older than Cadur and seven years older than Erinn, and he was a hothead who thought he was in charge of everything, that he knew better even than their father how to care for the kingdom, the people, his family, and above all, his sister. Braden was brilliant at strategy and battle plans, while Cadur was the strongest, bravest soldier in the kingdom, capable of fighting three men at once and triumphing while scarcely losing his breath.

And they both thought Erinn was still a baby, would always be a baby, that she needed protecting and coddling—and bossing around.

If she hadn't loved them so much, she would have gone mad by now. But she knew how to fight for every inch of her freedom, and most of the time her father supported her.

"Why is it that you are allowed to go beyond the castle gates at night at will, yet I have to answer to someone every time I choose to set foot outside the walls?" She stood up, poked a finger against Braden's chest, and grinned.

"Perhaps I should go to the inn and find some friends there to amuse me," she began, then started to laugh at the horrified expression upon his face.

"Inside with you—now," he ordered, but a grin tugged at his lips as she continued to laugh. He forced his mouth into a stern line. "It's too cold out here for you. You should be asleep before a warm fire. Not to mention the fact that—"

He broke off, but not before Erinn saw concern deepen the fine lines around his eyes.

"Not to mention what?" she demanded.

Braden shook his head. "I'm sure it's nothing."

"What's nothing?" Erinn persisted.

"I don't wish to worry you."

"You already have," she pointed out and stepped closer. "What is it now, Brade? Surely not . . . Tynon?"

"No, no." Her brother gave a grunt of satisfaction. "He's still licking his wounds from the last skirmish. It will take time for him to regroup his forces and attack again. But . . ." He hesitated, then continued, grimacing, "One of the guards at the gate thought he heard a splash in the moat earlier, yet he could see nothing, no one. Still . . ." Braden shrugged. "It is not for you to worry about, Erinn. I've set the guards on alert. No doubt it was only a goose that flew off before it could be spotted. Or perhaps a swan. Nothing to concern you. Now go—go to bed."

"Oh, Brade." She tilted her head up at him, and her rich green eyes glinted with amusement. "You're the one who's worried. By the angels, from the way you looked when you mentioned it, one would think Tynon himself had breached the moat and was sneaking into this very garden." There was a catch of laughter in her voice. "No doubt to ravish me," she continued with a grin, "and then single-handedly slaughter all our men while they sleep."

"Don't even speak of such things, Erinn." Braden caught her arm and gave it a shake, his face grim. "That bastard is capable of anything. Of course, I'd die before I'd let him get within a stone's throw of Marlbury Castle, much less you—"

Suddenly, even as he spoke the words, she heard a thwack, then Braden tumbled forward in the darkness, straight at her.

"Braden!" Erinn tried to catch him as he fell and somehow managed to break his fall, though she struck the ground as well, caught beneath his weight.

"Braden!" she cried again, trying to struggle out from beneath his arm, staring in horror at his closed eyes and unmoving form.

Before she could scramble free and see if he was all right, a dark shadow stooped down and tossed her brother aside as if he were no more than a log. A powerful arm seized her and yanked her to her feet.

For one instant, and one instant only, as moonlight spilled down into the garden, she stared into the face of the man who loomed over her. And went cold with shock.

It was his face—*his*. The man in her vision.

"Y-you!" she gasped, shock and terror vibrating through her body. He glowered back at her like the devil himself, his mouth twisting into a hard, mirthless smile.

"So you saw me coming, did you?" His voice was low, dangerous, containing a barely controlled fury that curdled her blood.

"For all the good it will do you," he added grimly.

Erinn screamed then. At least she tried to scream, with every ounce of strength in her body, but he was too quick for her. A heavy hand clamped over her mouth, squelching the scream, stifling her breath. Quick as a blink, he dragged her against him, and though Erinn struggled frantically, terror giving her fierce strength, there was nothing she could do to break the powerful hold that imprisoned her.

She kicked, bit, squirmed, elbowed—all to no avail. Her captor might have been a mountain, for all the effect she had on him. In short order, as terror for Braden and for herself swept through her, she was gagged and tied, a blanket was thrown over her head and wrapped tight around her body. Then she felt herself hefted in thick, suffocating darkness and tossed like a sack of grain over his shoulder.

Braden! Silent screams rocked her. Was he dead? Had this monster killed him? And who else? The guards . . . the knights asleep in the hall, the servants . . . Cadur . . . her *father?*

Panic filled her as she was carried through the garden, helpless and dazed, telling herself that her abductor could not possibly get out of the castle grounds alive. There were too many guards, and they had all been put on alert. Braden had told her that. The gates were closely watched, and the moat would be patrolled.

He would be caught, and she would be freed. And she would watch him get sliced into little pieces for what he'd done to Braden.

But even as she began to squirm and wriggle and try to make some sound to help alert the guards, she felt a queer sensation creeping over her. Her senses seemed to be swimming in murky greenish water. A sickening sweet stench reached her nostrils and made her feel ill. And sleepy. She couldn't move. Couldn't keep her eyes open.

He has drugged me, she thought wildly, as dizziness assailed her. Something in the fibers of the blanket was working upon her, enveloping her in a thick greenish fog that clogged her throat and stilled her body and made the world spin—and spin—and spin.

Until at last the world fell away, and there was only the poisonous sweet scent and the hot green darkness—and the man from her vision carrying her through the garden.

And then there was nothing. Nothing at all.

2

"WAKE UP, WITCH. Damn it, wake up."

The early-morning sun glittered down into the clearing along Marlbury's eastern border as Tynon knelt beside the sleeping figure of the girl. He had wrapped his gray woolen horse blanket around her to ward off the chill as she slumbered upon a pile of dead winter leaves. Her golden hair lay against her cheek, and with her eyes closed, she looked as peaceful and ethereal as an angel who had tumbled— mussed and lovely—to earth.

But she isn't an angel, Tynon reminded himself sharply. She might be delicate-looking, and more beautiful than any woman he'd ever set eyes on, but she was a witch—a cold, powerful, and most dangerous witch.

And she'd stolen his home.

He was only unsettled by the sight of her, he told himself, because she hadn't stirred since being overcome by the sleeping potion he'd steeped into the blanket. That was worrisome, though Albreth had warned him that the effect might be just so. Still, twice during the long journey from

Castle Marlbury, he'd stopped to make certain she was still breathing. There was a risk to these potions, so Albreth had told him. Death was unlikely, though not out of the question.

She must not die, Tynon thought desperately. His fists clenched, as if he could somehow use his strength and his fighting skills to summon her back to wakefulness. But he couldn't. She would awaken when the potion wore off, and there was nothing he could do to speed that.

Just so long as she didn't die.

It wasn't merely that he needed her alive to undo what she'd done, to restore Bordmoor Keep to its normal form. That was the most important matter, to be sure, but there was also the fact that he'd never taken a woman prisoner before, and it didn't sit well with him. Not in the least. He'd done it only because there was no other choice—she had put the damned spell on the keep, and now she could damn well take it off.

Be that as it may, Tynon didn't want a female's death on his conscience. He would let her live, once she'd done as he bade. Even though she was from the hated House of Marlbury, even though she was a despicable little witch. He wouldn't kill a woman. He would wait and exact his vengeance on her father and brothers, the whole damned lot of them.

Fine, sleep then, damn you, he thought. *By the time you awaken, perhaps we'll be at the keep. And you can lift the spell. Then I can be done with you.*

As if in defiance of his thoughts and his wishes, the perverse woman began to stir. Her eyelids quivered. A small moan escaped her lips.

Then her eyes slowly opened, and Tynon felt the breath rush out of him as if a giant had slammed a tree into his belly.

By the sun and the moon, she was beautiful.

He tried to catch his breath, and to tighten his resolve at the same time.

Rich green eyes gazed blankly into his. Her lips trembled, and what lush, inviting lips they were, pink as roses in contrast with her creamy skin. At that moment, the wind lifted a lock of her pale hair and tossed it playfully as Erinn of Marlbury studied him in dazed bewilderment.

"So, you're awake," he managed to choke out in a voice that sounded almost like his own curt, deep one, the one he used when barking commands to his men. She recoiled as if he'd struck her, and he saw the memories come flooding back, turning her eyes the color of an angry sea.

"You!" she cried, just as she had in the garden when he'd confronted her in the golden moonlight. "What have you done to my brother?"

"Killed him, I hope," Tynon answered grimly, and was surprised when she lunged up at him and struck him full in the face with the palm of her hand. But even as his arm shot out and captured her wrist, she fell back with a cry.

"Lie still, little fool," he ordered. "The potion leaves you dizzy until its power is gone."

Her eyes closed, and she took deep, steadying breaths, unable to move despite her anger and her fear. Her thoughts were a tortured jumble—terror for Braden, fear for herself, and wonder that this dark intruder who had come to her in a vision, perhaps the first in her life that had somehow signaled anything of importance, had somehow managed to smuggle her out of Marlbury Castle without being caught and instantly killed.

"Who are you?" she asked, her eyes still closed against the whirling dizziness.

"Don't you know?" His voice held an edge of mockery. It infuriated her that he was standing over her, watching her, while she couldn't even open her eyes to confront him face-to-face. This damned dizziness. Damned potion. Her fingers itched to claw his face.

"How in the world should I know?" she snapped, then realized too late that it was the wrong thing to say.

"You're a witch. You see things, don't you? *Know* things. It was clear that you recognized me back there in the garden."

Desperately, Erinn summoned her wits. "I recognized your face," she told him with the cool hauteur she felt worthy of a great witch. He thought her powerful, therefore she must keep up that illusion. It might be her only protection.

If he feared her, even a little, it might give her an advantage, a chance to escape.

"But the vision didn't offer your name." At least that much was the truth. She forced her eyes open, bracing for a fresh assault of dizziness, but the world had steadied, at least for now. She didn't know what would happen if she tried again to sit up.

He was kneeling beside her now, studying her, those keen blue eyes narrowed against the sunlight.

Oh, indeed, the vision had not lied. He was handsome. And large. Every bit as tall as Braden and Cadur, perhaps even more strapping in the shoulders. His hair was inky dark as in the vision, his features hawklike in a lean, sunbrowned face. A fighting man, confident and cool, in cloak and armor.

But who was he? What did he want?

"Here."

She flinched as he moved his hand toward her, but then saw that it held a flask. "Wine," he told her sternly, with a shake of his head. "Surely the great witch Erinn is not afraid of a sip of wine?"

"The great witch Erinn is not afraid of anything—or anyone, including a cowardly scoundrel like you who sneaks into gardens and steals ladies from their homes—and poisons them!" she flashed back. The eyes that had before peered at him blankly now blazed with green fire.

His mouth thinned. "It was a potion, not a poison. You're alive, aren't you? For the time being. Gad, woman, the potion may have made you dizzy, but it has not softened your tongue. So I assume your powers are intact as well."

"As intact as ever!" she informed him. Unfortunately this, too, was the truth, Erinn thought in despair.

She could suddenly bear it no longer—lying here, motionless, afraid to even move as this man studied her with insolent leisure. She sat up, more slowly this time, and was relieved to find that the dizziness had faded. The potion must be wearing off, thank the stars. The world held steady, the trees remained rooted in the ground, the sun, like molten amber, glowed in a fixed spot within the soothing blue sky.

She pushed the flask away as he held it toward her.
"No."

"It's not poisoned." He frowned. "You must be thirsty.
And hungry. A touch of wine will revive you."

"What kind of a fool do you think I am?" Erinn spat out.
"I will take nothing you offer, not food or drink. You are
not a man to be trusted."

"But I am a man to be reckoned with." His eyes narrowed. He stuffed the flask into a pocket of his cloak. "And
if you don't wish sustenance, that is well and good with
me. I brought you here for one purpose and one purpose
only. And you *will* do my bidding."

"Will I?" Through the pounding of her heart, Erinn managed a frosty little smile. "You forget who I am. Are you
not afraid that I will turn you into a toad—or perhaps a
worm?"

"If you were going to do that, I think you would have
done it already." His gaze was appraising. "Back there in
the garden—or when you first awoke."

"I might have." She took a deep breath. "But . . . I am
curious." She had to stand up, if only her legs would support her. She had to be ready to run.

Glancing around, she saw that his horse grazed nearby—
a huge black steed with long, powerful legs. She didn't
recognize her surroundings, and she knew Marlbury well.
Where was she?

No matter, Erinn told herself, though her throat was dry,
and not only from thirst. *If I can steal his horse and escape,
I will find my way back to the castle. Or come across someone who will help me get home.*

She rose warily, and found that the effects of the potion
had indeed faded. The world remained stationary, and she
tugged her cloak closer about her, chilled not by the new
dawn but by the cold eyes of the man who rose alongside
her, towering over her, blocking the sun.

"Why are you afraid to tell me your name?" she demanded, lifting her chin to meet those intense blue eyes
head on. "You must be shamed by it."

She was stalling for time, watching for an opportunity to
escape. To return to Marlbury and see if Braden was all

right. He *must* be all right, she thought frantically, and her heart tightened painfully at the memory of how her brother had fallen and lain so still and so silent.

She couldn't allow herself to think about that. She must think only of how to outwit this scoundrel and get back to her home.

The scoundrel took a step closer to her, which struck fear into her heart. He was too big, too strong. Too angry.

"You don't need me to tell you my name. You know it."

"I assure you, I don't." But even as she spoke the words, a horrible idea was forming in her mind. A suspicion that she tried to push away before it could even fully surface. No, no, it couldn't be.

Those keen eyes raked her. They were harder than stone, so penetrating that she somehow fell back apace under their scrutiny. He advanced suddenly and caught her by the arms, his voice low, taut with controlled fury.

"Did you truly think you could do what you've done and I'd not act against you? Did you think I would sit idly by while you enchanted my keep with your damned dark magic?"

"What are you talking about?" Erinn burst out, panicked by his words and by the viselike hold he had on her. "I have enchanted nothing. I know of no keep—"

"Bordmoor Keep." He bit the words out like nails. "I'd wager a fortune you've heard of that."

Bordmoor Keep. Her eyes widened. *Tynon's* keep? She stared up at him, her heart starting to thud and her breath catching painfully in her throat.

"*You* . . . are Tynon of Bordmoor?" To her consternation, her voice came out a whisper, hoarse and pitifully frightened.

She winced at the satisfied smile upon his face.

"Aye. You needn't look surprised. You could hardly expect me to let you abscond with my home without so much as paying you a visit. In fact, princess, I'm going to do more than that. I'm going to see to it that you reverse that spell and give me back Bordmoor Keep."

"You're a madman. I've done nothing to your precious keep."

"You're lying!" he snarled, and yanked her closer.

"If . . . if it caught fire or something, it was because of your own carelessness or that of your servants. I . . . I'm glad that your keep is gone," she lashed out at him, struggling uselessly against his far greater strength. "And I hope and *pray* that *you* will be destroyed as well—"

She broke off with a gasp as his hand went to her throat and the fingers tightened against her flesh.

"Enough," he said softly.

Erinn's breath came in short gasps. His hold was not yet painful, only taut, but the threat was clear. Hatred and terror warred within her, but she stayed perfectly still, fearing what he would do if she struggled, and wondering if Tynon of Bordmoor was truly mad.

"I think you are lying," he continued, his gaze raking her.

"I am not."

Her lips quivered. Tynan saw the fear in those glorious, widened eyes. He felt the tremors in her slender body, for the girl knew she was caught. Yet to his surprise she did not weep, or beg, or even whimper. She stood still, except for the trembling, and no word of appeasement came from her lips.

Reluctant admiration touched him. Yet he quickly reminded himself that she was no ordinary girl. She was a witch. Even now she might be planning some magical move of her own.

That was a risk he had to take. He had to get the keep back.

"You lie. If you did not cast the spell, who did?"

"That is . . . your problem, not mine."

Even with his hand at her throat, she would not give an inch. Tynon's mouth twisted. He dropped his hand and watched as her own flew to her throat. There would be no bruise, though the skin was delicate. He had not gripped her that hard. But her hands were shaking as she touched the place where his fingers had held her.

"Whether you cast the spell—which I would bet my sword and shield you did—or not, you are coming with me to undo it."

"Coming with you . . . where?"

"Where do you think? We're less than a day's ride from there now. We'll reach it well before sunset."

He watched her carefully as he said this, as if expecting those words to mean something to her, but Erinn didn't have any idea why they should. She only knew that she must have been asleep from the potion for a long while if they were so close to Bordmoor. The very name filled her with dread, and she had to swallow hard before she could speak again.

"Are we . . . still in Marlbury?"

"Not for long. We're at the farthest edges of the border, about to enter the llachlands. Aren't you curious? Don't you want to see the land your family has raided and tried to steal for a hundred years? The savages you have fought and slaughtered? Your brothers have seen it, but they've barely escaped with their lives every time they've attempted to conquer it."

"My brothers will find me. And they'll kill you in a most unpleasant way once they do. If you want to save your skin, you'll let me go right now. Then maybe you can get away before they swoop down on you."

Though she tried to sound confident, as if she expected Braden and Cadur to thunder through the woods at any moment and run him through, Tynon only gave a harsh laugh and dragged her toward his horse.

She held herself rigid as he tossed her easily into the saddle and then vaulted up behind her. The day was fair and scented with spring. Honeysuckle hovered in the air and the sun shone warmly upon the rough craggy land, where a few patches of grass strained to grow.

On such a day as this, she might have enjoyed a picnic with her ladies-in-waiting. They might have sat in the garden with their sewing, eating apples and listening to the birds. And dreaming of spring.

But there were no birds here in this daunting spot. Only gnarled trees and hard earth, and a man whose arms enclosed her as he spurred his horse forward.

Toward Bordmoor.

Erinn was all too aware of those powerful arms around

her as they rode, of his muscular torso at her back, his body intimately close to hers. Even through her cloak and gown, she felt the great strength of him, the warmth and power.

Never in her life had she felt so vulnerable and helpless. She'd always been carefully protected—guarded by her brothers as well as by her father's men. No one had ever dared lay a hand on her, certainly not a man like this, the enemy of her family for a hundred years.

Now her body was pressed against his, as he took her ever closer to another land, the land of her enemies. And she had no one to rely upon except herself. She would be unable to lift whatever spell had been cast upon his precious keep, and . . . what then? What would he do to her then?

Her thoughts churned in a wild jumble. And she couldn't stop thinking of Braden. Was he alive? Hurt? Who else had this monster harmed last night when he'd somehow breached the gate and the moat and sneaked into the garden?

Erinn clenched her hands before her, shivering despite the sun. She had to find a way to do something that her father and brothers and all the troops of Marlbury together never had done.

She had to best Tynon of Bordmoor.

3

Pink plumes of color had just begun to unfurl across the late-afternoon sky as Tynon reined in his destrier atop a rocky hill.

The long ride had been a blur—an endless, aching, silent blur. Erinn and her captor had not exchanged one word during the entire journey—and not long into it, she had begun to regret her hasty refusal of food or drink.

She had no notion how long it had been—one day, two—since her last meal, but the hunger creeping through her left her feeling weak and overwhelmed at the thought of what lay before her. And crossing mile after mile of unfamiliar forests, rolling meadowland, and narrow, icy streams had proved disheartening, for she knew that every mile they traveled away from Marlbury Castle diminished her chances of an imminent rescue.

Through weary eyes, Erinn saw a river flowing below to her left, its water a crystalline, translucent green. Yet as Tynon of Bordmoor lowered her from the saddle and then sprang down beside her, it was away from the river that he turned her—toward a towering black fortress perched on an opposite hillside some little distance away.

She gasped as she gazed at it, silhouetted against a sky of dazzling blue that had begun to glow gold and pink with streaks of sunset.

That was Bordmoor Keep? But how could it be? The name had always struck terror into her heart, for it was known far and wide as a massive, impregnable fortress—a fortress where the duke of Bordmoor kept his troops, his warhorses, his dreaded weapons, and his gold. Rumor had it that the keep was filled with tapestries and golden chests and riches far beyond those which Marlbury Castle had ever known, and she had always imagined it as a huge, terrifying stronghold where Tynon ruled from a throne studded with rubies and gold.

But this keep was a ruin. Its walls were scorched, black, and crumbling. They looked as if a mere breath would knock them over, and they were draped in smothering, decaying vines of ivy. The turrets were broken, the battlements no more than a pile of rock, and grime shrouded the mullioned windows. Huge rocks were strewn around the gates as though tossed by a giant, and the portcullis itself lay sideways with its giant spikes broken, rusted, and useless, as useless as the dry moat that surrounded the place, filled not with water but with dead and twisted weeds.

For one brief, dazed moment she wondered if her father's forces had somehow succeeded in bringing about the destruction of their enemy's stronghold, but then she knew this could not be. She would have heard—she would have known. There would have been days of celebrations and feasts, mass rejoicing throughout Marlbury if Bordmoor Keep had been brought to ruin.

Yet it had been brought to ruin. It was nothing but a broken and deserted pile of stones, decayed and sagging into the hillside like a smashed cake.

Behind her, Tynon's fingers tightened on her shoulders. "Change it back," he said softly, "if you value your life."

She whirled toward him. "You think I did this?" a hysterical urge to laugh nearly overwhelmed her.

She, who had once turned a squirrel into a wooden statue

in the garden when she'd been trying to transform it into a deer, could no more bring down a fortress than fly across that bone-dry moat and swoop in through one of the windows in the tower. In her wildest dreams she couldn't hope to achieve something like this.

But she managed to keep from blurting out that fact. If Tynon thought her powerful enough to cast such a spell, so be it.

"I wish I had been the one to do this to your precious keep." She drew the fur-trimmed folds of her cloak around her with dignity. "But I'm afraid it never occurred to me. I suggest you try to find the witch—or wizard—who did it and ask him or her to—"

"I'm asking *you*. No, I'm *telling* you. Change it back. *Now*."

"That's impossible. For one thing, I don't even know what it looked like originally, except for what I've heard, and—"

"*That*"—Tynon spun her around again and pointed at the keep with one hand, even as the other dug into her arm— "is what it looked like. As you damned well know. And that is what you are going to restore to me before this night is over!"

A chill swept through Erinn's blood as she stared where he pointed. Sunset was swirling, glistening through the sky, gilding it in pink and silver and gold just beyond the damaged keep.

Except that the keep wasn't damaged any longer. It now stood before her, glittering upon the hilltop as the sun dangled like a glowing orb behind it. The battlements and turrets were restored, the windows no longer obscured by grime. The fortress's stone walls rose solid and strong, free of ivy, and sparkling like towers of silver in the dying light of day. The dry moat was now brimming with water, the gate upright, gleaming, and manned by stout soldiers in black tunics trimmed in silver.

Indeed, inside the yard of the keep she glimpsed people moving about, talking, carrying buckets or pushing carts, horses being led toward a stable, and as she watched, a young boy appeared on one of the parapets. He waved his arm over his head, and she thought she heard faint words upon the breeze: *"Tynon! Tynon!"*

She blinked, blinded by the setting sun, and suddenly the restored keep was gone and the blackened, crumbling one stood in its place. Then as she stared in wonder, the first reappeared, flickering in and out of her vision—now glistening in its splendid glory once more, bustling with life and activity, now the dark ruin—and then again restored—until the exact moment when the sun disappeared behind the distant gray mountains.

Instantly, the gleaming vision vanished and did not return. The keep she had first seen was back—its turrets broken, the boy vanished, the moat and yard barren.

And as dusk whispered through the air, it stayed that way.

"I don't understand." Her voice shook. Whether from lack of food and drink, or from weariness, or from the power of the spell she had just witnessed, she couldn't say, but something had left her stunned and shaken.

She turned and peered into Tynon's face. "What has happened?"

He was gazing at her, those intense eyes blazing in the dusk. She saw the shock settle over his face.

"You really don't know, do you?" he said at last, and there was pain in the words. "I thought . . . I was certain . . . you *didn't* cast the spell, did you?"

"I told you I didn't."

"By all the fires in hell!" His jaw tensed as he swung toward the ruined fortress once more. "But if not you— who? I know of no one besides the Royal House of Marlbury who would do something so evil."

For a moment, seeing the desperation, fatigue, and pain that crossed his face, Erinn almost forgot who he was, who she was, and all that lay between them—an entire century of enmity. She thought how she would feel if her beloved Marlbury Castle was enchanted—changed, stolen from her, and transformed into a deserted ruin. She almost stretched out her hand to touch his arm, a sympathetic gesture that she quickly stifled, just in time.

"How often do you see the vision of it?" she asked instead. "When did this begin?" She wasn't asking for his sake, she told herself, only to satisfy her own curiosity.

"Every night at sunset—that is the only time the real keep appears. It lingers for only a moment or two, flickering in and out, until the sun sets behind the mountains."

"And the rest of the time, it is . . . like that?" she asked, glancing again at the monstrous ruin.

Tynon nodded grimly.

"Who is that boy? The one on the parapet calling your name?"

"My brother, Rhys. He's in there . . . and so is Marguerite . . . and I can't get to them. They're trapped—trapped in a vision, in a place that's no longer part of this world."

His mouth hardened as he once more rounded on Erinn, reached out, seized her arms. "But you can free them. And restore my home."

She'd been wondering dimly who Marguerite was, but at this she drew herself back to the matter at hand and spoke firmly.

"I cannot do what you ask. You must look elsewhere if you want to find the culprit, and the solution. I can't help you."

"You can, witch, and you shall." There was utter determination and a flicker of ruthlessness in his eyes that made Erinn swallow hard. "Perhaps you're telling the truth and you didn't cast the spell, but you can remove it. And you're not returning to Marlbury until you do."

"Don't you think my father and brothers will come after me? You're nothing but a fool! They will butcher you for having touched me. My brothers don't allow anyone to lay a hand on me, least of all a filthy savage like you and—"

She broke off as he hauled her up against his chest, fury glittering in his eyes. She forgot to breathe as she found her face only inches from his, as those mesmerizing eyes burned like blue flames into hers.

"I have outwitted and outfought them at every turn—even with your help. For one hundred years they have sought to dominate my people, to take that which is mine—do you think I'm going to relinquish anything of it to them now? No, they will not find you—or me, princess. My soldiers are lying in wait to attack them should they dare to cross the border. They are outnumbered three to one. You will not be freed until you do as I command."

"The day a princess of Marlbury takes orders from a llachlander of Bordmoor is a day you'll never live to see," she flashed back angrily, thinking how wrong he was about everything. It was the llachlanders who had tried to overrun Marlbury, to snare the lush farmlands and peaceful plains for their own use, to overpower her people and reduce them to little more than servants of a duke ruling from afar.

But even as she said the words, she swayed on her feet, and it was only the grip he had on her that saved her from tumbling forward. She saw the surprise in his face, and gritted her teeth, struggling against the weakness overtaking her in waves, but her knees buckled, and the next moment Tynon of Bordmoor had swept her up into his arms.

"Even a witch needs food and drink," he muttered as he began to stalk toward his horse. "I'm damned if I'll let you die on me."

Then they were in the saddle once more, and the great steed was galloping down the hillside toward the ruined keep.

Lavender shadows of night stole across the sky as they passed the fallen gate and entered the rock-strewn courtyard. Tynon left his destrier, slung his pack over his shoulder, and once more scooped Erinn into his arms.

"Set me down. I can walk," she protested, but he merely scowled at her and stalked toward the keep as if she hadn't spoken. In truth, she wondered if she *could* walk another step—her throat was dry, her spirit and body drained, and in Tynon's arms she found herself leaning her head weakly against his chest.

Yet her brain still worked, for it was filled with shock as they entered the portals of the great hall.

"Must we . . . stay in here?" she managed to utter, and he growled an incomprehensible sound of irritation.

"It's my home, what's left of it," he added, and Erinn could barely suppress a shudder as she gazed at the fallen pillars, broken stairways, and worst of all, the rats scurrying through the empty, darkened hall.

No furnishings appeared in the keep—it might have been a cave. Yet Tynon moved swiftly, as surely as if those keen eyes of his could pierce the darkness.

He headed up a staircase, moving without apparent concern over several broken steps, then entered a narrow corridor and kicked open a door that revealed a huge stone chamber, empty but for the barren hearth, one three-legged stool, and half a dozen bronze sconces.

"You'll have to excuse my poor hospitality, princess." There was mockery in his tone as he lowered her feet to the ground, then, still supporting her with his arm, tossed his cloak down upon the floor. "I can't offer you a feast, but like it or not, you're going to eat what's put before you."

Erinn shivered as she sank down upon the cloak he had draped across the stone floor. Even through its thickness the floor felt cold, so very cold.

"And no arguments this time," he added with a scowl. "You're no good to me dead."

"Are you always . . . so charming when inviting ladies to share your table?" Even to her own ears, her voice sounded faint and weak. How she wished she could sound fierce and fearless instead. It was humiliating to show weakness before him. To make up for it, Erinn frowned at him as he drew a bundle from the folds of his cloak.

"I'm not known for my charm. And even if I were, I wouldn't waste it on a witch of Marlbury," he replied almost absently as he handed her a hunk of hard cheese and an equally hard chunk of some thick, grainy bread.

Erinn no longer cared if the food was tainted with poison or some kind of potion. She attacked it with single-minded determination. She didn't even hesitate when he pushed the wine flask into her hands, but grasped it and drank deeply of the sweet dark wine, which burned its way down her parched throat.

It wasn't until she'd finished the last crumb of bread and cheese and drained the flask that she realized he was watching her. To her surprise, his expression was not hard as it had been before, but thoughtful, and searching.

It made him look different. Less harsh, and younger. And even more attractive.

None of that, she told herself, tensing. *Are you forgetting who he is? Tynon, who struck down Braden in the garden. Who wounded Cadur at the Battle of Three Rocks.*

Too bad he didn't look like the heartless monster she had always pictured him to be. He looked to be no older than Braden, surely not yet having reached his thirtieth year, and yet there was something careworn in his eyes, an odd weariness in that darkly handsome face.

It would be easier to despise him if he was homely or pompous or stupid as a troll, she thought in irritation. Still, she *did* despise him. With all her heart.

"Why are you staring at me?" she demanded. She felt stronger now, her spirit restored by nourishment.

"Why shouldn't I?"

"Staring is rude."

"Many men must stare at you." He grimaced. "Or do you pretend to be unaware of your beauty?"

Beauty? She possessed beauty? Erinn had all she could do not to gape at him. She had never glimpsed it in herself, and if the few men she had been allowed to converse with alone paid her a compliment she dismissed it as casual flattery to the king's daughter.

Of course, Stirling of Chalmers had told her that her eyes were exquisite, though she considered them quite ordinary. She'd assumed he was exaggerating for the purpose of getting her to let him kiss her, and since she'd been eager to try that herself, she'd not questioned him. She knew her fair hair to be of a pretty color, and it was soft, that was true, but it fell straight to her waist and refused to curl. How many nights had she practiced curling spells, all to no avail?

He was trying to trick her.

"Flattery will not get you what you want." She folded her hands primly before her. "I told you, I can't help you."

"If the great witch Erinn can't help me, surely no one can."

"It's out of the question. I'd be a traitor to Marlbury, to my own family."

"If you don't help me," he leaned toward her, and now there was only grim ruthlessness in his eyes, none of the thoughtful appraisal she'd glimpsed before, "I'll marshal my forces and lay waste to your precious Marlbury."

"You wouldn't—"

"Smoke from the fires will blot out the sky," he cut her off sharply. "And the land will be scorched, every dwelling and building set afire, every animal killed or herded across the border. I swear to you, witch, I'll see your people starve."

Erinn scrambled to her feet, nearly blinded by a red haze of fury and despair. He would make Marlbury suffer—and it wasn't Marlbury's fault! And she couldn't stop him any more than she could reverse the spell.

How did I ever feel a moment's compassion for him? she wondered frantically, the blood pounding in her temples. *He's a monster.*

If only I could *do magic. I'd . . . I'd . . .* She knew exactly what she'd do. She would tear one of those bronze sconces out of the wall by sheer will and send it crashing straight at Tynon of Bordmoor. If only she could . . .

Tynan rose, eyeing her warily, as Erinn fixed her gaze not on his handsome face but on the sconce nearest the door. She stared at it, stared harder than she'd ever stared at anything. Her eyes squinted with the effort, she felt her heart thundering, and her fingertips tingled until they grew numb. Everything in the room save that sconce was blotted out—the flickering candles, the dim, musty shadows, and the single mullioned window, broken and leaking in slanted bars of moonlight. She saw none of it—only the sconce, as her eyes narrowed and she concentrated every drop of her energy upon it.

Fly! Fly! she ordered it silently. *Fly right at him, strike him down!* To her amazement the sconce suddenly detached itself from the wall and hovered in the air. *Fly, fly!* she willed it again. *Fly hard and fast—strike that man where he stands.*

The sconce flew with dizzying speed—but straight at her. She ducked just in time, only to see it circle and swing back toward Tynon. But it was now moving so slowly, he didn't even have to duck. He watched it come, floating lazily through the air, and reached out a hand, effortlessly grabbing it.

Erinn could have wept. The one bit of magic she'd managed to summon faded as abruptly as it had begun. The sconce remained motionless in Tynon's grasp.

"What was that all about?"

"Nothing. I was merely . . ." Her voice trailed off. "Amusing myself."

"You Marlburys are a strange lot," he muttered. "If you're going to use magic, I suggest you do it for something worthwhile. Like breaking this damned spell that surrounds my home."

His home. The keep was a place of arms, wealth, and weaponry—not a home, not like Marlbury Castle was to her.

Or was it?

"I suppose you're going to tell me you miss your brother?" she said coldly. She saw the tension run through him.

"I do."

"And . . . Marguerite?"

"Of course. I'm worried about them."

"I'm worried about my brother, too."

"Don't expect me to apologize for that." His lips twisted. "And don't expect me to lift a finger to help you."

"I expect you to do whatever I tell you to do—if you want to go home again one day and find it as you left it." He crossed the distance between them in three quick strides and towered over her.

Erinn held her ground with an effort. The flickering candlelight and wavery silver moonlight revealed enough of his expression to make her draw in her breath. There was no trace now of the man of quiet reflection, of weariness, the man with pain in his eyes. This was a man who cared for nothing but his own needs and wants, a man accustomed to commanding, and to being obeyed. A man who no doubt took to the battlefield the way a bird takes to the sky.

His eyes blazed into hers, knocking her breath out of her lungs. They held a depth of determination that Erinn had never seen before, not in anyone, not even her brothers.

"Tell me you'll help me." The words were all the more dangerous because they were low and softly spoken.

"You'll get no help . . . from me—"

"Damn you!" His hands seized her arms, pulled her close. For a moment Erinn struggled to break free, but she quickly realized how useless that was. He was far too strong for her. He could break her in two if he chose, and he looked at this moment as if he *did* choose, as if that would please him above all else.

"I'm warning you. If you don't want to bring bloodshed and grief and destruction upon your people and to see your castle dismantled stone by stone—"

"No!"

"Then you'll do what I ask. Now, before another day—"

"Listen to me," she burst out, terrified of telling him the truth, yet panicked of what he would do if she didn't. "I have to tell you something . . . confess something. And it's the truth. It isn't fair to make Marlbury suffer."

"You are wasting time."

"No, listen, please. Don't punish Marlbury—it's my fault. Only mine."

"So it will be on your conscience when my men ravage your fields."

"No!" She felt tears burning her eyes. "I *can't* lift the spell," she gasped in misery. "Even if I wanted to. I . . . I . . ."

"You *what?*" His fingers tightened on her arms. "Tell me!"

"I can't do magic!" she cried.

Stunned amazement crossed his face, but it was immediately replaced by disbelief—and anger. "More lies." He shook her. "All the world knows of Erinn of Marlbury's powers."

"*That* is the lie, the only lie," she went on desperately. "I have no powers—at least, none worth mentioning." Her voice trembled with bitterness. "If I could do magic, don't you think I'd have struck you down with a spell the moment you stepped into the garden? My mother could have. She once turned an entire troop of men into rabbits as they were about to attack my father's camp. And she—"

"I'm not interested in your mother. I'm interested in you. You have a reputation as great as hers, you were the one who sent a hawk of victory circling the battlefield at Llachland Point, swooping down over your father's troops as if in salute, and it was then that the battle turned, just when I had him beaten."

"It was an accident that the hawk flew over. It wasn't my doing. But Braden and Cadur let word out that it came from me so as to encourage our men."

His eyes narrowed. "And the time that a lightning bolt sent a tree crashing over onto my camp before the engagement at Dunck Wood? It killed a dozen men—a sign, my knights believed, of imminent defeat. That was not your doing either?"

"No, I had nothing to do with it. But Braden and Cadur wanted to inspire fear in your soldiers, and hope in our people and they decided that by spreading tales of my powers we would . . . would . . ."

"Say it," Tynon ordered harshly as her voice trailed off.

"We would finally intimidate and defeat the llachlanders once and for all," Erinn finished defiantly.

And the truth of her words was apparent in her vivid, beautiful face.

It all made sense. Perfect sense. Yet it had never crossed his mind. Erinn of Marlbury's powers were legend. It had never occurred to anyone to doubt the veracity of all those tales. So all these years . . .

Numb, Tynon stared at the woman before him, the woman no longer struggling to escape his grip. He had breached the moat and braved the soldiers of Marlbury for naught. This slender woman with her golden hair, delicately sculpted features, and mesmerizing eyes was no more magical than he was. She couldn't lift the spell that imprisoned the keep any more than a mouse could fly.

She was afraid; he could see that in her eyes. Yet she held her head high and searched his face, no doubt wondering what he would do with her now. He wondered, too, even as frustration built inside him.

If Erinn hadn't cast the spell, who had? And who could break it? That was all he could think about, all he *must* think about.

So why was he staring into those vibrant green eyes as if hypnotized by their luminous depths? Why was he still holding on to this woman who was useless to him, utterly useless.

Suddenly her gaze shifted past him, and those lustrous eyes widened. And stared. True alarm showed in her face, and Tynon released her and wheeled around just as a huge red-bearded man slipped into the chamber, a cudgel gripped in his fat hand.

As Tynon watched, another man joined him, this one short and wiry, with straggly tufts of hair and a sallow face crisscrossed with scars. His gray tunic was ragged, but the knife he clenched gleamed like new.

Outlaws, by the look of them, Tynon thought swiftly. More and more they plagued the llachlands. If he wasn't always having to fight Marlbury, he reflected with bitterness, he could clear the scavengers from Bordmoor once and for all.

"I don't suppose they're f-friends of yours?" Erinn breathed at his side.

"Never set eyes on them before."

Erinn's heart skipped a beat as the two men glanced first at Tynon and then at her. The glint in their eyes made her queasy, and she knew instinctively that they were not men who would aid her in escaping Tynon. From the unsavory look of them, she had no doubt she'd be far worse off in their company even than in the llachland duke's, and with a little shudder she inched closer to him without even realizing she did so.

"Ho, ho, what have we here?" the red-bearded man muttered in a guttural tone.

"I smells a lady. A mighty pretty lady," the other smirked, and in the blink of an eye they had somehow positioned themselves so that they were blocking the chamber door.

"Keep quiet—and whatever happens, stay out of the

way," Tynon ordered in a low tone, and then he strode forward, placing himself squarely between Erinn and the two men, one hand resting lightly upon the hilt of his sword.

4

"GET OUT."

It was the warrior duke who addressed the intruders, and even they froze for a moment at the harshness of that commanding voice. They scanned the dark-haired giant—his braced stance, the firm mouth, the eyes that glittered like polished marble in the dank keep—and for a moment their courage deserted them. But only for a moment. Then they stiffened their resolve, remembering that he was only one man and they outnumbered him. Teeth clenched, they tightened their grips on their weapons and held their ground.

"Now, now, friend." Red-beard's voice grated like rough stones scraped together. "No need to snarl. We're simple travelers from Keege, looking for shelter from the night."

"We mean you no harm," his companion said with a smirk.

"You're not welcome here." Tynon spoke curtly. "Leave this place—now."

Bristling, the wiry man took a step forward. "We go where we please."

"Not here. Get out."

Erinn scarcely dared to breathe. How calm he sounded. And utterly confident. Yet the two men gave no sign of being intimidated. They continued to grin and smirk, fingering their weapons as if they couldn't wait to use them.

"If you don't leave this place now, you'll be sorry you didn't."

"Who are you to give us orders, eh?" the smaller man demanded.

"We don't much like getting orders from anyone," Red-beard said. "Maybe your woman puts up with it, but we're not about to—"

"You fools, he's the duke of Bordmoor," Erinn burst out, unable to keep silent any longer. She stepped forward to Tynon's side, extending her arm in a sweeping gesture. "And this is Bordmoor Keep. Leave now—quickly—and if you're fortunate he won't harm you."

But Red-beard gave a grunt of laughter. "Duke of Bordmoor, eh? And Bordmoor Keep?" He threw her a scornful glance. "And I'm the High King himself." He elbowed his companion in the midsection as they both chuckled. "Bordmoor Keep is a grand place—we've heard tell of it. Velvet curtains and golden goblets and a kitchen with stores to feed the entire llachlander army. And who might you be, wench?"

Erinn's chin lifted. "If you must know, I am Princess Erinn of—"

"Enough!" Tynon thrust her behind him again. "Leave her out of this. All that need concern you is that if you don't leave now, you'll die where you stand. Both of you."

Though he didn't move, didn't even draw his sword, there was no mistaking the threat he posed. His powerful warrior's body, his hard and determined face, those eyes that gleamed with such a fierce light. He *wants* a fight, Erinn suddenly realized. It hit her with a tingle of shock. *He's furious and frustrated about the keep, and itching to take it out on someone.*

But the two men seemed undaunted. They were looking beyond him, at her. Erinn had no way of knowing that she was the first woman they'd seen in weeks who wasn't old or gap-toothed. She had never realized that beauty shone upon her like the sun.

"You're the one who's going to die, you damned whelp." The scar-faced man showed Tynon broken, yellowed teeth. "But methinks we'll keep the woman alive—for a while," he added, and suddenly, with a yell, he leaped forward, knife outstretched even as his companion lunged toward Tynon at the same time, swinging the cudgel.

Erinn had no time to do more than gasp as the two converged on him, but somehow his sword was in his hand in a flash. Steel glinted in the candlelight, cutting a blazing arc through the air. There was a sharp whistling sound and a strangled scream as the sword caught the wiry man in the shoulder.

He reeled backward, blood spurting, and his bellow of pain and rage seemed to echo through the empty keep, from ceiling to floor and into every corner.

Then Tynon dodged Red-beard's cudgel and sliced the sword through the air again. With a grunt, the big man leaped back just in time.

Suddenly a third outlaw burst through the door. "What in bloody hell—" He broke off at the sight of his companions fighting for their lives against the strapping man in the black tunic. He surged into the fray, his shoulder-length muddy-brown hair flying as he clenched a dagger in each fist.

Erinn screamed as one of the daggers caught Tynon in the arm. Without thinking, she grabbed the stool, lifted it, and swung it straight at the outlaw.

It struck him full in the chest, and he toppled sideways, skidding into the wall.

"Get back, you little fool," Tynon yelled at her, but even as he spoke the man he'd wounded seized Erinn from behind, wrapped an arm around her slender waist, and pressed the blade of his knife against her cheek.

"Stop right there, you, or I'll cut 'er to ribbons," the outlaw shouted, holding her fast.

Erinn could scarcely breathe for the fear racing through her. The knife felt cold, so cold against her skin. An eerie silence fell over the chamber. As if through a haze, she saw the other two outlaws grinning at their comrade who held her, and then Red-beard edged slowly toward Tynon.

But Tynon didn't see him. He didn't even seem to notice or care that blood streamed down his arm from the knife wound. His gaze was fixed on her, and for a moment as their eyes met she saw a flash of fear in their depths. Fear . . . for her? Impossible.

Yet, a determination to survive or some other instinct must have spurred her to warn him. "Behind you!" She gasped, and the man holding her tightened his grip so painfully that she cried out.

Tynon wheeled around, leveling his sword at his advancing enemy. Red-beard halted, his tongue circling his lips as he eyed the glittering blade.

"Put it down, quick-like," the outlaw holding Erinn barked out. "Kick it over to them, or I'll slit the wench's throat."

Tynon looked at Erinn, his stomach clenching at her white face, her eyes vivid with terror. Then his gaze centered on the man who held the knife to her throat. He let his sword clatter to the ground.

"Ah, do you see this?" The long-haired outlaw loped forward. "I always fancied me a jeweled sword," he crowed and bent toward the weapon.

Erinn pushed the terror away and fixed her gaze on Tynon's sword, desperately concentrating all of her attention on it.

She'd been able to move that sconce, hadn't she? Not precisely the way she'd wanted to, but she *had* moved it.

The blade of the knife tingled against her cheek as she kept her gaze focused on the sword and willed it to obey with every ounce of her being.

Nothing happened.

Fly, she implored silently. Her brows drew together in fierce concentration as the outlaw's grimy fingers closed around the hilt.

Fly to Tynon!

The sword never moved. The outlaw smiled to himself, rubbing a finger over the encrusted emeralds and rubies glittering in the candlelight.

"By the stars and the moon—*fly!*" she shouted, and the outlaw jumped as the sword tore itself from his grasp and sailed upward through the air.

It swerved and angled, shooting straight toward Tynon of Bordmoor at a blinding speed. It nearly sliced off his head, but the llachlander ducked just in time.

Then the sword swung around and streaked toward Erinn and the man who imprisoned her. He cursed, releasing her as he dove toward the floor in his haste, and Erinn dodged the sword in time, shouting, "Stop! Stop!"

It slowed, and hovered, then began spinning about above their heads in a wild, careening circle—until suddenly Tynon stuck up his hand, grasped the hilt, and yanked it down.

Eyes bulging, Red-beard and the long-haired outlaw lunged toward him. Erinn whirled around to find that her former captor had dropped his knife. She scooped it up and brandished it before her.

"Don't move or I'll kill you, you filthy coward!" she warned him as she tried to keep her hands from shaking.

"You don't have the stomach for it, wench." Blood pooled at his feet as he dodged toward her, making a grab for the knife, but Erinn stabbed at him and managed to cut his hand. He jumped back, nearly slipping in the blood, then his eyes narrowed. He crept toward her again, more slowly, a cunning light in his eyes.

"You'll be sorry you did that, my lady," he gasped. "Sorry as you can be."

Behind her Erinn heard grunts and a crash and a curious gurgling sound, and she wondered how Tynon was faring against his attackers, but she dared not take her eyes off the man coming toward her.

He dashed in so suddenly that she gasped and struck out with the knife, but this time he caught her arm and twisted the knife away. Then he had it turned against her and came at her fast, but suddenly Erinn was tossed sideways and the room went spinning. When she glanced up from the floor where she'd landed, she saw Tynon standing over her attacker, who was sprawled in his own blood. Dead.

Tynon of Bordmoor wasn't even breathing hard, and his eyes were so cold that Erinn shivered.

Slowly, filled with horror, she struggled to her knees and glanced around the chamber where a short while ago she had eaten supper. Three bodies lay upon the cold stone floor, and blood flowed like a crimson river, soaking the stone beneath them.

"It's over." Tynon set down his bloodied sword and came to her. He reached down and raised her to her feet. She was trembling, this princess of Marlbury, and he knew she had never seen a man killed before, much less three of them.

"Are you hurt?" There was blood on her cloak and for a moment his heart stopped beating.

"N-no. But you are." Her dazed gaze turned to the blood still streaming down his arm.

"A scratch, nothing more."

"I must . . . tend it."

"Not here. This is no place for a woman."

Erinn had no wish to argue with him over this point; she longed to be away from here.

As he led her from the chamber, she carefully averted her gaze from the fallen outlaws. She felt oddly light-headed, and there was a sickening roiling in her stomach that made her long to lie down upon a soft bed and blot out this nightmare.

But she had a job to do first. A debt to repay.

The room he brought her to was down the corridor—a chamber somewhat smaller than the last—and nearly as sparse, but for the old bronze-framed mirror mounted upon the wall opposite the windows and the animal pelt draped upon a settle in the corner. He left her briefly, to retrieve his pack, which held salve, he told her, and while he was gone, Erinn made her way to the window, pushing the decrepit shutters open, breathing deeply of the cool night air.

She shivered as it touched her skin and blew her hair across her cheeks, but the chill of it helped to revive her from the sick sensation.

She gazed out at the land that surrounded the keep—peaceful-looking land, frosted silver by moonlight. In the distance there were meadows and fields, and the gleam of a great gray river. Near its banks she saw smoke curling from the roofs of a village.

The night sky gleamed with stars, hot blue stars that seemed to taunt her. These same stars, this same full moon, blazed above Marlbury, her home. Yet it was so far away.

She wondered with an ache in her throat if she would ever see it again.

At the sound of footsteps behind her, she whirled around. Tynon had returned, and he held a pouch that she guessed contained the salve and bandages that she would need to tend his wound. But he appeared to be in no hurry as he watched her from the doorway, despite the blood that soaked his sleeve.

"Plotting an escape?"

She lifted her chin. "Perhaps. Though I hope you'll have the decency to let me go, now that you know I'm of no use to you."

"But you are of use to me. The daughter of King Vort is a prize worth keeping. Or should I say a *pawn* worth keeping?"

She gritted her teeth. The cool air had revived not only her body but also something of her spirit, and she swept toward him with close to her usual composure. Snatching the pouch from him, she spoke in a low tone.

"Don't you think your time would be better spent finding whoever *did* enchant your keep instead of bothering with me?"

"It's no bother, princess."

"It will be. I assure you I can prove extremely bothersome if I put my mind to it."

His brows lifted at the challenging gleam in her eyes. "I don't doubt it. But I am a fearless warrior and will somehow endure."

"Don't be so certain!" Erinn retorted.

The way her eyes sparked green fire at him almost made him smile, but he caught himself in time. *Bothersome,* he thought with a sudden twinge of irritation. *That was a perfect word for this princess of Marlbury.* It was particularly annoying that she could appear so elegant, so assured, and so effortlessly beautiful after all she'd been through, even with her hair wild and tumbled around her face, even wrapped in a bloodstained cloak.

He wondered how she managed it.

Setting his jaw, he began stripping off his tunic and the chain mail beneath it, trying to focus on the throbbing pain in his arm and not on this golden-haired witch with the face of an angel.

Erinn dug the salve out of the pouch, far more disturbed about his threat to use her as a pawn than she had allowed him to see. But she nearly forgot about even that as she looked up and saw him standing bare-chested before her in the moonlit chamber.

By the stars and the heavens, he was splendid. More than splendid—mesmerizing, she thought in awe. His arms were corded with ropy muscle, and his wide chest and shoulders robbed her of breath. His stomach was flat and taut and, like the rest of him, bore many scars, she noticed on a gulp. Now the newest one would be the wound upon his right arm, a red, raw gash that had at last ceased to bleed. The knife had apparently not pierced as deeply as she'd feared, though the cut was ugly.

But the rest of him, Erinn observed, swallowing hard, was utterly magnificent.

Something fluttered deep and warm inside her, something she'd never felt before. Heat flooded her cheeks as she hurriedly raised her gaze to his once again, only to be confronted by those piercing blue eyes.

He wants to use you as a pawn, she reminded herself sternly, trying to focus solely on that. *He is despicable.*

But why couldn't he have been *homely* and despicable?

"My brothers were raised to believe it was wrong for men to use women as pawns in matters of war," she managed to remark with asperity. "Surely even you would not do such a thing."

"I'll do whatever I must to bring down my enemies."

"But your sole purpose in taking me from my home was to lift the spell, and it's clear I can't do that. So by all that is decent you must let me go."

"But perhaps you *can* lift the spell." He studied her thoughtfully. "From what I've seen, you have some magic in you. You're just not very good at controlling it. True," he added as she flushed, "you almost killed yourself and me, along with those scoundrels, but you did manage to send that sword flying. That's something. If you could develop those skills of yours a bit more," he went on with a gleam of speculation in his eyes, "it's possible you might find a way to restore the keep."

"I told you, I wouldn't help you even if I could. So kindly don't mention it again."

He watched that soft, full lower lip of hers push forward in a pout. An adorable pout. Unexpectedly, desire, hot and fierce, surged through him. He fought it even as he watched her dip her fingers into the salve. And as she began rubbing the balm briskly across his wound, it took all of his self-control not to seize her in his arms and kiss that sweet pout right off her lips.

The salve burned like hellfire, but as she rubbed it into the wound, the wound was not what hurt. The beautiful, sculpted features of his captive somehow seemed to blunt the pain—while creating an entirely different kind of torment.

Erinn deliberately ignored him, keeping her gaze focused on the wound. She pressed down hard, hoping to draw an exclamation of pain from him, to show him that even though he had saved her life, she had no sympathy for him, none whatsoever. She would tend his injury, thereby repaying her debt, and nothing more. Not one more measure of aid or comfort would she give him. Yet as she touched him, it was she who felt a kind of pain, an ache deep inside her. The tips of her fingers tingled. *It must be the salve,* she told herself. *The ointment is strong.* Biting her lips, she pressed even harder upon the raw center of the wound.

He drew in his breath, but made no sound no matter how hard she rubbed. His blue eyes were unfathomable. She knew the salve must burn, but she guessed that if he was like Braden and Cadur and most other men she'd observed, he'd rather bite off his tongue than admit weakness to a female.

"Does it hurt?" she asked innocently.

He smiled. "Your touch is too weak to hurt a warrior. Perhaps if you applied a bit of pressure."

"I *am* applying pressure," she snapped, then bit her lip as his smile slowly widened.

She yanked her hand away, but to her shock, he caught her wrist and held it.

"You said you would never help me, and yet you've just applied healing salve to my wound. The wound of your father's enemy."

"And of my enemy." Her eyes darkened with anger. "Make no mistake about that."

"Then why did you tend me?"

"You saved my life back there as well as . . . as . . ." Her voice trailed off as she recalled the vileness of the outlaws he had killed.

"As well as your virtue?" he finished for her.

"Yes, that, too." She flushed and favored him with a scowl. "So I owed you a debt. Now it has been discharged." She yanked her arm away, surprised when he let her. Dropping the salve back into the pouch, she pushed it against his chest.

"Here!"

Her fingers brushed his skin, encountering the rock-solid muscles beneath the dark mat of hair, and a jolt of something hot and wild ran through her.

Tynon seized her wrist again, imprisoning her hand as it rested against his chest.

"Your debt isn't yet discharged, little witch, much as you might wish. I saved your life; now you must save my home. That is a fair exchange, a fair repayment of your debt."

"Are you mad or merely a fool? I can't save your home. I don't know how. And even if I did, I wouldn't. What you ask is impossible!"

"Impossible, eh? When I was a boy, and Marlbury had twice the soldiers of my father, and twice the weapons and destriers, as well as friends and allies in all the kingdoms, my father was advised by a counselor from Ranue to cease the fighting, to sign a treaty with Marlbury and agree to whatever terms the king should demand. He was told that victory was impossible. But my father didn't believe that.

He fought on, fought with every man and steed he could muster, every sword, stick, and arrow. He fought to avenge all that had come before, and to protect those under his care. And now, he has been killed—killed by your father's troops, no less. Cut down little more than a year ago."

Tynon's eyes were the color of a storm-lashed sea, dark and furious. In them Erinn saw wrath, but also pain. The pain of loss.

"Yet he won many victories in his life, and so have I. Now it is we llachlanders who have the upper hand—and Marlbury that sees that victory is impossible."

"That is not true." She shook her head. "We will destroy you." But she feared he could see the doubt in her eyes. The tide had indeed turned against Marlbury. That was her fault . . . if only she could be of more use . . .

He laughed then, not a pleasant laugh but one that was harsh and mirthless. He released her so abruptly that she nearly stumbled.

But he didn't release her for long.

He only took the pouch from her and dropped it into his pack, then he drew out a length of rope.

Erinn backed away. But Tynon advanced with the rope, his mouth set.

"There is no need—" she began, a catch of fear in her throat, but he cut her off.

"There is every need. I must go and remove those stinking carcasses from my home. And tend to my horse. And I won't have you running off while I'm gone."

"I won't—I wouldn't—"

He laughed again, a sharp, cynical sound, and seized her even as she tried to dart away. With frustrating ease he bound her wrists behind her, then dragged her toward the settle, pushed her down to sit upon it, and tied the rope to one of its legs.

"I won't be long." He tossed the animal pelt over her and strode toward the chamber door, leaving her in the flickering darkness.

"You needn't ever return!" Erinn cried after him, fighting back tears of frustration.

"That wouldn't bode well for you," he called without

looking back over his shoulder. She heard his boots stamping through the empty corridor, then the silence of the darkened keep enclosed her.

She struggled futilely against the bonds, testing them, but they would not give. *Oh,* she thought, gritting her teeth, *why did I even touch Tynon of Bordmoor? He is a savage!*

Yet, she had to admit that though he had trussed her like an animal, the bonds were not overly tight. And never once, in all the times that he had seized her since the moment he'd taken her from the garden, had he hurt her with his strength, though well he could have.

And he *had* saved her life.

But only because he thinks you might be useful to him—if not as a witch, as a pawn. A shiver ran through her as she imagined her father's and brothers' desperation to get her back safely. They must be frantic, and even now organizing an army. But it would take time to bring together a force powerful enough to storm Bordmoor Keep—or what they imagined Bordmoor Keep to be. Days, perhaps weeks, to recall troops from Kaylantium and the ports. Tynon would anticipate that, of course. And Marlbury's forces would be blocked, perhaps ambushed. How many would die?

The only alternative was a ransom of some sort. But what would Tynon demand? How much would it cost Marlbury?

If only I could escape him and make my own way home, Erinn thought in despair.

But that possibility seemed hopelessly remote now, as she sat in the darkened chamber, shivering even beneath the animal pelt her captor had tossed over her. Tynon was a formidable adversary. He was far stronger than she, he was shrewd, careful, and he knew the llachlands well, while she was as lost and adrift here as a lamb in the center of the ocean.

Erinn closed her eyes, weariness creeping over her even as she pondered the futility of the situation, the dearth of choices available to her.

Her fate truly rested in the hands of Tynon of Bordmoor. Unless she could think of something . . . some way . . .

Her eyes closed, and her body, pushed beyond exhaustion, drifted into sleep. She never even heard Tynon return, never knew of the long moments he stood gazing down at her as the moonlight played softly over her face and set her hair shimmering like golden fire.

"You're not what I expected, Erinn of Marlbury," he muttered as he studied the delicate shape of her chin, the sweep of long silky eyelashes against cheeks as smooth and pale as cream.

She was beautiful, so beautiful, but there was more than that—there was a vibrance about her that was compelling, alluring. Though he hated all things Marlbury, he couldn't help but admire her fierce loyalty to her family and her kingdom.

Tynon had been too busy fighting Marlbury all his life ever to have the time to envision settling down with any one woman, though he had tasted the charms of many. But he found himself wishing for a moment that Erinn was a llachlander. She would be the kind of woman he would seek as a wife, and as the mother of his child. She was passionate, brave, spirited—and lovely beyond words.

But she isn't a llachlander, he reminded himself sternly, backing off a step. *She is your enemy.*

The fight had gone on for a hundred years, and now it was down to the two of them. He must use her, use her to find a way to break the spell, or to force King Vort to find someone who could.

She is a pawn, nothing more, he told himself. *A tool to use to free the keep from this damned enchantment.*

The worst thing he could do would be to start thinking of her as a woman. Then he would be susceptible to whatever feminine tricks or wiles she might employ.

He had to find a way to break the spell, and he had to extract as much as he could from Marlbury in the meantime. Now that his father was dead, the fate of the llachlands rested on his shoulders alone. The people depended on him. So did his brother.

Tynon had never been one to shirk responsibility. No, he had always taken on more than his share, and he excelled at whatever he endeavored to accomplish, be it swordsmanship, jousting, or leading men into battle. He didn't believe in half measures, and he had never tolerated fools.

He had always vowed to himself that one day he would bring the border wars to an end, and his people believed that he would do it. His brother believed he would do it, and so did Marguerite, his old nurse, who had first served Tynon's great-grandmother and who had lived through the wars for nearly all of her life.

What must they all be thinking now—trapped in a dimension that was inaccessible to the outside world? Not for the first time, he wondered if Rhys and Marguerite and the servants and soldiers in the keep could see him as he saw them.

He wished to hell he could get his hands on whoever had played this evil trick.

Just then, Erinn shifted in her sleep, and the animal pelt slid from her body into a heap upon the stone floor. He gazed down at her, realizing that he had yet to see her without that heavy cloak. His gut clenched as he wondered what she looked like beneath its dark, fur-lined folds— wondered if the rest of her was as exquisite as that breathtakingly delicate face.

Without knowing why, he took out his knife, then bent down and cut through the knot that held her trapped upon the settle. He lifted her in his arms and strode from the chamber, telling himself that what he was about to do would further his cause, that it had nothing to do with any softness he might be feeling toward his enemy's daughter, nothing to do with *her*. It was simply that a touch of goodwill from the princess of Marlbury could not but help his cause.

And except for the small warning voice in his head, he actually believed it.

5

Erinn came awake slowly, peacefully, the fleeting remnants of her dream lingering in her mind as she began to stir. She had dreamed that she was in her own velvet-canopied bed in Marlbury Castle. It was a sparkling summer day, and she was going to a fair. To escort her, her father had chosen a handsome stranger she had never seen before—a strapping knight with silky dark hair and a hard-planed face and fire-blue eyes—

Tynon of Bordmoor.

She jolted upright, fully awake, as memory rushed back and doused her with panic like a pail of ice water. She found herself not in her own bed but on a straw pallet in an unfamiliar chamber of Bordmoor Keep. And stretched out beside her was Tynon of Bordmoor. His eyes had snapped open at her sudden movement. Even as she stared down at him, he pushed himself up on one elbow and met her stunned gaze.

"You . . . you . . . we . . ."

Her heart sank. He was bare-chested, his silky hair tousled, his eyes calm and sleepy. He wore only his breeches, she noted, while she—

She glanced down, apprehension tightening her throat. With relief she saw that her cloak still draped her. For a moment she had feared to find herself stripped naked.

"What are we doing here? I . . . I was on the settle . . ."

"You looked uncomfortable. I thought you'd sleep better here."

She sprang up, trying to move away from him, but she realized suddenly that a rope was wound around her waist and the other end was knotted around *his* waist.

"I couldn't very well leave you unbound," he pointed out as she glared at him. "You might have tried to leave me while I slept."

"I shall leave you. You may be sure of that."

"Not before we've struck a bargain, little witch."

"I make no bargains with a savage like you—" Erinn began, but the words were cut off as with one hand Tynon yanked her down upon the pallet, and in a twinkling, before she could even draw breath, he was upon her. She struggled furiously, but she was pinned beneath him.

"Let me go! Savage! Brute! If I could, I would turn you into slime, into dust, into dirt beneath my very feet!"

"But you can't," he said softly. "And I, in turn, can do whatever I wish with you."

He spoke the words quietly, matter-of-factly, and they were far more devastating than if he had shouted them. He spoke the truth. Her own helplessness against his physical power was brought to bear fully as she felt vulnerable in the way only a woman could feel.

She stared up into his eyes, her own filled with a measure of fear that she could not hide, though she tried. From their gold-flecked depths, however, defiance still blazed even as she fought back tears of frustration.

"Are you ready to strike a bargain?"

She gritted her teeth. He leaned down toward her, his weight pressing her into the straw pallet. He brushed a pale tendril of hair from her eyes. For a moment his fingers lingered upon the silky strand, twining through it almost absently.

The intimacy of the gesture sent fear spiraling through her, but also a burning heat. "Let me go," she whispered.

"When you agree to my bargain. I made you comfortable last night, allowed you to rest, and did nothing to besmirch your virtue."

"How chivalrous."

"I hoped to earn your goodwill, but you are proving yourself to be ungrateful."

"Grateful? Should I be grateful that you kidnapped me from my home, struck down my brother, dragged me to this horrid place—"

"You should be grateful that I have found a reason to keep you alive."

"And what reason is that?"

As Tynon studied her defiant face, reluctant admiration tugged at him—along with a surge of red-hot desire. Holding her beneath him like this was tormenting him far more than her. It was pleasant, and could be even more so—if only she were willing. But he would not take her against her will. And besides, she was a Marlbury. He ought to be repulsed by her very existence instead of being attracted by the mere sight of her, by the way she moved and spoke, by the softness of that luxuriant hair that shimmered like the summer sun. The necessity of controlling the urges that gripped him was not lost on him, but the effort required was considerable. Strenuous even, he thought as he savored the soft curves of her body beneath him and saw the trembling of those lush, kissable lips.

"I want you to help me find a way to break the spell." Somehow he managed to speak in an even tone. "If you can't do it, you must know of someone who can. Together we'll find this person, be it witch or wizard, and bring him here. You'll assist in whatever meager way you can. But you won't go home, Erinn, until the enchantment imprisoning the keep is broken. And if—before that happens— your father and brothers dare to cross into the llachlands, their fates will rest upon your head."

"*Bastard.*" She struggled anew, but he held her firmly, trying to ignore the delicious squirming beneath him.

He waited until she grew still again, breathless and exhausted.

"Do you accept my bargain, witch?"

"Do you give me any choice, savage?"

"I must have your word."

Erinn's heart ached. Oh, how she hated him. He was cruel. Hateful. Yet a jumble of emotions warred within her, confusing her. Why did her heart pound so as she felt his body pressed against hers? Why was she fascinated by those cool eyes, by the thrust of his jaw?

She ought to feel only revulsion, and yet . . .

"You have my word!" She had to force herself to say what he demanded. Then she drew a deep breath as he moved off of her.

"Cut these bonds," she ordered as she scrambled to a sitting position.

Tynon shook his head. "If you're always this imperious, no wonder that you've not yet found a husband. Who would have such a sharp-tongued woman?" But as he spoke he sliced the knot with a swoop of his knife.

Erinn tore the rope from her and sprang up from the pallet. "I could have my pick of husbands, but I have yet to find one I *wish* to marry—or whom my brothers deem worthy of me. And you? Have you no wife? Or . . ." She remembered something abruptly and glared at him. "This Marguerite you mentioned—is she your wife? How would she feel if she knew her husband had spent the night upon a pallet with another woman?"

Tynon stood up, his bronzed chest gleaming in the vivid sunshine that filled the chamber. For the first time he chuckled without any trace of harshness. "Marguerite is *not* my wife." He grinned, pulling his tunic over his head.

"Then who is she?"

"Enough of your questions. We're leaving here."

"Leaving here?" Erinn regarded him suspiciously as he donned the rest of his garments. "Where are we going?"

"You'll find out when we get there—unless your powers of Sight are sufficient to reveal our destination to you."

Erinn's shoulders stiffened. "I don't have any powers of Sight—as you are well aware."

"You seemed to know me when I seized you at Castle Marlbury," he remarked. "We'd never met, but you recognized me even in the darkness. As if you'd known I was coming."

"I didn't know you were coming or I'd have been ready for you. The entire castle would have been ready for you." She pushed her tangled hair back from her face and tried to smooth the folds of her bloodstained cloak. "I did have a vision," she added in a low tone. "But not a very useful one. All I saw was your face, not that you were inside the castle grounds, getting ready to strike down my brother." She gritted her teeth. "All of my visions turn out to mean nothing. Why couldn't this have been one of those?" She shot him such a bitter look that Tynon grinned. And shrugged his big shoulders.

"Don't ask me, little witch—I'm a warrior, not a magician. I've no idea how such things work. But it does prove one thing. You're not completely bereft of magic." He reached out, cupped her chin, lifted her face so that she was forced to look into his eyes.

"Perhaps," he said slowly, "you can produce a vision of whoever performed the spell."

"One doesn't just produce a vision—at least, I don't." Erinn found herself getting lost in those deep blue eyes, and it was difficult to concentrate when his gentle touch seemed to be burning her flesh. She stepped back, breaking the contact. "That one vision I had of *you* was the first one that ever held any significance," she said, and not waiting to see whether it was scorn or pity that would cross his face at the admission, she straightened her spine and stalked past him toward the door. "And with my luck, it will be the last," she muttered ruefully over her shoulder.

Yet even as she swept out of the chamber, Erinn's mind was spinning. She couldn't help a twinge of wonder—and bewilderment. It was indeed strange, and more than a little unsettling, that the one vision that had actually meant something relevant to her life and the lives of those around her was the one involving Tynon of Bordmoor.

Why couldn't she have had a vision that *warned* her— so that she might have alerted Braden and spared him injury? So that Tynon himself could have been caught by her brothers and the guards, and then *he* would now be the prisoner, not she.

Oh, how she would love to see him locked in the dungeon of Marlbury Castle. If only her vision had been more useful.

She pondered this in frustration until they left the dimness of the keep and stepped into the sunlit courtyard. Spring danced in the air. Unlike the previous day with its chill and wind, today was a harbinger of the mild days to come. The air smelled of damp earth, the breeze carried the fragrance of distant flowers, and the sun shimmered like a gold coin in an azure sky.

She turned slowly, scanning the land that surrounded the keep. It appeared to be greening even before her eyes. Lovely, with its hills and moors and sloping meadows. *But,* she quickly told herself, *it isn't anywhere near as beautiful as Marlbury.*

Tynon gave her little time to embrace the day or take stock of her surroundings. Before she could even remove her cloak, which was far too heavy for so warm a day, he had her mounted before him on the black destrier and they were galloping south.

They flew past a sleepy village before she could glimpse more than a few low buildings, smoke curling from their chimneys, and a handful of people making their way with carts and horses. She heard the banging of a hammer, and from a cookshop came an aroma of fresh bread and buns. Geese and pigeons swooped and squawked, and a peddler's cart was stuck in the mud. But Tynon never slowed the horse, and the village was gone in a blink. They didn't stop until they had ridden well beyond the village and approached a house of timber flanked by many sheds and stables set amid groves of newly budding lemon trees.

"What is this place?" Erinn asked as Tynon pulled her down from the saddle.

"The home of a friend." Taking her arm, he drew her toward the door, but before they could reach it, a passel of children came tearing through the courtyard to surround them.

"My lord, have you broken the enchantment?" The tallest boy, with russet hair and bright freckled cheeks, asked, his gaze fixed eagerly on Tynon.

"Is the keep now back as it belongs?" A small girl pushed forward to peer up at the duke of Bordmoor.

"Papa has us say prayers every single night," another girl announced, folding her hands before her.

"Is this the witch of Marlbury?"

"Is she your prisoner? Will King Vort surrender?"

"My lord, did you know that Eadgyth is sick?" A boy with dirt-streaked cheeks and pale blue eyes piped up. "Mama cries every day and Nurse says Eadgyth might die."

"Hush, don't say that or you'll bring on the evil spirits," the girl with folded hands shrieked in alarm.

"What's this? Eadgyth is ill?" Tynon looked to the tallest boy. "This is distressing news."

"Aye." The boy nodded and ducked his head. "Even Papa is afraid, I think. He says only a miracle will—"

He broke off as the door to the house opened and a thin man with a lined, careworn face and the same russet hair as the boy stepped out.

"Tynon, thanks be to heaven, it is you. We have been waiting these many days for your return." He hurried forward, a bleak smile breaking across his features as he and Tynon gripped each other's arms.

"Is this her, then? The witch?" The man stared at Erinn as if he expected her to sprout black wings and a beak and peck his eyes out. She stood perfectly still, watching in silence as his gaze swung back to Tynon with eager hope.

"Does this mean . . . has she lifted the spell?"

"Not yet, Stephen. Things turned out to be more complicated than I first thought." *You have no idea how much more complicated,* Tynon thought, remembering how softly the little beauty beside him had nestled against him all through the night.

"But tell me, is it true that little Eadgyth is ill? What can be done?"

The lines on Stephen's face seemed to deepen, and his flesh looked gray in the morning light. "We've tried everything," he said in a low, defeated tone. "Hetta and her women have tended her ceaselessly, and the doctor comes each day. They say . . ." He took a deep breath. "They say they've done all they can, and know not what to do—how to help her." He lifted his hands helplessly. "The fever remains—and worsens. Would that I could take it on myself and spare the babe." For a moment his voice quavered, then he took command of himself. "But come, Tynon, come in. There is much to discuss."

As the children ran off, chattering among themselves, Tynon and Erinn followed their host inside the house.

He ushered them through the hall into a large, handsomely furnished chamber where tapestries covered the walls and sunlight spilled through mullioned windows.

"The servants will bring food and wine. But tell me, how can I be of service to you, Tynon? How can I help?" His gaze flicked only for a moment, warily, to the slender, silent woman whose rich cloak was stained with blood. Then his eyes settled upon his friend, searching his face with a worried expression.

"We need food and supplies, Stephen. I present to you Princess Erinn of Marlbury." Tynon's hand at her waist pressed her forward ever so slightly. "She is in need of your lady's care. It appears she'll be staying longer in Bordmoor than I first thought, and she has nothing but the clothes on her back. If Hetta can provide her with what she needs, I'll see that you're compensated."

"Of course, of course." Stephen held up a hand. "Only—" He moistened his lips, clearly uneasy. "How can we know that she will not put a spell upon my wife, upon my house—even upon my children?" he asked in a low tone.

"I swear to you, she will not."

Stephen hesitated, then gave a nod. "So be it, then. Your word is good enough for me." Still, he sent a quick, warning frown in Erinn's direction. "Whatever she needs, you can be sure, she shall have. And whatever you need, Tynon, you have only to ask."

So it was that Erinn found herself shortly after in a guest chamber of the house. Stephen's wife, a tiny reed of a woman with thick brown hair coiled around her head, came herself to see to her comfort, and after instructing a servant to bring a tub and heated water, she regarded Erinn with the same wariness as had her husband.

"The servants will clean your clothing and your cloak, and I will bring such garments as may fit you." Her voice sounded thin and raw as she took Erin's cloak from her and folded it over her arm.

"Thank you." As the woman lingered, regarding her uncertainly and with a desperate longing in her eyes, Erinn spoke quietly.

"I'm sorry to hear that your child is ill. Don't tarry with me. Please feel free to tend to her."

"Yes, my little Eadgyth. She's . . . only a babe," Hetta whispered, her hands clutched so tightly before her that her knuckles whitened to the color of bleached bones.

Seeing the pain and the fear in the woman's face, Erinn couldn't keep silent. "I heard that she has a fever. Have you tried camphor?" she asked quietly.

"Yes, yes. It did not help. Nothing has helped." The woman twisted her hands together, then suddenly spoke all in a rush. "I think it is meant that you are here today. I think you were sent here. To save her. I know that our peoples are at war, but you are a great witch. Surely you must know some way . . . some way to make her better." Desperation shone in her eyes. "Could you . . . would you . . . help her? Please, can you make my child well?"

Erinn's chest was tight. If only she had true power, if only she indeed were a healer. But she wasn't, and she couldn't bear to give this woman false hope.

"I am not a healer." She took a deep breath. "My powers are not . . . of that sort. But . . . I know something of children. And of medicines. I will see her and try, if I am able, to help."

Hope flickered in Hetta's eyes. Wild, heartrending hope. "Yes. Please." She hurried to the door. "This way, I beg of you."

The baby lay tucked in a cradle in an alcove of her mother's chamber. Her little body was wrapped tightly in a soft blue blanket. She was no more than a few months old, with wisps of soft red-gold curls framing a tiny face, a face that was flushed and hot with fever; and as she slept, she whimpered—pathetic, restless little cries that tore at Erinn's heart.

"How long has she had this fever?" she asked quickly, brushing a gentle finger along the baby's hot cheek.

"Five days now. She grows worse. And she has taken no milk. She cried at first all the time, cried loudly, pitifully, but since yesterday she is too weak to cry, except like this. And she is too weak to take nourishment."

The serving women all huddled together, motionless, and Erinn saw tears upon their cheeks.

"We've tried milkwort and lavendry, but the fever only worsened." Hetta's face seemed to grow even grayer, the shadows under her eyes darker. "Please, is there no spell, no magic that will lift the fever?" she begged.

Erinn was remembering something—one of the young village boys whose father had been killed in a battle. She'd visited the family with a basket of food and on the day she arrived, the boy—Ranulf—was sick with a fever and was believed to be near death. The midwife had come to treat him while Erinn was still there, and she had immediately prescribed a brew of myrrh and ginseng.

Erinn had returned the next day and found that the fever was broken, the boy was sitting up on his pallet, able to take broth from a spoon and even to smile when she told him of the cake she would bring him as soon as he was well enough to eat it.

"We must make a brew of myrrh and ginseng," she told Hetta quickly. "Do you have these things?"

"Yes, we have many herbs. But I never heard of this brew," the woman replied, her eyes wide.

"I have seen how it is made. I'll help you to prepare it." Erinn was already unwrapping the heavy blanket swaddling the child. The midwife also had instructed that such coverings were unhealthy for one with a fever, and since that time Erinn had more than once seen that she was right.

"Quickly, we must gather the ingredients and bring them to a boil, along with goat's milk and barley."

To her surprise, there was no hesitation, no doubt. The bond that flourished between women tending a sick child overcame every other consideration, and the women worked together with one single purpose in mind—a purpose stronger than hate or mistrust.

Once the baby had been fed a dozen spoonfuls of the brew, there was nothing more to do but wait. Erinn returned to her chamber, and a servant brought heated water for her bath while one of the women who had been tending Eadgyth laid out upon the bed a clean gown of finely stitched linen. It was too wide for Erinn's slender figure, but two servants set about sewing it to fit, and soon, having cleansed her hair and her skin, donned the soft pale-blue gown, and neatly plaited her fair hair down her back, threading it with a ribbon, she was led to the hall, where a long table had been laid and where Tynon of Bordmoor and Stephen waited.

Both men stood as she approached them, and she saw Tynon's gaze riveted upon her. His keen glance swept over her face, her plaited hair, the simple gown. She was conscious of the way the soft folds of the gown flowed over her curves. His expression was unreadable, but with a flicker of pleasure she saw a muscle clench in his jaw.

"At last," was all he said. She took her place beside him and said coolly, "You needn't have waited for me."

"What, and have you tell everyone in Marlbury—should I allow you to return—that the llachlanders have no courtesy for their ladies?"

"I am not your lady."

"I suppose I must thank the stars for that," he said curtly.

Stephen was watching the two of them uneasily. No doubt, Erinn thought, he feared that Tynon might provoke her into casting another horrific spell like the one that had claimed the keep.

She tossed her head and took a seat upon the bench without another glance at Tynon. Deliberately, she focused her attention on the platters of food set before her. Yet though the sun was already bright in the sky and she had not yet broken her fast, she barely tasted the bread and butter and cheese, the slices of cold venison, or the jellied eggs and nuts and wafers.

Tynon, she noted from the corner of her eye, didn't share her disinterest. He attacked his food with relish and spoke all the while with Stephen. There was no sign of Lady Hetta. Erinn kept glancing toward the doorway, wishing she knew if Eadgyth's fever was still high, if they had managed to give her more of the brew, if the little girl would recover.

No sooner had the last course ended than Tynon was ready to leave.

"We're going back to the keep? So soon?" she asked as Stephen led them through the hall and a servant appeared with her cloak.

"Of course. It's my home. It's where I belong. And where my messengers will come with their reports. Stephen has provided us with supplies that should last us until the keep is restored—"

He broke off as Hetta came hurrying down the hall, her face beaming and wet with tears. In her arms was a bundle—*Eadgyth*, Erinn saw with a surge of hope. The baby's eyes were closed, her breathing soft and even, and her cheeks no longer held the unhealthy flush of fever.

"Hetta," Stephen exclaimed, "what is it? The babe? She is better?"

"Yes, yes. Only look—the fever has broken. She awakened and was hungry and no longer frets. Oh, how can I ever thank you enough?" she burst out, turning to Erinn with shining eyes.

"I am glad—so glad." Smiling, Erinn peered down at the peacefully sleeping child.

"Are you saying that . . . a *spell* cured her?" Stephen stared at the pale-haired witch in his hallway. "I— I owe you my thanks then, lady . . . er, princess."

"No, no, it wasn't a spell. It was only a brew I know of, from my work with the children at home. I learned it from—well, never mind." She touched Hetta's arm, her gaze still fixed tenderly upon the baby. "I am only happy to have helped little Eadgyth," she finished quietly.

Tynon was staring at her. She refused to look at him, instead keeping her gaze upon the babe, only shifting it to Stephen and Hetta as they joyfully thanked her yet again.

It wasn't until she was sitting before him upon the black destrier once more that Tynon spoke, as the warm sun beat down upon their shoulders, bathing the spring day in softness. "You did a fine thing back there, healing the child," he said slowly.

"I did what I could. I would do the same for any child."

"One would not expect such gentle aid from—" He broke off. "Tell me the truth. Was it magic you used to cure the child?"

"No. I told you already. I learned of this brew back home."

"How?"

He had slowed the horse, and they were moving now at a leisurely trot. The day sparkled around them. She was surprised by how comfortable it felt to be here in the saddle with him, his arms around her as they rode. If she hadn't known better, she might have thought they were companions, part of a carefree group out for a picnic. But they weren't. They were enemies, and she couldn't forget that, not for a moment.

"There is a midwife in our village back home," she told him. "I have seen her prepare remedies for the children when they are sick. One day I happened to have brought a basket of food to the house of John, the silversmith and—"

"Why would a princess do that?"

"Bring food?" she asked in surprise. "Why not? My ladies and I frequently visit the homes of those who were lost in battle, trying to help the wives and the children. We have too many children like this—thanks to the brutality of the llachlanders—and I try to do what I can for them."

His arms tightened around her waist as he spurred the horse faster.

"Our land is filled with orphans and fatherless children as well."

"Then why don't you end the wars—surrender, call for a truce—and spare the lives of your people?" she flashed.

"Your father could do the same. If he were not so bloodthirsty and greedy to take over our land—"

"He is not! The war was started by the llachlanders—one hundred years ago and—"

"Is that what they told you? The war was started by Marlbury. Your great-grandfather, witch, began this war and spilled the first blood."

She twisted around in the saddle, her cheeks flushed with anger. "You're lying. I was told that your great-grandfather began the war!"

"That is the lie," he snorted. "And what reason was given to you for the start of the fighting?"

Erinn stared at him. "Reason?"

"Yes, the cause. What were you told?"

"I was never told the cause." Her voice faltered. The wind caught her hair, and a few glinting strands escaped the severe plait that bound it. "Were you?"

"I asked my father. He told me no one remembers."

He frowned, and Erinn sensed that he was weighing whether to say more.

"I thought that he might have remembered," Tynon admitted. "But he chose not to talk about it."

For a moment their eyes met, held. Then Erinn broke the contact and turned around in the saddle once again. "What does it matter? We were not the ones to start it, though. Of *that* I am certain."

"When it comes to war, one cannot be certain of anything," Tynon said grimly in her ear, and a shiver ran down her spine.

He spoke like a man who knew all too well about war, a man who had no taste for it. But . . . he was the consummate warrior. She had seen him fight in the keep, and his battle prowess was acclaimed even by his enemies. Then she thought of the easy way Stephen and Hetta's children had swarmed up to him, the concern he'd shown toward the baby, Eadgyth, and his gratitude for her help in making the child well.

It suddenly occurred to her that he was far more than a warrior. He was a man who was at ease with children. A man who could be gentle. Decent. That had indeed been fear in his eyes when he'd thought those scoundrels would kill her—fear for her. Had it been only because she was useful to him? No, something told her he had done it because he was an honorable man. Though he might be at war with her people, he had defended her. She was under his protection while she was his prisoner, and he wouldn't allow her death to be on his conscience.

Like her father, like Cadur and Braden, he had a noble side. A gentle side. And a quiet decency. Something twisted painfully inside her chest, an ache that went deeper than any physical hurt.

Suddenly she was more intensely aware than ever of his arms around her, of his powerful frame wedged against her back, of his presence, his strength, his warmth. Her heartbeat quickened, and the blood in her veins sizzled with a slow heat.

No man had ever made her feel like this before.

She took a long, shaky breath and decided that perhaps she would help him in earnest in getting his keep back—for the sooner he allowed her to return to Marlbury, to spare her family their worry and the possibility that they might walk into a trap, the better.

Because she herself seemed on the brink of falling into a trap, another kind of trap—one that once would have been unthinkable to her. But she felt herself tottering dangerously on the edge and knew that she had to get away from Tynon of Bordmoor soon. The man was too handsome, too intriguing, too *male*.

And too dangerous, by far.

If she hadn't known better, she'd have thought *he* was the one casting a spell—on her heart.

6

ERINN SPENT THE remainder of the morning exploring the ruined keep, going from chamber to chamber, roaming the corridors, trying to pick up some sense of who had cast the spell—and how—by gleaning what she could from within the enchanted walls. Tynon had wanted to accompany her, but she'd convinced him that he would only distract her from fully concentrating on what she was doing. So at last he'd relented, after demanding that she give her word she would neither hide from him nor try to run away.

She shivered as she prowled the tower and the great hall and the solar, all dim ruins of what they must have been before the spell was cast. Once she heard a boy's laughter, echoing faintly from the rafters, and wondered if that was Rhys. And what of the mysterious Marguerite?

She had no sense of a woman's presence, except once, as she returned to the chamber where she'd treated Tynon's wound and saw the mirror on the wall. For an instant, as she approached, she thought she saw a ghostly flickering within the glass—a woman with midnight hair that floated around a tear-streaked face—and for one chilling moment Erinn thought she could hear the sound of weeping. Then it vanished, and so did the image in the mirror. She walked closer, her skin prickling, but she saw only her own reflection looking back at her.

Thoughtfully, she returned to the sunlight to find Tynon conferring with a small group of soldiers beneath the shade of an acorn tree. The soldiers' horses stood nearby, great beasts whose coats glistened in the sun.

The men grew silent as she approached. All but Tynon regarded her with a mixture of distrust and dislike, much as she had seen at first in Stephen's eyes.

"So this is the infamous witch of Marlbury." The barrel-chested soldier nearest Tynon spit the words out with contempt. "Who would have thought such a little thing could bring so much evil? My lady is trapped somewhere inside there," he growled, jerking a thumb in the direction of the keep. "Should any harm come to her—"

"None will," Erinn said quickly.

All of the men, including Tynon, stared at her.

"So you say," the solider responded after a moment, his eyes slitted with suspicion. "But who can trust a witch who kills boys of twelve? My cousin met his death at Dunck Wood when the lightning struck. Your doing! His blood is on your hands—"

"Enough, Jared!" Tynon strode forward between the soldier and Erinn, his features taut. "Leave her be. You have your orders, all of you. Go now."

"But—"

"Go!"

Jared threw one last angry glance in her direction and turned away. Tynon waited until the men had all mounted their horses and ridden off over the greening ridge before he broke the silence.

"He's a good man, but he doesn't know the truth. Don't heed his words."

"I am sorry about his cousin," she said quietly, thinking that at twelve the boy was still so very much a child, not much older than those she visited with treats and trinkets in the village of Marlbury. She could understand the soldier's anger and grief—and his fears for his lady. She only wondered that Tynon hadn't told him the truth about her. She'd expected he would revel in her ineptitude at magic and assure all of his men—indeed, all of his people—that there was no witchcraft to fear from Marlbury, that King Vort and his troops had no magical advantage. For Marlbury's sake, she wanted to cling to her legend for as long as possible, but she'd expected Tynon to reveal its falsehood.

Yet he hadn't. Not to Stephen, and not to his men.

"Why didn't you tell him—any of them—about . . . me?" she couldn't help asking.

He gave her a long look, trying not to be distracted by the picture she made, a fresh, lovely picture on this golden spring day. "There will come a time for them to know. For everyone to know." He shrugged. "For now, let's just work on breaking the spell. Did you learn anything in the keep?"

"I learned that the spell, whatever sort it is, is not evil. That's why I could assure that soldier that no harm would come to his lady. Nowhere that I walked did I sense danger or evil. But . . ."

She paused, trying to find the words to explain what she'd sensed. "Sadness was there. A long-ago sadness. It lingers in the air, clings to the very walls."

"Sadness." Tynon shook his head, looking puzzled. "How does that help us?"

"I'm not sure. I wish there was more. I feel so helpless," she muttered. "I want to help you. So that I can go home," she added quickly. "But all I get are bits and whispers, not full pictures. That's all I've ever gotten." She took a deep breath. "I don't know if I can do this." The words rushed out, honest and unbidden. "I don't know if my meager powers will be enough."

"They will be." Tynon gave her a long, measuring look. "They have to be."

The calm expression in his eyes soothed her. For some reason the knots in her stomach eased.

"I'd best start, then," she said, surprised by the note of resolve in her voice, and she moved to a stretch of grass and settled down upon it, spreading her skirts about her.

She sat facing the keep, studying it intently as Tynon dropped down beside her on the soft grass.

But she was soon distracted by the sense of being watched, and her heart fluttered as she saw his gaze on her. "Surely you must have something better to do," she told him, smoothing back a wisp of hair that had escaped its plait.

"Not at all. I've given my men their orders, and messages are being sent even now to those in the field. Everything is under control—except this." He nodded toward the keep, just as several hawks swooped over the turrets, then soared toward the treetops and away.

"Has there been any sign from my father's troops?"

"They're marching toward the Marlbury border, but nowhere near the llachlands—yet. You have time yet to spare them."

The words chilled her, and a weight seemed to settle more heavily upon her shoulders. She focused her attention once more on the keep. She had to forget about Tynon and do *something*. But what? Closing her eyes, she tried to conjure up an image of whoever might have cast such a powerful spell.

"Perhaps Artho of Glaives," she murmured, half to herself. "He's a grand-wizard, also something of a trickster." Once when she'd been briefly under the tutelage of Cyrus the Sorcerer, Artho's nephew had been one of her fellow students. He had shown amazing promise, while she . . .

She groaned at the memory, and opened her eyes. Tynon lifted his brows.

"Something wrong?"

"I was just remembering the time I briefly took lessons from Cyrus the Sorcerer. Within a matter of days he sent me home, telling my father I wasn't up to the demands of his class. He took only the best, you see," she added with a wry grimace. "My mother was once his prize pupil. But he told me . . . oh, never mind."

"No, go on. What did he tell you?"

She took a deep breath. "That I had power of a sort not derived from sorcery. Whatever that means. He said that when it came to magic, I would forever be a tinkerer."

She scowled at the sky, fighting the desolation inside her.

"There are worse things," Tynon remarked evenly. "Do your father and brothers berate you because you're not a powerful witch?"

"No. No, of course not." She regarded him indignantly. "They're the kindest, dearest souls anyone could ever—" She broke off at his skeptical glance. "The strange part is that I wouldn't even care about the magic if only I didn't feel so useless. My mother, and her mother before her, were truly able to help our troops in the border wars, but I'm only a sham who can no more aid our troops than—" She bit her lip, remembering to whom she spoke. "Oh, never mind."

Tynon studied that lovely face, the full lower lip pushed outward in a pout, the eyes dark and moody as the sea. For a moment he forgot about the hundred years of battle between their two families, about the fighting and the deaths. What mattered was only the two of them—he and this entrancing woman with the silky hair—all alone in a grassy meadow on a soft spring day, enveloped by the sweet scents of earth and of distant wildflowers carried on the breeze. Pure silence surrounded them, but for the melody of a bluebird singing its heart out.

She thought she was a sham, but she was the most genuine human being he'd ever met. Honest, brave, defiant. And utterly beautiful.

"You're an enchanting woman, Erinn of Marlbury. That is a kind of magic in itself."

Now where did those words come from? he asked himself the moment he had spoken them. Yet they were true.

She gazed at him, her eyes widening. Her lips, those luscious berry-pink lips that seemed to beckon him, parted. "If I didn't know better," she said after a moment, her tone light, "I'd think you were trying to flatter me."

He fought the urge to close the distance between them, to push her down upon the pillowy grass, to lie with her, upon her, and taste those lips.

"I'm speaking the truth." With a jerky movement, he pushed himself to his feet before he did something he'd regret. "Should we go in search of this Artho of Glaives, or of Cyrus the Sorcerer? Could he himself have done this?"

"Cyrus?" Something jolted through her, something hot and pulsing. *Truth.*

She spun about and examined the keep. "Yes, yes, he could," she exclaimed. "Cyrus is a master—a genius of sorcery, the very best wizard I've ever heard of. He could have, indeed. And . . ." she said wonderingly, her eyes lighting with excitement, as the pulsing flickered wildly through her. "I think he did. It feels . . . *right.*"

"I've never even met him. Why would he want to do this to me?" Tynon demanded.

"He didn't do it out of malice, that much I do know from walking through the keep."

"Then why?"

She shook her head, as baffled as he. "I can't begin to imagine."

Tynon's face was grim. "How do we find him?"

"We don't. Don't even think about attempting it, Tynon. Tracking Cyrus down won't work. He is too powerful. You'd never get close enough even to catch a glimpse of him if he didn't want you to. It's not the way." She saw how his mouth was set tight with determination and knew with a surge of uneasiness that he was unswayed by her words. *Stubborn man.* Without thinking, she clutched his arm. "If you anger him . . . no . . . *no,* I won't let you."

Her small hand upon his muscled arm held Tynon rooted to the spot. A surge of heat crackled through him at her touch. At her words.

"What is this?" he asked, studying her sharply. "Don't tell me you care that he might turn me into a rock or a tree?"

"N—no, of course not. But I'm as anxious to end this as you are—to go home and keep my family safe. Let me see what I can do."

"And what do you think you can do?"

"I'm going to review all of my undo, cancel, and reverse spells," she told him. "I may not have power, but I have memorized every spell I've ever heard of or read about.

Not that I can do them—at least, not the way they were intended," she admitted. "But I can *try*."

"And if that doesn't work, we'll go after Cyrus?"

"If that doesn't work, I'll find a way to approach him. Alone. You'll have to trust me to handle it."

He frowned down at her. "I'm not accustomed to letting others handle my concerns."

"Then you'll have to *become* accustomed to it."

From anyone else, at any other time, he'd have struck down the very notion, but when it came from her, he felt not irritation, anger, or resistance, but only amusement and a tug of something stronger, more intriguing. *Attraction.* He was attracted to her, Tynon acknowledged grimly. Attracted to her beauty, her directness, even her stubbornness. But it was only attraction, he told himself hastily. Nothing more.

Wasn't it? he asked himself with a jerk of panic.

All he knew was that by all that was holy, he wanted to kiss her. He ached to kiss her.

"Try, then," he managed to say, using all of his self-control to resist the urge to sweep her close to him and see once and for all how sweet those saucy lips of hers tasted. "There are still several hours until the sun sets. But if you can't come up with something by then—"

"I will." Erinn dropped her hand from his arm and gave him what she hoped was a confident smile. She stepped back swiftly, shaken by the way she felt when she was near him, when she touched him. Golden sparks seemed to fly between her flesh and his when they touched. Burning sparks, sparks that were not painful but pleasant. *Too* pleasant.

"Whatever happens, don't interrupt me," she told him, backing away from him, returning to sit upon the grass, facing the keep, focusing all of her attention upon it.

Tynon sat down a little way from her and began plucking blades of grass as the sun rose higher in the sky. It felt strange to be sitting quietly, doing nothing. *Useless.* He was accustomed to *doing* things, not *waiting* for things. Planning strategy, ordering the placement of his troops, riding into battle.

Sitting still on a golden day, doing nothing, with a beautiful woman only steps away was a new experience for him. Nights he often spent with women. Days, no. Usually he wasted no time persuading them to give him what he wanted—they were only too eager to oblige. He seduced them the same way he fought a battle—with confidence, experience, and his rapt, undivided attention. But doing nothing—that was harder than leading a charge, harder than fighting three men at once.

Especially when there were plenty of things he *wanted* to do with his kidnapped princess from Marlbury.

Still, sitting here with her, enjoying the quiet of the peaceful spring day, wasn't all that unpleasant. Except that he knew it would be even more pleasant if he was kissing her.

I suppose this is what life would be like should the border war with Marlbury ever end, he thought suddenly. *There would be time . . . time to find a wife, start a family, groom an heir. Time to see to the needs of the people, to watch the villages flourish, to plant and to build. And in the evening to stroll with my wife through the halls of the keep as the sun sets and to hear the laughter of our children—*

He gave a start. For when he pictured that fabled wife of his imagination she looked just like Erinn.

His mouth tightened with the memory of all that lay between them, and he pushed the image away.

But his gaze shifted right back to the Erinn before him, the one whose pert countenance was fixed intently upon the looming keep, her eyes narrowed and unblinking.

"I'm going to try something," she muttered suddenly.

"What?" Remembering the sword circling crazily above his head in the chamber, he wasn't sure if he felt eagerness or fear.

"Maybe you should tell me what you're doing first."

"It's a reversal spell." She still hadn't taken her eyes from the crumbling walls of the keep. "It's quite simple, really, and it could work on a transformation such as this."

She stood up, and raised both arms before her, stretching them outward toward the keep, her fingers arced upward.

"Keep quiet and don't move," Erinn said in a commanding tone. "Don't even blink."

Tynon tensed, watching—without blinking—as she began to speak in a low, rhythmic tone.

> *"Winds of change, hear my call.*
> *I summon you—undo it all.*
> *What has been wrought, shall be lifted and tossed,*
> *Blown like leaves before the frost.*
> *I beg this spell be borne away,*
> *Blown and tossed by light of day."*

No sooner had she uttered the last words than there was a huge clap of thunder. Then a wind tore across the bluff and the meadow, roaring like a storm. It lifted Erinn clear into the air, swept her high off her feet, and threw her backward, straight into a clump of thick grass, upon which she landed with a thump, flat on her back. The wind died instantly and the clearing was quiet again, except for the stamp of Tynon's boots as he sprang toward her.

"What the hell—! Are you hurt?"

He knelt beside her, his face taut with concern.

Erinn stared up at him shakily. "I don't . . . think so." She swallowed. "Did the keep change back?"

Tynon glanced toward the bluff. He hadn't even looked before now. He'd been too stunned when he saw Erinn swept through the air as if she weighed no more than a feather. Now he saw that the spell had had no effect on the keep at all.

"No change." He kept his tone neutral.

"Ohhh!" She sat up and looked for herself. Then she clenched both fists in frustration as she glared at the ruin of the keep. "I don't understand," she muttered between clenched teeth. "I did it exactly right, I know I did. It should have worked. Only they never work!"

"It worked, it worked—in a way," he said hastily as he saw the frustration and distress in her eyes. "You did blow yourself backward. That's something."

"It is *not* something. It's nothing! Blowing myself backward was not what was supposed to happen. What kind of a witch performs a spell on herself? What kind of a witch sends herself flying backward only to crash into the earth?"

Tynon felt the grin start at the corners of his lips and spread. He couldn't stop it. The sight of Erinn, along with her sputtered words of outrage, struck him hard, and he could only stare at the woman who just hours ago had left Stephen's home so elegantly attired and coiffed. The tremendous wind had blown her hair loose from its plait; in fact, it had sent the ribbon sailing into a tree, and now it hung over a branch, flying like a miniature banner. Her hair tumbled wildly around her cheeks, which were filmed with dust, and her glorious eyes were shimmering with self-reproach.

She looked disheveled and adorable, and as he stared at her, it occurred to him that this was the witch of whom his troops had so long been terrified, this passionate, delightful girl whose spells never worked as they ought to had inspired fear in a thousand men.

He started to laugh—at the absurdity of it, of his men, himself, and at how infuriated she looked right now with the world. He couldn't stop even when he saw her staring at him, saw the fury darken those magnificent eyes. He laughed harder because she looked so angry, and so damned appealing.

"How dare you! I'm trying to help you—against my better judgment and everything I've always believed—and you . . . you're laughing at me. Stop laughing. *Stop*, do you hear me?"

But as she beat a fist against his chest, and then another, doing nothing but hurting her knuckles, and his laughter only doubled, she suddenly felt laughter bubbling up within her as well. She looked at Tynon, at his handsome face creased in a grin from ear to ear, heard the deep rumble of laughter echoing from his massive chest, saw him helplessly clutching his middle, and she burst into laughter herself.

"Stop laughing," she gasped again, but this time she was laughing even harder than he.

They both sank to the ground, unable to control the dizzying mirth, and before either of them realized it, they were tangled upon the grass, rolling together. And suddenly Tynon had somehow rolled atop her and she was laughing beneath him, her cheeks flushed like apples as she gasped for breath.

Then, abruptly, Tynon stopped laughing. His muscled frame above her went still, and she realized that his face was only inches above hers. He reached out a hand and slowly smoothed a tendril of pale hair from her eyes. His touch was gentle, so very gentle.

Erinn stopped laughing. She almost stopped breathing.

Their gazes met, and neither could look away. They could only look ever more deeply into each other's eyes, glimpsing things they had never allowed themselves to see before.

"Erinn." Tynon's normally deep, steady voice was a hoarse croak.

She opened her mouth to speak, but no words came out.

He leaned closer, hypnotized by the wonder in her widened eyes, drawn by lips that begged for a kiss. One kiss. Just one.

Or so he told himself.

He leaned down toward her, unable to resist the allure of this delicate woman whose tousled hair was fanned out like golden velvet upon the grass.

"Tynon . . . no . . ." she whispered, finally forcing the words out through trembling lips. She searched his eyes and tried to remember all the reasons she should not let him kiss her, all the reasons she should not feel anything but hatred for this dark warrior of Bordmoor, but she could only remember the way he'd saved her from the outlaws, the way he'd gazed at her after she'd helped little Eadgyth, the way they'd laughed together just now while lying upon the grass.

"Please don't tell me no, Erinn," he said very softly. "Tell me yes."

And though a voice inside her screamed at her to struggle, to refuse and push him away, her heart bade her be still. Then he was leaning closer, closer still, and his gaze held her captive.

By the angels, she heard herself breathe, "Yes."

He smiled, a smile that made her heart flip over, just as he kissed her.

It was a kiss like none she had ever known. Like none she had ever imagined.

And as it began, a wind started to blow.

At first Erinn didn't even notice the wind. She only noticed the kiss, that exquisite kiss. No quick, cautious peck was it, like the one she'd shared with Stirling of Chalmers. Nor was it rough and wet and unpleasant, as when Sir Rudyan had kissed her. Tender as the morning was Tynon's kiss. Gentle and bursting with need. Heat flared like a torch within her as the kiss seemed to go on forever—*or perhaps*, Erinn thought dazedly, *time is standing still.* She only knew that she was drawn into a realm of dark, potent pleasure as his warm mouth slanted to hers, and she began kissing him back, kissing him eagerly, with a yearning she'd never known before, and a wish that this warm, spiraling pleasure would never end.

And then the kiss changed, heightened somehow, as he took it deeper. It became possessive, commanding, as Tynon explored her mouth with a questing intensity that vanquished all thought, sense, and reason.

And all of her defenses collapsed.

His tongue thrust cleverly against hers, and sparks flamed inside her. Erinn could do naught but surrender to the onslaught of sensations taking hold within her, sensations that Tynon stoked into a glorious burning fire. Kiss followed kiss, touch followed touch, and then he was raining hot kisses upon her throat, her cheeks, her eyelids, and Erinn was clasping her arms around his neck, plunging her fingers through his hair, drawing him closer and closer.

By the time he stopped kissing her, her limbs felt melted, her senses swam like stars in a midsummer night's sky.

And she couldn't speak at all, could only stare dazedly into eyes that gleamed like bolts of blue fire into hers.

"Perhaps I'm not . . . such a failure at kissing after all," she murmured shakily, and heard a rumble of laughter.

He rolled off of her and scooped her into his arms. Before she knew what he was doing, he had leaped to his feet, still holding her, and begun to spin her around, laughter still booming. "You're not a failure at anything, Erinn of Marlbury. Even your magic is as unique and unpredictable as you are. By all that is holy, you are enchanting. Beautiful and enchanting!" he shouted, spinning faster, and it was only then that they both noticed the wind that was blowing around them, a high, powerful wind with shrieking gusts that sent dust motes and bits of twigs swirling.

Tynon stopped spinning and cradled her closer. Joy shot through her as she saw the tenderness in his eyes. But sudden doubt swirled within her, too, just like the whirling dust and twigs all around them. *What have we done? What are we doing? I shouldn't have* . . .

And then, over his shoulder, she saw something that drove everything else, even that mad, glorious kissing, from her mind.

The keep was engulfed in a whirlwind. And slowly, slowly, as the whirlwind swept over it, through it, and past it, even as she watched, the blackened ruin disappeared before her eyes, the ivy blew away, the crumbling walls were no more.

The wind died as suddenly as it had begun and the keep of Bordmoor glistened before her, grand and imposing, as it had appeared in the shimmering moments of yesterday's sunset. Its stone walls were high and strong. Its towers spiked toward the skies, and even from this distance she could smell roasting meat on cookfires and hear the whinny of horses, the din of voices from the courtyard beyond.

"Tynon—*look!*"

He had already spun toward the sounds, and now stood with her clasped in his arms, staring, staring at the keep he had always known. His fortress, his home—strong and whole and vibrant with life and vitality.

First disbelief and then joy lit his face. As if stunned, he set Erinn down and wheeled back to feast his eyes on the sight of Bordmoor Keep.

"But only a moment ago it was a ruin. The spell must have just been broken. Just now." In wonder, her voice dropped to a whisper. Tynon dragged his gaze from the keep and looked into her eyes. He saw that they shone with happiness. Happiness for him.

"Yes. It broke just now. It broke while we were kissing." He gripped her arms and grinned down at her as he pulled her against his chest. "Don't you see, Erinn? *We* did it. We did it together. We broke the spell."

"I don't see how!"

"Magic." He laughed and dropped a kiss on the tip of her nose. "Come on, I must see Rhys . . . and my steward, and the bailiff . . . and Marguerite." Grabbing her hand, he began to run, pulling her with him toward the tall, upright gates and the full moat where swans swam upon the still, clear water.

But Erinn tried to pull back. "Wait, Tynon. Please, stop."

He obeyed and turned to face her, his hand still holding tight to hers. "What's wrong?"

"You must tell me something . . . before we go in there." She lifted her gaze to his and moistened lips that felt suddenly dry. "Who is Marguerite?"

Tynon's brows drew together in puzzlement. "What does Marguerite have to do with anything?"

"Is she your . . . your lady? You said she wasn't your wife, but is she . . . important to you?"

"By all the fire in hell, yes, she is important to me." He caught her chin in his hand and kissed her quickly on the lips. "She was my great-grandmother's nurse. And mine as well. And she's nearly as ancient as the sea."

A smile trembled across her lips, coming straight from her heart. She began to laugh again, even as he once more pulled her toward the keep. They ran together, side by side, he matching his long strides to hers, their hands clasped as if they would never let go of one another.

And moments later, Erinn of Marlbury passed with Tynon of Bordmoor through the raised gate, crossed the courtyard bustling with llachlanders, and entered the restored and gleaming Bordmoor Keep.

7

THE SUN SANK in a fiery red-gold sky as Erinn brushed her hair before a flickering fire.

She was in the same chamber where last evening she and Tynon had spent the night, bound together by a rough rope upon a meager straw pallet. Only now, instead of cold stone walls and a pallet, the chamber glowed with every evidence of comfort and beauty. The mirror hanging upon the wall was framed in burnished gold, and there were tapestries flanking it, and adorning the other walls as well—intricate embroidered tapestries such as Erinn had never seen.

Instead of a pallet, there was a huge bed draped in rich blue velvet, with gold-fringed pillows piled upon it. Sweet-smelling reeds covered the floor, and candles glittered in golden sconces everywhere she looked. Then there was the fire—roaring cheerily in a scrubbed hearth, its welcoming warmth banishing the chill of evening.

The silver brush that she was drawing through her hair had been resting on a small mahogany chest alongside a trio of golden candlesticks. There was a platter of berries and cheese, and a silver goblet of spiced wine had been brought to the chamber as soon as she had stepped into it.

This Bordmoor Keep with its halls full of soldiers and servants, its treasures of wealth displayed from the solar to the tower to each chamber and anteroom was far different than the stark shell of a keep where she and Tynon had fought Red-beard and his fellow outlaws.

And what had broken the spell, and restored Tynon's home to its former glory? What had thrust it back into the world, rescuing it from the shimmery mysterious dimension to which it had been confined? Had it been the kiss, she wondered? *Their* kiss? Her hand paused in midair as memories returned of all the sensations and emotions that had rushed through her, igniting her soul during that long, heart-stopping kiss.

A knock sounded upon the door, and a maidservant entered.

"Duke Tynon requests your presence," she said with a curtsey. "I will escort you."

Duke Tynon requests your presence. Erinn was stunned by the way her heart leaped at the words. *What a fool you are,* she told herself as she set down the brush with a clatter and rose, smoothing the skirt of her gown. *One kiss from the man and you're desperate to be with him every possible moment. Have you forgotten who he is? Do you wish to be a traitor to your family, to your home?*

But she already was, she thought heavily. The truth was that she was in love with her enemy. Something in Tynon of Bordmoor drew her inexorably to him, made her want to kiss him again, to be held by him, to be the one to make him smile.

Did he feel the same?

No, why should he? He made it clear at the start that you are nothing but a pawn. But that was at the start, a voice inside her argued. That was before the laughter, before the kiss . . .

She felt heat and hope pulsing through her and pushed away all thoughts of the kiss as she followed the maidservant in silence.

When she and Tynon had first entered the courtyard of

the keep, they'd been greeted by a swarm of soldiers and servants alike, all clamoring, jostling, welcoming, and it was then that she and Tynon had learned that no one in the keep had even been aware that to those in the outside world, the grand keep of Bordmoor was *gone*. To them, the rest of the world had looked the same, except that the spell had locked them within the keep and the boundaries of the courtyard. Everything had appeared as it had always been to them, and they were not afraid—but they knew they couldn't leave the castle, for an invisible wall prevented anyone within from passing through the gates. After trying again and again to no avail, they'd settled down to wait—waiting for Tynon to return home and rescue them from whatever enchantment had claimed the keep and locked its inhabitants within those thick, protective walls.

Even stranger, they hadn't been able to see what was going on beyond the moat—they hadn't once glimpsed Erinn or Tynon or his men or the horses. They had only a view of trees and hills, the same view they looked upon every day. Even Rhys, waving on the balcony, had not seen his brother—he had only been waving and calling Tynon's name to try to summon him quickly, should he be near.

Rhys. As Erinn followed the maidservant through a maze of torchlit corridors she couldn't help but smile as she thought of Rhys. The boy was a miniature version of Tynon himself—darkly handsome, with bold, intelligent eyes and a direct, outspoken, and aggressive manner that he clearly had learned from his brother. Rhys had thrown himself into Tynon's arms, hugged him tightly around the neck, then jumped back as he saw Erinn, her pale hair atumble, her gown still strewn with grass.

"Is this the witch? You forced her to break the spell? What are we going to do to her now?" he demanded, his eyes flashing at the slender woman from the land of the enemy.

"*We* aren't going to do anything to her, Rhys. She wasn't the one who cast the spell. But she did help to break it."

"How? How'd she break it?"

"Her power is very great," Tynon said gravely as those who were gathered around them in the great hall murmured and fell back. Then Tynon glanced over at Erinn, and a slow grin curled around the corners of his mouth. "Do you want to tell him how you did it, or shall I?"

"It was . . . a lucky accident, nothing more," Erinn explained hastily. She fixed Rhys with a flustered smile. "Your brother helped me. We . . . did it together."

Over the boy's head, her gaze met Tynon's. His grin made her knees tremble.

"You did, eh?" Rhys eyed her as if he didn't believe a word she said. He spun back toward Tynon. "So now do we lock her in the dungeon until Marlbury surrenders?" he said eagerly. "How do we know she won't cast another spell on us? A *worse* one. I think we'd better order Biddlow to lock her in the dungeon right now. I'll go with him and—"

"There will be no dungeon, Rhys."

"But—"

"The lady is my guest," Tynon said sharply, and his gaze became stern as he glanced first at his young brother and then at all the other servants and soldiers gathered around them. "Princess Erinn of Marlbury is my *guest*," he repeated, raising his voice over the stunned murmuring that had greeted his words.

Rhys looked incredulous, but there was no mistaking the iron in Tynon's voice. "Is that clear? You will treat her, all of you, with the respect due any guest in our land."

And then he had propelled her before him into the hall, directed that she be made comfortable in one of the royal chambers, and gone off with his men, hammering questions at them as they followed him through the keep.

Now she herself had been summoned. She had no idea what to expect next.

The maidservant rounded a corner and ushered her down a flight of dizzily winding stairs, then along a corridor to a low-ceilinged chamber where Tynon sat at a long table with his steward. He was studying a sheaf of papers, but he looked up, then stood as Erinn stepped into the room.

"Thomas, you may go," Tynon told his steward. All the while his eyes were fixed on the woman who had paused just inside the doorway.

Even as the steward slipped past Erinn, Tynon strode forward and drew her into the room. A jumble of emotions beset him as he gazed at her. She appeared to be poised and elegant, but her eyes were filled with worry despite her obvious efforts to appear serene.

He took her into his arms, his chest feeling as though it would explode as she came willingly, her own arms twining around his neck. He breathed in the sweet womanly scent of her and bent his head to kiss her again, but she flinched away from him.

"No, Tynon, no. How can we?" Her voice throbbed. "Have you forgotten who we are—and all that lies between us?"

"Damn what lies between us. I want you, Erinn of Marlbury, and from the way you kissed me back there on the hill, you want me, too."

"But it cannot be." She shook her head. "You know that as well as I. It isn't possible—"

"I'll tell you what isn't possible," he said roughly. "It isn't possible for me to wait another moment to kiss you again." Then his mouth claimed hers, cutting off her protests. In his arms, with his hot kisses melting her bones, Erinn no longer remembered the list of reasons why they should never kiss again.

The world flew away—and there were only the two of them, holding each other, clinging to the sweet passion tearing through them both. Until they heard a gasp just behind them that sent them jumping apart.

A scrawny twig of an old woman with gray hair that fell in stringy coils to her pointed chin stared at them, her seamed face nearly as ashen as her hair. By her plain clothes and stooped shoulders she looked to be a servant, and she held a silver tray of wine goblets in hands that trembled.

"Ah, so it *is* you, my lord duke." Though she had obviously seen them kissing, after that one gasp she made no mention of it. Nor did she glance more than a moment at Erinn's flushed cheeks. She hobbled into the room, the skirts of her brown kirtle rustling like dry leaves, and spoke in a low, rusty tone. "You *are* back with us. For a moment

I thought you were a ghost—you and the lady."

"A ghost, Marguerite?" Somehow Tynon didn't seem the least bit disconcerted to have been caught kissing the princess of Marlbury. He spoke casually. "It's not like you to indulge fits of fancy."

With a quick, reassuring smile to Erinn, Tynon went to the old woman and gently took the tray from her hands, carrying it to a side table. "You look weary. Are you unwell?"

"Sleep eludes me. It always has . . ." she mumbled sadly. "But never mind me, my lord. I am an old woman, given to strange thoughts and restless dreams." She sighed as he took her arm and led her to a settle. But even as she sank upon it, she was studying Erinn, taking in her delicately sculpted features, the grace of her figure, the curtain of pale hair.

"You've heard that Princess Erinn is my guest?"

"Aye. 'Tis why I brought the wine. I wanted to see for myself the lady from Marlbury here in Bordmoor Keep."

"That's well and good—but you're too old and frail to wait upon me, Marguerite. Your days of work are done. You should be resting and letting the kitchen maids bring wine to *you*."

"I wanted to come. I wanted to see *her*."

Tynon went to Erinn, took her hand, and drew her toward the old woman. "Here she is, then." He smiled as Marguerite continued to stare.

"Marguerite has lived in Bordmoor Keep for nearly one hundred years now—longer than any other servant," he explained as the old woman continued to study the girl before her. "Her mother was a kitchen maid in the time of my great-grandfather, and Marguerite lived here with her even as a child. And when she was grown, she served as lady's maid to my great-grandmother, and then became my mother's nurse. And eventually, mine, as well."

"I am pleased to meet you, Marguerite." Erinn spoke kindly, puzzled by the way the woman continued to stare at her. "Perhaps you would like a cup of wine," she offered, turning toward the tray, for the woman still looked weak and shaky. But the elderly servant shook her head.

"Nay, no wine, child. I'm off a bit, true, but 'tis only that it has been a long time since I've seen a lady of Marlbury inside this keep," she murmured. "A very long time."

Marguerite continued to gaze at Erinn intently, her gentle blue eyes looking as wrung out and faded as a much-washed rag, as if they had seen too many unhappy things in their lifetime.

"If the truth be told," Erinn said quietly, "I don't believe any lady of Marlbury has ever set foot in Bordmoor Keep before."

"Aye—one did. That I know." The woman nodded sagely. "She was dark, like my lord duke here, not fair like you." Her voice became dreamy. "But she was here. She was the one who started it all. My own dear lady, Olivia." She shook her head. "Such a long time ago."

"Olivia?" Tynon frowned, studying her with concern. "My great-grandmother? You're confused, Marguerite. She was never a lady of Marlbury. She came from Gwent."

Marguerite suddenly became aware of his piercing, questioning glance, and she stiffened. The little color that remained in her ashen cheeks vanished, and she shook her head quickly. "Never mind, my lord. You are right. I was mistaken." But she said it too quickly, and there was a furtive glint in her eyes.

"Perhaps 'twas only a ghost," she added in a low tone, ducking her head, but not before Erinn saw a film of tears in those sad old eyes.

She hurried forward, unable to contain herself. "What is it, Marguerite?" she asked. Something in the woman's words set off a strange thrumming inside her. She knelt and touched the old servant's gnarled hand. "There's something more, isn't there? You're unhappy—why?"

"*She* was the one who was unhappy," the old woman whispered, her lips barely moving as she spoke. "I only felt for her—felt her pain, her guilt, like it was my own. It all came back to me when I saw you there, kissing my lord duke. Aye, it all came back . . ."

Her voice trailed off, but as Erinn and Tynon looked at one another, puzzled, Marguerite suddenly yanked her hand away.

"Never you mind," she gasped. "I won't tell you about it. I never told a soul."

Erinn bit her lip, for some reason unable to tear her gaze from the servant's pale face. Marguerite seemed confused, but her unhappiness was all too real. Something seemed to buzz in the air, a tension, a humming. There was something here, something important. *If I were a better witch, it would be clear as glass*, she thought, and suddenly, unbidden, there came into her mind the image of glass—a looking glass—a looking glass she had noticed in walking through the keep earlier, when she'd seen that brief flicker of the midnight-haired woman and heard the sounds of weeping.

"Was that Olivia?" she asked suddenly, and took a deep breath. "Marguerite, I think I saw her. Olivia, I mean. In the looking glass in one of the chambers."

"I have seen her there oftimes, too." She nodded. "Weeping. Always weeping. Because she felt it was all her fault."

Erinn glanced questioningly at Tynon, wondering if he wanted her to continue, and he nodded quickly. Once more she touched the servant's hand.

"What was her fault, Marguerite?" she asked gently.

"The war, of course. They were fighting over her. If she hadn't come here that day there never would have been a war. But how was she to know?" Marguerite's faded eyes fixed themselves on Erinn's face. "She didn't mean any harm," she sighed. "My lady always meant to go back to Marlbury, she swore to me she did, and I believed her."

"Do you mean to tell me that you know what started the war? The war between Marlbury and Bordmoor? How can this be, Marguerite?" Erinn breathed, her heartbeat quickening. "Even my father claims not to know."

"Maybe he knows and maybe he doesn't. No one spoke of it, not ever." The old woman peered up at Tynon now, her eyes glimmering with sorrow. "Your great-grandfather wouldn't allow any whispers, not a word said against her. That was to his credit. But some knew. Some heard rumors. *And I saw.* I saw the whole thing. I was the only one."

For a long moment Tynon could only stare at her in amazement. Then he stepped closer. "What did you see, Marguerite? The time for secrecy is past. I must know."

She stared into his eyes, her own seeming to glow suddenly from within. They grew keener, sharper, and yet they held an unmistakable fondness for the tall young duke whose family she had served for nearly one hundred years.

"What did I see? Ah, my lord, I saw exactly what I saw today when I first came into this room." Her voice quavered. She glanced back and forth between the two young people before her, then leaned wearily back upon the settle.

"I saw a kiss."

8

ERINN'S HEART BEGAN to race. She rose and stood beside Tynon, gripping his hand as the old servant continued to speak, her voice so low and raspy it was almost as if she were speaking to herself.

"I came upon them by accident. I wasn't spying, not intentionally," she murmured with a shake of her head. "She and Dugal were in a chamber—near the gallery, it was—and they were kissing. Their arms were wrapped around each other—ah, so sweetly. Oh, the picture they made!" Marguerite's gnarled hands lifted toward her heart, resting upon her thin chest. "She loved him, you see, had loved him since she was a girl. It wasn't her fault that her family had arranged for her to be married to King Leiff of Marlbury. What was she to do?" She gazed imploringly at Tynon and Erinn, then went on before either of them could say a word.

"Leiff and Dugal were friends in those days. They lived upon neighboring lands and often hunted together. That day, only three days before King Leiff and Lady Olivia

185

were to be wed, your great-grandfather"—she flicked another glance at Tynon, whose expression was unfathomable, though he gripped Erinn's hand tightly—"invited Leiff and Olivia and the entire court of Marlbury to a banquet in honor of their wedding. If he hadn't . . . ah, if only he hadn't, everything might have been different."

"How?" Erinn asked as Marguerite lapsed into a dejected silence. "What happened at the banquet?"

"Something terrible. Something that changed the course of the next hundred years." Marguerite spoke heavily. She was no longer looking at either Erinn or Tynon. She was looking toward a spot near the window, seeing something neither of them could see. "During the course of the evening, Olivia and Dugal slipped away together," she said sadly. "To say their last farewells. She was going to honor her parents' wishes and marry a man she didn't love, but she wanted one last moment with the man she did love. Just one moment. Was that so terrible?" She sent Tynon a pleading look, and then her gaze swept to Erinn, who was listening in amazement.

"No," Erinn whispered. "No, it wasn't terrible." She tried to imagine how it had been for the dark-haired Olivia, loving one man, about to be bound in marriage to another.

"What happened to her? To them?" she asked softly.

"A horrible thing. They were discovered. I came upon them from a connecting chamber, nearly stumbled into them, but I saw them in time and ducked behind the curtain of the anteroom. I ought to have left, but I . . . I couldn't. I was a mere child then, sent on an errand by my mother, but when I saw them locked in each other's arms, I forgot everything else. And she was weeping. My poor pretty lady was weeping. But then, before I could back away, before they could draw apart, King Leiff himself came upon them."

Marguerite was trembling now, and her voice was so low they had to strain to hear it. "I believe he must have come to love her as well in the days before their marriage, or else it was just pride that ripped through him and brought the black rage upon him. He was a prideful man. He drew his sword, and the next moment Duke Dugal drew his, and they fought, fought nearly to their death, as Olivia stood screaming. Soldiers from both lands rushed in. Ah, there was such confusion, such blood and mayhem as you've never seen. But King Leiff and his company were at last driven from the keep. And only Lady Olivia stayed."

Marguerite hugged her arms around herself. "She stayed with Dugal, for Leiff had vowed to kill her for committing treason against him, and Dugal would not let her go. That was the start of it, the start of the war. The hatred of those two men grew over the years, and the battles grew fiercer. They were determined to destroy each other. And my sweet Olivia," she murmured sadly, "she wept for all the blood and all the dead. She felt the cause of it rested all upon her shoulders. Now she was free to marry the man she loved, and she did marry him, but she had brought dishonor to her family, and war to both kingdoms, and death and suffering to many. I still hear her weeping, my poor pretty lady."

The old woman peered at Erinn, tears now glistening like diamonds in her eyes. "Aye, at night when the wind is calm, I hear her. And sometimes I catch a glimpse of her in the looking glass. She can't rest, methinks, 'til the war is over. I wish she might."

There was a long silence as she finished the tale and sank back with a shudder upon the settle.

"I wish she might rest, too." Erinn spoke very quietly. She glanced at Tynon, and he moved closer to her and slid his arms around her waist, pulling her near to him.

Marguerite looked at them both, then lifted her hands helplessly. "One hundred years of war. How will it end?" she asked in despair.

Tynon turned to Erinn. Her heart leaped as she saw the glinting determination in his eyes, the resolute set of his jaw.

"How indeed," she whispered, trying to search her thoughts for a solution. But he shook his head.

Slowly, he brought his mouth down to hers, and his lips brushed hers with tenderness, a tenderness that never failed to surprise her in a man so fierce.

"I swear to you, Erinn," Tynon muttered for her ears

alone. "This war will end. I will see to it. It will end here
and now, the same way it began. With a kiss."

He came to her when the castle was asleep. The moment
he rapped softly upon the door she knew it was he, knew
even before she saw him. He slipped into her chamber without a word, and Erinn ran to him and tilted her face up to
his.

"It took you long enough, my lord duke." But her smile
was warm and for him alone.

"After being locked out of my keep for more days than
I care to count, I had matters to attend to, my princess."
He grinned. "But now my work is done, at least for the
night. And it's time to pursue matters of a different nature—more pleasant ones."

As he spoke, his gaze ran admiringly over her slender
figure, clad in a delicate nightshift that a maidservant had
brought to her. It was of softest white linen and floated
loosely down to her dainty ankles. Her hair was unbound,
free, flowing pale as the moonlight that glimmered upon
her fine-boned face. Her eyes glowed up at him, filled with
hope and a kind of hunger that sent heat surging through
his loins.

"Far more pleasant ones," Tynon muttered and caught
her to him with single-minded impatience. So beautiful was
she that she took his breath away. As she threw her arms
around him, he knew only that the past be damned. Nothing
would stand in the way of his having her.

"Kiss me again, Tynon, for I'm starving," Erinn
breathed, blushing when he chuckled. She clutched him
close, stood on tiptoe, and stretched her mouth up toward
his. Perhaps she should have been shocked by her boldness,
she reflected dizzily as his mouth crushed down upon hers,
but she wasn't. She didn't care. She knew only that his
kisses felt right, that they felt wonderful. They were everything she could have ever wished for, and so was he.

Except that he was a llachlander.

But as he kissed her, as his arms tightened around her,
she knew with a certainty that none of that mattered. And
it would never matter again. There had been too much

death, too much pain, too much grief between their kingdoms. Tynon was right. It was time to put a stop to it.

They *must* put a stop to it.

Somehow.

They kissed in the moonlight that bathed the room, long,
needy kisses that left her gasping and weak. And wanting—
wanting more.

"Stay with me tonight." The words spilled out urgently
against his lips and she thrilled at the hard tremble that ran
through him.

"Only try to make me leave, princess," he breathed in
her ear.

"That's the last thing I want you to do. The very last
thing." She touched his jaw, that strong jaw that was rough
now with a day's worth of stubble, which only served to
emphasize the rugged beauty of his face. His eyes gleamed
down at her, making her heart race.

"Tynon, how did this happen to us? How did we come
to feel this way for each other? How did kissing you, touching you, being with you, come to feel so right?" Erinn
asked wonderingly.

His hands slid down her body, caressing the curve of her
breasts, the tiny waist, the lushness of sweetly rounded hips.
Heat and need roared in his blood and began to pound
relentlessly in his temples. "The same way it came to happen for Dugal and Olivia one hundred years ago," he said
huskily.

"Yes, like Dugal and Olivia." Erinn nodded. "I know
now, oh, how I know what they must have felt, what they
must have gone through."

Tynon's hands gripped her shoulders suddenly, and his
eyes darkened. "I've learned all too well that death can
come quickly in this world, and so can grief. And so, it
seems, can love," he said softly, staring into the piquant
face that stole his breath away. "Love apparently has the
power to come where it is least looked for and least expected. Yet it comes. It comes like a storm."

Love. A thrill shot through her. *Love.* She smiled. "So . . .
you love me?" It was a whisper, a whisper that held a world
of hope and yearning in the single word. But there was also a

glimmer, a mere glimmer of doubt that clouded those magnificent eyes, and he knew suddenly that she needed to hear the words.

And he needed to say them.

"I love you, Erinn. More than life. More than this keep," he added with a hoarse laugh. "More than the llachlands. I love you and want you, and I swear to you, I will have you no matter what I have to do for us to be together."

"I'll hold you to that, my lord duke." She clung to him, shaking, and as she laid her head against his powerful shoulder, lightning seemed to flow between their bodies, and she felt all of the warmth and fire and strength of him sear her, and seem to penetrate her very soul.

"Because I love you, too. Though there is so much in our way, and I can't see how we're going to overcome it—"

"Don't speak of it tonight." He cupped her chin and stared into her eyes, his own intent. "Tonight is just for us. Tonight the world will go away, and there will be you, Erinn, and me, and this chamber. Just for tonight."

"Yes," she whispered, tenderly wrapping her arms around his neck and pulling him down to her, sweeping her lips against his with a need that could no longer be contained. He was right. Tonight was theirs.

"Just us, Tynon." The words were a promise. "Just for tonight."

And so it was.

As the moonlight gilded the reed-scented chamber, they undressed one another and explored one another with joy and with need. There was no need for words, no need for thought or for questions. There were only the princess, in every way set free, and the man who had first come to her in a vision. There was only fire and passion and tenderness such as neither of them had ever known, and there was pleasure deeper and wilder than the sea.

They tossed and rocked upon the velvet-covered bed, as the stars burned in the sky. She found what it was like to touch and kiss that magnificent bare chest that had so mesmerized her before, and Tynon took his time discovering all the soft, sleek places of her glorious body. When he loved her breasts, and stroked her thighs, Erinn moaned with delight in a most satisfactory way, and when she touched her fingers and her lips to his flesh, he thought he would explode with madness.

Their kisses came from the heart, and their lovemaking came from the soul, and Erinn felt not a wisp of fear as Tynon of Bordmoor touched her as no man had ever touched her and surged inside her to make them one. Their bodies burned with a savage fire, but there was tenderness in every kiss, in every touch. Still, the need took its toll, in sweat and in desperation. In urgency and in speed. Locked together as one, they climbed hard and fast past desire, past heat and naked want, to a joyous fulfillment that rocked through them like thunder. When the thunder died down and the lightning subsided, they were left spent, breathless and shuddering. Their bodies sheened with sweat, they clung to each other, breathing in the air of love and of night and of discovery sweeter than the most delectable wine.

They lay entwined thus all through the night, holding each other as if they might never hold each other again, and just before a topaz sun peeked through the sky they made love once again, even more tenderly than before and far more slowly, listening to their hearts beating as one.

And Erinn held her midnight-haired warrior and stroked the thick silk of his hair. She thought of Dugal and Olivia— and wished that she knew a spell that would make the night last forever and would eternally banish the sun.

9

In the end, they did it Erinn's way, despite Tynon's misgivings. He wanted to ride openly to the gates of Marlbury Castle—only the two of them—but she insisted they go in through the secret passage, the one known only to the royal family and the captain of the guard.

"This is far easier than the way you came in last time," she told him as they made their way through the secret tunnels that ran beneath the castle. Suddenly she stopped short and turned to him in the dense blackness that was lit only by a single torch. "Which reminds me, how *did* you come in last time? Past the moat and the gate and the guards, all the way to the gardens undetected?"

He grinned in the darkness, the dancing gold torchlight illuminating the sharp planes of his face. "You don't want to know." Low laughter rumbled softly as he steered her ahead of him. "Let's just say it wasn't as simple as this."

"You must agree that this is much better than riding up to the gate and having them take you prisoner before the blink of an eye," she whispered back, her feet padding softly along the dank, twisting corridor.

192

"Aye, so far, my love." Tynon tried to keep the dryness from his tone. This wasn't going to be easy. Whatever influence Erinn thought she might have over her father, he fully expected to be taken prisoner one way or another, but if it pleased her to get them to her father's chamber before anyone else discovered his presence and clapped him in irons, so be it.

Whatever happened, he and Erinn would have to find a way to overcome all of King Vort's suspicions and hostility. He wasn't about to let the finest thing that had ever happened to his life slip through his fingers because one hundred years ago his great-grandfather had indulged in what he believed was one last kiss with the woman he loved.

"I think this is the last turn." Erinn rounded the corner and peered ahead as Tynon held the torch aloft. "Yes, there's the secret door. It opens into the anteroom of my father's chamber. Ban, his chamberlain, sleeps there."

Her voice, even to her own ears, now sounded less than steady. She was afraid, deeply afraid, but not for herself. For Tynon. Perhaps they should have found another way— but this was her way. Direct and honest. She would appeal to her father, make him see the truth, and with him behind her, behind both her and Tynon, they could then convince Braden and Cadur that there was no cause to continue battling Bordmoor. No cause to bring death and fear and suffering to the people of both lands.

"Afraid, my love?" Tynon spoke softly in her ear as she hesitated at the door, summoning her courage.

She turned and gazed up into those keen eyes. "My only fear is of losing you," she whispered.

With his free arm, he pulled her close. "You won't. If I have to fight my way out with you at my side, I will—and take you back to Bordmoor—where you'll stay with me for the rest of our lives. No one will come between us, Erinn, I swear it."

"And I swear I will come with you if . . . if we cannot make them see."

But he recognized the grief shimmering in her eyes. And he knew it would slowly kill her if she were cut off from her father and brothers, if she were thought a traitor to her home. That was the fate that had befallen Olivia, and as he stared down at the brave golden-haired woman who stood on tiptoe to press her lips to his, he vowed he would never let it befall his lovely Erinn.

"Don't worry, my love. It won't come to that."

He knew it sounded like a vow, and he meant it that way.

She kissed him again, a soft, urgent kiss that made him feel he could slay a hundred men with a thrust of his sword, and then she pulled away abruptly and pushed open the door.

King Vort was snoring in the adjoining bedchamber as they crept into the anteroom. Ban, the chamberlain, jerked awake, his eyes going wide as he stared at the shadowy figures near the foot of his bed, yet even as he opened his mouth to shout, Tynon's fist slammed into his round, fleshy face, and he slumped back, as if he'd never awakened from sleep.

Her heart thumping, Erinn stared in dismay at the kindly servant, and would have taken a step toward him, but Tynon held firm to her arm and drew her along.

Her father's snoring grew louder as Erinn approached the great velvet-curtained bed.

"Father," she whispered. "Father, wake up."

King Vort's eyes fluttered open. As if dreaming, he stared at her vaguely, and then a smile dawned across his lined and haggard face beneath the tousle of bristly white hair. "Why, Erinn, my girl, you're back. Even if 'tis only a dream, stay with me, child. How I have longed to see your face."

"It's not a dream, Father. I'm here. I must speak to you. Wake up."

The last fog of sleep lifted from his eyes and the king sat up, his Adam's apple trembling above the scarlet collar of his long linen nightshirt. He stared at his daughter with pure joy for one breathless instant, then his eyes fell upon the second figure in his bedchamber, a very tall, very broad-shouldered figure who stood just behind her.

Up and up went the king's gaze as he stared in shock at

the giant clad in dark cloak and breeches and boots, the giant who held aloft a torch that revealed the face that Vort of Marlbury had glimpsed often enough in battle. Dimly he heard Erinn's voice, saying something to him, but he was damned if he knew what it was—he could only stare at that damned devil of a face. He'd seen that face from a distance, it was true, but it was not a face he would ever forget.

It was the face of his enemy.

"Bordmoorrrrrrrrr!" the king bellowed, and sprang from the bed with the alacrity of a much younger man.

"No, Father, listen," Erinn cried in horror as the shout echoed through the castle and she instantly heard the sounds of running feet and deep-throated yells.

"Behind me, girl!" her father roared and reached to grab his sword from its scabbard.

Tynon stopped him, jerking the scabbard out of reach. "King Vort, we beg you to listen to us. Your daughter has something she wants to—"

But before he could finish the words, the door burst open and a dozen men surged into the chamber.

Braden and Cadur were the first, of course, Erinn noted in dismay, and as they set eyes on Tynon, every man as one drew his sword.

"Lower your weapons, all of you!" Erinn had whirled to face them, and she stepped purposefully in front of Tynon, who had exercised every ounce of self-control he possessed to keep from drawing his own sword instinctively. He smothered the torch, but did not drop it, holding it loosely in one hand as his gaze shrewdly assessed the fighting men confronting him.

There was shock and fury in their faces as they looked upon Erinn and him.

"Erinn! You're alive, thanks be to heaven," Cadur croaked out.

"What has he done to you?" Braden leaped forward and reached toward her as if to yank her behind him, but Tynon moved faster, seizing the prince's arm, spinning him around and shoving him back into his brother.

"Don't touch her," Tynon said grimly. "Just listen to her."

"Braden, Cadur, please—" Erinn held her hands out beseechingly, but the sight of Tynon of Bordmoor standing feet apart beside their sister in their father's bedchamber within the very heart of the castle stirred her brothers and the soldiers to rage beyond reason.

"Kill him!" Braden ordered, and the men surged forward. Her own father yanked her out of their path as, with swords raised, they rushed at Tynon.

Instinct took over, and he drew his sword in a flash. Then the room became a blur of swords and shouts and grunts, and Tynon was at the center of it, trying to fight them all off with sword and torch as terror ripped through Erinn's soul.

She closed her eyes tight and whispered, "Begone, begone, rough weapons begone. Tarry not in angry hands, by all that's just, heed my commands."

The next instant the swords flew out of the hands of all the men, Tynon included, and streaked up toward the ceiling. A burst of wind blew the shutters wide, and the swords all veered straight toward the open window.

In a blink they were gone, flying out into the darkness.

Everyone froze, staring at her. "What are you doing, girl?" her father gasped. "We're trying to protect you from this . . . this savage—"

"No, you're not, Father. You're trying to kill the man I love."

Erinn faced him, stunned that the spell had actually worked, but knowing she'd best make use of the pause in the fighting while she could.

Her words seemed to turn every man in the chamber into a statue, including her brothers.

"Braden and Cadur, you may stay, but everyone else— except of course, *you*, Father—must leave. Tynon and I wish to speak to you."

"Erinn, what has he done to you?" Braden asked again. He came toward her and placed his hands gently on her shoulders, fear glinting in his eyes. "By all that is holy, this is my fault. I let him steal you—"

"I'm glad he didn't hurt you, Braden, but for once in your life," Erinn said impatiently, "will you listen to me?

I'm not a child who needs protecting. And I don't want you or anyone else finding me a husband. I have found him on my own—the only one I shall ever want. Tynon and I are going to be married. We will join our lives for all time, and we'll bring an end to the enmity between our lands."

"Never. Not so long as I have breath." Braden spun on Tynon, his face a mask of fury. "I'll see you in hell before I let you touch my sister."

"I'll see you in hell before I let you stop us." Tynon's voice was low, but there was no mistaking the deadly conviction in his words, or the determination glittering in those keen warrior eyes. For a moment, looking at him, even Erinn felt a jolt of fear, but as his glance shifted to her, his eyes softened and she saw in them the depths of desperation and love that matched her own.

"Erinn, you can't mean this," Cadur exploded. "You know who this man is—what he's done!"

"He has done nothing worse than what you've done, Cadur, or Braden or Father. He's fought wars. Now he's ready to make peace. The question is—are you?"

King Vort stared at her blankly. "Peace?"

"Do you know what started the wars between Bordmoor and Marlbury, Father?"

The king shook his head dazedly. He was staring at his daughter as if he'd never seen her before.

"Do you, Braden? Cadur?"

Grimacing, they shook their heads, and with a sudden glimmer of hope, Erinn saw the curiosity spark within their eyes.

"Then dismiss the knights and let us gather around." Her voice gentled, and in it all the men in the chamber could hear the echoes of hope, hope that had been wilting for years within their own war-weary souls. As King Vort waved the soldiers away and they departed in wonder, they glanced back over their shoulders at the princess whose words stirred something near forgotten in their hearts.

Princess Erinn went to her father and touched his arm.

"Tynon and I have a story to tell you. All I ask is that you listen. And listen well."

"I . . . will listen." Once more King Vort looked upon the

beloved face of his daughter as if seeing her for the first time. Dazed, he tore his gaze from hers, glanced at Tynon of Bordmoor and shuddered. But he addressed his sons in tones of command.

"You shall listen, too. Both of you. It won't hurt, I suppose . . . to listen."

As her brothers glowered, Erinn led her father to a chair and eased him into it. "It all began with your grandfather, Father. And his bride-to-be. She had dark hair and came from Gwent. Her name was Olivia."

When she finished speaking, there was a long silence in the chamber. It was Tynon who broke it as he moved to Erinn's side and slipped an arm around her shoulders.

"King Vort, Erinn and I have made our choice. We will marry and will be husband and wife for all of our days. Nothing under the sun or moon will stop us. But now the choice is yours to make, yours and your sons'," he added with a level look at both Braden and Cadur. "If something as small as a kiss can bring either peace or war, then I say let it bring peace."

Tynon dropped a kiss upon the top of Erinn's head as King Vort looked on, his hands clenched at his sides.

"I say the same, Father," Erinn said softly, and as she gazed at her father, her heart was in her eyes. "What do you say?"

Before he could reply, there was a rush of wind and a great clatter, and all the swords Erinn had sent flying out the window came soaring back into the chamber. Tynon dragged Erinn against the wall and shielded her, while the others dived for cover as the swords streaked around the chamber and then crashed down in a heap upon the king's own bed.

"I was afraid that would happen," Erinn muttered disgustedly as Tynon eased away from the wall.

"I never doubted it would." He wrapped his arms around her.

King Vort scowled at the shining swords piled upon his bed. His sons did the same, and then glanced from the swords to Erinn and her llachland duke, snug in each other's arms.

"By all the saints, what is the world coming to?" the king muttered, scratching his head. "Flying swords and my daughter in love with a llachland savage. What to do, boys, what to do?" he grumbled.

Braden and Cadur gave no answer at first. They were too busy glowering at the possessive way Tynon had his arms around their sister, but they couldn't help noticing that Erinn *did* look happy—happier than they'd ever seen her. In fact, she was radiant.

"Peace or war," Braden muttered. In his mind's eye he saw a bloody battlefield. If he never saw another one it would be too soon.

"It seems for the first time in one hundred years we have a choice." Cadur pursed his lips, thinking of the fetching noble's daughter he'd encountered in the village only a week ago. If he didn't have to spend all of his time fighting and riding from one battleground to the next, always trying to find ways to gather more men, more horses, more wealth to wage the wars, he might have time to think about finding himself a wife.

King Vort thought back to his grandfather, a man he dimly remembered as having a black temper. He'd never much liked the man. Then he looked at Erinn, who smiled at him with such hopeful pleading in her eyes.

"Peace . . . or war." He cleared his throat. "If Tynon of Bordmoor will negotiate a fair treaty with me, then . . . we shall try . . . I suppose . . . for peace," he announced doubtfully, nearly choking on the words.

Erinn flew to him and kissed his cheek. Then she embraced both of her brothers, melting even their scowls as she smiled at them with glowing pleasure.

But it was to Tynon that she went with outstretched arms, and pulled his head down to hers. It was a decorous kiss, at least compared to the way she really wished to kiss him, but even then she heard the muffled groans of her brothers and her father's sigh.

"Never should I have doubted you," Tynon told her,

smoothing her hair. "You worked your magic on them, just as you did on me and on my keep."

"It wasn't magic. Only love. They love me, and no matter how much they despise you, they want me to be happy," she said with a grin. "And I can't take credit for the keep," she objected, touching his face with tenderness. "We lifted that spell with our kiss. Don't ask me how, but—"

"The only thing I'm going to ask you is *when*. When will you marry me?"

"On the first of May." She snuggled deeper into his embrace. "Under one condition."

"And what is that?"

"Promise you'll never let Rhys lock me in the dungeon," she told him, laughter bubbling in her throat.

"Done." He grinned and pulled her closer, staring deep into her eyes. "Don't fret, my love. You'll see. It won't be long before Rhys loves you as much as I do. . . . Well, almost as much," he finished softly, and this time when he kissed her it wasn't decorous at all.

10

It was a spectacular wedding. Attended by nobles and common folk from two kingdoms, it took place upon a shimmering spring morn when the very trees seemed to shine with silver light and the wind was softer than a baby's breath. Though the ceremony was solemn, and silence reigned throughout the candlelit ceremony at Marlbury Castle as Princess Erinn and Duke Tynon duly repeated their vows before nearly a thousand onlookers, the wedding feast and festivities that followed and that went on for days were anything but sober. There were minstrels and jugglers, acrobats performing handsprings, singers accompanied by viol and flute, and fragrant spices set burning for seven days and nights throughout all the castle and the village square. Masses of flowers, torches, tapestries and garlands adorned Marlbury Castle—but no adornment was more lovely, the duke of Bordmoor told his bride after their first breathless matrimonial kiss, than she.

Indeed, the bride was resplendent in a gown of palest blue, the color of a sunrise sky, and embroidered with tiny amber flowers. She wore a mantle of golden lace and a circlet of gold upon her head. Gazing into her eyes after the ceremony, for that one fragile moment before they were swept up in the pageantry and gaiety, Tynon felt the last weight of darkness and loneliness slipping from his massive shoulders.

This lovely girl with her smile and hapless magic, and her heart of pure gold, had saved him—offered him a reprieve from war and darkness—and granted him a future brighter than anything he had ever imagined.

For the folk of Marlbury and Bordmoor there was dancing and laughter, and spiced wine by the barrel, as well as food beyond compare—boar's head and capons and ducklings by the hundreds, mutton and beef, all manner of fruit and spices, cheese and eggs and frosted cakes and savory puddings.

So rambunctious and joyous were the festivities as peace for the first time in one hundred years was celebrated in conjunction with the marriage, that no one noticed when shortly before midnight the bride and groom disappeared. But disappear they did—slipping away from the strains of flute and harp, from the toasts and laughter, making their way to the bridal chamber that had been prepared for them.

Tynon, not trusting the hearty celebrants to leave them in peace, barricaded the door with a vast chest and turned to grin at his bride as she stood near the elaborate velvet-swagged bed. Candlelight glowed upon her creamy skin and illuminated her eyes with a glowing, eager fire.

"You don't really think they'll try to intrude on us, do you?" Erinn asked as he strode toward her.

"Not if they know what's good for them."

She laughed. And threw her arms around her bridegroom. "I have been waiting for this moment since I opened my eyes this morning. You and I—married . . . and alone."

"I have been waiting for it too—even more for what comes next."

And he began to kiss her, long, possessive kisses that burned with hunger and with happiness and with a desire that melted right into their souls. Their lips never parted as he swept her up in his arms and carried her to their marriage bed.

And the night was filled with love and heat and passion, and the days to come were filled with happiness—and children—and, for the first time in one hundred years, with peace.

"That's quite enough." Cyrus lifted a hand, and one by one the lit candles he'd planted in a circle in the earth extinguished themselves. As their light vanished, so did the vision of the newlyweds in their marriage bower that had flickered momentarily within the magic circle.

Ophelia blew a wayward lock of red hair from her eyes and sighed dreamily. "That was the most impressive magic I've ever seen." She glanced at her instructor, incredulity mixed with admiration. "With one spell and one spell alone, you brought the wars to an end."

"But how did you know that Tynon of Bordmoor would believe that Erinn of Marlbury had cast the spell on his keep?" Barnaby asked in an awed tone.

"And how did you know that he would go after her and . . . and that they would actually kiss, enabling the spell to be broken?" Elwas's pointed ears quivered as he leaned forward eagerly toward his mentor. "It *was* the kiss that broke the spell, wasn't it? I thought that's what you intended—"

"Of course it was." Cyrus's robes whipped around him as he surveyed each of his pupils by the glow of the moon. "Your lack of knowledge becomes more apparent by the moment. Obviously none of you have thoroughly studied the basic textbook of this and every class—*The Wizard's Handbook*. Now have you?"

Ophelia flushed, even her freckles growing redder. "I skimmed the last few chapters," she admitted. "I was busy practicing Visions, so I suppose I could have missed something—"

"I only had time to read every other chapter because I was trying to master the transformation tables," Barnaby sighed.

Elwas chewed his lip. "I lost my book. It wasn't my fault—there was a gnome hanging about and I think he—"

"No more!" Cyrus turned on his heel and paced across the cliff and back, struggling to keep his temper under control. He tried to remind himself that one day, with training, these three would be mature, talented wizards making great magic of their own. But they had a long way to go before *that,* he reflected darkly.

"You are all going to repeat Level Three of your training. And you will not advance until I know with certainty that you are ready. We'll begin tomorrow morning—at ten minutes before dawn."

He ignored their groans and downcast eyes. "But first you will repeat for me the cardinal rule explained on the last page of *The Wizard's Handbook*—the page none of you apparently bothered to study. It is the creed of every great wizard, and none of you will ever achieve more than ordinary power, fame, or notice until you know it to be true."

He looked at them expectantly, but they gazed back at him with nervous unease. "Excuse me, sir, but how . . . how are we to repeat the creed to you if we don't know what it is?" Barnaby ventured at last.

"You do know what it is. I just showed you what it is. Princess Erinn . . . Duke Tynon . . . the keep . . . the wars . . . By Merlin's light, did you learn *nothing* from my demonstration?"

Suddenly Ophelia blinked and sat up straighter. Elwas clasped his hands together, and his ears twitched forward. Barnaby's expression changed from glum confusion to a sudden dazzling smile.

"Go ahead." Cyrus nodded at each of them. "Ophelia, the first word, Elwas next, and Barbaby the last."

They all three rose to their feet. Ophelia cleared her throat. "Nothing . . ."

Elwas grinned. "Is . . ."

Barnaby raised his hand, and a lightning bolt, just a tiny one, exploded from his fingers as he spoke. ". . . *impossible!*" he announced, unable to resist imitating the dazzling confidence of his teacher.

Cyrus nodded. Then he raised both arms, and there was

a flash of silver smoke. He vanished in its midst. But they heard his voice clearly in the stillness that followed as the smoke tumbled out toward the sea.

"That is correct. And don't ever forget it if you would do great things, for love, and hope, and all things magical stem from this truth and this alone—*nothing is impossible.*"

SEALED WITH A KISS

Ruth Ryan Langan

1

"THE INVADERS HAVE fled, my laird. The Highlanders routed them." A lone rider cupped his hands to his lips and shouted to the stooped figure standing high above on the castle tower. "Praise be. Once more our land is safe from the barbarians."

Gordon Douglas gave a long, deep sigh of relief as he turned away. But before he could go below and survey the damage done to his keep, his eldest daughter, Arianna, stepped out onto the parapet.

Her father could tell by the look in her eyes that she'd heard the news. " 'Tis true, then, Father? The Highlanders are victorious?"

"Aye, lass." At his words he saw a shudder pass through her slender frame.

This should have been a time of rejoicing, for once again the villagers had been spared. The Douglas keep, which had kept guard over this soil for generations, had withstood another assault. Despite the destruction of stables and outbuildings, and the loss of animals trapped by the fire of the invaders' torches, many more had managed to break free. Flocks of sheep still grazed on the hillsides. Crops waved, full and lush, in the fields.

Only Arianna and her father knew the price that must be paid for their good fortune.

"Please, Father." Though she struggled to hold the tears at bay, her eyes swam and her lower lip quivered. "Release me from this hellish promise you made."

Sorrow etched his features as he shook his head and reached out a hand to her. She shrank back, avoiding his touch.

Seeing her reaction, he spoke on a sigh. "I've given my word to Duncan MacLean."

"Aye." She'd seen the man when last he visited their keep. A bloated goat of a man, with watery eyes and a beard as white as the snows that dusted the Highland peaks.

Arianna shivered. "The thought of being wed to such a man, and sharing his bed, is more than I can bear."

Her father swallowed back his own revulsion at the image that came to mind. "Can you bear the thought of your sisters being brutalized by barbarians, lass? For that is what would happen without the MacLean's warriors. Our land stands at a crossroads, between lowland and the hills beyond. We have no natural fortifications, as do the Highlanders. Worse, I am without sons, and therefore am at the mercy of invaders. Out of the goodness of his heart, Duncan MacLean gave his word to defend my land against the barbarians. In return, I promised him that he could take as wife my beloved firstborn."

Arianna knew, by the gruff tone, the depth of her father's emotions. He had entered into this agreement in desperation. The invasions by barbarians were growing more frequent; the invaders more determined. She understood that her father had made this bargain to ensure the safety of those he loved. Not only his family, but also those villagers who looked to him for protection. But that knowledge did little to make her sacrifice less painful.

The old man's tone softened as he turned away to look over the fields. "So much destruction. This time the barbarians advanced to our very doorstep. Had it not been for the courage of our Highland protectors, we would have surely lost not only our home but our very lives."

Arianna knew that her father spoke the truth. She had watched from the tower as the Highland warriors had engaged the invaders in battle. Even from this distance, she'd seen the flash of sunlight as sword met sword. Had heard the bloodcurdling shrieks and cries, and later the moaning of those who lay dying. Had witnessed the mangled limbs, smelled the sharp, acrid stench of death that permeated the air. Through it all she had marveled at the courage of those who had come to protect strangers.

Now, with the battle won, and the villagers burying the dead where they lay, an eerie silence spread over the land. No birds cried. No insects buzzed. Even the breeze had gone still.

As Arianna and her father descended the stairs and walked into the gardens, her younger sisters, Glenna and Kendra, came dashing through the tall grass.

Glenna shouted, "Father! They're coming."

For the space of a heartbeat the old man went deathly pale, and Arianna could feel the tremor that shot through him. "So soon the Highlanders come?"

"Aye, Father. Look." The lass pointed to the long column of riders just topping a nearby ridge. Even from this distance they were an awe-inspiring sight.

As they drew near the girl lowered her voice. "Giants they are. Look at them. Their shoulders wider than broadswords."

"And their faces," sighed her sister Kendra. "So fierce."

That remark brought a sharp rebuke from their old nurse, Nola, slightly out of breath from her efforts to keep up with her young charges. "Hush, now. 'Tis unseemly to say such things about our protectors. The two of ye step back here out of the way now and mind yer tongues."

Properly chastised, the two younger girls followed the old woman to stand slightly behind their father and older sister.

Since the death of their mother four years previous, Arianna had taken charge of the household, overseeing the cleaning and cooking and acting as her father's hostess whenever he entertained the lairds and ladies from neighboring clans. For years she had been more of a mother to the two younger girls, since their own mother's health had been fragile.

Arianna thought herself prepared for any situation, but the sight of these Highlanders filled her very soul with terror.

As the mounted men halted, their leader slid from his horse. He was so tall that both father and daughter had to lift their heads to see his eyes. Fearsome they were, like the sky before a storm. His cheeks and chin were covered by a growth of stubble. Dark hair fell to his shoulders. Shoulders so broad they blocked the view of the men behind him. He was dressed no better than the barbarians, his arms and legs bare, his torso barely covered by a blood-stained length of plaid. On his feet were sturdy boots, laced with strips of hide that crisscrossed his powerful calves. The jeweled hilt of a sword glinted from the scabbard hanging at his waist.

It was easy to see how he and his men had bested the barbarians, for they were a truly frightening band.

He lifted a hand in greeting. "I am Lachlan MacLean, nephew of Duncan MacLean, who sent us to do your bidding, my laird."

"We are grateful to you and your warriors, Lachlan MacLean. I am Gordon Douglas, and these are my daughters Arianna, Glenna, and Kendra."

Weary from the battle, Lachlan barely acknowledged the introductions with a curt nod of his head. "My uncle said we were to rout the invaders, and when we were assured of your safety, we were to return to our own land with your payment."

The older man turned slightly, indicating the keep. "If you will follow me inside, I'll see that your men are fed."

Lachlan shook his head. "I thank you for your kind offer, but many of my company have been away from family, flocks, and fields for too long. We will hunt what we need as we journey homeward. If you will see to the payment agreed upon, we will be on our way."

"Did your uncle tell you what the payment would be?"

Lachlan MacLean paused for just a moment. "Your first-born daughter."

"Aye." Ignoring the gasps uttered behind his back, Gordon Douglas cast a sideways glance at his eldest daughter, then squared his shoulders. He'd known how the two younger lasses would react, for they adored their sister. And so he'd kept knowledge of the bargain from them until this very moment, hoping to avoid a torrent of tears.

To cover his pain, he turned to the young woman beside him and issued a stern command. "Daughter, you will go with Nola and fetch your traveling cloak."

Arianna knew it was useless to protest further. Ever since she had first heard of the agreement her father had entered into with his protector, she'd fought him bitterly. Now the moment of reckoning was here. With a toss of her head she followed her nurse into the keep.

Minutes later, head still high, she stepped through the doorway wearing the hooded cloak, lined with ermine, that had once belonged to her mother. Her old nursemaid, trailing behind, was also dressed for travel.

Gordon Douglas put a hand under the elbow of each of his younger daughters. "Bid good journey to your sister."

"Nay." Glenna, at ten and five, was beginning to emulate her older sister by constantly testing her father's patience. "I'll not wish Arianna such a thing, for I don't want her to leave."

"Nor do I." Kendra, at ten and three, was becoming increasingly headstrong. "It isn't fair, Father. Why must Arianna leave us? Why must she be wed to a stranger? If you'd given us swords, we'd have routed the invaders ourselves. And then we could live in peace and have Arianna here with us always."

Behind her, several of the warriors could be heard chuckling at her suggestion that these small females could have bested the savages.

Seeing the fire in their father's eyes, their older sister drew them into the circle of her arms to silence their protests. With her mouth pressed to their hair she whispered, "Hush now. 'Twill do you no good to argue. You know Father has no choice now but to abide by his agreement, or be called a liar and a cheat by all who know him."

Kendra was weeping, big wet tears that slipped from her eyes to roll down her cheeks. She hated that the Highlanders were here to witness her weakness. "We'll never see you again. I can't bear it."

At that Glenna burst into tears as well.

"Shh." Arianna brushed her thumbs over their cheeks, and tipped their faces up so that she could look into their eyes. "You mustn't cry for me. We'll be together again very soon. I promise you."

"You promise?"

"I do."

Glenna's eyes widened. "Oh, Arianna. Do you have a plan?"

Even before the words were out of her mouth, Arianna was pressing a hand over her lips to silence her.

"Not one word, do you hear? Just take comfort in the fact that I will soon be home with you."

The girls caught hands and looked at their older sister with growing admiration. Arianna had always had a mind of her own. They would trust her to find a way out of this impossible situation.

A servant came forward leading a horse.

Gordon Douglas took his daughter's hand in both of his. "Know always that it breaks my heart to send you away, but I have no choice. I am nothing if not a man of my word."

Arianna nodded. "I know that, Father."

The old man looked up at the Highland leader. "Your uncle valued my daughter as a prize beyond gold, beyond flocks, beyond crops. A fairer maiden you will ne'er find in this land. See that you keep her safe."

The Highlander nodded. "You have my word as a MacLean on that."

Gordon Douglas drew her close and pressed a kiss to her cheek. "Safe journey, my daughter." He then helped her into the saddle.

After arranging her skirts, she took the reins from the servant and allowed her gaze to move slowly over her father, her sisters, and finally the towering keep that had been her home for all of her ten and seven years.

She loved this place. Loved everything about it. The stones in the courtyard, polished to a high shine by the hooves of generations of horsemen. The servants, most of whom had been here since before she was born. The gently rolling hills of her father's land, covered with heather and dotted with flocks of sheep. The church bells that welcomed them each morning and evening, calling the faithful to prayer. How could she leave it? How could she live without it?

Worse, how could she bear the harsh, primitive Highlands, with their towering granite cliffs and icy streams? How would she fare with warlike giants who dressed like savages and reveled in battle?

There was no time to soothe the pain in her heart. No opportunity to mourn her loss or dread her future.

At a shout from Lachlan MacLean, the Highlanders wheeled their mounts and started off, with three men on either side of Arianna's horse. A servant helped the old nurse, Nola, into the back of a wagon piled with animal skins and trunks of clothing. With one of the Highlanders driving the team, they trailed the band of horsemen up the curve of hill.

Within minutes their little party was lost from view as horses and riders became swallowed up by the mists of the forest. But even as her home slipped from her sight, Arianna could still hear in her heart the sobs of her sisters. And feel, deep in her soul, the terrible, searing pain of separation.

2

"PEMBROKE." LACHLAN CALLED to the man who rode in the middle of the line of horsemen.

"Aye, Lachlan." Circling back, the fair-haired young man brought his mount beside that of his friend. The two had grown up together in the Highlands, sons of warriors. After losing their fathers, both Lachlan and Pembroke Drummond had been taken in by Lachlan's uncle, to be trained in the art of warfare.

"What is it, friend?"

"I'd feel better if you rode up ahead and kept a sharp eye out for trouble."

"You think some of the invaders took to the forest?"

"It wouldn't be the first time."

Pembroke touched a hand to his sword. "Let them come." He glanced over, surprised by the grim look on his friend's face. "What's this? I never thought I'd see the day when you would grow weary of the fight, my friend."

"Not weary. But I'll not be careless." Lachlan's eyes narrowed on the surrounding brush. "For we've a treasure to deliver to the laird."

"Aye." Pembroke couldn't keep the smile from his voice. "And what a treasure. Like a queen, she is. Did you look at her, Lachlan?"

Seeing his friend's scowl deepen, he regretted his question. He bit back whatever else he was about to say and urged his horse into a run. "I'll ride ahead and call out a warning if I see anything."

Lachlan reined in his own mount and waited until Arianna Douglas and her escorts rode past. Then falling into line behind them, he held the reins loosely, resting his hand on his thigh.

He thought of his friend's question. Aye, he'd looked. And was looking still.

Never had he seen a fairer lass. Eyes as green as a Highland loch. A mouth so perfectly formed it made his throat dry just to look at it. Skin so pale and flawless it could have been carved from alabaster. She'd tossed back the hood of her cloak, and the breeze caught the ends of her hair. Hair the color of fire, spilling in waves to below her waist.

He'd seen, before she covered herself with the traveling cloak at her father's keep, just how trim a figure she had. High, firm breasts. A waist so small, his hands would surely span it with room to spare.

His grasp tightened on the reins, and he found himself thinking about how it would feel to touch her. To rake his fingers through her hair. To draw that lithe young body against his and press his mouth to hers.

The mere thought of it had heat curling through his veins. And with the heat, a wave of guilt for the things he was thinking.

He owed his life to his uncle. Had it not been for the generosity of Duncan MacLean, Lachlan's widowed mother would have been consigned to a life of poverty. Instead she'd spent her last years in the luxury of Duncan's Highland fortress, with servants to attend her when she'd finally breathed her last. She'd died knowing her son would always have a place in his uncle's heart and in his home.

Furthermore, he was a warrior. Hadn't he given his word to his father that he would let nothing and no one distract him from his goal of becoming the finest warrior in all the Highlands?

Lachlan deliberately turned his gaze away from the woman and studied the passing forest. He almost hoped for some sign of the invaders. A skirmish would be a welcome distraction from the forbidden thoughts he was entertaining.

Still, as daylight hours lengthened into late-afternoon shadows, and gentle hills became steep mountain passes, he found his gaze drawn to her again and again. She remained in the saddle without complaint, never asking for a moment's respite from the discomfort she must surely be feeling. She spoke not a word, though her mind was no doubt filled with questions about the unfamiliar land that held her future.

There was such strength in the lass. In the way she sat, stiff-backed, chin jutting like a young warrior facing her first joust. Lachlan had admired the way she'd comforted her sisters, even though her eyes had revealed a painful inner conflict. And though she'd been unable to mask the sadness and disappointment when facing her father, she'd managed a civil departure.

He grinned at the memory. She'd looked like a monarch being banished to the tower. Resigned, but unflinching. And far from defeated.

Perhaps she was unaware of the opulent lifestyle that would be hers in the Highland fortress of Duncan MacLean. In his youth the MacLean had been considered the strongest and most feared warrior in the Highlands. Now, with advancing age, the old man left the fighting to his men, while he rarely left his keep. But he was still considered the strongest, bravest man around, and out of respect for his accomplishments, he was referred to as the laird of lairds.

His woman would want for nothing. Servants to see to her every need. Food fit for a king. Best of all, peace of mind, knowing hundreds of warriors would be willing to lay down their lives to assure the safety of the laird's bride.

Bride.

The word scraped across Lachlan's nerves. He tried to imagine the lovely Arianna Douglas in the arms of Duncan MacLean. Sitting always beside him at his table.

Lying in his bed.

Lachlan's chest rose and fell, and he cursed when his horse stumbled on the rocky trail. He quickly pulled his thoughts back to the task at hand. He had no business letting his imagination play such tricks on him. But as he reined in his mount and watched the trail of horsemen move ahead, his gaze fell on Arianna again. He could see why his uncle had offered for her. Duncan MacLean may have lived a long life, but he was still a strong, virile warrior. No man in his right mind could resist such a treasure.

When at last the gathering shadows signaled an end to daylight, Lachlan sent a band of warriors into the forest to hunt their supper. He gave the command to the others to make camp beside a rushing stream.

One of his men helped Arianna down from the saddle, and he saw her press her hands to the small of her back. A simple gesture, but it caused a twinge of guilt. He'd been so busy with his own thoughts, he'd given not a care to her comfort.

He hurried forward. "Forgive me, my lady. I'll have my men prepare a shelter for you and your nursemaid. Because we've yet to cross into our own borders, we'll have to remain close, for your own protection. But know that my men and I respect your privacy and will see to your every need."

His demeanor was so formal, she seemed to consider a moment before replying, "I thank you. But Nola and I will be quite comfortable in the back of the wagon."

He bowed. "As you wish."

His warriors returned bearing a stag, and soon the fragrance of roasted meat filled the night air. While Arianna and Nola sat on a nest of furs in the wagon, eating their fill of venison and drinking ale to warm them, the Highlanders sat in a circle around the fire, talking in low tones.

Arianna noted that warriors stood on the various hilltops around the camp, keeping watch. Though they were merely looking out for her safety, they served another purpose as well. If she were inclined to attempt an escape, they would surely spot her.

Not that she intended to sneak away like a thief in the night. Where would she go? If she were to return to her home, her father would simply send her away again, this time no doubt to be dragged to the Highlands, bound hand and foot like a prisoner.

Nay, she had no intention of running away. But neither did she have any intention of becoming the bride of a tired old Highland laird. She understood her father's need for protection. That was why she was so determined to find a way to escape her fate without bringing shame to her family.

"Ye're quiet tonight, lass." Nola touched a hand to Arianna's forehead. "Are ye feeling a bit feverish?"

"I'm fine." Arianna turned away, composing her features. The last thing she needed was her old nursemaid hovering over her through the night. She forced a yawn. "Just weary after so many hours on the trail."

"And why not?" The old woman's brow wrinkled with disdain. " 'Twas a hard day. We'll both be glad when we reach the Highlands."

Arianna blocked out Nola's words as she studied the men around the campfire. She needed to choose her target well. Someone young and brash and fair of face. Someone foolish enough, or arrogant enough, to be considered irresistible to maidens.

As if in answer to her thoughts, Pembroke Drummond turned from the fire and caught sight of her.

At once he hurried over. "Is there something you need, my lady?"

"Nay, I . . ." She brought a hand to her throat, unsure how to broach the subject. "Do you . . ." She swallowed. ". . . have a wife?"

"Not yet." His smile was quick and warm. "But soon, I hope. There's a lass in our village. Lana is her name. I've decided that when I return to the Highlands, I'll speak with her father."

"I see." Her heart fell. He seemed the youngest man here, and certainly fair of face. "Are all the men wed, then?"

He shrugged, glancing at his comrades. "Not all. There's Vinson, whose wife died in childbirth." He pointed to a young man, extremely wide of girth, who was busily stuffing venison into his mouth. "His grief is so deep, he scarcely speaks of her at all. His only consolation is in food."

His smile returned as he caught sight of his friend returning from the river. "And there's Lachlan, of course. Though there are many maidens in our village who sigh over him, he swears the woman hasn't been born who will claim his heart."

Arianna followed the direction of his gaze. The giant leader of their group had obviously just come from a bath in the river. His dark hair was plastered to his neck and beaded with droplets of water. The plaid had been scrubbed clean of dirt and blood, and left to dry while he bathed. It was now draped across his chest and wound around his hips, leaving his arms and legs bare. He was carrying two buckets of water, one in each hand. Though they were filled to the brim, he carried them with ease as if they weighed nothing at all.

"And why is that? Does he dislike women?"

"Nay, my lady. He enjoys them well enough. But he made a vow to his dying father to dedicate himself to becoming the strongest, bravest warrior in all of Scotland. And to that end, he must avoid losing his heart. For to do so would be a distraction he could ill afford."

Arianna crossed her arms and tapped her foot, deep in thought.

Oh, the warrior wouldn't do at all. He was too strong. Too dedicated to the task of war. What if her plan went awry and he overpowered her?

She lifted her head and studied him through a fringe of lashes. There was something dangerously attractive about him. Perhaps it was the darkness, the hint of quiet strength, that had her heart beating so erratically.

Still, he would be a fearsome foe.

Without giving herself time to change her mind she gave the young warrior a smile. "Perhaps you could ask your leader to bring me a drink of water from that bucket."

"Aye, my lady. 'Twould be my pleasure."

Pembroke hurried away.

Moments later Lachlan approached the wagon, holding a dipper. "Your water, my lady."

"Thank you." Arianna was dismayed when, instead of handing the dipper to her, he merely held it to her lips. As she drank she was uncomfortably aware of the way he studied her.

The hand holding the dipper was big and rough and calloused. A warrior's hand. The eyes watching her were shuttered, though she thought she detected curiosity. His skin smelled clean and fresh, and the plaid wrapped around him held the hint of evergreen. She'd been right to think he was all wrong for her plan. Up close he was simply too overpowering.

Every sip was an effort. What she really wanted was to turn away and forget her silly plan. But unless she saw it through tonight, all would be lost. She would find herself in the Highlands, wed to Duncan MacLean. That thought, and that alone, kept her from bolting.

"Your friend tells me you are unwed."

"Aye, my lady."

His deep voice seemed to warm with unspoken laughter. That caused her to back up a step. Yet she could read nothing disrespectful in his demeanor.

"Is there not some village lass awaiting your return?"

"None that I know of."

"Your friend . . ."

"His name is Pembroke."

She nodded, and almost lost her nerve. She took a deep breath. "Aye. Pembroke tells me there are many maidens who smile at you."

He shrugged. "A maiden's smile can mean many things. Take yours, my lady."

She felt her smile slipping and forced herself to meet his eyes. "What do you read in my smile?"

"I would hope it means that once you are wed to my laird, you and I can be friends."

"Friends." Out of the corner of her eye she could see the men going about their evening chores. Tending the horses. Slipping away to the loch to bathe. Though none were staring, they had to be aware that Lachlan MacLean was speaking in low tones to the laird's betrothed.

It was too late to change her mind. Her plans were already being put into motion.

"Aye, Lachlan MacLean, I would like us to be friends." Arianna took a step back and gave him a hesitant smile. "I'll bid you good night now."

He inclined his head. "And you, my lady. Rest in the knowledge that my men and I will keep watch through the night."

Keep watch through the night.

His words rang ominously in her ears as he walked away. Arianna leaned weakly against the side of the wagon. If she thought that first part had been difficult, it was nothing compared with what she planned to do when the others had fallen asleep.

3

In the back of the wagon Arianna lay in the nest of furs, listening to the sound of Nola's breathing beside her. It had seemed an eternity before her nurse had drifted into sleep. And even now the young woman dared not move, for fear of disturbing the old dear.

She peered cautiously over the edge of the wagon bed. The fire had burned to embers. In the glow she could make out the shapes of the sleeping men. A short time ago she had watched as Lachlan MacLean had chosen a spot a little away from the others, beside a tall boulder. It was so perfect, it had to be fate.

After a glance at her old nurse to assure herself that she was sound asleep, Arianna eased herself up and over the side of the wagon, all the while holding her breath. One misstep now and she would have the entire encampment awake too soon. Oh, she intended to wake them. But only after she'd positioned herself beside their leader, in a provocative and incriminating pose. Then she would let out a bloodcurdling scream loud enough to wake even the dead.

Nola would be shocked. Scandalized that one of the laird's own men would compromise the woman Duncan MacLean had chosen for his mate. Arianna would, of course, assure her old nursemaid that it had not gone beyond a touch, or perhaps an attempted kiss. In that way, her honor would not be violated. But even this hint of scandal would force that righteous old woman to return Arianna to her father. Duncan MacLean would have to find another maiden to wed. Arianna's reputation would remain intact. And her life would go on much as it had before.

Oh, it was so simple.

She flattened herself against a rock and peered around, first at the men asleep around the fire, then at the men standing guard on the distant hillsides. When she saw the sentries turn away to study the forest, she covered the space that separated her from Lachlan's bedroll.

Moving quietly, she knelt beside him and watched the steady rise and fall of his chest. All she need do now was snuggle in beside him, and the deed would be accomplished.

In the manner of all warriors, Lachlan slept lightly. His years of training had taught him to identify the distinct sounds of the forest. Even with a mind numbed by sleep, he was able to chart the soft footfall of a deer, the rustle of a fox's tail, the barely perceptible slither of a snake.

Someone was standing over him. Not one of his men. The footsteps were too light. He felt the grass ripple as the figure knelt. Curious, he opened his eyes and watched as Arianna Douglas unfastened her cloak and began to settle herself beside him.

Once he'd assured himself that he wasn't dreaming, his hand snaked out, capturing her wrist. "What game is this you play, my lady?"

He saw her eyes widen. As she opened her mouth, he clapped a hand over it, stilling her cry. When she brought her hands to his chest to push away, he caught them, pinning her against him.

She'd expected strength. But she'd never before known

anyone to be this powerful. With absolutely no effort on his part he had her restrained and helpless.

"I ask again." His words, whispered against her ear, sent icy splinters down her spine and brought a strange curling deep inside. "What game do you play?"

She moaned in frustration, but he kept his hand firmly over her mouth as he began to work his way toward answering his own question.

"You have no weapon. Therefore, you meant me no harm. Or did you? There are other ways to harm a man besides a dirk or sword." He suddenly understood. "You little vixen. You thought to use me to gain your freedom."

He saw the truth of his words in her eyes.

His own narrowed in fury. "Did you not think beyond the moment? What this would mean to my laird? Did you not realize he could have me flogged or worse, hanged, for sullying his betrothed?"

If he weren't so furious he might have noted the look of consternation that clouded her face, followed by the dawning of truth and pain. But all he could see was a sly female out to entrap him in her own little web of deceit.

Anger had his blood running so furiously, he could feel sense and reason begin to slip behind a veil of red-hot mist. "I see. You thought only of your own fate and gave not a care to mine. I was simply to be a pawn in this little game of yours. So be it. If I'm to pay the price, then at least let me enjoy the crime."

As he lowered his head Arianna felt her heart stop. Felt the breath back up in her throat. Sweet heaven, he was going to kiss her. And she was helpless to stop him.

She'd never expected it to come to this. She'd intended to cry out, wake the entire company of warriors, and flee to the safety of her nursemaid's arms.

Fool, she thought, as his mouth hovered inches from hers. She was nothing more than a fool.

And then, before she could put together another coherent thought, his lips were on hers in a kiss meant to punish. A kiss that unleashed the storm swirling inside him. All heat and flash and fury.

If she'd been struck by lightning, Arianna couldn't have

been more stunned. The moment his lips covered hers, there was an explosion of color behind her eyes, as if the stars had collided in the heavens and were sending off millions of fiery sparks.

A cry escaped her throat. He swallowed the sound until it was little more than a sigh. But that was enough to have him lifting his head.

He looked down into eyes that had gone wide with absolute terror. He experienced a moment of vindication. But that was almost immediately followed by a rush of remorse. Arianna Douglas was a maiden. An innocent. And from the looks of her, one who'd never before tasted a man's lips. That knowledge was both humbling and deeply arousing.

He was her first. Her only. It was the sort of thing that filled a man with not only an odd sense of pride but a deep sense of responsibility.

Without even realizing what he was doing, he nuzzled her lips, teasing, tasting, until they softened and opened to him.

"Oh, my lady." He breathed the words inside her mouth as he nibbled the corner of her lips.

"Please." She tried to turn her head away. "You mustn't. We mustn't . . ."

"Too late." With his hands framing her face, he stared into her eyes and took the kiss deeper.

He saw the way her eyes widened before the lashes fluttered closed. Felt the way her skin flushed and heated at his touch.

It was the sweetest of torture to lie with her here, feeling that slender body beneath his, chest heaving, hands trembling as they found their way around his waist. And clung.

He thought he could remain just this way, with her hands touching him, her sighs filling him, until the morning sun burned away the mists of the forest.

He could feel the imprint of her body on his. The soft curve of breast. The flare of hip. Despite her innocence, there was no denying her reaction to his kiss. He could taste her passion. Was well aware of her first stirrings of desire. It wasn't something she had learned to hide, the way a more experienced woman might.

He took the kiss deeper and heard the soft, guttural moan that seemed to come from deep in her heart. That only inflamed him more, until he was lost in her.

Lachlan thought of himself as a worldly man. The battles had taken him to many villages. There were always females willing to offer comfort to weary warriors. He'd kissed more women than he could remember. But none of them had ever tempted him to forget his vow as warrior. He was a man who took what he wanted and gave nothing of himself in the bargain. His heart was never in danger of being bruised.

Never had he tasted a woman like this. Here was sweetness. Here was rare beauty. Not just the beauty that came from a perfect body and a flawless face. There was an inner beauty in this woman. A goodness that set her apart from every other woman he'd ever met.

This was a woman he could love, with all his heart and soul. A woman a man would be proud to call his own. As that thought flashed through his mind, he wondered that the heavens didn't open up and swallow them both.

Was he so weak that one small woman could make him forget the promise he'd made to his father?

He was fully into the kiss, and completely aroused, when he felt her tears.

Tears?

On a wave of self-revulsion he drew a little away and touched a finger to her lashes. "Please don't weep, my lady. I never meant for this to happen."

"Nor I." The tears came harder now. Faster. "But I cannot allow what has happened between us to change what I must do." She pushed away, dragging air into her starving lungs. "I'll tell you this now, Lachlan MacLean, so that you will understand. I'm truly sorry for what I'm about to do. I didn't realize how it might affect you. Still, I must do whatever necessary to escape my fate so that I may return to my home and my sisters."

Before he could stop her she let out a sharp cry that had the warriors around the campfire sitting up and reaching for their weapons.

While he watched in consternation, Arianna leaped to her

feet, clutching her cloak around her. Her nursemaid was out of the wagon and across the clearing within seconds, demanding to know what had happened.

"The Highlander, Lachlan MacLean, tried to . . ." Arianna burst into tears.

Lachlan got to his feet and watched in silence as the old woman gathered her young charge into her arms.

"Here now, child. Ye must tell me what has happened."

When there was no reply, the old woman murmured words meant to soothe.

The tears fell harder now. Faster. There was no need for Arianna to pretend to weep. It was enough to give in to the feelings of shame and remorse that swept over her, nearly swamping her with their intensity. She allowed herself to weep openly, aware that all could see.

As the warriors gathered around, they glanced uneasily at their leader while Arianna gave a halting account, between sobs, of his attempt to seduce her.

"Did he succeed?" Nola's sharp eyes darted from Arianna to the man she'd accused.

The entire company of men seemed to hold its collective breath, awaiting the lady's reply.

"Nay." Arianna looked at the ground, refusing to meet the old woman's eyes. "But he . . . lay hands upon me. And . . . lips upon mine. I have been sullied in the eyes of the man to whom I am betrothed."

The men were grim as they waited for their leader to deny the charges.

Instead, he held his silence, staring at Arianna with a look so dark, so damning, it sent icy fingers prickling along her spine.

To escape him she turned her face into her nursemaid's shoulder. "We must leave this place, Nola, and return to my father's keep."

"You would break your father's solemn vow, child?"

"But I've been sullied. What Highland laird would want me now?"

The old woman smoothed her hair and drew her a little away. "Ye're young, Arianna. Innocent. Ye've yet to learn the ways of men and women. But a touch, a kiss even, would not be enough to release a man from his vow of betrothal. 'Tis said that the Highland laird is a fair man. And a wise one. Duncan MacLean will not be swayed from his intention to wed ye."

At her words Arianna went rigid with shock. "You can't mean this, Nola."

"I do indeed." With a sigh the old nursemaid led the way back to their wagon, where she bundled the shivering young woman into the nest of furs and sat stroking her hair. "Rest now, child. When we reach the Highlands, ye'll be greeted like a fine lady. Like a queen."

"I'm not a fine lady. Nor am I a queen." Arianna choked back more tears and lay wallowing in abject misery. What had she done? Oh, what had she done?

She'd been absolutely shattered by that kiss. She'd never known a man's lips could be that sweet. There had been lads in the village who had kissed her. Quick pecks on the cheek, or a stolen kiss on market day, which more often than not missed her lips and landed on her chin. But this had been a kiss that stirred her blood and melted her bones.

She tried to tell herself it was because Lachlan MacLean was a man, not a lad. He was older, more experienced in the ways of the world.

Each time she thought about the way it had felt to be held in his arms, his lips moving on hers, she was forced to endure again that quick, dizzying rush of heat, and that amazing tightening deep inside her.

She hadn't been surprised to find such strength in Lachlan MacLean. His power was obvious. What had caught her unawares was the tenderness. That had been her undoing. Even when he'd figured out her little scheme, he'd refused to condemn her.

He could have denied everything, of course. Though he'd had every right to call her on her lie, he had held his silence. And that silence had made her feel small and selfish.

And the look in his eyes. A look of misery laced with impotent fury. She couldn't bear it. Nor would she be able to bear looking at him ever again.

After this night, he would have to face the ridicule of

his own men. And worse, he would have to answer to his laird.

At the thought of him enduring a flogging tears filled her eyes once more. She blinked them back. She had no time for foolish weeping. No right to mourn her childish attempt to escape the dictates of her father. Now she must find a way to make things right. Not for herself, but for this innocent warrior.

As for her, she must accept the fact that she would spend a lifetime wed to a man she didn't love.

It would be all the worse now that she had felt Lachlan MacLean's strong arms around her and had tasted his firm, clever lips.

The look in his eyes, gazing at her with such tenderness, was an image that would remain with her forever. As would the look of icy hatred that now branded her.

4

As MORNING SUNLIGHT filtered down to the floor of the forest, Arianna remained in the back of the wagon, her eyes averted, while the Highlanders broke camp and prepared to move on.

From beneath lowered lashes she watched as Lachlan shouted orders to his men. It was odd that something as simple as a kiss could have changed so many things. Not just the way her heart felt, tight and crowded inside her chest, but also the way things now looked to her. The day seemed shiny-bright. Fresh and new. She couldn't recall a day quite like this ever before. And yet it brought her no pleasure.

Then there was the man who'd kissed her. Though she had initially been offended by the sight of his naked limbs, she now found them beautiful. There was a wonderful sort of grace to his movements. Like a wild creature at home in the wilderness. Now that she'd touched him, she understood the ripple of muscle beneath the plaid that draped his torso. The smooth, easy stride as he crossed to a group of warriors. She still found it amazing that a man of such extraordinary strength could have been so gentle with her.

If he was suffering from her betrayal, he gave no indication. Not once did he look her way as he moved about the camp, seeing to the endless details. The sound of his deep voice issuing commands sent shivers along her spine.

There was venison that needed to be carefully wrapped in lengths of hide and parceled out to those who would ride ahead. Weapons to be checked and horses to be fed and watered at the loch before departing. No detail was too small for his inspection.

He issued his orders in a voice devoid of emotion. But from the steely look in his eyes, his men knew better than to argue. Temper simmered just below that icy-calm surface, and Arianna found herself thinking of the way his voice had sounded whispering in her ear, growling against her mouth.

He assigned the man who would drive the wagon's team, and the six men to ride on either side of the laird's intended.

"The laird's intended." Arianna flinched at those words, snapped out like cracks of a whip.

Still, she was filled with quiet hope. A man as tender as Lachlan MacLean would surely be open to her explanation.

She carefully rehearsed the apology she would whisper to him when he came to help her mount. Uppermost in her mind was the need to make amends for what she'd put him through. Though there would be little time, she was determined to make the most of it. Then he would forgive her. Would smile upon her. And the day would feel sunny and bright again.

When it came time to move out, Lachlan pulled himself into the saddle and joined those who would ride ahead, leaving Pembroke to see to the women.

Arianna's heart sank. The Highland leader was making it plain that he had no intention of being alone with her again.

As Pembroke offered his hand and helped her to the ground, she could see the faint flush on his cheeks. "Good morrow, my lady."

Despite this young man's polite demeanor, Lachlan was

his friend. And she had besmirched that friend's good name. She mumbled a greeting, wishing she could bury herself beneath the furs in the back of the wagon. Instead she settled herself in the saddle and lifted her head in a regal manner as she started off on another grueling day.

On either side of her, the Highlanders exchanged sidelong glances. She ignored them and forced herself to stare straight ahead. What filled her vision was Lachlan, astride his mount. The width of his shoulders. The chiseled profile when he turned to call to one of his men.

As she focused on him, she could see the anger in the way his hand clenched at his side. In the stiff, taut line of his back. In the sharp tone he used to the warrior beside him.

It humbled her to know she'd caused so much turmoil in that good man.

Suddenly her horse stumbled. Though she was an excellent equestrienne, she'd allowed herself to become distracted. It took all her skill to keep from being thrown as she struggled to calm the rearing animal.

At a shout from one of her escorts, Lachlan wheeled his mount and hurried to her side, grasping the reins.

"Are you hurt, my lady?" His anger was forgotten, replaced by concern.

"Nay. It was nothing. I was caught by surprise."

"You're certain?" He nearly reached out to her before he caught himself and lowered his hand to his side, where he clenched it into a fist.

"Aye. It was but a misstep. I'm fine. Truly."

He drew in a breath before unleashing his temper on the men riding beside her. "You were given but one order. To see that the woman would be unharmed." He studied each of them in turn. "Does any man here wish to be relieved of his duties?"

The warriors were quick to shake their heads in denial.

He fixed them with a look meant to freeze their blood. "See to the lady, then." He nudged his horse aside, waiting until they passed him, then falling into line behind them.

Though the rest of the day passed without incident, the Highlanders were uneasy, knowing their leader was watching them, ready to pounce on the first one to make a mistake. His temper, which he had kept carefully banked, was now ready to ignite into full-blown fury.

They all knew the reason for his anger. It was because of the female in their midst.

As for Arianna, she could feel the tension, sharp as a blade, that kept the entire company on edge. When they stopped at midday, the men stood in clusters of four and five, watching in silence as she and her nursemaid took their meal on a cloak spread in the shade of a tree. Within the hour they were back in the saddle, following a narrow trail that seemed carved out of sheer rock.

By the time twilight shadows began to drift over the land, they had made camp on a high, heather-strewn meadow. Despite Lachlan's gloom, his men were in high spirits now that they were drawing near their home.

Pembroke reached a hand to assist Arianna from the saddle. "It's been a long ride, my lady." The young man gave her a gentle smile. "By this time on the morrow, you will be welcomed into the laird's fortress."

"Aye." She glanced away quickly, to hide the fear she knew would be in her eyes. As she did, she caught sight of a magnificent waterfall, and beyond it, a rainbow. "Oh." She couldn't help clasping her hands together. "How splendid."

The young man looked pleased at her reaction. " 'Tis a familiar sight to those of us who live here in the Highlands. The falling waters and the loch below are said to be enchanted."

"Enchanted? In what way?"

Pembroke pointed to a high cliff above the waterfall. "That is the sight of a bloody battle between one of Scotland's bravest warriors and a band of barbarians who had left a trail of death across the land."

"Was this warrior alone, without comrades?"

"He was, for he'd come here with his family to enjoy a day of frolic, and suddenly they were attacked without warning. The warrior was a fierce fighter, but he was badly outnumbered. When he realized he was mortally wounded, he knew he could no longer protect his wife and small son.

So he tossed them from the rock into the falling water, where they were carried into the loch below."

Arianna put a hand to her mouth. "Didn't he fear they would drown?"

"Aye." The young man nodded. "But he thought drowning a far better death than being brutalized by the barbarians, for he had seen what they did to their prisoners. Especially women and small children. As his family struggled in the loch he could hear their cries, and he longed to go to them. But he knew that duty and honor must always come before love, and that he was bound to stay and fight until his last breath."

"Did he die?" Arianna was spellbound by the tale, as was her old nurse beside her.

"He did, my lady. The invaders tossed his body off the cliff into the loch, where it's said he waits to this very day for the invaders to return so that he can have his vengeance. Some have seen him, shimmering in the summer's moonlight. Others have even heard his moans on cold winter nights."

That had Nola shivering and crossing herself.

Arianna looked up at the young man. "And his family?"

"They survived the falling water and the loch. Until the day she died, his woman spoke proudly of his courage. His son followed his example and became a man of similar courage."

Arianna sighed. "I'm glad, Pembroke. Glad that something good could come from such a noble sacrifice."

"No sacrifice is ever in vain, my lady." For the first time he met her eyes, and she thought she could see sympathy, and more, understanding, in those soft blue depths. "Warriors are not the only ones who must risk all for the sake of others. No unselfish act, done out of love for family, friend, or country, will ever go unrewarded."

It soothed her heart to know that this young warrior understood what was being asked of her. Before she could thank him for his kind words, he caught up the reins of her horse and walked away.

Arianna followed Nola to the shade of a tree, where the two women settled themselves in the cool grass.

"I'm told we'll reach the fortress on the morrow." The old woman was watching Arianna's eyes as she spoke. "Ye'd best choose yer finest gown so ye'll look beautiful for the laird."

"Do you think it matters what I wear, Nola?"

The old woman flushed and looked away. "Nay, lass. But 'tis a sign of respect."

Arianna tossed her head. "I've no desire to look beautiful for the laird."

"Then ye'll do it for yer father, lass. To make him proud."

The old woman could see that her words had the desired effect, and she gave a sigh of relief. Though Arriana had always been headstrong, she'd never been anything but kind and fair. The lass would see this thing through, if only for the sake of her father's good name.

The nurse motioned toward the fire. The enticing fragrance of roasting meat was making her mouth water. "Come now, child. We'll eat, and then we'll make ready for the coming day."

Arianna followed, keeping her head bowed as she passed a cluster of warriors. But she knew by their sudden silence that they had been discussing her. And why not? She was the stranger here. Would always be the stranger in their midst.

Anger replaced the guilt that had held her in its grip all day. Let them talk. Let them say whatever they pleased. If she couldn't control her destiny, at least she could take charge of this, her last night of freedom.

She turned to Nola. "I have no need of food. I wish to go alone to the river and wash myself."

The old woman shook her head and glanced around for Lachlan. "The Highlander will never permit it."

"It's not his right to say aye or nay, Nola."

"He is responsible for yer safety, lass."

"I'm responsible for myself."

"Aye. That ye are. But at least wait until dark, so the men can be warned to stay away from the river, to protect yer modesty."

Arianna was about to argue when she saw the pleading look in the old woman's eyes.

She nodded. "So be it. But I'll not be dissuaded from this, Nola."

Her nursemaid breathed a sigh of relief. She'd bought enough time for the Highland leader to take charge. After that little incident of the previous night, the old woman was certain he would never permit Arianna to be alone, for she might plot another means of escaping her fate.

But as daylight faded and darkness spread its cloak over the land, the Highland leader was nowhere to be found.

When at last the warriors began rolling themselves into their plaids around the fire, Arianna rummaged in the trunk and removed a clean gown. "I go to the river now, Nola."

"Nay. Not alone. At least let me go with you, child. Who knows what danger lies beyond the firelight? Ye heard what the lad told ye. The river and the falling water are enchanted."

"I care not for such things, Nola. I'm not the enemy. The ghost of the brave warrior would have nothing to fear from me."

Seeing the fierce determination in her eyes, the old woman caught her hands. "Give me yer word, child, that ye'll make no attempt to flee."

Arianna looked down at the gnarled hands, then into the wide, pleading eyes. "I give you my word, Nola. On the morrow I go willingly to the laird of lairds, to fulfill my father's promise. But tonight is mine. I'll not be denied this, my last night of freedom." She gave her old nurse a gentle hug before turning away. "Have no fear. There are guards posted. No harm will come to me. Sleep well, Nola. I will return at dawn."

Draping the fresh gown over her arm, she followed the sound of the rushing water until she came to the banks of the loch. Undressing quickly, she dropped her soiled clothes into the water and washed them, hanging them on low branches to dry. That done, she sat in the shallows, scrubbing her body all over, and then her hair, before walking into the deep.

The heavens were awash with millions of glittering stars.

Clouds scudded across a fat golden moon. Arianna looked up, wondering if Glenna and Kendra were watching this same sky. Were they missing her as much as she was missing them? She felt a wave of such homesickness that she nearly began to weep. She looked around, wondering if she would ever feel as though she belonged in this wild, primitive place.

With great effort she shook off her melancholy. Tonight was hers. Only hers. She would allow no unhappy thoughts to mar this special time.

She held her breath and ducked beneath the water, then scrubbed her fingers through the tangles until her hair was rinsed clean. Surfacing, she began swimming toward shore.

When her feet touched bottom, she stood and began to walk. Water lapped gently against her breasts. She looked up at the moon and found herself smiling.

At a sound on shore she paused, the smile fading from her lips.

At first she thought she detected the shadow of one of the guards. But when she glanced up, she could see them, still high above on the cliffs, keeping watch. The waterfall protected her modesty.

Perhaps the tall, silvery figure was the ghost Pembroke had described. Tall he was, like a giant. He stood, feet apart, sword lifted as though asking a blessing from the gods. The plaid was tossed rakishly over one shoulder. The breeze caught the hair at his neck and feathered it about his face. A face lifted to the sky, lost in contemplation.

Suddenly the clouds drifted away, leaving the figure bathed in moonlight.

Neither guard nor ghost, Arianna realized. The shadowy figure was Lachlan MacLean.

5

Lachlan's first thought when he saw the figure in the loch was that this was surely some sort of spell. With moonlight trailing a ribbon of gold across the water, bathing her in a golden halo, she looked like a goddess.

He blinked, certain that she would disappear. Instead she seemed to come into even sharper focus, until all he could see was Arianna. Hair hanging in fiery ropes around her face and shoulders. Eyes looking too big in her pale face. A face so beautiful it took his breath away.

Though the water covered her, he could see the outline of her breasts beneath the waves and the darkened cleft between them.

Heat rushed to his loins. His throat was dry as dust. He forced himself to swallow, and, in defense, his mouth twisted into a fierce scowl.

"Woman, why are you here?" His tone was as harsh as the look in his eyes.

"Your friend Pembroke told me this place is enchanted." She saw something flicker in his eyes and wondered about it. Not fear, she reasoned, but some deeper emotion. As though he both loved and hated this place. "Perhaps you think I foolishly came to seek release from my father's promise."

When he said nothing, she sighed and decided to confess the truth. "Since my future is now out of my hands, I decided to spend this, my last night of freedom, alone."

He inclined his head. "Then I'll leave you to your solitude, my lady."

As he turned to leave she waded onto the shore and, ignoring her nakedness, lay a hand on his back.

He flinched. And froze.

Arianna absorbed a blow to her heart. "Is my touch so offensive to you, Lachlan?"

He kept his gaze averted. "Is a flogging not enough for me? Is it your intention to have me killed by my laird as well?"

"Oh, Lachlan." His name was torn from her lips. "How can I ever make you understand how sorry I am about last night? It's true I wanted to use you to gain my freedom. But it was never my intention to have you punished in my stead."

His tone softened, but just a little. "In truth, I'll not mind the punishment. A beating is little enough price to pay for the pleasure of your kiss, my lady."

Her heart leaped to her throat. "You . . . aren't angry?"

"At myself, perhaps. For being such a fool. For those few precious moments, I allowed myself to think you enjoyed the kiss as much as I."

Before he could step away she caught his hand. "Look at me, Lachlan."

"Nay." He shook his head. "I'm in enough torment. To look at you, to see you as my laird will see you, would only bring heartache."

"Lachlan." She spoke quickly, afraid if she didn't, she might lose her nerve. "I did enjoy that kiss. As much as you. More, perhaps."

He turned. The sight of her standing before him, water sluicing from her hair and sheeting down her body, stunned him and sent his heart reeling. The need for her was so sharp, so demanding, it nearly staggered him.

"I've never felt that way before." She saw the way his eyes narrowed in suspicion. "Nor will I ever again. You were my first, Lachlan."

"The first to kiss you." His voice hardened. "But not the last. On the morrow you will belong to my laird."

"Aye." She lifted her chin. "That I cannot change. But tonight, I belong to myself. Tonight whatever choices I make are mine. I thought I wanted to spend this time alone. But now that you're here, I realize what I truly want. I want, more than anything, to lie with you. To love you, Lachlan."

Already he was shaking his head. "So that you can rouse the entire camp and accuse me of something far worse than a kiss?"

"I would never do that, now that I know what your punishment would be." Her voice lowered to a whisper. "I know I have no right to ask you to trust me. Not after the cruel trick I played on you. But I swear on my mother's grave that I had no idea of the consequences of my action." She lifted a hand to his mouth and traced a finger over the frown that carved his lips. Lips that trembled at her touch.

The thought that she could make this brave warrior tremble made her heart thunder. "I would give anything—anything," she repeated with a fierce whisper, "to bring the smile back to your eyes."

He could feel the jolt clear to his heart. And though he warned himself that he would be a fool to trust her again, the need to taste those lips was more than he could resist.

He closed a big hand over hers, stilling her movements. "I could easily snap your bones like twigs."

"Aye. And if I betray you, Lachlan, that should be my punishment." She shivered at the strength in him.

Seeing it, he misunderstood. "You're cold, my lady." He took the plaid from his shoulder and wrapped it around her, drawing her against the length of him.

"It isn't the cold that makes me shiver, Lachlan. It's you."

"Do you fear me, then?"

She shook her head. "Nor is it fear that has me trembling.

It's the wanting. I want you, Lachlan. Only you. And I have, from the moment you kissed me."

His hands gripped her upper arms roughly, holding her a little away from him. His eyes were narrow slits of doubt and anger. "You must stop this talk. You're a maiden. Betrothed to my uncle."

"Aye. And if I must spend the rest of my life in a loveless marriage, at least let me have my memories of tonight."

"You're mad."

"Perhaps. If loving you, wanting you, is madness, then surely I'm possessed of it. And I've no one to blame but myself. For I was the one who shamelessly used you in my little scheme."

He ran his hands up and down her arms, staring into her eyes with a look so intense it made her heart race and her skin heat. "We're both mad, then, my lady. For I haven't the strength to walk away from what you offer."

"You'll stay with me this night?"

He nodded and drew her close, pressing his mouth to the tumble of damp hair at her temple. "God help me, Arianna. God help us both. I'm too weak to resist."

He tangled his fingers in her hair and drew her back, so he could stare into her eyes. The look he gave her was so hot, so fierce, she felt her heart constrict. "When first I looked at you, I felt a need I'd never known before. I tried to deny it. But that kiss shattered my heart."

A thrill of triumph shot through her, piercing her to her soul. "It was the same for me. No other man will ever have my heart, Lachlan."

But the knowledge that another would wed her sent pain, swift as an arrow, crashing through him. He thrust aside that knowledge. For now, for tonight, they would forget about what lay before them and take what pleasure they could.

He brushed hot, wet kisses across her cheek to her ear, holding her as if she were a fragile doll. "I want to be easy, Arianna, for I know you're a maiden. But all through the night, after that kiss, I lay awake, dreaming of the ways I'd like to love you."

She shivered at the warmth of his breath and wrapped

her arms around his neck, pressing herself to him. "Show me, Lachlan. Teach me the ways."

Still he held back, his hands gentle, his mouth hovering over hers. "I'm afraid I'll hurt you."

She stepped back to frame his face with her hands. "I'm not a child. I'm a woman."

His smile was quick and dangerous. "Oh, my lady, I'm well aware of that."

"Then kiss me. Now, before my poor heart stops beating."

His mouth covered hers, and he heard her quick intake of breath before she poured herself into the kiss. It seemed to spin on and on until they were both breathless and gasping for air. And still it wasn't enough. He kissed her again, feasting on her lips as though starved for the taste of her. And all the while his hands, those strong, clever hands, moved over her, lighting fires wherever they touched.

The heat that surged through his veins had him moaning and taking the kiss deeper, until he was nearly devouring her.

Arianna had never known such feelings. She was hot and cold, and her legs were trembling until she feared they might not hold her. Her fingertips tingled from the mere touch of the hair at his nape, and she wanted more. She wanted to touch him everywhere, as he was touching her.

He lifted his head and she felt bereft. But seconds later he nibbled kisses down her neck to the hollow of her throat.

She felt a strange weakness taking over her limbs. All she could do was arch her neck and thrill to the pleasure as his mouth roamed her collarbone, then lower, to the swell of her breast.

When he took one erect nipple into his mouth she gasped and clutched blindly at his waist.

Half mad with need he lifted his head. "Did I frighten you, Arianna?"

"Nay." She could barely get the word out, over a throat clogged with passion. "Well, perhaps." She smiled then. "But I wouldn't mind if you did that again."

He chuckled and covered her mouth with his. Now their

kisses grew more heated, their sighs more muffled as they lost themselves in each other.

Lachlan tossed his plaid to the ground, then caught her hands and dragged her down with him. He lay beside her, loving the way she looked, shimmering in the moonlight.

His fingers played with the ends of her hair. Hair that glinted like fire. Her eyes, as green as a Highland loch, were fixed on him with such intensity, he felt she could peer into his soul. She smelled as fresh and clean as the evergreens in the forest.

Water slapped against the banks, a steady, rhythmic sound that neither of them heard. Somewhere in the distance a horse stomped and whinnied, but they took no notice. All they could see was each other. All they could hear was the thunder of their two hearts. All they could feel was the glorious wonder of their newly discovered love.

"I have so little to give you, Arianna." And so he gave her kisses, soft and light, until she relaxed in his arms.

"I need nothing more than this." She returned his kisses. "Only this, Lachlan."

He fought the needs that warred inside him, forcing himself to go slowly. To taste, to savor. If this was all he could give her, it would have to be enough to last a lifetime.

Responding to his tenderness, she lifted a finger to trace the outline of his lips. Growing bolder, she brought her mouth to his throat and pressed soft, moist kisses there until, with a groan, he dragged her into his arms and kissed her mouth, her throat, her breast.

What had moments earlier been a purr turned into a gasp. Pleasure now bordered on something so intense she couldn't put a name to it. The heat between them became an inferno, until even the coolness of the grass, and the rush of night air on their skin, did nothing to put out the fire that raged.

Lachlan stared into her eyes and could see the desire that burned there. Could taste the passion on her lips. Could feel the need that struggled to be set free.

He framed her face with his hands and kissed her deeply, fueling the hunger that demanded to be fed.

"Know this, Arianna. I love you. Only you. And will love you for all my life."

She reached for him, desperate now for release. "And I love you, Lachlan."

He drew her closer, and she could feel the thunder of his heartbeat inside her own chest. A heartbeat that was as out of control as her own.

He'd wanted to be gentle, but now there was no stopping the demon that had taken over his will. He had to possess her. Body. Mind. Soul. He was like a madman as he entered her. Then, hearing her gasp of surprise, he went deathly still.

"What was I thinking? You're a maiden. Arianna, forgive me . . ."

She pressed a hand to his lips to stop his words. Then without speaking, she drew him in and began to move with him. Climb with him.

He held on to her as he took her higher, then higher still. Together they raced across the darkened sky, beyond the moon, to the distant stars, where they shattered like diamonds and drifted slowly to earth.

"Did I hurt you?" Lachlan lay, his face buried in her hair.

"Nay." It was the only word she could manage. Despite the fact that her heart seemed so full, her body felt weightless.

"I tried to be gentle but . . ."

With a smile she lifted her hand to his mouth. "Shh. Lachlan, it was so wonderful. Is it always so?"

"I'm told, if the love is true, it can be so."

"Have you ever known love?"

"Never before."

At his admission she went very still. "Pembroke said you took a vow."

"It is one I made to my father, before he died. That I would dedicate my life to being a warrior worthy of his name. To that end I decided that I would never lose my heart to a woman, for to do so would be to weaken my resolve on the field of battle."

"I don't understand."

"In battle, only one thing matters. Survival. If a man is distracted by love, it can cost him his life."

"Was your father distracted by love?"

"He was. That love, that determination to protect those he loved, cost him his life."

"And so you will journey through life alone."

"Aye, my lady."

Arianna sighed. "Knowing that makes me treasure all the more the memory of this special time with you."

He nuzzled her throat. "You speak as though our time is over."

"Isn't it?" She ran her hands through his hair to still his movements.

But he continued nuzzling her throat until she wriggled beneath him. "We've only begun, Arianna."

She went very still as the meaning of his words became clear. "We can . . . again?"

"And again and again." He lifted his head and with a knowing smile looked down into her eyes. "You said we had the night."

"Aye. But your vow?"

"Has already been broken. I've already lost my heart to you." He brought his lips to hers. The words he whispered inside her mouth were warmed by equal parts of love and amusement. "So, since we have the night, let's not waste a moment of it, my love."

With but a kiss she found herself sliding back into a world of dark, mysterious tastes, and even darker passions. A world known only to lovers.

6

ARIANNA AWOKE IN Lachlan's arms. As her lids fluttered open, she found him watching her. In his eyes was a look of such intensity, she sat up in alarm.

"Why did you let me waste our precious time together in sleep? Why didn't you wake me?"

"You looked so peaceful, love."

Love. The endearment wrapped itself around her heart. She knew what it cost this strong, brave warrior to admit such a thing.

She glanced up at the sky, where the first faint ribbons of dawn were just beginning to paint the horizon. How cruel of the night to flee so quickly. "You must hasten to camp before your men find you gone."

"First, my love, a kiss." He drew her down to him and kissed her long and slow and deep.

They'd spent the night loving. At first they were seized with a quiet desperation, as though frantic to store up whatever memories possible. And so they loved just as desperately. But as the night wore on, they became soft and easy with each other, as comfortable as old lovers who had all the time in the world.

They talked, eager to learn all they could about each other. They spoke of their childhood, hers spent in happy play with her sisters until the death of her mother, when she'd been thrust into the role of housekeeper and hostess. During his childhood he had learned the ways of war from his uncle, who had taken him in after the death of his father. Lachlan's skill with sword and knife had become legendary. As had his insistence that no woman would distract him from his true calling.

"Tell me something, Arianna." He played with the ends of her hair, as they lay whispering together in the darkness. "Why did you not choose someone fair of face like Pembroke for your little scheme? Didn't he seem a far easier man to ensnare?"

She was grateful that he couldn't see the flush that stole over her cheeks. Even now it pained her to think how she'd trapped this good man in her little scheme. "Pembroke told me there was a lass who owned his heart."

"Lana."

"Aye. I feared that the scandal might cause him grief."

He smiled at the evidence of her gentle heart. "And so you chose me."

She sighed. "I was thinking only that you had no woman who might be hurt. I truly never thought about what this might do to you."

"My sweet, honest Arianna." He drew her close and kissed away the little frown that marred her forehead.

And when she finally slept, he watched her, memorizing everything about her, and wondering how in the world he could bear to let her go.

She was everything a man could ever want in a woman. Spirited and strong-willed. And blessed with a quick, inventive mind. Had she been more worldly, she might have succeeded in her attempt to escape her fate. And yet, it was her innocence that had first endeared her to him. When she realized the punishment that would befall the innocent victim in her little plan, she was filled with remorse. There was such goodness in her. He'd seen the tender way she dealt with her younger sisters. Best of all, there was such passion in her. After only one night in her arms, he knew that no other woman would ever satisfy him.

Before meeting her, he had believed he would always travel a lonely path through life. But now that he'd tasted her love, he knew he was doomed to much more than loneliness. He would live a life filled with regret at what the fates had denied him.

"I can't leave you yet, my love." His hands began moving over her.

"Lachlan." She was as breathless as though she'd been running across a Highland meadow into the arms of her lover. "You know what this will lead to."

"Aye." He gave her a heart-stopping grin. "I'm counting on it."

He drew her down and kissed her again. And then, as they rolled over and over in the cool grass, they showed each other, in the only way they could, all the things that were locked in their hearts.

Arianna watched as Lachlan stepped out of the loch and picked up the length of plaid from the low-hanging branches. She'd never known a man's body could be so beautiful. Broad of shoulder and narrow of waist. Tall and slender, with muscles that rippled at every movement. He tossed back his dark hair, like a great shaggy hound, sending a spray of water dancing around him. Then he wound the plaid around his waist and threw it over one shoulder before securing his boots.

He picked up his sword, crossed to her, and caught her hands. "Can I not change your mind?"

"Nay." She forced a smile to her lips. "We must not return to camp together. It's better this way. I'll bathe and dress, and return shortly." She lifted herself on tiptoe to brush her lips over his. "Now go, love."

He was so staggered by her kiss he wondered if his legs would carry him. He turned away, then returned to gather her roughly against him and kiss her with such fervor that both their hearts were hammering. "Know always that I love you, Arianna."

"And I love you, Lachlan." She bit down hard to keep her lips from quivering as he strode away.

This time he refused to turn back, knowing if he did, he would never be able to leave her.

By the time he returned to camp, his arms were laden with logs he'd collected in the forest. He deposited them on the hot coals, wiping his hands on his plaid. Then he moved around the fire, waking his men.

They were breaking their fast when Arianna stepped into the clearing, head high, features composed. She was wearing her best gown, of emerald velvet, with a softly rounded neckline and a long skirt that brushed the tops of her kid boots. The sleeves were tapered and dusted with little points of lace that fell over the backs of her hands.

As she made her way to the wagon, she could feel Lachlan watching. She kept her gaze averted and prayed there would be no betraying blush on her cheeks.

"Ah, child." Nola paused in the act of folding the furs that had cushioned her through the night and gave a nod of approval. "I see ye took my advice and dressed for the laird."

"Aye, Nola."

The woman tossed the fur into the back of the wagon. "I'll fetch ye some food."

"Nay." Arianna touched a hand to her stomach, to still the flutter of nerves. "I've no appetite this morrow, Nola."

"I understand." Her nursemaid glanced around at the sudden flurry of activity, as the fire was banked and the warriors began pulling themselves into the saddle.

She caught the young woman's hand. Squeezed. "It's glad I am that ye had yer night of solitude, child. Ye seem calmer this morrow. And more ready to face yer future."

"Aye, Nola." Arianna gave a deep sigh and turned as Pembroke approached with her horse.

Across the clearing she caught sight of Lachlan as he shouted orders to his men. For a moment her smile slipped, and she wondered if she had the strength to see this thing through. Then she was being helped into the saddle, and as their company moved out under the canopy of forest, she emptied her mind of all thoughts save one. This day, the

man she loved would deliver her into the hands of his uncle, Duncan MacLean, the laird of lairds. Before this day
was over, she would be wed. And her heart, so filled with
love for the one, would be pledged for all time to the other.

By midday they could make out the turreted fortress in the
distance.

As they drew near, Arianna's throat was so constricted
she could barely swallow. Fear and dread lay heavy on her
heart.

On a far meadow she could just make out snug cottages
and huts, and hillsides dotted with sheep. The pretty picture
was in sharp contrast to what she'd been expecting. After
all, these Highlanders were a warlike people. She had expected that their lives would be as harsh and unforgiving
as this primitive countryside they called home.

Their party entered a paved courtyard, the horses and
wagon clattering across the stones before coming to a halt.
Almost at once a door was thrown open, and a servant came
rushing toward Lachlan as he slid from the saddle.

"Oh, praise heaven you've returned."

While the others watched, he caught the woman's hands.
"What is it, Brinna?"

"We were invaded. Our laird called up what men were
left in the village, and managed to rout the barbarians, but
he was . . ." Her composure slipped, and she began weeping
softly. "He was gravely wounded in the battle."

Lachlan was already striding across the courtyard and
through the open doorway. Over his shoulder he commanded, "See to the laird's guests, Brinna. I must go to my
uncle."

While their company disbanded, each warrior leaving for
his own home to be reunited with family, Arianna and her
nursemaid were led through the keep to a suite of rooms
on an upper floor.

Everywhere she looked, Arianna was surprised by the
luxury of the place. Tapestries lined the walls, telling of
the history of the MacLean clan and their many glorious
deeds on the field of battle. Chandeliers blazed with hun-

dreds of candles, and fires roared on every hearth to chase the chill from the rooms.

Their own suite consisted of a large sitting chamber, with sleeping chambers on either side of it. Chaises were pulled near the fire, and fur throws covered the wooden floor and softened the walls.

In the sitting room a serving wench bowed before offering them goblets of wine and cold meat and cheese, as well as a plate of biscuits and jam.

"Thank you." Arianna sipped the wine and settled herself before the fire. "How fares the laird?"

The girl was too timid to look up. Keeping her gaze averted, she said hesitantly, "We fear the worst. He can no longer be roused."

When the serving girl was gone, Arianna pretended to inspect her sleeping chamber, while Nola unpacked their trunks. She needed some time alone, to sort through her thoughts. Though it seemed wrong to take comfort from another's sorrow, she couldn't help but be buoyed by the realization that she had somehow earned a reprieve. With the laird gravely ill, there would be no thought of a wedding.

Just as daylight began to fade, word spread throughout the fortress that the laird had given up his battle with death. From belowstairs a great cry went up that could be heard throughout all the rooms. A low keening, that grew louder as each new voice joined in, until it seemed that all of Scotland must surely be mourning the death of the laird of the MacLeans.

Nola found Arianna standing on a balcony, watching a parade of torches that seemed to stretch for miles, all of them moving like a sea of lights toward the fortress.

"You heard, child?"

Arianna turned. "Aye. The laird is dead." She paused a moment, gathering her courage, before adding, "I hope you won't think me evil, Nola, but I can't help but rejoice that I am now free."

"Free? What are you saying, child?"

"With the laird dead, I'm no longer bound by my father's promise. I can return now to my home."

"Come here, child. Sit and listen to me." The old woman took her hand and led her inside to a chaise by the fire.

At the gravity of her demeanor, Arianna felt a chill of unease.

When she was seated Nola stood for a moment staring into the flames. Then she turned. "The laird's death makes no difference."

"I don't under—"

Nola lifted a hand. "Ye were promised, not to Laird Duncan MacLean but to the laird of the MacLeans."

"But the laird is dead."

"Aye. And the people cannot be without a leader. That is why the men of the village make their way here even now. Ye saw their torches. By the time the old laird is in the ground, a new one will have been chosen to take his place."

"But I . . ."

"Ye will be bound by yer father's promise, just as the new laird will be bound by the promise made by Duncan MacLean to continue to protect yer family and yer people."

"Is there no way out of this, Nola?"

"There is. If the new laird should already have a wife, ye will be returned safely to yer father's keep, and a new bargain will be struck."

"And if he is old, and his wife dead and buried?"

The woman said nothing. But her silence spoke more than words.

Arianna got to her feet and stepped out onto the balcony, to gaze down at the flickering torches undulating in the darkness. These men would unknowingly seal her fate.

Throughout the evening she and Nola kept to their chambers, catching bits and pieces of information from the serving wenches who brought their supper. The MacLean was being mourned and honored with many tankards of ale, while his clansmen debated his successor. The two names most often considered were Winfield MacLean and Powell MacLean.

"Are these men wed?" Arianna paused with the goblet of wine halfway to her lips.

"Nay, my lady. Winfield's wife, my mother's cousin,

gave him thirty years of faithful service and seven sons, before going to her grave. Powell was wed briefly to a lass who ran off rather than endure his bad temper." At once the girl looked embarrassed by her slip of the tongue. "Forgive me, my lady. I must see to my duties." She hurried from the room.

An hour later a great cheer could be heard coming from below.

Nola stuck her head out the door and stopped a servant. "What was that?"

He paused, his arms laden with wood for the many fires that must be stoked. "It can only mean that a new laird has been chosen."

"Do ye know the laird's name?"

He shook his head. "Nay. I've not heard. But by morning, word will go out to all the villages, and we will bury the old laird and pay homage to the new."

Arianna hurried to her sleeping chamber in a panic. A short while later Nola entered and found her pacing.

"Come, child. No need for that now. The worst is behind ye. There's naught to do but sleep. On the morrow, ye'll learn yer fate."

Dazed, Arianna allowed herself to be helped into her nightdress. While Nola held the blanket, she slipped into bed and watched her nurse snuff out the candle.

In the darkness she listened to Nola's footsteps as she crossed the room and let herself out.

Silence settled over the fortress, and Arianna lay still as death, willing sleep to take her. But she could only hear Nola's words over and over. How could she lie here and calmly await her fate?

Suddenly she sprang up and began to prowl the room, pressing her fingertips to her temples. She could stay here no longer.

She knew it was the coward's way, but she had to flee this place. The thought of being wed to an old man—or worse, a cruel one—was more than she could bear.

Moving carefully in the dark, she located her gown and slipped into her kid boots. Rather than risk waking the servants, she began fashioning a rope of bed linens. When it was long enough to reach nearly to the ground below, she tied one end to the rail of the balcony and tossed the other end over the side. With her heart pounding, she pulled herself over the balcony and began the long slide to the ground.

In the courtyard she found several horses. Catching up the reins of a black mare, she led her out into the darkness, then pulled herself into the saddle.

She hadn't given a thought to where she would go. Her only intention was to be free. But with the fortress at her back she turned the mare in the direction they had come that day, watching for familiar landmarks in the darkness.

She had found peace and contentment in Lachlan's arms on the banks of the enchanted loch. Perhaps, if her luck held, or if the loch truly was enchanted, she could find her freedom there as well.

7

THE DARKNESS WAS both a blessing and a curse. A blessing because it hid the horse and rider as they made their way through rough terrain and headed deep into the forest. A curse because it hid branches that slapped without warning at Arianna's face and tugged at her hair.

She was without her traveling cloak, since she would have risked waking old Nola if she had tried to retrieve it. The only gown available had been the heavy emerald velvet, now snagged and torn. She'd been forced to hike it up between her legs in order to sit a man's saddle.

When the trail took a dangerous dip, she slid from the saddle and began leading her mount. The velvet flapped at her ankles, slowing her movements, and the sharp edges of rocks bit through the kid boots until she found herself limping beside her horse.

She could hear in the distance the roar of falling water, and it gave her hope that she would soon reach the enchanted loch.

At the top of the high cliff the mare tossed her head wildly, eyes wide, nostrils flaring.

"Here now. Hush. Don't be afraid." Pushing aside her own fears, Arianna paused to soothe and coax the animal, finally persuading her to start down the steep trail that led to the loch.

The rush of water was so loud here that it drowned out every other sound as Arianna picked her way carefully over rocks and through thick foliage until at last she and the horse reached the banks of the loch.

Instead of heading to the water to drink, the mare suddenly reared up, pulling the reins out of Arianna's hands. Before she could retrieve them, the horse ran off into the forest.

Dazed, Arianna turned, intent on giving chase.

She stopped in mid-stride when she found herself facing a line of strangers. All of them holding swords and knives.

Too late, she understood the mare's skittishness.

"Well, well. What have we here?" One of the men, barefoot, wearing little more than a strip of fur to cover his nakedness, stepped closer. He held a knife in one hand. "A female? Traveling alone, are you?"

The others laughed.

The sound of their high-pitched laughter scraped Arianna's nerves. She knew, from the manner of speech and dress, that these were the barbarians. Routed from the Highlands, they'd taken refuge at the loch. And she had foolishly walked right into their camp.

She took several steps backward, until she felt the splash of water over her ankles.

"Come to amuse us, have you, woman?"

Again the laughter as the others began to circle her, sniffing like dogs with the scent of prey in their nostrils.

Without a weapon she had only her wits to save her. With false bravado she lifted her head and faced the leader. "My warriors will be here soon. If you value your lives, you'll leave now, before they come upon you."

Her regal manner and tone of voice caused the men to step back from the water's edge and look around in alarm.

"Warriors?" The leader threw back his head and cackled. "What kind of warriors would send one puny female ahead to scout for them?"

At that the others relaxed and joined in the laughter.

"I am betrothed to the laird of lairds. My life is precious to him. Do you think he would allow me a midnight ride without his warriors following to protect me?"

"I think—" The leader's smile vanished, and he grabbed her wrist. "—you're nothing more than a tasty morsel among starving men." He looked around. "What say you, men?"

"I'll have my fill of her," one shouted.

"I'd even settle for what's left over," called another with a chilling laugh.

The leader dragged her close. She gagged with the stench of him. But it was the look in his eyes that made Arianna's blood turn to ice. He shot his men a look of supreme confidence. "I'll take her first. Then you can all have what's left of her."

She surprised him by pulling free and turning to dash into the loch. With each step she was nearly dragged to her knees, and she cursed the heavy velvet gown. If it made walking through water difficult, it would make swimming impossible. Still, she would rather drown than face being brutalized by these barbarians.

"Little fool. Do you think you can outrun us?" The leader reached out, catching a handful of her hair.

With a cry she fell backward, choking and sputtering as she sank beneath the surface.

He dragged her up and pinned her in his arms. His eyes were hot, fierce with a mixture of fury and lust. Holding her a little away from him, he swung his big hand in an arc and slapped her with such force that her head snapped to one side. She blinked furiously, trying to see through the shower of stars that danced before her eyes.

"Now you will pay, woman." His hand clamped around her upper arm, and he started back toward shore, dragging her along beside him.

Arianna dug in her heels, determined to fight him every step of the way.

"You dare to defy me again?" He closed his hand into a fist and Arianna steeled herself for the blow to come.

Suddenly a great wind came up, churning the water

around them until the waves rose higher than the trees that ringed the shore. Arianna found herself thrown free of the barbarian's grasp. And though the water around her smoothed and settled, it whirled even faster around him, tumbling him about like a leaf in a storm.

A shimmering dark cloud rose up from the foam. As the wind disbursed the cloud, a Highland warrior could be seen in the darkness.

He clamped an arm around the barbarian's throat.

With a gasp, his victim clutched at the arm, desperate to dislodge it. But his strength was useless against the superhuman power of the Highlander. Within minutes the barbarian slipped into the water, his lifeless body carried away on the waves.

The moon, which had been covered by a bank of dark clouds, suddenly broke free, illuminating the figure in the loch.

Arianna gave a gasp of recognition. "Lachlan. Oh, my beloved! It's you!" She started toward him, arms outstretched.

He spoke not a word as he lifted a hand, indicating that she should stay where she was. Then he turned and unsheathed his sword. The jeweled hilt winked in the starlight as he strode to the shore to face the rest of the bloodthirsty band.

The barbarians were ready for him. Having witnessed the murder of their leader, they circled him and attacked as soon as he stepped out of the loch. The battle was fierce, and should have ended quickly. But the Highland warrior refused to give up, no matter how many wounds he suffered. Despite the fact that there were a dozen men, he managed to slowly whittle away at them as one after another fell from the blows delivered by his mighty sword.

"You must die, Highlander." One of their number raised his broadsword and caught the warrior on the side of the head, knocking him to the ground.

"Nay!" From her place in the loch Arianna gave a cry as she started forward, still cursing the heavy skirts that slowed her progress.

The barbarians swarmed over the figure lying in the dirt,

knives and swords glinting in the moonlight as they inflicted mortal wounds.

Through a haze of blood and pain the Highland warrior struggled to his feet and continued fighting until only one of the enemy was left standing.

The lone barbarian gave a chilling smile. "You're too badly wounded to fight on. You'll feel my sword, Highlander. And then your woman will be my reward."

Arianna watched as her champion swayed, too weak from his wounds and too blinded by blood to defend himself. She stumbled over a rock in the shallows, then bent to pick it up before rushing forward, determined to fight for the man who had risked his own life for hers.

The barbarian lifted his sword and charged. At the same instant Arianna threw the rock. When it struck its target, the barbarian looked stunned and paused. That was all the time the Highland warrior needed to thrust his sword, driving his attacker backward, where he lay among his fallen comrades.

Arianna caught the Highlander just as he was dropping to his knees.

"Oh, Lachlan. My darling. You saved me." She cradled him in her arms, crooning to him as he lay, still and silent.

Up close she was horrified by the amount of blood. It soaked his plaid and ran in rivers, staining her gown and the ground beneath them.

"Please, my darling. Please don't die."

Desperate to save him, she began tearing strips of her gown and petticoats, tightening tourniquets, binding his wounds. But as quickly as she stopped the flow of one wound, she would spot more. Dozens of them. It was more than any mortal could endure.

He was slipping away from her. She could feel his life slowly ebbing with each drop of blood. And there was nothing more she could do, except tell him what he meant to her.

She bent close, pressing her mouth to his ear. "You gave your life for me, Lachlan. Perhaps it is my punishment for choosing love over honor. But I will never regret a moment of the time I spent with you. If I can never know love again in this world, know this: What I feel for you will be enough to last me a lifetime. My only regret is that our time together was too short."

She could feel the shallow rise and fall of his chest, and she knew that soon he would breathe his last. Tears filled her eyes, but she blinked them back. There was so little time, and so much more she wanted to say.

"Because of your love I can be strong enough to go back and face whatever fate is to be mine. If the new laird of the Highlands wishes me to honor my father's promise, so be it. It matters not where my duty takes me, Lachlan, for this night you taught me the importance of honoring that duty. Wherever I go, you go with me, in my heart. For I am comforted by the knowledge that I have been loved by the finest Highland warrior in the land. That love will sustain me in my time of need."

Though his eyes were now blind, he lifted a hand to her cheek, as though struggling to see her face. His lips moved, trying to form words.

She clasped his hands and bent her ear to his lips.

His voice was little more than a raspy whisper. "I know now that . . . love is not a weakness . . . but a gift. Tell . . . him that."

"Tell who?"

Arianna felt his hand go limp in hers. Saw that his chest no longer rose and fell.

An icy wind churned up the loch until it foamed and frothed with all the fury of a storm.

Her grief was all-consuming. She gathered him close and wrapped herself around him, burying her face in his neck. The tears she'd been holding back now spilled over and flowed in a torrent of misery and self-hatred.

She had cost her lover his life. It was her fault that he'd followed her here and engaged the barbarians in a battle that had been doomed from the start. How could any warrior, even the finest in the land, hope to defeat more than a dozen armed men?

She'd brought about this slaughter through her own cowardice. If she had stayed at the laird's Highland fortress and faced her fate with dignity and honor, none of this would have happened. Instead, she'd behaved like a coward, and the man she loved had been forced to pay the ultimate price.

She'd thought this loch enchanted. Instead, it was cursed. As was she. Cursed for having drawn an innocent man into her web of deceit, and ultimately, love. A love he'd fought from the beginning.

Lachlan had wanted to keep his focus on battle. Love, he believed, was a distraction. And now, because of her, he was dead.

Still holding his lifeless body, she tasted the bitter tears of her loss.

8

IN A DISTANT part of her mind Arianna seemed to hear a drumming of horses' hooves, drawing near. She was so drained by grief it seemed too great an effort to rouse herself. Through sheer effort she managed to lift her head.

Brilliant morning sunlight reflected off the smooth surface of the loch and illuminated a figure on horseback. Blinded, she held a hand to her eyes and struggled to see the one who dared intrude upon her grief.

Broad of shoulder he was, with dark hair brushing his shoulder, where a length of plaid had been tossed rakishly. The jeweled hilt of his sword shot a dazzling display of color as he slid from his horse and started toward her.

She sat up and felt her head swim. She rubbed her eyes. Was she dreaming?

"Lachlan. How can this be?"

"Oh, my darling." He hurried forward and gathered her into his arms. "When I found your bed empty and realized you'd fled the fortress, I was so afraid of what I'd find."

She framed his face with her hands, peering deeply into

his eyes. "But you were here with me. Fighting the barbarians. I saw you die."

His mouth curved into a wide smile. "What dreams you have, my love."

"'Twas no dream, Lachlan. When I reached the enchanted loch, my horse bolted and ran away."

"Aye." He pointed to the mare, tied behind his stallion. "I found her in the forest and feared the worst. You've no idea what that did to my poor heart. I imagined you lying somewhere, hurt and unable to go for help."

"It was much worse than that. The horse bolted because she sensed the presence of the barbarians."

At her words he glanced around and saw the bodies nearly hidden in the tall grass by the water's edge.

His smile faded. "Sweet heaven, love. How did you survive?"

"It was you, Lachlan. You rose up out of the loch and strangled the leader, who was dragging me back to shore. And then you engaged the others with your sword. You killed them all, Lachlan. But in so doing, you gave up your own life."

The look in his eyes was now hot and fierce as he set her on her feet. It was the same look she'd seen last night when he'd come to her rescue.

She took a step back from him, hands clenched at her sides, determined to make him believe her. "I held you in my arms until you'd breathed your last. And I wept bitter tears until I cried myself to sleep."

He pointed. "I see the spot where you slept alone."

"Not alone. You were . . ." She glanced down at the grass that still bore the imprint of her body. The spot was empty, except for a length of faded plaid.

She picked it up and stared at it, stunned. "Last night this cloth was wrapped around you. It bore the damage of a dozen knife and sword wounds. It was soaked with your blood, Lachlan. As were the grass and my gown."

She looked down at her skirt in disbelief. There were no bloodstains. Her eyes went wide with sudden fear. "Lachlan, I swear to you, I wasn't dreaming. There was a Highland warrior. It was he who slew the barbarians. And he looked so much like you, I was certain I'd lost you forever." She pressed her fingers to her trembling lips. "Am I losing my mind?"

Without a word he took the plaid from her hands and pressed it to his mouth in a gesture so loving, so tender, she could only stare. She saw a film of moisture in his eyes.

Tears? From this hardened Highland warrior?

Seeing her look of fear, he caught her hands. They were cold as ice. He drew her close and wrapped his arms around her. Against her temple he murmured, "I understand now. This was no dream, love. Nor was it a trick of the mind. I must tell you something."

She drew away a little and looked up into his eyes.

"Pembroke told you this loch is enchanted. Did he tell you why?"

"Aye. He said that a warrior gave up his life to save his wife and son from the barbarians."

Lachlan nodded. "It's true. That warrior was very brave. But something kept him from enjoying his eternal reward. There was something he needed to do before his spirit could be released from this place. And so he remained all these years, waiting for the chance to finish the task given him."

She nodded. "Pembroke said he remained here to slay the barbarians. But why now? What was so special about my life, that he should rise out of the loch to protect me?"

"He did it for me, love."

Arianna looked at him in confusion. "I don't understand."

"He saw us here, and felt the love between us. He knew how important it was to me that your life be spared."

"But what is your life to him?"

He smiled then. A smile so tender, she felt it touch her heart. "I am his son. His only heir. He gave his life once for me, when he tossed me into the falling water, along with my mother, so that we'd have a chance to live. And now he has given up his spirit as well, so that the woman I love will be spared."

"Your father?"

He nodded. "When you saw me standing on the banks

of the loch, with my sword uplifted, I was uttering a prayer that my father would show me a way to keep my honor, while still having that which my heart most desired. That desire was you, Arianna."

She closed a hand over his. "Oh, Lachlan. I had no idea. But now I understand the words you . . . your father spoke as he lay dying in my arms."

His eyes burned with an inner fire as he caught her roughly by the shoulders. "Tell me what he said. I need to know."

"He said that love is not a weakness, but a gift."

For a long while Lachlan looked out over the smooth waters of the loch, as though searching for some sign of the man he'd loved and lost. Then he looked down at the hand on his. So soft. So perfect.

"Until you kissed me, Arianna, I'd thought of nothing but the next battle. I had vowed that no woman would ever rob me of my heart, for I feared that it would distract me from my task as a warrior. My father's last words to me, when he tossed me into the waterfall, were that I must become a warrior worthy of his name. In order to keep my promise to him, I'd closed my heart to everything but war. My promise to him has consumed my life." He looked into her eyes, seeing the love there. "And then we lay together, here on the banks of the enchanted loch, and I knew what it was to love."

With a sob Arianna lowered her head, unable to bear the look in his eyes.

He caught her chin, and forced her to look at him. "What is it, love? What is the pain I see in those depths? Is there more that you haven't told me?"

She swallowed. "While my brave warrior lay in my arms, I made a vow."

When Lachlan said nothing, she forced herself to go on. "I was convinced that I'd lost you, my love. And I believed that it was my punishment for having fled the laird's fortress in the night like a coward, rather than staying and honoring my father's promise."

He gave her a gentle smile. "Now you know otherwise. I'm still here, Arianna. Your brave warrior was from the spirit world, sent to serve you in your hour of need."

"Aye. But that doesn't release me from my vow."

"What is this terrible vow that brings such pain to my beloved?"

She took a deep breath. "I made a solemn vow that I would accept my father's will and wed the laird of lairds." She felt tears spring to her eyes, but she blinked them away. She had to be strong enough to get through this. "And though it will break my heart to be wed to another, I will do so. Not only because I have promised it, but because it is the honorable thing to do. I owe that much to my father, and to my people."

His eyes narrowed on her, and she felt again the strange intensity that she felt whenever he looked at her. As though he could see clear through to her soul.

"After all that we've been through, you would wed another, Arianna?"

She touched a hand to his. "Please don't make this any more painful than it already is, Lachlan. I fled once like a coward. Now I must do what is right. But know always that I will carry you forever in my heart."

At a thundering of hooves they looked up to find the entire company of Highland warriors riding toward them. Sunlight glinted off weapons as the men dismounted and hurried forward.

Pembroke halted a few steps away and looked from his old friend to the woman beside him. "Praise heaven you found the lady unharmed."

"Aye, Pembroke. I see her nursemaid gave you my message."

The young man chuckled. "The old woman was ready to sit a horse and join us."

"And why not?" Lachlan's voice warmed with humor. "She is aware of the treasure she guards."

The two shared a smile.

Lachlan lifted a hand. "And now we must return the lady Arianna to the fortress, for the laird of lairds is planning to introduce her to his people before they are wed."

Arianna glanced up at him sharply. "You find this amusing?"

"I do, my lady. As shall you." He turned to one of the warriors and called, "When we're gone, see that those bodies of the barbarians are disposed of."

The man gave a stiff bow of his head. "Aye, my laird."

Arianna glanced from the man to Lachlan. "My laird?"

He was smiling broadly now. A smile that reached his eyes, warming them like the morning sun had warmed the earth. "It was not my choice to lead my people. But once chosen, I could not refuse. Though it humbles me, I will do my best to serve not only the Highlanders but your father and his people as well. For the promises made by my uncle will be kept by me."

He pulled himself up into the saddle, then reached down and lifted her into his arms. He lowered his voice, so that she alone could hear. "It gladdens my heart to know that my woman has vowed to wed me, regardless of how old I may grow, or how fearsome I may look."

She swallowed back the laughter that bubbled up. "Take care, my laird. If you ever keep such an important secret from me again, I may make you sorry that you ever met me."

"That will never happen, Arianna."

With his entire company of warriors watching, he lowered his mouth to hers and kissed her until her head spun and she felt the earth tilt.

As they started off through the forest, she leaned back, feeling the warmth of his arms enfolding her.

"I feel as if I'm dreaming, Lachlan."

"If this be a dream, it is one we both share." He urged his horse faster. "I've already sent a carriage to your father's keep."

"A carriage?"

He leaned close. "I thought you would enjoy having your father and sisters with you when we are wed."

"Oh, Lachlan." She turned and wrapped her arms around his waist, pressing her lips to his throat. "You own my heart. And have since first we kissed."

"It was all part of a grand plan by the fates, my love." His words wrapped themselves around her heart, and she knew they were true.

She wouldn't question the fates. She would simply take what they offered, and be grateful.

9

Sunlight burned off the mist, leaving the Highland meadows bright with heather. The hills echoed with bells ringing in the tower of the kirk, announcing the wedding of the laird and his bride.

From miles around, the villagers came to the kirk high in the hills to see the woman who had won the heart of their laird.

Already the love of these two had become the stuff of legends. Everyone enjoyed hearing about the young lass who had defied her father and fled rather than enter into a loveless marriage. The warriors who had ridden with Lachlan MacLean had added to the lore by telling of the barbarians, dead at the hand of the ghost of the enchanted loch.

It was said that these two had been fated from the beginning of time to be together.

In the knave of the kirk, Nola fussed and fidgeted over Arianna, while Glenna and Kendra flitted around their sister like bright butterflies.

"Oh, Arianna. Look at you!" Glenna couldn't stop touching the gossamer gown.

"Step aside now, the two of ye, while I dress yer sister's hair."

"I think it should be braided." Glenna picked up a length of white ribbon.

"Nay. Brushed long and loose," Kendra insisted. "And no ribbons. I think she should wear wildflowers in her hair."

"She'll wear a veil," Nola said firmly. "As did her mother, and her mother before her."

The two girls watched as she set a length of fabric as delicate as a spider's web on Arianna's head, and secured it with a jeweled comb. Then she led the bride to a looking glass. "What think ye, child?"

"Oh." Arianna studied her reflection before nodding. "Aye. My mother's gown and veil are perfect, Nola." She caught the hands of her two sisters. "Soon enough, you'll both be wearing this as well."

"Kendra was eyeing a fair warrior just this morrow." Seeing the fire in her sister's eyes, Glenna giggled. "And when she walked away, he turned and watched her."

"He did?" Kendra's anger at Glenna's tattling evaporated, and she grabbed her younger sister by the shoulders. "Truly?"

"Aye."

"Oh, Arianna." Kendra looked at her big sister hopefully. "Do you think you could learn his name?"

"I suppose I could. If you don't mind waiting . . ."

She looked up at a quick knock on the door. When her father stepped through the doorway the others fell silent. He stood there, studying his firstborn daughter.

Kendra was the first to speak. "Doesn't Arianna look beautiful, Father?"

He found it difficult to speak over the stone that had become lodged in his throat. "Aye. She reminds me of another." He crossed the room and bent to kiss her cheek. "I've never seen you glow with such happiness, Arianna. Does this mean my promise to the laird of the MacLeans no longer displeases you?"

She gave a delighted laugh. "Oh, aye, Father. How could I be displeased with Lachlan MacLean?"

"Now that I've had time to get to know him, I quite agree. He seems an honorable man. His men consider him the finest of warriors. His people speak of him with love and pride." He caught Arianna's hands and looked into her eyes. "And best of all, he makes you happy."

"Aye. He does, Father."

They could hear the sounds of happy voices as the villagers filed into the kirk and took their places alongside the many lairds and fine ladies.

Gordon Douglas gave his oldest daughter a final kiss, then draped an arm around each of his younger daughters and beckoned to Nola to follow. "It's time we joined the others."

Arianna kissed her sisters, then hugged her nursemaid.

Nola paused in the doorway. "Perhaps I should wait here with ye."

Arianna shook her head. "I need a moment alone, Nola."

The old woman nodded in understanding, then turned away and followed the others from the room.

Arianna walked to the window, which overlooked a walled garden with stone benches scattered here and there among fragrant roses.

It didn't seem possible that on this day she would be wed to the man who owned her heart. All the darkness of the past seemed to have been swept away in one rare burst of sunshine.

Hearing a sound, she turned to see Lachlan standing in the doorway. At the fierce look on his face she hurried toward him.

"What is it, love? Is something wrong?"

"Wrong?" He shook his head. "I was afraid I would blink and find you gone. How can someone so beautiful be real?"

She laughed. "Oh, I'm real enough. Touch me, Lachlan."

He reached out to touch her cheek, and she moved against his hand like a kitten.

"You see?" She turned bright, shining eyes to him.

He nodded and lifted his other hand to her face. She was stunning, with all that fiery hair framing a face so lovely it took his breath away. Her eyes seemed even greener, with the gown and veil spun of stardust.

The music of a lute could be heard, and they knew it was time to make their way up the aisle. Still, neither of them moved. They stood perfectly still, staring into each other's eyes, as though there they could read the answers to all of life's mysteries.

His voice was little more than a whisper. "Before the priest and people, I will swear my love to you, Arianna. But know this. The words I speak can't say all the things that are in my heart."

She felt her throat fill with such love, it was impossible to speak.

"I love you, Arianna, with my heart, my soul, my entire being. And I give you my word that I will do everything in my power to make you happy here in my home."

He touched his mouth to hers. Just the sweetest of kisses, and she felt the heat all the way to her core.

It had begun with a kiss. A kiss that had shattered her heart, and left it in pieces. And now it would be sealed with a kiss. One that would bind her to him for all time.

"Come, my love." He caught her hand, and together they started up the aisle, while the entire assembly smiled its approval.

Arianna walked proudly beside Lachlan, the laird of lairds, and felt her heart swell with love.

She had feared leaving her home and family to begin life in this strange new place. But what she had found was everything her heart desired. This man. His people. Enough love to last a lifetime and beyond.

She'd expected to find herself lost in a savage wilderness. Instead, she'd found paradise.

Her heart soared as she spoke the vows that would make her his wife.

She hadn't left home after all. In fact, in Lachlan's arms she'd found it.

KISS ME, KATE

❧

Marianne Willman

To the women everywhere who have turned frogs into princes through a little magic—and a lot of hard work.

*And to Nora, Ruth, and Jill
and our very own princes
Bruce, Tom, Larry, and Ky*

Prologue

THE MOON EMBROIDERED the night in black and silver while the stars sang a song as old as time. It was spring solstice, that magic night when the door between worlds opens. A mystic wind danced high over land and sea, carrying the starsong to the earth's four corners.

For those who heard it, life would never be the same.

In Chicago, at midnight, Kate Singleton heard it as she lay snuggled in her bed beneath a warm down comforter, dreaming her favorite dream. The one where her ex-fiancé broke out in warts, her boss promoted her to senior editor, and she won ten million dollars in the state lottery.

As the music wove itself into Kate's dream she smiled and turned over.

In England, near dawn, Michael Bellamy heard it as he walked through the ruins of Kingsbury Castle. He paused beside a windowless stone arch, looking out toward the shadow of the man-made hill where legend said ancient kings lay buried. Yes, there it was again, music both lovely and poignant, yet so faint he wondered if he imagined it. He closed his eyes and listened intently. But the harder he tried to hear, the more indistinct the song became. Suddenly restless, he whistled for his dog and turned toward home.

In that same moment, a tall figure materialized beside the man-made hill, with the same song ringing in his ears. Light winked from the gems in his slender gold crown and the jewels at his throat.

He stared in wonder at a night sky that was not a hollowed sapphire studded with diamond constellations—the only kind of sky he'd ever known till now—but a real sky, limitless and glowing with an infinity of stars.

Gauzy ribbons of mist gathered around him, then vanished in a flash of brilliance as the first rays of dawn struck the spot. Gathering his courage he stepped across the tenuous boundary between this strange new world and his, passing from shadow to light.

And turned into a frog.

The creature sat there in amazement, blinking its golden eyes. It tried a hesitant leap and landed wrong-side-up, with its pale belly exposed. The frog gave an indignant croak and righted itself after a short struggle.

After a series of more-or-less successful leaps, it vanished into the tall grass of the meadow.

1

Chicago

KATE WOKE EARLY on the first day of April, convinced
for at least twenty seconds that she had actually won ten
million dollars in the state lottery. When the dream faded,
her first keen disappointment gave way to the firm belief
that the dream was an omen. Something wonderful was
going to happen today; she was sure of it.

Instead, everything that could go wrong, had.

She hurried along Navy Pier in the gathering twilight
toward the soft lights of the Café Roma, like a storm-tossed
ship heading for safe harbor. The gusty wind followed her
inside, whipping her sleek dark hair against her cheekbones
and billowing the edges of the white tablecloths out like
miniature sails.

She spotted Jenny, her roommate and best friend, in the
cozy end booth by the fireplace and slipped in opposite her.

Jenny looked up from her handheld computer where she'd been crunching numbers.

"You're early, Kate. Should we ask for the menu or would you rather start off with wine?"

"Wine. Buckets of it."

Jenny's thin face lit up. "You got the promotion to senior editor!"

"No." Kate took a deep breath. "I got fired."

"What?"

"As of today, Hartland Press no longer has a children's book division." Kate fought to keep her voice level. "In fact, there is no Hartland Press. The conglomerate that bought it last month decided we weren't profitable enough."

Indignation sparked in Kate's violet eyes. "Seventy-five years of creating modern classics for children, tons of prestigious awards—and we're dumped by a company that makes glow-in-the-dark toilet paper!"

Jenny winced and reached across the table to touch her hand. "Oh, Kate! I just don't know what to say. I am so sorry."

"I don't know what to say, either. Or do. I've been walking around the city for hours, mulling over my options, and they're damned few. I can't think of anything outside of publishing that I want to do."

"You could go to New York. I know you've considered it before."

Kate's face brightened. "It might be time for a change. I suppose I could live off my savings while I look around for a new position. But whether in New York or Chicago, something interesting is bound to turn up."

Jenny clapped a hand to her mouth. "That reminds me. Something did!"

She pulled a thick white envelope from her purse. "This came special delivery for you. From London. It must be really important: the postman wouldn't hand it over until I signed for it in blood and promised him my firstborn child."

Kate laughed. "What was his name, Rumpelstiltskin?" She took the letter with its colorful stamps bearing the face of the queen of England. "Plunkett, Plunkett and Ritchie," she said. "Doesn't ring any bells."

666 KISS ME, KATE ➴ 281

"Read it, for heaven's sake. I'm dying of curiosity!"

Jenny signaled the waiter and asked him to bring a carafe of the house wine, while Kate opened the envelope and pulled out several sheets of impressively heavy vellum.

25 March 2002

Dear Miss Singleton,

It is my sad duty to inform you of the death this past November of our most esteemed client Agatha Culpepper. It has been the privilege of our firm to represent the late Miss Culpepper for more than sixty-five years. Under the terms of the will (a copy of which is enclosed herewith), you are chief beneficiary of the Culpepper estate, which consists primarily of Frogsmere, a furnished manor house with extensive gardens, situated upon twenty acres of land in East Sussex. There are also items of a more personal nature, such as jewelry and private journals, which she specifically willed to you.

Due to the unfortunate delay in locating you, there are now urgent matters that must be set in order with all good speed, and that will require your presence in England at your very earliest convenience.

All travel expenses will, of course, be charged against the estate. My secretary, Miss Golunka, will be delighted to make any and all arrangements for you.

I shall look forward to hearing from you in the very near future.

Sincerely yours,
Alfred Plunkett IV

Kate was dumbfounded. She read it a second time. *A manor house with extensive gardens, situated upon twenty acres of land!*

Then she realized what day it was and tossed the letter down. "Very funny, Jenny. You had me going. For a minute, I really believed I'd inherited an English manor."

Her friend stared at her blankly. "What are you talking about?"

"It's April first. You had one of your E-mail pals overseas send this letter as an April Fool's joke."

"No, but I wish I'd thought of it! I'm not that creative." Jenny laughed. "Which is why you're the writer and I'm a CPA."

Kate's heart was pounding so hard her hands shook. She held out the sheet of heavy paper. "You won't believe it unless you read it yourself."

While Jenny read the letter, Kate took a big swallow of her wine. A warm glow radiated through her, from the crown of her head to her toes, and it wasn't from the wine.

"I can't believe it. It's like a fairy tale!"

Jenny frowned at the sheet of vellum in her hand. "Too much so for comfort. Who exactly is this Agatha Culpepper?"

"My fairy godmother evidently." Kate's eyes danced. "And a pretty terrific one. An English manor house. *Much* more practical than a pumpkin coach and glass slippers."

"Are you saying you don't know her from Adam?"

"That's right." Kate poured more wine into both glasses. "She must be a cousin; my great-grandparents did come over from England. If my parents weren't off digging up dinosaur bones in the wilds of Brazil, I could ask my mother about it. She knows all the ins and outs of the family relationships."

"You're taking this seriously," Jenny worried. "You know what they say—'anything that seems too good to be true, *is*.' This could be a scam."

"Yes, I thought of that." Kate shrugged. "But it's not as if they're asking me for money."

". . . yet."

"Come on, Jenny. What happened to make you so cynical? Didn't you ever believe in Santa Claus, or look for elves under toadstools, or make a wish on a star?"

"Sure. Until I was six and learned that my mother was the tooth fairy." Jenny made a wry face. "And a cheap one at that—I got quarters when all the other kids on the block were getting dollars."

"Oh, the disillusionment!" Kate teased. "That explains everything."

"I may be a cynic," Jenny retorted, "but you're a hopeless romantic."

Kate grinned. "Why does 'hopeless romantic' sound like 'complete idiot' when you say it?"

"Admit it. If you found a frog on the front doorstep, you'd kiss it just in case it might be a prince in disguise."

"It would be worth risking a few warts," Kate said. "Princes are in short supply these days."

Kate checked the name and address on the envelope again. "I suppose it could be a case of mistaken identity—there's bound to be another Katherine Singleton in a city as big as Chicago. But," she added, "I'm sure Plunkett and Whosis had me checked out before sending the letter. Agatha Culpepper was probably some long-lost relative."

"Right. Or my mom the tooth fairy." Jenny's face went serious. "All I'm asking is that you look at this objectively instead of floating off in daydreams."

Kate shook her head. "The trouble with you, Jenny, is that you're always expecting a lightning bolt to zap you, even when the sun is shining. Sometimes marvelous things like this happen, right out of the blue."

"Only in the movies. You're like the kid in that old joke, digging through manure because you're sure there's a pony hidden inside it."

Kate put her chin in her hand and didn't reply at first. After staring at the letter a moment, she sighed. "All right, you've convinced me."

She slid out of the booth and went to the fireplace and held the envelope out to the fire.

Jenny bolted up and snatched it from her. "Wait! Save that address! Even if it is a scam, you owe it to yourself to contact this Alfred Plunkett. Just in case."

"There's hope for you after all!" Kate laughed. "I wasn't really going to burn it. Oh, Jenny! If this is genuine it could be the answer to my prayers."

England! Colorful images flowed through her mind. Castles and crowns. Bold knights, dragons, and maidens fair. Wicked wizards and magic spells. In fact, all the wonderful things she loved most about the old fairy tales.

Not to mention that furnished manor house—and the twenty acres with extensive gardens. Kate had always dreamed of having a lavish garden. Snug in her apartment during the snow and cold of Chicago winters, she loved to go through gardening catalogs, planning the one she hoped to have one day: masses of purple and blue larkspur, pink and white hollyhocks, velvety roses, and spiky lavender set in frothy masses of baby's breath.

She could scarcely contain her excitement. "What's the time difference between Chicago and London, Jenny?"

"Seven hours."

"Rats. It's midnight there now." Kate thought a moment. "I'll make you an offer you can't refuse. I'll spring for dinner tonight, if you'll see if you can find anything on the Internet about Agatha Culpepper, and the law firm of Plunkett, Plunkett and Ritchie."

Jenny made a wry face. "Actually, I was already planning to do that. There are some questions to ask."

Kate finished off her wine. "Why Agatha Culpepper, apparently a complete stranger, would will her estate to me?"

"Bingo."

"I don't know," Kate said, "but I *will* find out."

"Good answer."

"That little voice that whispers dire warnings in your ear talks to us optimists on occasion, too," Kate added.

And right now it was shouting at her: *"What's the catch?"*

2

MICHAEL BELLAMY PULLED his battered Land Rover
up near the edge of the cliffs and got out. The wind came
in fitful bursts, whipping his blond hair back from his forehead. The *whump-whump-whump* of helicopter blades echoed back from the ruins of Kingsbury castle and the
sandstone walls of King's Meadow Hall.

"You'd better call your crew in," he shouted to the figure
leaning against the tailgate of a pickup truck. "There's one
hell of a storm blowing up."

The other man, short and intense, turned to watch the
chopper as it circled over the white-crested waves of the
English Channel and came racketing up over the cliffs toward them. He took another drag on his cigarette.

"Can't do it, old man. The photographer isn't half done,
and this is the perfect time of day to catch the shadows of
old foundations or soil disturbances."

Michael's green eyes blazed. "Don't be a fool, Peter.
They're not familiar with the weather on this coast. I am.
The storms blow up out of nowhere, and the wind comes

barreling through the straits like a sonic blast."

Peter Jones, the producer of *Dig It*, the British Broadcasting Company's unexpected hit show, threw his cigarette stub down and ground it beneath his boot.

"Look here, Bellamy. You don't understand what producing a television series like this entails. It's not just coordinating the profs from the university with the directors and my cameramen and the sound and lighting crews."

There was always the worry that they might spend weeks digging up the place, only to find nothing more interesting than a crumbled wall dating back fifty years. The thought of it made his stomach clench.

The helicopter made another tight pass over the narrow river valley and the half-abandoned village of Frogsmere. Michael watched it swoop low, felt the reverberations of the engines in his bones, and tightened his windbreaker against the blast from the blades.

"Damn it, man, they're likely to catch a downdraft that will send them right into the cliffs!"

"If you want the BBC to underwrite a dig season at King's Meadow," Jones said, "we have to get on with the job. They're already talking of going back to the other site. I don't think you want that to happen."

Michael's jaw hardened. "I don't. Having the property surveyed and investigated by your team of specialists is certainly important. But it's not worth losing human lives."

Jones shrugged. "It's their job. They know the risks."

Evidently they did. When he signaled for them to go round once again, the chopper came down low and fast instead, shaking the ground with its thunder. So close that Michael could see the wide grin and rude gesture the pilot sent the producer.

The photographer was still shooting as the billed cap that Jones wore went whirling away, revealing the large bald spot in the center of his trademark long dark curls.

"Bastards." Jones suspected they did it just to get his goat.

He stalked off to retrieve his cap, then got in the pickup and drove off toward the place where the helicopter would eventually set down.

Michael looked away toward King's Meadow Hall. Slanting light glittered from the windows of his home and highlighted the more distant ruins of the fortified castle that had once guarded the coast.

He was dedicated to restoring King's Meadow to its former grandeur, but it was the land that he loved with a passion. He'd roamed the downs and meadows, fished the streams, and looked for buried treasure as far back as he could remember. And now it was his.

The estate had been in his family since Girard Bellemè had come over from Normandy in the train of William the Conqueror. Over the centuries it had thrived—according to some, on fortunes made smuggling French brandy across the Channel. Others claimed it was because the Bellamy ancestors had chosen their brides wisely, marrying for wealth as well as status.

Michael's father had been the exception.

At thirty-five, William Bellamy had fallen for a beautiful American actress, mistaking her childishness for innocence. He'd married her for love. The resulting divorce settlement had emptied the family coffers and left him an angry, bitter man.

Michael's mouth went hard. He had no memory at all of his mother, and wanted none. She'd abandoned him shortly after his second birthday, and had died in a car crash in California when he was seven. Her legacy to him had been a lonely childhood, a father distracted by financial worries, and a fear of losing his home.

It had been a struggle to keep King's Meadow in the family at all, much less in half-decent repair over the years, and Michael was determined to use every tool that came to hand in his battle against time and neglect. Agreeing to let the television show excavate on the estate was only the latest one.

The wind rose, buffeting him, and dark clouds swept in, killing the light. He turned back when he heard the off-kilter *whack-whacka-whack* of the helicopter and watched it tilt alarmingly. The pilot fought the throttle and brought it down safely in the east meadow in a cloud of dust and whirling leaves.

Damned fools. They cut it close!

Beyond the still-rotating blades, the chimneys of Frogsmere rose in silhouette against the angry sky. Agatha Culpepper had thrown his plans awry, leaving Frogsmere to someone in the States.

He frowned and wondered what the unknown heiress was like, and what she'd think of the old place. Not much, he hoped, once she discovered how out of the way it was and how very inconvenient an old house could be to someone used to the level of comfort with which most Yanks grew up.

While most Americans he knew had a reverence for the past, they were also too fond of central heating, shopping malls, and modern conveniences to put up with an antiquated place like Frogsmere for long. If he was lucky, she'd take one look at it and hotfoot it back to Detroit or Milwaukee or whichever Midwestern city was her home base.

Light flickered in the green depths of his eyes. Despite inheritance taxes and repair bills, he'd managed to guard and protect the assets of King's Meadow and consolidate the estate's holdings. Long ago, Frogsmere had been a part of it.

He had no doubt that if he was clever and played his cards right, Frogsmere could still be his.

3

London

KATE FINISHED OFF the last of a buttered scone and put down her linen napkin with a sigh of contentment. Through the wide windows she had a panoramic view of the Tower Bridge and the busy water traffic on the Thames.

Yesterday she'd been in Chicago's O'Hare airport, drinking ersatz cappuccino from a disposable cup. Today she was in a four-star hotel in England, sipping Earl Grey from bone china.

She jumped when the phone rang, hoping it was Jenny with some information—any information—on Agatha Culpepper before she met with the attorneys.

It was the concierge. "Your car is here, Miss Singleton."

"Thank you. I'll be right down."

Grabbing her purse from a side table, she hurried down to the small jewel of a lobby and out the glass doors. A black car with a uniformed driver was pulled up to the sidewalk carpet.

One more reason to be grateful to Miss Golunka, she thought happily.

The doorman conjured up a folded umbrella as neatly as a stage magician pulling paper flowers from his sleeve.

"Rain this afternoon, Miss."

She looked up at the cloudless blue sky. "How can you tell?"

"This is England, and it's April, Miss." The doorman smiled as he opened the car door for her. "Also, I saw the weather forecast on the telly this morning."

He shut the door and rapped on the roof to signal the driver that she was safe inside. The chauffeur saluted and shifted into gear. Kate's heart raced as they set off through the morning snarl of cars, trucks, and red two-decker buses. Everywhere she looked there were historic buildings overshadowed by tall glass-and-steel skyscrapers. Ornate medieval structures and centuries-old churches stood cheek by jowl with office towers filled with the electronic bustle of modern businesses.

It's like a time warp, she thought in wonder, and leaned back to enjoy the view.

Kate had imagined that Mr. Plunkett's offices would be in Temple Bar and the Inns of the Court, where the characters in her favorite mystery novels all seemed to work. Instead the driver continued on into the Bloomsbury district and pulled up opposite a large square filled with flowers and trees, enclosed by a high wrought-iron fence.

"Here you are, Miss." The driver held the door open as she got out.

Kate gazed at the impressive Georgian facade of number 66, all gray stone and white trim, with a glossy black door beneath a decorative arch. It looked more like the home of aristocrats than law offices.

"Are you sure this is the right place?"

"Oh, yes, Miss. There's the placard affixed to the wall d'you see?" Sunlight winked off a discreet brass plaque PLUNKETT, PLUNKETT, AND RITCHIE, BARRISTERS AND SOLICITORS.

Kate tipped the driver, took a deep breath, and approached the place. She was looking for the bell when the door was suddenly flung open by an elderly porter in a black suit.

The man bowed her into a dark-paneled hall floored in marble squares. A brass and crystal chandelier hung in the dimness above the staircase. It was like stepping into an old Agatha Christie novel. She half expected to see Hercule Poirot and Miss Marple both waiting to greet her.

Kate suddenly felt underdressed and hopelessly modern. A setting like this called for immaculate white gloves, a discreet strand of perfectly matched pearls, and a whimsical little cocktail hat with a polka-dot veil.

Not to mention a pistol in my purse with one bullet gone, she thought. *Or an enormous ruby plucked from the eye of an ancient idol.*

"Miss Singleton?" The voice shattered the mood as a figure materialized out of the shadows at the back of the hall. "You're very prompt. I am Miss Golunka, Mr. Plunkett's secretary."

Kate blinked. From Miss Golunka's telephone voice, Kate had pictured her as a thin, elderly woman with a pursed mouth and flat bosom. Despite the secretary's Gibson girl hairdo and her retro ankle-length skirt and jacket, she looked to be the same age as Kate. She had an impressive chest beneath her crisp white blouse, and a waist that Scarlett O'Hara would envy. Thick rimless glasses magnified her green eyes rather alarmingly.

"Thank you for taking care of my travel arrangements," Kate said.

"My pleasure, Miss Singleton. Please come this way."

She led Kate through a reception room and down a hall past enormous waterscapes and pastoral scenes in heavy gilt frames. The only portrait was of a beautiful young debutante dressed in Edwardian fashion. Kate caught just a glimpse of it as she passed.

Miss Golunka opened the door at the far end and ushered her into an office filled with leather furniture and lined with bookshelves. The blinds were half-open, bathing the room and its occupant in watery spring light. They might have been in any year of the past two hundred. No computer, no multiline telephone cluttered the pristine surface of the mahogany desk. Kate wondered if the quill pens in the gilded inkstand were there for more than decoration.

The portly man behind the desk leapt up from his leather wing chair. "Welcome to London, Miss Singleton!"

He made a courtly bow over her hand. "Alfred Plunkett at your service."

His elegant manners and air of complete delight at meeting her made Kate feel like a princess. In the dimness and the excitement of finally being there, it took her a moment to realize that he, too, was dressed in a style of years past. Beneath the dark green frock coat, a vest of tobacco-colored brocade stretched over a rotund belly festooned with a gold watch chain that gleamed in the filtered light.

He led her to a chair beside his desk. "And how was your flight?"

"Extremely comfortable, thank you."

"And the hotel is to your liking?"

"Very much so."

"Excellent, excellent. Haven't stayed there myself, although I hear it's quite the thing these days." He puffed out his cheeks. "We Plunketts always put up at Claridges."

He took his seat and regarded Kate appraisingly. A slight frown formed between his brows. She felt exactly the same way she'd felt in seventh grade, when Sister Mary Columba called her to the office for some infraction of the rules.

Mr. Plunkett let his breath out in a long sigh. Kate had the sinking feeling that he was going to say that he was sorry but there had been a terrible mistake. She was sure of it. "Have any relatives of Miss Culpepper come forward to contest her will?"

"Alas, she was the last of her noble branch. There were only the two children born of her parents' marriage. Honoria was the elder. A great beauty. She received offers of marriage from princes and kings."

"What happened to Honoria?"

Mr. Plunkett shook his head. "She vanished one fine summer morning, along with one of the footmen. It created a dreadful scandal. Agatha told her distraught parents that

Honoria was safe with the man she loved, and that they should be happy for her."

"I hope they were." Kate slipped a packet of documents from her purse. "I've brought everything you requested: my birth certificate and my parents' birth certificates with official seals, and a notarized copy of their marriage license."

Mr. Plunkett examined the papers gravely while she held her breath.

"All in order." The solicitor smiled. "Well, then. You've a long day ahead. I'm sure you'd like to get down to the business at hand."

He opened the desk drawer and took out an ancient-looking key ring and a manila envelope. "The keys to Frogsmere. This large ornate one opens the front door."

Kate reached out her hand. The moment her fingers touched the heavy brass key she felt a jolt of current race up her arm. For a split second the world tilted, then it righted itself. She took a deep breath and convinced herself it was only a combination of jet lag, excitement, and static electricity.

Mr. Plunkett didn't appear to notice anything unusual. "Inside the envelope," he continued, "are the keys and papers to the automobile we've hired for your use during your stay. You'll find a map with the route clearly marked and suggestions of places you might care to stop along the way."

He favored her with a wide smile. "It's not much above an hour's drive to Frogsmere, unless it rains—one never knows this time of year, does one?—or unless you run into heavy traffic leaving London."

He rose, indicating that the interview was over. "I believe that is everything for now, Miss Singleton. Please feel free to call me if you have any problems or questions."

Kate was startled. "But . . . shouldn't there be a reading of the will or something?"

"Been watching the legal shows on the American telly, have you?"

He smiled, and his tawny eyes gleamed with good humor. "Miss Culpepper's will went through probate last February. It's really more of a formality now. I'll come down to Frogsmere Monday afternoon, and we can go through everything, if that's agreeable to you?"

"Yes, of course. Thank you." She took the envelope from him. "Will I be staying at the house or at a nearby hotel?"

Plunkett chuckled. "I don't think you'd care for the amenities of the Jester's Arms—the taproom tends to get rather loud of an evening. I arranged for Mrs. Bean, Mrs. Culpepper's former housekeeper, to get the place ready for your arrival. She's agreed to come in daily. The linens will be aired and the fridge well stocked. Should you require anything more, there's a butcher shop and a greengrocer in the village. Miss Golunka has set up an account with them to cover your expenses."

Kate was impressed. "You seem to have thought of everything."

"We want your stay at Frogsmere to be quite comfortable. Oh, and should you run into problems with anything mechanical, there's Eames, who lives in the old gatehouse. He used to be coachman, and later chauffeur, to Miss Culpepper. He'll come round to look after the gardens and do odd jobs. He's quite elderly but still active. A positive wizard with anything that has gears or a motor."

She pumped the attorney for more information. "I'm still baffled as to why Mrs. Culpepper chose me as her heir."

Mr. Plunkett smiled. "I am quite certain that she had her reasons. She was inordinately fond of Frogsmere, you know, so she must have reposed a good deal of confidence in your ability to manage the place."

Kate hoped she'd live up to it. "Frogsmere. That's a very interesting name. Do you know anything about its origin?"

"I've never given it any thought. Perhaps you'll discover something in Mrs. Culpepper's journals to satisfy your curiosity," he said.

Kate had forgotten that she'd inherited her benefactor's private papers along with the other contents of the house. "Are there many of them?"

"I should say so!" The attorney's eyes sparkled. "Miss Culpepper filled a volume every year or so. And then, of course, there are her mother's journals, and her grandmother's . . . and her great-grandmother's," Plunkett added, guiding her inexorably toward the foyer.

Excitement sent shivers up Kate's spine. The same golden shivers she'd felt whenever she found a book that she wanted to acquire for Hartland Press. If these journals were any good at all, she might be able to edit them and sell them to a small publishing house.

"How far back do these journals go, Mr. Plunkett?"

"I'm not exactly sure . . . early 1700s, I believe. Miss Culpepper's ancestors believed in equal education for females, you know, and the maternal line was very strong on record keeping. And there are the household inventories going back a good way."

Kate was so excited about the journals and lists that somehow she found herself at the open front door without realizing how she'd gotten there. Mr. Plunkett held out his hand.

"A safe journey to Frogsmere, Miss Singleton. Godspeed."

There wasn't much more she would get out of him, Kate realized. "Thank you. Until Monday, then."

"Yes. I shall look forward to hearing your impression of Frogsmere."

His voice resonated with quiet reverence, but there was a glimmer of something else in his face. Kate couldn't quite place it.

"Is it very beautiful?" she asked.

This time she caught a distinct twinkle in his eye. "My dear Miss Singleton, I believe you'll be both surprised and delighted with the old place: Frogsmere is not only beautiful . . . it is utterly enchanting."

Alfred Plunkett IV stood at the window and watched from behind the net curtain until the hired car drove off with Kate inside. When the vehicle vanished around the corner, he strolled back down the corridor.

Miss Golunka was waiting for him beneath the portrait in the hall. All the former reserve between the attorney and the secretary vanished. She smiled up at him.

"Well, Alfred, what do you think?"

"My dear Sophie, she is perfect. A true lady, just as Miss Culpepper promised."

"And very pretty! Oh, Alfred, I think we may just pull this off."

The grinning porter joined them bearing a silver tray with three cut-crystal glasses of brandy. He took one himself.

"To the queen!"   •

"To the queen!" They each took a sip, then lifted a toast toward the portrait in a salute. "To Miss Culpepper," the porter said.

"To Miss Culpepper!" the others agreed.

They downed the brandy, well-pleased with their day's work. "Bring the carriage around, Frederick," Mr. Plunkett said.

"You mean the automobile," Miss Golunka corrected.

"Ah, yes. Thank you, Sophie. I miss the horses, you know," he confided, "but I find automobiles a much more satisfactory method of travel."

"And the radio and CD player," Miss Golunka added. "What marvelous inventions!" She was particularly fond of Broadway show tunes. "I'll bring the score to 'Once Upon A Mattress' along today."

She wandered off singing a tune from the musical about the rarity of genuine princesses. Her voice was slightly hoarse, and the last refrain ended in a bit of a croak.

Mr. Plunkett stood alone in the cool dimness of the hall, beaming up at the portrait. He cleared his throat.

"Well done, Agatha!" he murmured. "Oh, very well done indeed!"

4

Kᴀᴛᴇ ᴄʜᴇᴄᴋᴇᴅ ʜᴇʀ watch. "So far, so good."

She was feeling pretty cocky. Another quarter hour or so and she'd be at her destination. Once she'd gotten used to the steering wheel being on the wrong side of the car, her solo journey had been a snap—sunshine and a straight shot along the A21 from London, southeast across the rolling green Sussex Downs.

One of the first things she intended to do, after unpacking, was to look for those journals written by generations of female Culpeppers. There should be a lot of interest in them at the major publishing houses. Historians would be ecstatic but Kate hoped she could make them fascinating for everyone.

I'll sit out in the garden and read through the journals. If I'm lucky there might be enough for more than one book.

The scenery kept distracting her thoughts. Every house and shop and village she passed was awash in flowers, from pots of geraniums, painted window boxes, and handkerchief gardens in front of row houses to sprawling borders spilling along brick paths and lining the drives of private estates.

The farther she got from London the fewer houses she saw. From time to time she caught glimpses of the sea, like a soft smudge of pale blue watercolors in the distance.

Twenty minutes flew past before she realized that something was wrong. The turnoff should have taken her past the village of Battle, where William the Conqueror had defeated King Harold in 1066 and changed the course of history.

Instead she saw nothing but the undulating downs, a few ancient stands of trees that had escaped the iron foundries a hundred years earlier, and a lone cottage with a thatched roof. There wasn't even another car on the road.

Gray clouds scudded in, smattering the windshield with fat droplets. Within minutes it turned into a deluge. Kate pulled over in the shelter of a ridge and groaned. She was hungry and jet-lagged.

And very possibly lost.

She had two choices: to press on and hope she would come to a village where she could get something to eat, or turn around and go back the way she had come.

"There must be something nearby." She tried to turn on the map light. There was a faint click, but no illumination. She swore again and opened the glove box. No flashlight, but she could just make out the lines on her map in the dim glow of the small light.

Her finger traced the route she'd taken. There should have been a country lane branching off to the valley below, leading eventually down toward the sea and the village of Frogsmere.

"Damn!" That rutted "cattle track" she'd passed a half hour ago was probably the lane where she should have made a right turn.

She frowned at the map. There was a hamlet just a few miles ahead. The thought of hot food spurred her on. She put the car in gear and started up the hill. She was almost at the crest when headlights pierced the gloom.

They were headed straight at her.

Kate wrenched the wheel as far as she could toward the hedgerow. Twigs popped and cracked, their broken ends screeching along the fender, scrabbling at her side window like leafy claws.

She gripped the wheel, heart pounding louder in her ears than the sound of the driving rain upon the roof. The car fishtailed in the muck as she slammed on the brakes, and then broke through an opening in the wall of green. It careened to the right and bumped over something solid while she wrestled for control. A tremendous jolt threw her forward as the car lurched sideways. Despite the seat belt, her chin hit the steering wheel.

The headlight beams shone upward at an odd angle, illuminating the top of a stone wall. She was vaguely aware that the engine had stalled.

The passenger door jerked open. A man leaned in, his face all angles and shadows in the faint green glow from the dashboard. "Are you injured?"

"N . . . no."

"Good." All the concern vanished from his voice. "Then perhaps you might tell me what in hell you thought you were doing?"

His anger shocked Kate out of the strange calm that had come over her. "I was trying to avoid being run down by you! You were on the wrong side of the road."

He lifted an eyebrow. "I beg to differ. This is England. Unlike you Yanks, we drive on the left here. Something you would be wise to keep in mind—if your auto still runs once it's winched out of the drainage ditch!"

"Oh, God." Kate felt all the color drain from her face. She leaned back against the seat. In the disorientation of the rain and her fatigue, she'd automatically pulled off to the right, as she would have in the States.

"I am so sorry! I hope you didn't suffer any injury to yourself . . . or damage your car."

He shrugged. "A few more dents will make little difference to me—and none at all to the Land Rover. Give me your hand. I'll help you out."

She realized the car was canted at a steep angle. "I'd be grateful."

Snagging her purse with one hand, she reached the other out to him. A reassuringly firm grip closed over her fingers, and she was hauled up toward the passenger side. His arm curved around her waist, surprisingly hard and strong, as he lifted her out of the car. He set her down on the road, and Kate stood in a daze with wind and rain lashing at her skin and whipping her short hair against her cheekbones.

"This way. Careful now!"

He steadied Kate and led her across the muddy road to a battered Land Rover parked on the verge with its hazard lights blinking.

As he helped her clamber in, she had her first good look at him. A strong face with good cheekbones, firm mouth, and lean jaw. His skin was deeply tanned, his blond hair dark with rain, and his eyes the deep, shadowy green of a forest.

He raised his eyebrows. "Do I pass inspection?"

She flushed with embarrassment. "I'm sorry, I didn't mean to stare. I think I'm still in shock."

"It's my turn to apologize. I should have realized that." He frowned suddenly. "You've cut your chin," he said, turning on the dome light. "You're bleeding."

Kate raised her hand to her face. "I thought it was just rain."

He turned her face toward the light, then dabbed at it gently with a folded handkerchief. "Nothing serious. Let's get you somewhere warm before you catch your death of cold."

He turned the key in the ignition, and Kate felt a welcome blast of warm air from the heater. "I'm sorry I was so rough with you," he said. "I was afraid for a moment that you'd done yourself a serious injury."

"I understand. When I was twelve I went to the park with some friends, but decided to stop at the library on my way home, without telling anyone. When I finally got home my parents were in an uproar. They were so happy to see me safe and sound that they blistered my ears and grounded me for a month."

He smiled at her story. "I seem to recall a similar incident in my own youth. Where are you headed?"

"To Frogsmere," she said.

He sent her a surprised glance. "The village that time

and tourists have forgotten? It's very much off the beaten track."

"I'm not exactly a tourist. I'll be staying at Frogsmere Manor for a bit."

Lightning danced between the clouds, illuminating the countryside with a great blue-white flare. A look of guarded curiosity flickered over his face.

"You're the mysterious American to whom Agatha Culpepper left her estate? We're neighbors, then. I'm Michael Bellamy, of King's Meadow."

"Kate Singleton," she said, offering her hand.

He took it, enfolding her slender fingers in his, and felt a tingle race like a current between them.

She wasn't at all what he'd expected. Her voice and manners had the cheerful openness he associated with Americans, but none of the airs that seemed to imply that a country which produced fast food, video games, and air-conditioning was vastly superior to the one that had produced the Magna Carta.

No ring, he noticed. That boded well. A single woman would be less inclined to consider staying on at Frogsmere.

And despite the fact that he found her violet eyes and sense of humor attractive—or perhaps because of it—he hoped she would return to the States soon.

He smiled and released her hand. "My business in Battle can wait. I'll take you to the manor. Normally it's a fifteen-minute drive, but the bridge is out for repair. There's no telling how long the detour around it will be in this weather."

"That's very nice of you—especially after I almost caused a wreck."

"Always happy to rescue an heiress in distress," he said coolly, and put the Land Rover in gear.

He drove with the skill and ease of someone totally familiar with both his vehicle and the road it traveled. Between the roar of the engine and the howling storm it was impossible to carry on a conversation, so Kate settled back and listened to the sigh of the wipers and the clatter of the hard rain pinging on the roof as they drove through the storm.

I'll just close my eyes for a minute, she thought.

The next thing she knew, the car was jouncing through a pair of high wrought-iron gates. Bellamy muttered something she didn't quite catch.

"I beg your pardon?"

"Sorry. I thought you were still asleep."

"I wasn't sleeping."

In the light from the dash she saw amusement flicker over his face. "You dozed off a good half hour ago."

God. Kate brushed a strand of hair from her eyes. He was right. The rain was gone, and ribbons of blue threaded the scattering clouds. *I must have really been out.*

"I hope I didn't drool."

"Do you usually?"

She hadn't realized she'd made the comment out loud. Her face burned with a hot rush of embarrassment. "No one's complained so far."

"Good. Beautiful heiresses should never drool in their sleep. Or any other time, come to think of it."

"I'll make a note of that," she said, "for future reference."

Now they were driving along a cliff road with a wide view of the English Channel and the Straits of Dover. The clearing sky melded with the steel sea, without any line of demarcation between them.

"Look. You can see the village from here."

She peered out and down to the toy village below. There were a few tile-roofed buildings of local sandstone, some with half-timbering, leaning against one another shoulder to shoulder. They marched down one side of the river valley to the narrow strip of beach, where several fishing boats were pulled up on the strand. The streets looked completely deserted.

"I see why you called it the village that time forgot."

"It hasn't changed much since it was built five hundred years ago. Descendants of the original families still live in the old houses, although there are fewer and fewer of them every year. Not enough work or excitement to keep the younger generation here."

Although he intended his voice to seem casual, Kate was aware that they were strung like beads on a thin wire of tension. She thought she understood why. King's Meadow was listed in all the best guidebooks, along with the notation that it was still in the hands of the Bellamy family after almost a thousand years.

"You'd like to see the old ways preserved."

"Yes. Selfish of me, I know. But once they're abandoned they're gone forever."

Kate considered. "The best of the past should be preserved and the worst of it remembered so we don't repeat it. All the same, I'm glad to live in the present time. The world is an exciting place these days."

"And growing smaller by the minute, what with E-mail and faxes and cell phones."

"I suppose that's why I'm so delighted about inheriting Frogsmere. I can work there and still keep in contact with home."

"Then you intend to keep Frogsmere?" he asked abruptly. The moment the words were out he regretted them.

"I hope so. Does that surprise you?"

"I imagine it would be difficult to keep the place open, unless you mean to hire it out?"

Kate turned to look at him. His gloved hands were tense upon the wheel. She realized he wasn't making small talk: her answer mattered to him. She had a flash of intuition.

"Are you interested in the property yourself?"

Michael kept his eyes on the road. "Naturally. My lands adjoin it."

She didn't know why, but she suspected he wasn't being completely truthful with her.

The Land Rover's rear end fishtailed in a spray of mud, but Michael kept control. "Agatha Culpepper knew how to guard Frogsmere," he murmured. "These ruts are better than a bloody moat for keeping people out."

"I understand that she was a very private person."

"That's putting it mildly. I don't believe that she allowed anyone but the housekeeper, the handyman, and myself inside the house these past ten or fifteen years."

Kate's stomach sank. *Ah! There's the catch!*

She wished now that she'd had a room reserved at the

village inn. "Should I prepare myself for rooms filled from floor to rafters with boxes of old clothes, empty cookie tins, and stacks of yellowing newspapers? And dozens of emaciated feral cats, all yowling for their supper?"

His laughter was warm and rich. "Miss Culpepper was a most particular woman. I believe you'll be pleasantly surprised."

He slowed for a curve around a stand of hardwoods. "There's the house. You can just see it through the trees."

Frogsmere revealed itself in dappled sunshine. Surprise was Kate's first reaction. Somehow she'd formed a picture of a formal facade with turrets and a multitude of brick chimneys rising above the roofline.

The only thing she'd gotten right was the chimneys.

Frogsmere was amazing—a giant's version of a typical English cottage. Sandstone walls with great half-timbered gables and square window bays, and topped by a tiled roof speckled with moss. Leaded-glass windows sparkled in the sunlight, their diamond-shaped panes reflecting blue sky and scudding clouds.

The Land Rover pulled around the end of the house and into a cobbled courtyard formed by two wings of the structure. Michael came around to open her door and help her down.

"Go on in. I'll fetch your luggage."

Taking her purse and laptop case from the seat beside her, Kate went up the brick walk that wound through a lush perennial border. The door was of thick oak, heavily carved, beneath a tiny peaked gable.

A single marmalade cat lay sunning itself on a wooden bench beside the door. It stared at Kate, then stretched and vanished amid the tangle of greenery.

As Kate approached, the door swung open of its own accord, as if in greeting. She took it for a good omen.

She stepped into an immaculately clean hall with a stone-flagged floor and a ceiling of ornamental plasterwork between huge beams. An ancient refectory table, mellow and black with age, stood in the center surrounded by high-backed chairs covered in faded tapestry. There was nothing of the museum about it. This was a living, breathing house. It's energy was unmistakable.

The air smelled of baking pie crust—cinnamon and apples?—and the same old-fashioned furniture polish she remembered from her grandmother's house.

It was like coming home.

Michael followed her in with the suitcases and set them down on the stone floor. "Here are your bags, Miss Singleton. Shall I carry them upstairs for you?"

"Thank you, but I have no idea where Mrs. Bean has put me."

He glanced at the watch on his tanned wrist, where fine golden hairs caught the sunlight through the open door. "I'd best be on my way. I hope you'll enjoy your stay at Frogsmere, Miss Singleton."

"You sound rather doubtful."

"Life here follows the old, slow country rhythms. I imagine you'll find the pace a bit slow."

Kate lifted her chin. "I'm not that easily bored, Mr. Bellamy."

"I hope not, for your sake." His smile was pleasant but didn't quite reach his green eyes. "Good-bye, Miss Singleton."

She watched him walk away to his Land Rover, thinking how still and peaceful the countryside was in the afternoon sunlight. The only sounds were the engine starting up and the crunch of wheels on gravel as he drove off.

Kate shut the door and turned back to the hall. "And now the adventure begins!"

5

"Mrs. bean?"

There was no answer.

And there were no cats or piles of newspapers. Everything was neat and clean and so perfectly preserved it seemed as if at any moment the lord and lady of the manor might come strolling through, she in a gown of cut velvet, with a ruff of white lace framing her face, he in doublet and tights, a short cape swinging jauntily from his shoulder.

She glanced over to the staircase and did a double take. "Good grief. A suit of armor."

It was cold to her touch and wonderfully crafted, the chest plate intricately chased with a design of Saint George slaying the dragon and the helm inlaid with gold and copper. And the top of it came just to her shoulder. The owner had been a good deal shorter than her five feet five.

She tried to lift the visor to peek inside and found it heavier than she'd expected. It slipped from her grasp and shut with an alarming clang.

"That suit belonged to Sir George Culpepper, and was

worn at the Battle of Agincourt," a stern voice said from the shadows.

Kate gasped and whirled around. An older woman stood in the open doors to the parlor, her hands folded neatly at her waist. A silver chatelaine of keys hung from her black-garbed bosom.

"Mrs. Bean? I'm Kate Singleton."

"Good evening, Miss. I thought I'd stay on until you arrived, and make sure everything was set."

"That's very kind of you," Kate said, although she had the distinct impression that the housekeeper had remained for the sole purpose of judging whether or not Kate was worthy of inheriting Frogsmere.

From the woman's stiff posture and the slight frown between her brows, the jury was still out.

"I've put you in the Rose Bedchamber," Mrs. Bean announced. "It was Miss Culpepper's personal wish that you be installed there, rather than her old suite."

Although Kate was taken aback, she tried not to show it. "If Miss Culpepper selected it for me, I'm sure I'll be quite happy there."

There was a slight softening of the housekeeper's face. "The Rose Bedchamber was always reserved for the eldest daughter of the house."

Kate was touched. "How thoughtful of Miss Culpepper!"

Mrs. Bean nodded. "The mistress was ever a great one for planning, you know."

"I don't know anything about her," Kate replied. "We never met. In fact, I have no idea why she left the estate to me."

An expression flickered behind the housekeeper's pale blue eyes and vanished. "I've no doubt you'll discover it in time."

Kate had the distinct feeling that Mrs. Bean knew more than she was telling.

"You'll want to freshen up after your travel," the housekeeper said, and escorted her up the carved staircase. "Was that the Land Rover from King's Meadow that dropped you off?"

"Yes. Mr. Bellamy came to the rescue when I drove into a ditch in the rain."

"Did he, now? Well, isn't that just like him. Master Michael was always a good lad." A sudden flush rose up her face. "Or rather, as I should say, Sir Michael, as he is now."

"I stand corrected."

She followed Mrs. Bean into a charming bedchamber with painted furniture and a mirrored armoire. A marble-faced fireplace graced one wall, a wide window seat overlooking the extensive gardens the one opposite.

Kate looked out the window and was dazzled by the view.

The growing season in England was well advanced from Chicago's, and the flower beds were filled with the dappled colors of an impressionist painting. It was the garden she'd always dreamed of having, but ten times larger. And not a weed in sight. "Is there a gardener?"

"Eames takes care of the lawns and flower beds. But it was Miss Culpepper who always decided which plants went where and such."

A door on one side led to an adjoining bathroom with a dressing table and a claw-footed tub, and another opened to a bright sitting room with a view across the cliffs to the sea.

Kate's eye was drawn to the portrait over the fireplace. It portrayed a young woman in a summer dress of white chiffon, against a background of greenery. She was lovely.

"What a beautiful woman! Is that Miss Culpepper?"

"It is her sister, Honoria."

"The sister who ran away," Kate said. "Mr. Plunkett mentioned her."

"They were twins, you know. Born here at Frogsmere, minutes apart. Honoria on the stroke of midnight and Agatha shortly after."

The shadow of a bird passed by the window, and Kate looked out. The Channel was a wide swath of blue silk hemmed in by the green velvet cliff tops. A broken gothic wall thrust up against the paler sky.

"What is that ruin?"

"That would be the south wall of the lady chapel at

Kingsbury Castle. It's on the grounds of King's Meadow."

"King's Meadow. That's where Mr. Bellamy"—she caught herself—"where Sir Michael Bellamy lives?"

"Yes, he moved home two years ago, after old Mr. Bellamy died. And good it is to have him there!"

She checked the watch pinned to her bosom. "If there's nothing else you want, Miss, I'll be off home. If you're feeling peckish, there's a nice stew of beef and some sliced ham in the fridge, and a caramel flan with poached pears for pudding."

Kate was so delighted she could have hugged the woman. "So that's the wonderful fragrance that greeted me when I came in the door. Thank you so much! Left to myself, I can't do much more than make coffee and toast and peanut butter sandwiches."

The housekeeper looked horrified. "Since I'll be coming in daily to pick up, I'll cook up a little something for you before I leave, the same as I used to do for the old mistress. I'm one as likes to keep her hand in, and there's no one to cook for at home these days, with all my lads gone off to work on the North Sea oil rigs.

"I'm off for home now, Miss. I'll lock up behind me when I leave."

Kate was still at the window looking down at the garden when she heard the sound of the front door closing. A short time later she saw Mrs. Bean on a bicycle, pedaling along a path that led down to the village.

A stillness descended upon Frogsmere, and a sense of welcome wrapped itself around Kate like a warm chenille shawl. She went through the house, peering into a dim library, a large formal dining room, and a long drawing room with windows opening to a terrace and the gardens beyond.

As she looked around, Kate was mentally putting her stamp of ownership everywhere. The small parlor would make a wonderful study, with her laptop set up on the table in the window bay, and her photos and favorite books on the shelves flanking the fireplace. She could envision herself working on the book of fairy tales she'd start writing here, free of the noise and distraction of city life. Oh, if only she could keep Frogsmere!

Don't get too excited, she cautioned herself. *You have no idea if you can even afford to pay the inheritance taxes, much less the upkeep on a place like this, even for a short time.*

She went upstairs to unpack, and the white bed with its rose and white curtains looked so comfortable that Kate couldn't resist trying it. She imagined spending rainy nights reading tucked in it, with a fire in the hearth and a glass of wine on the skirted table beside the bed.

Thwump!

Thwump! Thwump!

"What on earth?" Kate went to the window and looked out, but couldn't discover the source of the sound.

Down in the maze of iris and gladiolus stems, a small green frog attempted another leap for the sill of the open library window. It missed. Again.

Thwump!

The frog sighed disconsolately, and hopped softly away to nurse its aching head.

6

THE VILLAGE OF Frogsmere dozed in the sun as the elegant old touring car drove along the cobbled High Street. Miss Golunka picked up the speaking tube.

"Frederick, let me out by the greengrocers, if you please."

Mr. Plunkett put a hand on her arm. "My dear Sophie, do you think that is wise?"

"I missed my lunch," she said, eyeing the display in the window, where a cloud of fruit flies hovered over a platter heaped with ripe peaches and plums and glistening clusters of grapes.

Mr. Plunkett sighed. "I fear you have more than lunch in mind."

Miss Golunka smiled. "You needn't worry, Alfred. I know what I'm doing."

The town car glided to a stop beside Michael Bellamy's Land Rover. "I'll only be a minute," she promised.

The inside of the greengrocer's shop was dim and her mouth watered at the lovely scents that hung rich upon the air. Her green eyes shone and her pink tongue curled in anticipation. She sidled toward the window, unnoticed by either Michael or the elderly storekeeper, who was weighing a bag of peaches on his balance scale.

"When I was a lad," the merchant said, "everything sold here was grown in and around Frogsmere. Not like today, when it comes from foreign places." He shook his head at the wicked ways of the world.

Michael smiled. "It's hard to see the old ways go, Jenkins. But I must say I'm delighted to have peaches in April and asparagus in February."

"Hmmmph," the old man said. "I'm agin change. It won't be the same with somebody new at Frogsmere Manor. Miss Culpepper was a true lady. The last of her generation."

"I think you'll like the new owner," Michael answered, as he took the bag of peaches. "She's American. Very pleasant and quite striking."

Jenkins grinned suddenly. "Aye, Miss Culpepper showed me a photograph of the lass once. Pretty as a May morning. Between having a new mistress at the manor, and all those BBC people running about, things are bound to get lively this summer."

Miss Golunka glanced over at them from where she'd been discreetly sampling the delicacies in the greengrocer's window. Something in Michael Bellamy's voice had caught her attention.

So, he is interested in her, is he?

She smiled to herself, realizing there were ways to use this knowledge to her advantage. She gave a dainty wave of her hand and two heads of cabbage transformed into pink geraniums in green glazed pots. Next she produced a tiny vial from her handbag, and took off the silver cap.

A shower of golden sparkles dusted the leaves and petals of the geranium on the left. It sparkled for several seconds and became the most lovely geranium in all the world. A veritable queen of geraniums.

Miss Golunka smiled and took the other pot up to the counter. "How much for this, Mr. Jenkins?"

The shopkeeper frowned. "Where did you find that?"

"Over by the door. It will make a lovely gift."

Michael was on his way out, but he caught sight of the other geranium in its solitary glory. He picked it up and turned back to the counter, smiling absently at Miss Golunka as she passed him on her way out.

"Add this to my bill, Jenkins."

When he was alone again, Mr. Jenkins came around from behind the counter, scratching his head. He couldn't for the life of him figure out where those geraniums had come from.

Nor where all the flies had gone.

Meanwhile, Miss Golunka reached the town car and got in. Mr. Plunkett was surprised. "I thought you were going in for lunch, not posies."

"And why not both on such a lovely day?" she said, and burped daintily into her lace handkerchief.

Something rolled out of her pocket to the floor of the car, and he bent to retrieve it. "Oh, dear, Sophie. The lid is loose on this vial you dropped. I hope it wasn't your Love In Bloom potion!"

"Do you think I would be so careless with such a potent spell? And, even if I were, it only works on those who are already attracted to one another."

"Ah, then there is no danger."

Miss Golunka folded her hands in her lap. *I wouldn't say that,* she said, but only to herself. She smiled at her reflection in the window.

One does what one must.

After unpacking, Kate went exploring. Somewhere in this wonderful old house must be clues to why she'd inherited the place. Perhaps Miss Culpepper had left her a note or letter tucked away.

Kate searched the desk in her sitting room and the one in the master suite that had belonged to Agatha Culpepper, to no avail. The library was next on her agenda, and she descended the stairs just in time to see the Land Rover pull up in the drive.

A thrill that was part nerves and part pleasure ran through

her as Michael Bellamy got out. Kate moved away from the window and opened the door.

Sunlight glinted from his fair hair as he came up the brick walk, carrying a potted geranium in a pot of glazed celadon. "A housewarming gift," he said, presenting it to her. "I saw it in the village, and thought of you."

"Thank you, it's lovely."

No more so than you, he thought. A flush rose over his face. For a horrible moment he was afraid he'd spoken aloud. He felt confused and off balance. He couldn't recall the last time he'd brought a woman flowers on the spur of the moment—nor the last time he'd blushed like a schoolboy in one's presence.

"I hope that you are fond of geraniums. Some people don't care for their scent."

Kate shook her head. "I love their odd, peppery fragrance."

"I'm glad. They smelled a bit like cabbage, I thought."

She bent her head over the blossoms, and as she inhaled she had the odd sensation that she breathed in tiny sparkles of light. "They do, just a little bit."

Their eyes met over the top of the bright blooms. It seemed impossible for either to look away as the seconds stretched out. *How green his eyes are,* she thought, and felt her heart flutter.

The spell was broken as something came flying off the little bench beside the door and shot between them. Kate stepped back, stumbled, and almost dropped the flowerpot. Michael caught her in one arm and the geraniums in the other.

He was quick and strong, and as his mouth hovered near hers briefly, she had the burning desire to kiss him. She fought it and regained her balance.

"Thank you. Now you've saved me twice in the same day."

"Wretched frog," he said, eyeing the creature half hidden in the grass. "Go away, you beastly creature, before you find yourself dipped in breading and popped into a hot frying pan."

The frog blinked and bounced away as if on springs.

"A frog? I wasn't sure what it was," Kate said. "I just had a glimpse of something dark and glittering."

"He's gone now. I'll be on my way again," he said. "I just wanted to warn you that there will be a good deal of noise around here in the coming weeks. There's going to be a BBC film crew following a team of archaeologists around while they do some preliminary site work at King's Meadow."

Kate was immediately interested. "What are they looking for?"

"High ratings for the show," he said with a laugh. "At least for the producer and the director."

"I was thinking more of historic finds," she said wryly.

"The archaeologists will find an embarrassment of riches. In addition to the ruins of the medieval church, there could be any number of other eras on the property, from prehistoric hut circles to traces of the Roman occupation of the area. Mrs. Crane, the lead archaeologist, says that there have likely been settlements in the meadow going back to the Stone Age. They'll be here all summer, so I hope the noise won't be too much of a bother," he said.

"It's no problem," Kate assured him. "After all, how much noise can a team of archaeologists make?"

"More than you would imagine," he said. After an exchange of good-byes, he walked back to the Land Rover and drove off toward King's Meadow. His nose still prickled from sniffing the geraniums, as if he'd breathed in sharp little golden stars.

Where the devil did that come from? he thought. He'd never been one for fanciful flights of imagination and it couldn't be spring fever. He was well past the age of mindless infatuation. Had Kate Singleton managed to get under his skin in the very short time they'd spent together? Or was it something entirely different?

He headed down the road, uneasy and scarcely aware that his vehicle held the faint odor of cabbages. As he pulled into his own drive a few minutes later, his mind wasn't on flowers or vegetables, but on Kate Singleton.

He wondered what she would have done if he'd given

in to that almost overwhelming urge to kiss her.

There was, he decided, only one way to find out.

Kate was restless after he left. She could still feel the strength of his arm around her as he'd saved her from falling. She could still feel that dizzying impulse to wind her arms around him and touch her lips to his firm mouth.

Spring fever, she thought, as she slipped out through the terrace doors.

A pale slice of moon rose just above the trees in the darkening sky. The soft sounds drifting in were so subtle that she couldn't pinpoint when she'd first become aware of the low chorus of frogs and tree toads singing in the gathering dusk.

Chirr-chirr.

Ritchie-ritchie-ritchie.

She followed the brick path in the twilight, through the formal beds and down stone steps to the lower level. One side held a kitchen garden behind a painted fence, the other an old-fashioned knot garden of herbs and flowers. The lowest level was the cutting garden that ran all the way down to the meadow.

The amphibian chorus was just warming up as she reached it, one group starting up and another joining in, like a choir singing roundelays:

Ritchie-ritchie

Zeet-zee-zeet-zee

Chirr-chirr-chirr.

And the counterpoint of a lone bullfrog: *Ga-lunk. Ga-LUNK!*

It brought back happy memories of summers spent on her grandparents' farm in Indiana with her cousins, chasing fireflies and watching for falling stars.

It was full dark now and the stars were out in force. The air had turned chill while she listened to the peepers singing, and she hadn't taken a jacket along. Kate decided to go back, and hurried up the path and into the house. There was a rustling in the shrubbery. A frog came leaping in great, desperate hops through the wild grasses to where Kate had stood only a few moments earlier.

The frog sat on a tuft of grass, its yellow throat pulsing. The creature hopped up to the terrace, sucked in a deep breath and filled the night with its ardent call: *Kizzmee, kizzmee. Kizzmee, kizzmee.*

A light went on in the kitchen at the back of the house. The frog hopped closer. *Kizzmee,* it sang. *Kizzmee.*

Although it sang its heart out, the door remained firmly closed.

For several minutes the frog stared up at the house with its great bulgy eyes. Then the frog turned and went leaping away toward the meadow, the jewels in its tiny gold crown flashing in the moonlight.

7

KATE WAS INURED to the noise of city traffic, but an earsplitting racket snapped her out of dreams and left her disoriented. She groped for her watch on the nightstand. Seven A.M. on a Saturday morning.

If there isn't a law against it, she thought indignantly, *there ought to be.*

Then she blinked. She wasn't in her apartment, but at Frogsmere, out in the middle of nowhere. So what on earth was that ungodly noise?

She tottered to the window and pushed the heavy draperies aside. A bulldozer rumbled toward the lower garden in a way that meant business. Further on she saw another two men conferring beside a yellow machine with a long arm ending in a clawed metal bucket.

She threw on jeans and a cable-knit turtleneck, ran a brush through her straight dark hair, and went outside to discover what was going on.

The cool morning air reeked of diesel fuel and echoed with the clank of metal treads. Cutting past a garden shed and a row of beehives, she let herself out through a wooden gate and into the meadow. The dozer made another pass, this time with lowered blade, and sliced the top layer of soil away as neatly as a knife scraping frosting from a cake.

He was also peeling away a wide swath of the herbaceous border planted there. Yellow daffodils, purple Siberian irises, and bright English primroses lay uprooted and crushed among the clumps of damp earth. Kate started running. The mechanical beast ignored her and began tearing off another strip.

Kate waved her arms and shouted. The driver slowed and put the machine in idle. He tipped his yellow hard hat in her direction.

"Begging your pardon, Missus, but you hadn't ought to go running out in front of me like that. You might get hurt."

"What are you doing?" she called up to him.

"Laying the first trench," he said, as if that explained everything.

"Through the middle of the flower beds?"

"Well, that's where the foundations are," the man told her.

"Miss Singleton!"

Kate turned and found her rescuer of yesterday beside her. She hadn't heard his approach over the roar of the bulldozer. "They've dug up part of the garden," she said indignantly.

"I am so sorry, Miss Singleton," he said to her. "There's been an error made."

He addressed the driver. "The site map is wrong, Harry. It was marked on a piece of clear acetate, and the tech who photocopied it reversed the image. You're to begin the trench off the other side of the ruins."

"Yes. Right." The man tipped his hat to Kate and put the dozer into gear. It clanked off across the meadow.

"What on earth is going on?" she asked, watching the machine's treads flatten the grasses and wildflowers.

"He's with the *Dig It* crew the BBC sent down." He saw her blank look. "It's a television show. They'll spend the weekend laying test trenches and uncovering foundation walls or other sites deemed of archaeological interest. The real work will start later."

Kate frowned. "I thought they had to be so careful—dental picks and sable brushes—but they're using heavy equipment!"

"Once they get the turf stripped, it will be painstaking trowel and brush work. There are indications of both a Bronze Age settlement and a Roman fortified villa in the meadow, and they're hoping to make significant finds."

She was interested despite herself. "What are they expecting to uncover?"

Bellamy smiled. "A mosaic floor or a gold torc or two would do very nicely. Anything that will further knowledge and keep the public entertained—and, hopefully, interested in funding future projects. There is a lot of history to salvage in the area."

Kate knelt down beside a clump of shredded lilies. "Well, there's no hope of salvaging any of these poor plants. The roots are destroyed."

"Make me a list of what you've lost," he said. "I'll see that they're replaced."

She rose, brushing damp earth from her palms. "Thanks, but I won't hold you to it. Mainly because it would be a waste of my time to try and dig through that huge mound of dirt in search of torn stems and crushed petals."

He nudged a mass of undefinable vegetation with the toe of his boots. "Yes, it would be effort wasted." He regarded her intently. "If I can't replace the plants, will you at least accept an invitation to dine at King's Meadow with me this evening? I was thinking of having a small dinner party."

His invitation had caught her off guard, and Kate was flustered. "That's kind of you. I'm not sure how I should address you, Sir Michael . . ."

He flashed her a smile. "Just Michael, please. I believe you Americans don't put much stock in titles."

"You're pulling my leg. We're the biggest title snobs in the entire universe," Kate laughed, "and I can tell from that twinkle in your eye that you know it's true."

"All the more reason to dine with me, then."

Kate still hesitated. "I really didn't bring anything suitable for a dinner party."

His smile deepened, and his green eyes crinkled at the corners in a way that charmed and disarmed her.

"Are you picturing a formal party with footmen in powdered wigs? If so, you'll be disappointed. I have something simpler in mind: just salad and chicken Florentine, with a little wine thrown in. The BBC photographer invariably shows up in black denim jeans and turtleneck."

She smiled up at him. "I think I can handle that."

"Good. I'll send the car for you at seven. And now I'd better see what the crew is up to."

Kate said good-bye and watched him lope away, her heart beating just a little faster than it had before. She found herself attracted to him, and had the impression that it was mutual. And there was something so familiar about him . . .

He moves like a runner, she thought as he bounded down the steep slope to the meadow. *All economy and fluid grace.* But by the time he reached the BBC crew he was limping slightly.

Suddenly she remembered why his name and face seemed familiar. She should have recognized him from the news reports. Michael Bellamy was the triathlete, who'd lost his shot at an Olympic medal when he pushed two children out of the way of a speeding car. CNN had shown coverage of the tragedy over and over. The terrible injuries he'd sustained had ended his promising career and opportunities for lucrative endorsement deals.

Most people had called him a hero, but some had called him a fool.

He'd vanished from the public eye during his long months of physical therapy. The queen had knighted him for valor. Kate had seen photos of him at the ceremony three years ago. A KNIGHT IN SHINING HONOR, one newspaper had captioned it.

But except for the occasional "Where Is He Now?" feature on TV or in magazines, people seemed to have forgotten his existence.

Kate never had. His bravery and sacrifice of his dreams

had touched her and she was glad to know he'd recovered so well despite everything.

She watched him as he moved among the crew, talking to first one and then another, and she smiled. He lifted his head and waved to her, and a thrill ran through her.

In an age when being famous for "being famous" was considered a virtue, real heroes seemed to get lost along the way. But Michael Bellamy was different. He seemed to be a man of high principles and great courage. *Knowing him,* Kate thought, *is a privilege.*

He had character, integrity, and charm. *Not to mention those gorgeous, gold-lashed green eyes,* Kate murmured as she strolled back to the house.

A few seconds later, the pile of torn earth and ripped plants trembled, and a small green frog popped out. It had lost its jeweled crown amid the debris. With a leaf stuck to its head and a piece of grass hanging down crookedly over one eye, it looked like an amphibian version of a drunken pirate.

Shaking them off, the frog jumped over the mangled flowers and headed after Kate.

8

As KATE JOGGED back toward the house, she almost tripped over a fat frog squatting squarely in her path. The creature tried to leap up, but its aim was off. The silky green body flipped in midair and tumbled end over end before landing on its back.

"Poor little thing. You can't hop very well, can you?"

Kneeling beside it, Kate scooped the frog up in her hands. It rolled its eyes in alarm, but didn't try to escape. There was an odd dent running in a circle around the top of its head.

"You're in no shape to take care of yourself."

Cradling it gingerly against her, she went back to the manor.

When she reached the house, she realized belatedly that she had no idea of how to apply her first-aid skills to a frog. Didn't they have to keep their skin wet? She wasn't sure. The only thing she knew about their needs was that— oh, God!—they ate live bugs. "I hope you're recovered by morning," she told it, "or you're going to starve."

She went through the side entrance to the kitchen, a large, comfortable room with a stone floor and glass-fronted cupboards on two sides. There was a lumpy armchair pulled up near the old red-enameled AGA, with its intimidating multiple burners and triple oven. In Kate's world an AGA was like nuclear power: its inner workings would forever remain a mystery to her.

She placed the frog in the center of an empty fruit bowl on the scrubbed kitchen table and slipped a plate over it to keep the creature in while she searched the kitchen for a more suitable container.

As she rooted around in the cupboards, Kate realized a phone was ringing faintly somewhere. She found it, old-fashioned and heavy, on a stand in the hall. "Hello?"

Jenny's voice came crackling over the line. "Aren't you supposed to say 'Frogsmere Manor' or something a little more dignified?"

"Obviously you've confused me with a butler."

"Well, no one who knew you would ever confuse you with a cook," Jenny said, laughing. "Did you get my E-mail?"

"No. I haven't even taken my laptop out of its bag yet." A line formed between Kate's brows. "I wasn't expecting to hear from you by phone. Is everything all right?"

"I'm fine. How's your adventure going?"

Kate laughed softly. "Far better than even an optimist like me could ever have predicted. Frogsmere is lovely, the weather has cleared—and I've been invited to dine at the private home of Sir Michael Bellamy."

There was a tiny gasp from the other end of the phone line. "Well, that puts my news to shame! Tell me he's grown fat, bald, and cranky."

"No can do." Kate's face grew warm. "He's gorgeous and charming."

"My news isn't nearly as exciting," Jenny said, "but I have solved the riddle of why Agatha Culpepper left you her estate. I've been fishing the deep waters of the Internet, and I reeled in some big information. Does the name Trixie Pickering ring any bells?"

The name instantly conjured an image of a thin, white-haired woman with wire-rimmed glasses and a wide straw hat, standing before a rioting mass of larkspur and foxglove and hollyhocks.

Kate smiled. "You know it does. It took two years, but I acquired the American rights to her books for Hartland Press."

Trixie Pickering had been a writer and illustrator of award-winning children's books. The characters from her delightful *Hedgehog Chronicles* and *The Fairies in My Garden* series had been loved by children and adults for more than fifty years.

Although they'd never met, Kate and Trixie Pickering had corresponded through the writer's London publisher and developed a friendship. After that, letters had flown across the Atlantic like clockwork, decorated in the margins with clever little sketches of elegant fairies and of cuddly woodland creatures dressed in high Victorian style. Kate had treasured and saved every letter.

"Trixie passed away last winter at the age of ninety-three," she said softly. "I was very fond of her, and I miss her very much."

"She must have liked you, too," Jenny said. "Because that's why you got your inheritance."

"I'm confused. Was she a friend of Agatha Culpepper?"

Jenny's laughter came through the phone as though she were standing beside Kate. "Closer than that. Listen to this: Trixie Pickering's birth name was Agatha Beatrix Pickering Culpepper. Agatha and Trixie were one and the same. She must have thought you knew."

"She never said a word." Tears choked Kate's voice. "I'm practically speechless."

"That would be a first," Jenny teased. "Next thing I know, you'll be learning to cook instead of nuking frozen food when it's your turn to make dinner. Is there a microwave at Frogsmere, or are you dining out of a peanut butter jar these days?"

"I've hit the jackpot," Kate said. "Her name is Mrs. Bean and she's promised to cook for me every day. It would break your heart if I told you about the beef stew and caramel-pear flan I had for dinner yesterday. So I won't say another word."

"Just don't let her quit until I make it to England in June."

They talked another ten minutes and finalized their plans for Jenny to come out and spend several weeks at Frogsmere. When they hung up Kate was bemused.

All the pieces were in place now, and she saw the pattern: Trixie Pickering, as Agatha Culpepper, had not only gifted her with a wonderful estate, but with the opportunity of a lifetime.

Kate could stay on at Frogsmere and edit those journals Mr. Plunkett had mentioned. The news of their existence would make a big splash in the publishing world.

But first she'd have to find them.

Kate dried her eyes, blew her nose, and tried to assimilate everything she'd learned. If Agatha Culpepper's journals showed any of the flair exhibited by her writings under the name Trixie Pickering, Kate hadn't the slightest doubt that she could get them published.

She lifted her chin and addressed the air, where she was sure the shade of her benefactor hovered. "I'll fulfill your trust in me," she said. "I'm going to read your journals and edit them, just as you intended. And I'll take good care of Frogsmere," she added fiercely. "I swear it."

A thunk from the table made her jump. She'd forgotten the frog. It leapt up in the ceramic bowl, hitting its head against the plate on top. She rose and peered beneath the plate. The frog was lying on its back, stunned.

First things first. After searching through the cupboards a bit more, she discovered a footed glass trifle bowl.

Kate put some water in it, set it on the countertop, and put a tile trivet in the center to make an island. She then placed the frog in the bowl. "Here you go, fellow."

The frog splayed its front feet on the trivet and leapt on top. It overshot the mark and toppled off the other side, where it lay panting.

"Not too bright." She picked it up carefully and set it on

the trivet. "Really, I don't know what to do to help you," she said.

The frog gazed up at her raptly. *"Kizzmee, kizzmee."*

She laughed out loud. " 'Kiss me'? Whatever happened to plain old 'ribbet'?"

Was that odd little croak where the fairy tale of the frog prince started? she wondered.

"Kizzmee, kizzmee," the creature said, even louder this time.

Kate leaned down and looked into those round golden eyes. "Sorry, Your Majesty. I'm afraid you've got the wrong girl."

And that was when everything happened.

The frog gave a mighty leap and smacked her right in the mouth. She grabbed at the table for support, but the oilcloth tablecloth came off instead. The glass bowl went flying against the ancient AGA, where it broke into a dozen pieces, and Kate fell back against the cupboard behind her, banging her head. The air sparked and sizzled like a downed electrical wire.

When the dazzle of light vanished, so had the frog.

A man dressed in shiny green silk from head to toe lay in the shadows beneath the table, blinking up at her.

9

"I'M DREAMING!" KATE said. "I must be."

She closed her eyes tight. When she opened them again, there was nothing on the floor but the dirt she'd tracked in on her shoes and the small green frog.

Kate stared at it. The frog stared back.

She closed her eyes again and counted to ten. When she opened them, it was still just a frog.

Then she realized that the long green form on the floor was the oilcloth she'd pulled off the kitchen table when the creature had leapt at her.

"Jet lag," she muttered, rubbing her temples. After all, it was the middle of the night back home in Chicago.

Her mouth felt numb where the frog had collided with her face. She'd have to ice it down, or show up at King's Meadow tonight with a fat lip.

"You're more trouble than you're worth," she scolded. She scooped the frog up again, opened the screen door, and carried it to the edge of the shady terrace. "And you're better off out here. As for myself, I'm going back to bed."

The frog heard the door lock firmly into place, and hopped disconsolately away into the garden.

Kate was too revved up to go back to sleep. Life at Frogsmere was proving to be a lot more interesting than she'd expected: first the early wake-up call via bulldozer, then the revelations about Agatha Culpepper, followed by that peculiar optical illusion that had made her think, for one startled moment, that the frog had changed into a prince!

And this evening she'd be dining with a very attractive man—a knight, no less—and the director and crew from a BBC production.

She could hardly wait to see what the rest of the day would bring.

Kate fixed herself coffee and toast, and ended up scalding one and burning the other. She opened the casements and set off to search out Agatha's journals while the smoke cleared.

The shelves of the library were filled with an assortment of books jostling for space: mysteries, romantic intrigue, fantasies, and other popular fiction stood cheek by jowl with volumes of history, poetry, and classical literature. There was no sign of the journals she sought among them.

On her way through the house, Kate discovered a door she hadn't noticed before, leading off the great hall. It was set so cleverly into the paneled wall that she wouldn't have seen it, except that it stood slightly ajar.

She pushed it open and found herself in a narrow passageway that ended in a charming room with a stone fireplace and thick rounds of bull's-eye glass in the windows. Kate realized that this ancient room with its wide-planked flooring and serene air was part of the original Tudor house. She stepped closer to read the letters carved above the hearth: HEART'S HOME.

A long table at one end served a single chair pulled up in the center. A leather tray held a neat stack of papers to one side and an old-fashioned ink stand of gilded brass and cut glass sparkled in the light.

She knew that this was where all the Trixie Pickering books had been written.

She admired the satiny wood of the Welsh cupboard, which was familiar to her from the books' illustrations, and took down a tall china cup. There was a folded scrap of paper inside. She opened it and scanned the sentence written there:

"This is where Pixie Jack hid from the children in the first of the Hedgehog books."

She unlatched the casement window and looked out. The view framed in the window was familiar from the Fairy Garden series. Kate leaned over the sill. And yes . . . she broke into a smile. "There's the bronze sundial where the little lost fairies sunned themselves."

Kate hadn't known that the places in the famous books were taken from real life. She doubted that anyone had.

She knew then that she had found her life's work. Not only would she edit the journals, she would have the privilege of writing the definitive biography of Trixie Pickering, one of the world's most beloved storytellers.

In her mind's eye, she saw a fabulous book that she would put together, with Trixie Pickering's luminous illustrations set side by side with photographs of the actual places that had inspired them.

She knew that she could never, ever, sell Frogsmere. Of all the places on the face of the earth, this was where she was meant to be.

Heart's Home.

Kate was nervous as she waited for her ride to King's Meadow. She'd changed her clothes three times, but nothing she'd brought with her seemed suitable. She'd finally gone with pale gray slacks and matching jacket and a red silk shell, hoping it struck the right balance of informal chic. A pair of strappy Italian sandals had won out over the others she'd brought in her suitcase, but she was still rethinking them when she saw the flash of a silver BMW through the drawing room windows.

She was surprised to see Michael Bellamy get out from behind the wheel. He was dressed in beautifully tailored slacks and a crisp white shirt and carried a leather aviator's jacket slung over his shoulder.

There was approval in his face when he saw her. "You look lovely," he said. "And you're prompt. I was expecting to cool my heels a bit."

She raked a hand through her smooth, straight hair, and it swung back into place. "Foolproof hair," she told him. "Something every career woman should have."

He escorted her out to the BMW. "You're an editor of children's books, I understand."

"I was with Hartland Press for six years. Unfortunately the company ceased to exist three weeks ago."

"That's too bad," he told Kate. "I'm truly sorry to hear it."

And yet, she thought, *he doesn't seem particularly sorry.*

In fact, for a fraction of a second his smile had widened before he'd caught himself. She was woman enough to hope that meant he was interested in her, and looking forward to her staying on at Frogsmere for a while.

They arrived at King's Meadow as the sun was setting in a wash of golden light. It was an impressive time of day to view the estate, with long shadows stretching away and every window seemingly on fire.

"It's beautiful," she said, awed by the impressive facade.

"Not as old as Frogsmere, but it has its charms."

"Frogsmere could be dropped into it three or four times, with room to spare," she said.

"Yes, it's far too much space for a bachelor like myself," he admitted, answering the question uppermost in her mind.

The inside of King's Meadow was as well proportioned and beautifully cared for, all mellow wood and muted colors, with antique furnishings polished to a satin sheen. The Oriental rugs and cozy chairs in the drawing room had the comfortable shabbiness that comes with long and loving use.

"Your home is very lovely," she said. "I can't imagine what it must be like, to live in such a beautiful place, surrounded by so many family heirlooms."

"I spent fifteen years on a sheep station in the Outback," he answered. "That helps me keep a sense of proportion. King's Meadow will, presumably, be standing here another three hundred years, when I am nothing but a name in the family Bible. I remind myself every day that it has only been loaned to me, in trust."

Kate was so busy taking it all in while he poured her a glass of wine that it took her a minute to realize there were no signs of other guests.

"Where is everyone?"

His green eyes danced with mischief. "If you must know, I decided I would rather have you all to myself on your first visit to King's Meadow. There will be plenty of time to meet them in the days ahead."

Kate regarded him over the rim of her glass. "I don't know if I should be flattered or annoyed that you lured me here under false pretenses."

"Take your pick—although I'd prefer you to feel flattered. I meant it as a compliment." Again that flash of amusement came and went. "I admit it was selfish of me— but I can only listen to so much talk of potsherds and soil disturbances and f-stops without going mad."

"I see. You provide the dinner and I provide the entertainment?" Her smile softened the words.

"Something like that," he agreed. "And just in the nick of time, before you can relay the poor opinion you've formed of me, here is Martindale to announce dinner."

She looked up and saw a silver-haired butler standing just inside the door. "As you say, sir," the man intoned. "Everything is in readiness."

He withdrew discreetly and with a distinct air of disapproval.

Kate glanced at Michael Bellamy. The butler's steely response hadn't fazed her host one bit.

"Your butler doesn't like me," she commented.

"It's not you. Mansfield lets me know at least once a day that I'm much too informal and undignified to suit him. We're still feeling our way to some sort of truce."

"How long did it take you to get used to being addressed as Sir Michael? Or is that an impertinent question?"

"Five minutes, to answer the first," he said. "And no, to answer the second."

Michael was glad she'd accepted his invitation. He liked her quick wit and ready smile, and those violet eyes did serious damage to his personal armor. If he wasn't careful he might make a mistake that would cost him more than he was willing to give.

Taking her elbow, he escorted her down a side hall to a pretty parlor, where a candlelit table was set up before the marble hearth. The low flames burnished the heavy sterling flatware and darted in points of light from the cut-crystal goblets and the bond of fragrant roses.

"Do you always dine so splendidly?" she asked. "Even when you're alone?"

She was teasing him and he knew it, but his answer was serious. "Only when I'm trying to impress a guest."

Tension flickered between them, like tiny flames. Kate could feel the heat of it against her skin. She tried to defuse the situation. "I suppose this is my cue to ask why you want to impress me—and then you can tell me that this time I *am* being impertinent."

"Something like that," he said, smiling.

The strain vanished in their mutual laughter, and they sat down to enjoy the meal. The talk was easy throughout the meal, and Kate couldn't remember the last time she'd been so relaxed with any man. Michael Bellamy was well read and a clever conversationalist. They loved the same authors and seemed to share a similar philosophy of life. Not to mention the same type of subversive humor.

The evening flew by, and he seemed as reluctant as she to end it. "Thank you for your company tonight, Kate," he said as he escorted her to her door.

"Thank you for inviting me. Dinner was lovely, and so is King's Meadow."

"And so are you." This time it was right to say it.

For a moment they stood still in the moonlight, staring into one another's eyes. Even the chorus of frogs ceased. In the sudden stillness, elfin music drifted on the summer breeze, faint and far away.

He leaned down and touched his mouth to hers. It was entirely unplanned, and he knew it might ruin everything. But the moment his lips touched hers, he couldn't think of anything but kissing her again. And thoroughly.

A shiver ran through Kate. Half surprise, half sudden

awareness that the spark of his kiss had ignited a flame. It burned in the pit of her stomach and spread out along her limbs until she was burning with need.

Her arms wound around his neck, and he pulled her tight against him, feeling the softness of her mold against his hard muscles, feeling the fire burst out between them in a flare of desire. He realized that he'd wanted this moment all evening, and that he wanted far more.

Kate lost herself in the kiss, in the iron circle of his embrace. He kissed like an expert, and she knew he would make love the same way. She wanted him to prove her right, but she fought against her own desires, cursing herself for a fool while she did.

The moment she pushed against him he released her. The only thing he could think of to salvage the moment was to make light of it. "I'm sorry," he said. "I never kiss on the first date."

She gave a husky little laugh at his joke, and he joined in. They laughed so hard they clung to one another for support. The next thing they knew, the laughter was gone, and the passion was back, hotter than before.

This time he moved away first. His eyes were heavy with need. "Sleep well, Kate."

"And you, Michael."

She stood in the open doorway and watched him drive away. She knew that if he came back she wouldn't shut the door on him. It shocked her to realize that. And yet—it had felt so right to be in his arms, as if she belonged there and always had. Kate was certain that he felt the same.

She saw the taillights of his car slow and stop when he reached the lane. He sat there for two or three minutes, and she waited. When he pulled away toward King's Meadow, she didn't know if she was more relieved or frustrated.

For all her romanticism, Kate was cautious where her heart was concerned. She valued herself and knew she didn't need a man to validate her existence. She didn't want a physical relationship with him or with any man just yet. Plus, moving too fast could jeopardize their chance of friendship and anything deeper that might develop in the future.

But she knew that if he kissed her again and the same fire bloomed between them, they would become lovers.

10

Kᴀᴛᴇ ᴡᴀꜱ ᴘᴜʟʟᴇᴅ up from dreams by someone pounding on the front door. She slipped her robe on and padded down in her bare feet. *Mrs. Bean must have forgotten her key.*

"I'm coming," she called as another series of knocks sounded.

Left on her own, she probably would have slept until noon. She'd lain awake most of the night thinking of Michael Bellamy, wondering where their attraction to one another would lead them, and then she'd finally fallen into a heavy sleep just before dawn. Mr. Plunkett had called sometime in the interim, to say that he was not coming down until the afternoon, and Kate had rolled over and gone back into her dreams.

Dreams of walking beside Michael Bellamy along the shore of a lake as black as glass. She couldn't recall much. There'd been an island in the center of the lake, with a splendid castle. And then there was that odd bit about the frogs in the meadow below the garden. They'd covered the ground like a biblical plague, hopping and milling about, and singing so loudly that the low sound vibrated through her bones.

Like a bizarre choir afflicted with severe laryngitis, she thought.

She opened the door to golden morning light and Michael Bellamy on the doorstep. He was dazzling in the sunbeams, and she turned her face away from the brilliance.

"Wait. Please!" He thrust out a florist's cone of flowers. It was amazing what old Jenkins was selling these days. "A small act of contrition for my ungentlemanly behavior last night."

Kate pushed her hair out of her eyes and took the flowers. It was an old-fashioned bouquet of pansies, violets, and miniature roses framed by a lace paper doily and all of it tied up in blue satin ribbons. She inhaled their fragrance— and once again felt prickles, as if she'd inhaled champagne bubbles.

"I don't have anything to give you to apologize for mine," she mumbled. "I don't exactly remember you forcing me to kiss you back."

His smile was blinding. "Then give me a cup of coffee and we'll call it even?"

"All right." She stepped inside, still half asleep. "I'm afraid the conversation won't be very stimulating. I was up most of the night. I don't know why . . ."

"Don't you?" Michael looked down at her, with her hair all tousled and her mouth soft with sleep. "I didn't sleep either," he said quietly. "I doubt I'll sleep tonight again. All I could think of was you. How you look and move and talk. How it felt to hold you in my arms."

"Things are moving too fast," she said.

Or not fast enough, her body told her. Beneath the silky robe and skimpy gown, her flesh warmed to him. She felt her breasts tingle and her loins contract. No man had ever had such an effect on her.

When she'd read books and manuscripts in which people felt and acted in the heat of impulse, she hadn't quite believed it. Now she knew it was true. She wanted his mouth on hers, his hands on her body, with such a fever she felt she would soon burst into flame.

He ached for her with a fierce desperation. His voice was still low, but fueled with passion and need. "I want to make love to you, Kate. But only when you're ready. I'll wait as long as it takes."

"I might never be," she said. "I'm not the kind of woman who can take a hour's pleasure and walk away without a backward glance. I don't pass myself around like a plate of hors d'oeuvres."

"I didn't think so." The laughter in his eyes replaced the dark desire she'd seen there only a moment earlier. But it still pulsed in the air between them. "But if you did . . ."

He willed her to him and her body swayed. He held his arms out, and she took another step toward him. He wanted to sweep her up in his arms and kiss her face, her white swan's throat, the succulent curve of her breasts. Wanted her so much he was shaking with the need of it.

Kate closed her eyes and stepped into his arms.

He felt the heat of her breasts against his chest, smelled the musky woman scent of her, and was lost. His mouth was hot and urgent, and she responded to him without reserve. Whatever power it was that he held over her, she surrendered to it eagerly.

He filled his fists with her hair and kissed her senseless, then nibbled a line of exquisite sensation along her jaw and throat. She curved against him, and he felt a pull deep inside that sent every thought pinwheeling out of his mind. Nothing existed but the two of them, the fire of their passion, and the spiraling need to be consumed.

The phone rang three times before either of them noticed.

"Shall I get it, Miss?" a voice called from the kitchen.

"Mrs. Bean!" Kate stepped away reluctantly. "I didn't know she was here."

Michael swore, kissed her again, and swore some more. "Dinner tonight?" he whispered in her ear.

Kate thought a moment. "Only," she said, "in a very public place." After he was gone she couldn't believe the way she'd fallen apart when he touched her. The way she'd fallen apart when he stopped.

She could feel every imprint of his hand on her body, as if the sensual pleasure of it had seared her skin.

She damned Mrs. Bean to perdition: they'd been one scene away from Rhett Butler sweeping Scarlett O'Hara up in his arms and carrying her up the stairs.

"Why do I react so strongly to him?" she wondered aloud as she climbed up to her room. Was it hero worship, or the attraction of a sophisticated man of the world? The lure of potent pheromones? Or plain old physical lust?

Michael was wondering the same thing as he drove down the coast to meet the developers. This was the third meeting that had been set up between them, and the first one he was keeping.

There'd been less room in his mind for everything else from the moment he'd set eyes on Kate. She was smart and funny and pretty and nice—but so were a hundred other women of his acquaintance. What was it about her that had suddenly turned him into a mass of raving hormones, as if he were a boy of sixteen again?

No, it was more than just hormones. It went deeper than that.

Which made Kate Singleton a very dangerous woman.

The bell on the door of the little flower shop tinkled as a young couple went out with six pots of violets. "Only a handful of blossoms left," the woman Kate knew as Miss Golunka said with satisfaction. "It's been a very successful day. And Mr. Jenkins wants more pots of flowers for his shop."

"It was clever of you to think of this, Sophie," Mr. Plunkett said. "And such a nice little apartment above. I've grown quite fond of it."

She stared at him. "You're not wanting to *stay* Above, are you, Alfred? Because the queen would never forgive me!"

"Of course not," he said quickly. "However it's always nice to be comfortable, don't you think?"

Miss Golunka sighed. "I won't be comfortable until this is over and the prince is safely home again."

Another tinkle heralded a new customer. She went out

through the curtain and wrapped a cone of flowers for the elderly woman who'd wandered in and stayed to buy. "That will be seven pence, please."

"Pence?" The woman laughed. "You mean pounds, surely."

"Of course!"

"Still, very reasonable."

After the money changed hands, the woman looked about. The sign on the window read YE OLDE FLOWER SHOPPE, GOLUNKA & PLUNKETT, PROPRIETORS, in faded gold letters.

"It's very odd," the woman said, shaking her head. "I've lived in the village my whole life, and I don't recall there ever being a flower shop here."

"And you won't remember it being here today," Miss Golunka said and croaked a strange little phrase. The air twinkled briefly.

The woman was suddenly on her own front doorstep, her arms filled with flowers. She couldn't for the life of her figure out where she'd gotten them. Her memory wasn't quite what it used to be lately, what with X-rays and radios and televisions—and now microwaves and cell phones sending signals through the air. It was no wonder a body became forgetful at times.

"I'll just go round to the clinic and see Dr. Potter tomorrow," she said firmly, and went inside to put the blooms in water.

When the door of the flower shop was locked and the window shuttered for the day, Mr. Plunkett came out of the cooler with a cloud of baby's breath. "I thought you might like to wear these gypsophilia blossoms in your hair for the ball tonight, Sophie. They'd be most becoming."

"Thank you, Alfred." Miss Golunka took them from him. "I'm not sure if I'll be attending the ball."

"But . . . but it's *required*. And what if the prince should return? You'd want to be present for that, wouldn't you?"

"For all the good it would do me I might as well stay here," Miss Golunka said in a low voice. "In any case, one of us must keep an eye on him in case he needs assistance."

Mr. Plunkett made sympathetic noises. "He's young yet.

Give him time. It's only natural that the prince sows some wild oats before he decides to settle down. You mustn't hold it against him."

She turned away. "It is no business of mine whether the prince falls in love a dozen times—as long as he returns before the Summer Solstice. With, or without, a bride!"

Frederick came in from the back room, where he'd been reading a battered copy of *Wind in the Willows*. "Marvelous book," he told them, setting the volume back on a shelf. "By the by, did one of you take my vial of Spring Fever Powder? I was sure I'd left it right by the carnations."

"Didn't I tell you?" Mr. Plunkett asked. "I used the last of it up on the posy that Sir Michael purchased for Miss Singleton."

Miss Golunka's eyes popped. "Good heavens," she exclaimed. "I'd already sprinkled half the vial on it earlier!"

She clasped her hands to her fine, wide bosom. "Oh, dear. That's *far* too much. Especially when there is already such a strong attraction!"

Mr. Plunkett was so distracted he didn't even react when a fat fly settled down on a wall nearby. "I've never heard of anyone taking so large a dose of it. What do you suppose will happen?"

She bit her lip. "I suspect that there will be two fairly besotted young people mooning about between Frogsmere and King's Meadow for the next few days."

"You Victorians are so prissy," Frederick said. " 'Besotted'? 'Mooning about'?"

He winked. "That's not what we called it in *my* day."

Miss Golunka huffed and pushed upon the door leading up to the apartment. A few minutes later they could hear the sound of water running in the old claw-footed tub. "She always does that when she's distressed," Frederick said.

"Yes, there is nothing so soothing as water. Unless it's water and moonlight." Mr. Plunkett sighed. "I'm afraid that dear Sophie is not taking this to heart as she ought."

Frederick eyed him shrewdly. "I believe she is taking it very much to heart. She's been in love with the prince from the time she was a tadpole."

11

THE ROAR AND rattle of the bulldozer filled the June air, but Kate was used to it now. That didn't make it any easier for her to roll out of bed, though. After fortifying herself with a hot shower and scalding hot coffee, she went outside to watch the BBC film crew and archaeological team at work. This was the first official day of filming.

While the 'dozer stripped off the upper layers of turf in one section of the wide meadow, two men quartered another marked-off area with metal detectors. She saw Michael Bellamy before he saw her. It affected her the same way it did every time they met. A hot rush of eagerness, a giddy little spurt of joy, followed by caution and regret.

Their relationship hadn't progressed since the morning when Mrs. Bean had interrupted them. If anything, it was in a strange state of suspended animation. Kate felt the same strong attraction to him she had almost from the beginning, but it was a one-sided effort. Michael was friendly enough. He even seemed to court her good opinion and to go out of his way to be pleasing to her, but there was an invisible line he never crossed.

She'd resigned herself to nothing more than friendship on his part.

In the past weeks she'd strolled along the river with him, or joined him at the dig site. He'd invited her to dinner at King's Meadow twice, once with Alicia Kane, the lead archaeologist, and BBC officials, and another time with his Australian mates and their wives who were visiting England. Kate had taken her cue from him and kept the tone of their meetings cordial and impersonal.

It was driving her crazy.

She knew with a woman's instinct that he was as drawn to her as she was to him. It showed in the light in his eyes when they rested on her, in the touch of his hand on her arm, and the flush of blood beneath his tan when their gazes met. She wondered if he had a girlfriend or lover. It kept her awake nights. Still, when he called to her across the meadow, she found her pulse racing as she waved back.

He met her at the bottom of the garden. "This should be an interesting day. They've decided to give up on the hut circles—nothing but a few potsherds so far—and run a few more test trenches while the cameras are rolling. Either the Roman villa area, or the medieval village."

Kate had seen the aerial photos taken earlier in the year, where ditches and walls showed up in lighter or darker areas of turf. The circles of Stone-Age huts were cut through by rectangles indicating the foundations of a Roman villa. Traces of the medieval village overlay both.

She pointed to the long, low hill that ran north to south at the far end of the meadow. Half of it was covered with trees and thick brush. "I thought they were interested in that long hill. The barrow, Alicia Kane called it. She thinks it's a burial mound."

Michael nodded over at the red-haired archaeologist in charge of the dig.

"Alicia is excellent at what she does, and I have the utmost respect for her—but believe me when I say that it is nothing more than a midden heap, where generations of Bellamys have thrown out their trash."

Alicia heard him and came over. "Even so, there are bound to be interesting items there, since your family has been here forever! I do wish you'd let us have a go at it, Sir Michael. I'm certain there's a megalithic barrow grave beneath all that vegetation."

"There do seem to be an awful lot of frogs around here," Kate said. "They're everywhere. I find them in the house from time to time."

Michael looked startled. "Don't kiss them, whatever you do."

Alicia Kane cocked her head. "Afraid Kate will catch warts, Sir Michael, or that she'll find a handsome prince and run off with him?"

Before he could respond, Peter Jones joined them, slapping his baseball cap against his leg. "This is it. We need to make a big find, Sir Michael, or the season will be a bust. Just let us have one crack at a test trench across the end of that barrow."

"You're persistent, Jones, I'll grant you that. Very well. Keep one group working on the villa site, and have your operator run a test trench across the southern point of it. But if you don't find anything by day's end, you'll give up and leave me in peace about it for the rest of your time here."

Kate went along to watch as the 'dozer set to work, delicately peeling layers of turf and soil with its steel blade. "Found something!" The director shouted, and everyone came running over.

The scrape of shovels was followed by careful digging away with garden trowels. "Looks like a piece of porcelain," Peter Jones said. They went at it with renewed energy and revealed—a broken washbasin. The let-down was great. Over the next hours they turned up linement bottles, a cast-iron bathtub, two cracked boiler plates, and a case of smashed canning jars.

"It looks like you're right," Alicia Kane said with disappointment. "Nothing here but the detritus of generations of Bellamys."

Suddenly a shout went up from the direction of the Roman villa traces. "Something big here!"

Kate could hear the wild pinging of the metal detectors. Several archaeologists huddled around the spot and one began to trowel off the upper layers. "It's more than a handful of coins," Alicia said. "Could be the treasure trove of a Roman legionnaire, buried for safekeeping when he went off to war."

"Or a bloody ten-year-old bit of broken plow," one of her compatriots teased.

"Bite your bloody tongue!" the director snarled. "They won't renew our program if that's the kind of find we turn up."

Kate waited eagerly while they worked their way down through the sandy soil. It didn't take long to unearth the artifacts. First was a leather sack with a rotted drawstring threaded around its neck.

"Something metallic inside," one of the men said. "Better let Alicia do the honors."

Their chief grinned and reached carefully inside. The pouch contained two glass amulets, a ring of heavily corroded silver, three bronze cloak pins green and fragile with age, and a variety of coins.

"First century," one of the archaeologists said.

They passed the coins around but the jewelry expert took the cloak pins and set them in a special box, while the crew gave opinions on whether their owner had been Roman or Briton.

Kate held the blackened ring on her palm. The green glass stone in its center was frosted and badly pitted, but she found it amazing and beautiful.

Michael hunkered down beside her. "You look mesmerized. What thoughts are running through your head?"

"It's like reaching through a window in time to touch the past." She closed her hand over the ring. "Who was its owner?" she said softly. "Why was it hidden? And why didn't the person who hid the sack and its contents ever come back for it?"

"Yes." Michael turned a gold coin over in his hand. "That's the romance and magic of it. The link to those who lived here centuries ago. I always find myself wondering what their stories were . . ."

". . . and how they ended," Kate finished for him.

Their eyes met and held. He smiled at her in a way that warmed her from head to toe.

"I'm glad you were here to share this moment with me, Kate."

She felt her color rising. "I am, too."

He cupped her chin in his hand and gazed down into her eyes. The excited chatter of the BBC crew faded away into a low, background hum. There was nothing but the two of them. They were in total harmony with one another, even their hearts beating in time. Then he leaned down and kissed her.

It was a long kiss, deep and passionate. Kate felt the need rise inside her and knew it did the same in him. She could tell by his quick intake of breath, the tightness of his arms as they wound around her and pulled her close. If they were alone they'd be tugging at the clothes that separated them, bringing the long weeks of growing tension to the culmination they both wanted.

He looked down at her, and all the heat of passion that she felt in his kiss was there in his eyes. Mingled curiously with regret. "Ah, Kate. I've tried so damned hard not to rush you again and frighten you off!"

She smiled up at him. "I don't frighten easily."

"And I don't kiss women in public. But I'm going to do it again." Sliding his fingers through her shining hair, he lifted her face for a kiss that seared her lips and left her gasping.

"I suppose," he murmured in her ear, "it would look a little conspicuous if we suddenly left together."

Kate realized she was trembling. "I don't care."

He pulled her into his arms and they kissed again. One of the cameramen cheered. "That's a quid you owe me, Peter."

Kate flushed and Michael released her quickly.

Peter Jones joined them. "Glad to see you're enjoying yourself on the dig, Miss Singleton," he said smoothly. "You weren't so pleased with us when you first arrived."

"I didn't understand what you were doing that day," she said. "I do now."

"That's gratifying." His flicker of a smile was almost a

nervous tic. "Then you won't be upset with me when we run a test trench through the gardens."

"*My* gardens?"

"That spot where you came flaming down like an avenging angel when we first began working the site," Jones said, indicating the scarred turf where the bulldozer had plowed through the day after her arrival. "The richest finds will be there, so I'm afraid it will have to go."

Kate folded her arms across her chest. "You needn't be. Surely you have enough places to dig on King's Meadow property, without encroaching on Frogsmere."

The director looked from Kate to Michael. "Er . . . uh . . . I believe I'd best leave the explanation to Sir Michael. Got to get back to the job at hand, you know."

Jones tipped his baseball cap to her and started away down the slope, shouting something to one of the archaeologists below.

"He looks," Kate commented, "like a small boy who's just batted a ball through his neighbor's plate-glass window and is making his escape."

"Not a bad description," Michael said wryly.

"And," she added, "you're the one left behind to answer the awkward questions."

"Yes. Well." He rubbed a hand along his jaw. He felt like throttling Peter for forcing this on him.

"This is damned awkward. We need to talk, Kate, but this isn't the right time or place. Perhaps we could have dinner together tonight. There's a little restaurant down the coast that serves wonderful food . . ."

Something in his voice had Kate's instincts on alert: whatever he was going to discuss, she wouldn't like it. "I think we had better talk it over now." She regarded him levelly. "Why does Peter feel it's your permission he needs to dig up *my* garden?"

Michael flushed but held his stance. "Because," he said, "it's actually *my* garden. I own all the property from your pond down to the river."

She stared at him in astonishment. "That can't be true."

"I'm not in the habit of making up such things. I'd hoped that we wouldn't have to cover this ground just yet, but perhaps it's better to get it all out in the open."

"This past December, Agatha Culpepper sold off her acreage to me—everything but the house itself and the three acres of park and gardens immediately surrounding it."

"No. That's not possible." Kate was indignant. "I met with her solicitor before I came down here. Mr. Plunkett said nothing about any property being sold, and he specifically told me that the acreage came with the house."

"I'm afraid that's in dispute. Your Mr. Plunkett has reservations regarding the sale of the property—according to him, there's a question of whether Miss Culpepper could legally split the land off from the house to sell separately."

A wash of relief flowed through Kate. "Well, there you are. Mr. Plunkett knows everything about Frogsmere, and he must certainly know the law."

Michael frowned. "It would seem so—on the surface. However, his contention goes back to a small phrase written more than three hundred years ago in the last will and testament of Josiah Culpepper. I, on the other hand, have a signed and notarized purchase agreement between myself and Miss Culpepper dated a few months ago. And while I don't wish to cause you any distress, it's only fair that you should know I intend to follow through on it."

Kate leapt on that. "Then the sale was never completed?"

"I gave Miss Culpepper the check in good faith. She failed to endorse or deposit it, and it was found among her effects."

"Maybe," Kate suggested, "she'd changed her mind, and intended to return the check to you."

"There is no way of knowing either way. In the end it may be up to the courts to decide."

She froze. "Is this your way of saying that you intend to sue me?"

"No. Only that it may require a judge to render a ruling based on interpretation of the law."

Kate felt used and betrayed and deeply angry. She was so distraught that she could hardly bear to look at him.

"I'm very sorry," he said. "I haven't handled this very well."

Her eyes were hard as diamonds. "Why didn't you explain it to me that first morning, when I came charging out of the house?"

"I expected that you knew." Michael shrugged. "When I realized you didn't, I thought it wiser not to bring it up just then. It was a mistake on my part and I feel badly that you're upset, Kate."

"*Upset* is too mild a word for what I'm feeling: Now I know why you asked if I intended to sell Frogsmere! You're not content with just the land—you want the house, too!"

"I won't deny it. If you choose to sell the place I'd be first in line to buy it."

"A property involved in legal action can't be sold or traded until the matter is resolved. I couldn't sell even if I wanted to!"

"That's only partially true," he said. "You could sell it to me and end the dispute. I hope you'll consider it."

"Oh, I will," Kate said coolly. "Sometime between the return of the dinosaurs and the moment that hell freezes over."

She turned and stalked off up the meadow path.

12

MRS. BEAN TOOK one last look before letting herself out the front door. Frogsmere was clean as a wink, and she'd left a nice bit of scalloped potatoes and ham in the refrigerator for Miss Singleton.

Satisfied that she'd done everything that needed doing, she picked up her carrier bag from the countertop and headed for the front door. She fumbled for her key, not noticing the fat little frog a step beyond the threshold.

She didn't see the frog hop through the open door just before she locked it up with her key either.

It sat a moment, then bounded across the hall and and didn't stop until it reached the concealed door to the study where Agatha Culpepper had written the Trixie Pickering books. The frog blinked three times and the door opened. Just a crack, but enough for the enterprising creature to fit through.

Those great jeweled eyes gazed around the chamber. The frog had heard of this room and knew he'd find help here. He gave a happy croak: *Kizzmee, kizzmee.*

A few short hops brought him to the quiet shadows beneath the trestle table, and he settled down to wait, ignoring the tasty fly dozing on the wall. He was thoroughly sick of flies. And gnats.

What he really desperately wanted was a glass of ale and some stuffed pheasant—or at the very least, a good steak-and-kidney pie.

Kate slammed the door behind her with such force that china knickknacks wobbled and clinked on their shelves.

Jenny's right. I am a romantic fool. How could I possibly have imagined anything deeper than a surface attraction to Michael Bellamy?

She decided to spend the rest of the day indoors, blocking out the sounds of the bulldozer and backhoe chewing up the meadow.

It's high time I found those journals.

They were hidden in plain sight, among the household ledgers in the desk. She opened one of the older-looking volumes and saw the date inscribed in ink that was brown and faded: 1603.

It gave her a little jolt to think that another woman had held this same volume in her hands four hundred years ago in this very room.

Kate closed the journal and carefully put it back. The only thing she knew about handling documents this old was that they were extremely fragile and that she'd need to seek expert advice before she went any further.

The newer ones didn't have the same potential problems, so she selected a fresh-looking volume and opened it to the title page. It was dated only a few months ago and had been written by Agatha Culpepper shortly before she died. She turned to the last entries:

Tuesday. A cold wind off the sea, but very sunny.

Mrs. Bean is making a pot of ox-tail soup and quantities of restorative tea, in hopes I will regain my old vigor. A futile attempt, but kindly meant. I am ready and have no reservations about going on to the next

*waystop on my immortal journey, only a very great
curiosity to see what mysteries lie beyond.*

Wednesday. Rain.
   *Mr. Plunkett down from London this morning to fi-
nalize papers. A visit from Sir Michael Bellamy. He is
adamant about the terms of our agreement. It must be
his way, he says, or he will not sign the papers. After
a long discussion, which became at times rather
heated, everything is settled between us. I am sure
Honoria would agree that this is for the best.*

Kate's heart sank. Was she referring to the sale of her
acreage? She couldn't tell, and realized she was in no mood
to read about it. As she started to close the journal, her own
name leapt out at her from the page opposite.

Friday. Cloudy and colder.
   *Another delightful letter from Kate Singleton in
America. How I envy her the opportunities available
to young women nowadays. I must make a note to
answer the letter and let her know what I have done
regarding Frogsmere. Also I must remember to tell her
about* The People Under the Hill. *Things are coming
along well after much work. I believe that Lady Eu-
genia's role will have to be greatly enlarged in order
for it to end up as I have planned.*

Kate's heart sped up. That must be the title of the new
manuscript the elderly widow had been working on at the
time of her death.

The entries ended abruptly two pages later without mentioning either Kate or the *People Under the Hill* again. Kate
decided to search for the manuscript in the little room
where Agatha Culpepper had written the Trixie Pickering
books.

As she crossed the great hall, a thought struck Kate. Who
owned the rights to the Trixie Pickering books? Were they
part of the estate she'd inherited? There was no specific
mention of them in the will. She saw she would have to

start writing down all the questions she had for Mr. Plunkett to answer when he drove down from London.

It didn't take long to find the manuscript. It was in an embossed leather folder on the Welsh cupboard.

"Not many pages," she said, leafing through the hand-written document. Kate stifled her disappointment, sat down in the lone chair and began to read.

It was a first draft, with words and phrases struck out here and there, and others inserted. Also a few indecipherable notes in the margins. Kate read the dedication. "To my sister, Honoria, who showed the courage of her convictions."

The People Under the Hill

Constellations of diamonds studded the sapphire sky, twinkling like stars. The queen leaned against the balcony rail and smiled.

She remembered stars.

They were one of the few things she missed from the world Above.

The lilting strains of a waltz wafted through the open ballroom door. The leaves of the crystal trees in the garden shimmered and tinkled in three-quarter time. The queen hummed along in spite of herself. Everyone in the kingdom was in the mood for romance.

Everyone but the Crown Prince.

The problem with her son was that he was too coddled and protected. His father had never allowed him so much as a glimpse of the world Above, which made it all the more alluring.

Perhaps his father is afraid it will appeal too greatly to his human side, *she thought,* and that he won't come back to us. He is wrong. Arthur may be spoiled and inexperienced, but he is deeply loyal. In the end, he will always do what is right.

Everyone in the kingdom had, at one time or another, made their choice. Certainly she did not regret making hers.

She turned as her husband approached. "I cannot find our son anywhere," the king said.

"There he is, my dear, sitting by the lake, staring at nothing in particular."

The king frowned. "He is supposed to be dancing with the guests! All the fairest maidens in the land are here, and he has not danced with any of them. I don't know what has come over him."

"I think I do." The queen's pretty mouth curved upward. "He is very like you at the same age, you know. Our son is tired of having to meet everyone else's expectations. And he is restless, as all young men are. He wants to see the world. The world Above."

"No! I forbid it!"

She put a hand on her husband's sleeve. "Every young man needs to sow a few oats before he settles down. Arthur has never had that opportunity. He has never smelled a real rose, or eaten bread hot from the oven. He has never known the warmth of the sun on his face or the cool kiss of the rain.

"It's dangerous Above," the king said slowly.

She saw the look on her husband's face. He was afraid for Arthur, although she thought it was rather dear and silly of him to be so worried about his only son. Not that Above didn't have its drawbacks.

People fell ill.

Grew old.

Died.

Soon there would be no one left of those she'd known in her own girlhood. But in the five hundred years since the kingdom was founded, not one member of the royal family had been lost during a pilgrimage to the other world. Except, *she reminded herself with a shudder, for the one who was run over by the ox-cart.*

"He must make his own choice," she said. "We cannot do it for him. And he should see Above, just once before settling down."

"Do you miss the world Above, Honoria?"

The queen touched her husband's cheek. *"I miss stars and summer nights and kittens. But I must admit that I like staying young and beautiful and never having to worry about eating too much chocolate."*

The queen leaned her head against the king's broad shoulder. *"It's high time that you had your father-son talk with Arthur. About his going Above. I believe it's exactly what the boy needs. Just a little taste of adventure before he settles down. I am confident he will make the right decision."*

"But, Honoria—surely it's too soon. Why, he's only a lad."

The queen laughed. *"Oh, Edgar. You were exactly the same age when we met and fell in love."*

The king thought a moment. *"By Jove, you're right. I'll do it."* The king sighed. *"I'll talk to Arthur when the ball ends at dawn. He knows what must be done if he intends to go Above. But I must say I don't think he'll be very happy about being turned into a frog . . ."*

Kate was dismayed to find the next page blank. So were all the rest. Unless there was another copy of the manuscript floating around somewhere at Frogsmere, it appeared that it had never been completed.

She didn't know quite what to make of it. It was an odd little story, half Coming of Age and half Frog Prince. And curiously, it wasn't written for young children like all the rest of the Trixie Pickering books.

Despite her annoyance, Kate wanted to know the answer to that all-important question that kept people turning the page: What happens next?

While she'd been reading, the sounds of the heavy equipment had faded into the background. Now, as she straightened the sheets of paper and slipped them back into the folder, the clank and roar came back with a vengeance.

Kate hurried outside to see what the noise was about and stopped dead in her tracks.

"The bastards!"

They were uprooting a tree.

And she didn't care what Michael Bellamy claimed—
that tree was on her property.

13

KATE HEARD THE car pull up as she was heading for the gardens. "Mr. Plunkett!" The very man she needed.

She went around to the front and greeted him.

"Country life must agree with you," Mr. Plunkett said. "You've fresh roses in your cheeks since last we met."

"I'm afraid it's anger that has my face glowing," she told him. "At this very moment, Sir Michael Bellamy and a BBC archaeological crew are digging up Miss Culpepper's garden and ripping out trees. You have to stop him!"

"Oh, dear, oh, dear. I rather thought you would like Sir Michael. This will make everything so awkward."

Kate eyed him with growing suspicion. "He claims that he bought the property from Miss Culpepper before she died."

"That's true. Up to a point. I am contending, on your behalf, that the sale should be set aside, since the check was never cashed. Unless," he said hopefully, "you wish to accept the terms that were negotiated and complete the transfer of property."

"No. I want to keep the estate intact. I won't sell off so much as a foot of it unless I'm forced to do so." She folded her arms. "And I wouldn't sell it to Sir Michael Bellamy even then."

She led him into the drawing room, with its fine view of the gardens. He smiled with approval at the vases of flowers on the mantelpiece and the roses in their fluted crystal bowl. "Charming, my dear Miss Singleton. Quite charming!"

Kate offered refreshments, which he declined. "I lunched at a pub in the village. If you like we will get down to business."

She took the chair opposite him by the fireplace. "Let's start with the unpleasant part and get it out of the way. How bad will the estate taxes be?"

Mr. Plunkett cleared his throat. "I'm afraid the news is not good." He named a sum that made Kate's stomach bounce up into her chest before dropping like a lead weight.

"I'm stunned," she said at last. "I don't have those kinds of funds available to me." She grasped at other possibilities of raising money. "I've been meaning to ask you. Who owns the rights to the Trixie Pickering books?"

"You do, Miss Singleton. In an equal partnership with Sir Michael Bellamy."

"Him again!" She knotted her fingers together. "He seems to have had a very close relationship with Miss Culpepper."

"Oh, yes, indeed." The solicitor's voice was mild. "Sir Michael helped Miss Culpepper with her affairs after his return from Australia. Her health had been failing for some time, and she said on more than one occasion that she didn't know how she would have managed her finances without him."

She drummed her fingers on the arm of her chair. "What was the sum he offered her for the property?"

"One hundred pounds per acre."

Kate felt sick. It was an old story: a handsome and charming young man, an older woman in poor health needing assistance in managing her money—and a tidy bequest to the man in question when the old lady passed on.

"Do you really think him capable of such a thing?" Mr. Plunkett said, watching her face intently.

"No," she said at last. "You're right. I can't see him purposefully setting out to turn things to his advantage. It was hers to dispose of as she pleased."

"Perhaps you might offer some of the antiques at auction. Items that perhaps you have no use for that would fetch a tidy sum."

"But wouldn't I have to pay more taxes on the profit?"

Mr. Plunkett considered her objection. He tented his hands. "By Jove, I believe I can find a way around part of the problem. You might set up a trust to maintain Frogsmere, and place the funds from the sale in the trust. That would enable you to keep the house up, yet the rate of taxation would be much lower. Shall I look into it?"

"Yes, please." Kate remembered the other matter she wanted to discuss. "I found a partial manuscript among Miss Culpepper's journals. Does Sir Michael also share an interest in them?"

"No. Her papers and unpublished manuscripts are yours exclusively."

That was encouraging. Kate was familiar enough with the Trixie Pickering style of writing to complete *The People Under the Hill*. She would need only notes or a plot outline to tell her how the story was to go. She intended to send out feelers to different publishers to find out how much interest there would be in a new Trixie Pickering story, and in the biography she proposed to write.

Mr. Plunkett coughed his gravelly cough. "Would it be possible to see this manuscript?"

"Of course. It's in her study." She led him across the hall and through the hidden door. "Welcome to the world of Trixie Pickering."

As she opened the door she saw a frog sitting squarely atop the pages. "Oh! How did you get in here?" She scooped the frog up and went to the casement window. "Out you go, pal."

The frog landed in a patch of goat's beard and leapt away as if jet-propelled.

Mr. Plunkett smiled. "No damage to the pages. He was just trying to read them, I suspect."

"You have quite a sense of humor."

"One has to, in my business."

Kate hesitated. "I'd like to talk to Sir Michael before I make any final decision on the property."

"That's wise of you, Miss Singleton. I'll await your directions."

When he was gone Kate went through the drawing-room doors into the summer garden. Alicia came up the path from the dig site, her red hair frizzing to a halo in the heat. "The fellow's here to measure for the car park. I thought I'd better warn you."

"What car park?"

"For the King's Meadow Convalescent Center." She frowned. "You did know that Sir Michael has sold the place, didn't you?"

Kate just shook her head. "I don't believe you. He loves King's Meadow!"

"He can't afford to keep it, with the death duties and all. That's the only reason he let us near his place—for the fees. Quite stiff ones, I might add. He's an excellent negotiator."

"Don't I know it," Kate mumbled.

"This way," Alicia went on, "he retains an interest in the property when it becomes a children's rehabilitation center."

"I imagine he'll make a tidy profit on it," Kate said bitterly.

The older woman looked surprised. "He's not making a penny on it. In fact, he's donating the property. Remarkably generous of him, when his investments are just beginning to pay off the debts his father incurred."

Kate stared at her. It didn't make sense. "Thank you, Alicia. I'd invite you in, but . . . but I have to see Sir Michael on urgent business."

It was a quick walk across the meadows and through the fallow fields to King's Meadow, but it gave Kate time for some heavy-duty thinking. The butler gave her shorts and tank top a look of disapproval, but ushered her into a small book-lined study. Michael looked up from a ledger but didn't say anything when she was announced. Kate waited until Mansfield closed the door.

"You don't look happy to see me," she said.

"You caught me off guard. I wasn't expecting you." He folded his arms and waited for her to explain the reason for her visit.

"You're not making this any easier for me." Kate's violet eyes met his. "Whatever contract you negotiated with Miss Culpepper was between the two of you. I won't raise any road blocks regarding your purchase of the acreage."

He raised his eyebrows in surprise. "I see."

"I thought you'd be glad to hear it. You look disappointed."

Michael shook his head. "I'm conflicted. Until the business I have under way is finalized, my pockets are pretty much to let."

"I beg your pardon?"

"Vacant," he said. "Empty of money."

"Then why on earth did you persuade Miss Culpepper to sell you her land?"

Michael came around the desk. "You're under a misapprehension. The transaction went against all my better instincts. It was she who persuaded me to buy it."

Kate felt lighter than air. She'd misjudged the situation entirely. Misjudged him. "Then why did you agree?"

"Out of friendship. Loyalty. Duty. All the things that have gone so out of style these days."

"They never go out of style." Kate crossed the rug to his side. "If you feel it's a mistake, then, I won't hold you to it. Your call, Michael. Either way."

He stepped forward and pulled her into his arms. "To hell with Frogsmere and King's Meadow. We've got other business at hand."

His kiss sizzled right down to her toes. "God, I've missed you."

She laughed against his mouth. "It's only been two hours since we quarreled."

"Far too long," he said, and kissed her again. "Do you believe in fate, Katherine, my love? Because I knew the first time I saw you that you were destined to be mine. Just as I was meant to be yours."

"I think I've always been yours," she said. "Because I'm most alive when I'm with you."

Her arms were around his neck, her fingers tangled in his hair as she pulled his face down to hers. His mouth was hot, his body hard beneath his clothes. She felt her own melting against him, melding into the heat of his passion.

Her fingers worked open the buttons of his shirt, her mouth pressed against his bare flesh, and his embrace tightened so she could hardly breathe. He sensed it immediately, murmuring apologies against her throat as he loosed his hold, intoxicating her with his touch.

The world tilted from vertical to horizontal. She could feel the brush of the Oriental carpet against her bare back and realized her tank top was at her waist. Then his hands and mouth were on her breasts, and she was arching up to meet him, willing and eager for more. She felt the buttons pop on her shorts as he tugged them loose, heard the soft rustle of his own clothes as he stripped them off.

He started with kisses on her eyelids and worked his way down. By the time his mouth skimmed over her midriff she was on fire with need. Burning, burning with delicious sensations, and wanting more. Much more.

She caught his face between her hands and lifted it. "Make love to me, Michael," she said fiercely. "Take me now!"

He answered with a hard, hot kiss on her mouth as he stretched his long frame beside her. There was such power in his restraint that the air hummed with it. He teased her into higher arousal. His fingers moved down, explored, retreated. Her body shuddered with pleasure. He touched her again, once, and the world splintered into wild, dark colors that she'd never seen before.

"Now," she demanded.

"Now," he said, and settled his weight over her. She felt him slip inside her, thrust deep in the perfect moment. Fire danced through their veins, and roared through their bodies. They were locked together, fused by the glory of their passion.

"I love you, Kate," he said after, when they lay heart to heart.

"Don't," she said. "Don't promise anything now. It's too soon."

"You don't seem to understand," he said, looking down into her eyes. "What's between us isn't infatuation. It isn't lust. This is forever."

14

THE MOON WOVE strands of silver through the trees, and long shadows stretched away from Frogsmere to the dark woods beyond. Kate sat on a garden seat sipping a glass of Riesling, listening to the soft ruffling of the wind and the chirping of the frogs.

After Michael drove her back to Frogsmere, they'd made love again. Then they'd devoured Mrs. Bean's home cooking, finished a bottle of wine, and made love again. "Will you stay the night?" she'd asked as they lay entwined.

"I have to leave in a few minutes," he told her, his voice heavy with regret. "I'll be back before midnight, if you'll let me in."

"I'll be waiting."

But here it was, almost one in the morning, and there'd been no sign of him. Doubt crept in like little shadows. She didn't know him well enough to begin a relationship. She'd rushed in too fast and gone too far.

She brushed the doubts away as if they were gnats. No. This was real. And right. He was right. This was their destiny. Fate had taken a hand in their meeting in the first place. "And Agatha Culpepper," she said aloud.

Something plopped softly on the stone bench beside her. She turned and saw a little frog looking up at her with round, imploring eyes. Before she could react, he leapt into her lap. She set her glass down, then picked him up and put him down in the grass. He—or his identical twin, she thought—was back a moment later.

"Persistent, aren't you?"

"Kizzmee. Kizzmee."

She held him in her cupped hands. "Are you one of the frogs I have to kiss before I find my prince? Because you're too late. I've found him."

"Kizzmee. Kizzmee!"

"All right." And she did.

It was just like before, in the kitchen. The air sparkled and fizzled into a bright white mist. There was an odd sound, like a lightbulb popping—and a man in a green tunic and tights went sliding off her lap, pulling Kate down into the grass with him.

"What the hell . . ."

He rolled to his knees as she thrashed around in the grass. As she struggled to rise, he caught her hand in his.

"Lovely Lady, Thy kiss has released me from the spell of enchantment that kept me from my true form and bound me in the guise of a lowly frog. In return, I pledge my heart and sword to thy most gracious service. How may I serve thee?"

"By letting go of me! Who the hell are you? How did you get here?"

"I am a noble prince, and now thy sworn champion. By thy chaste and merciful kiss, released me from the spell of enchantment laid upon me. The spell that kept me from my true form and bound me in the guise of a lowly frog. Name any task, whether it be to slay a fiendish monster or lead thy gallant knights in battle, and I shall accomplish it in thy name. I pledge my heart and sword to thy sweet service."

"First, stop repeating yourself. Second, let go of my hand."

Kate pressed her fingers to her face and closed her eyes. It was the wine. It had to be the wine. But when she opened her eyes again he was still there.

She reached out and pinched him. He was solid as a brick.

"Ow!" He did an undignified little dance. "That was a lousy thing to do."

Kate stared. " *'Lousy'?* What kind of language is that for a prince? What happened to your *'thys'* and *'thous'* and *'wherefores'*?"

He looked sulky. "I've been watching the telly down at the pub. There isn't much else to do when you're a frog. Except in the mating season, but I've been a frog since the bloody solstice, and haven't met any others inclined to it. Not that I was inclined," he added hurriedly.

She was having difficulty taking it all in. Yes, he was dressed like Robin Hood—except for the ermine cape and the crown on his dark head—and he felt real enough. He even cast a shadow in the bright moonlight. That didn't mean he was real. It meant that although she rarely drank more than one glass of wine, tonight she'd had four and she was having hallucinations.

"I know what you are," she said. "You're a pink elephant."

"Am not!"

"Yes you are."

"Nyah-nyah!" the prince said, sticking out his tongue.

"Have you been watching cartoons?"

"How did you know?"

"You looked just like Bugs Bunny for a minute there." Kate squinted. "I can still see the ghost outline of big furry ears hovering near your head. And you shouldn't make faces like that. Not very princely, you know."

He looked dejected. "It's the shape-shifting spell. The one that made me into a frog. I'm out of practice." He brightened suddenly. "Don't worry, though. I learn quickly. I should have it well under control in another CROAK-CROAK—damn. Another—*ritchie-ritchie*—sorry. Another day or two."

"I'm going back inside," Kate announced. "You do whatever it is that princes who were frogs do. Good night."

But when she got to the door of the drawing room, he was right there beside her. "You can't come in," she told him.

"But it's going to rain!" And the wind rose up on the heels of his words, spiraling through the treetops. A few drops splattered on her arm.

"Did you do that?" Kate's eyes widened.

She watched him wrestle with his conscience. "No."

"Good. I wouldn't want to be turned into a frog myself."

"I don't really know any spells," he told her. "We leave them to the women and the wizards. The primary function of princes," he explained, "is rescuing fair maidens. That and dragon slaying."

"That seems very hard on dragons. I'm rather partial to them myself."

She felt sorry for him, standing there in his silks and jewels without a friend in the world.

"All right. You can come inside." At least she would find out some of the answers to her growing list of questions.

They went in through the side door to the kitchen, and his face lit up when he smelled the aroma coming from the oven.

"Is that . . . is that steak-and-kidney pie?" He was practically drooling.

"Yes, and you can have it all if you're hungry. Sit down and I'll fix you a plate."

She took out a crockery dish and silverware, then slipped on mitts and pulled the pie from the oven. Rich gravy bubbled up through the flaky crust. He sighed with anticipation as she fixed a portion for him and served it.

"Do you want any steak sauce with it?"

"No, thank you. But if you have a few flies . . . ?"

"What a shame," she said wryly. "I used the last of them up at lunch."

The prince tucked into his dinner, and Kate sat down on the chair opposite him. It was going to be a long night.

15

"NOT FAR NOW," the prince told Kate. "The entrance is at the end of the hill."

He led her through the dark thicket toward the mound that stretched across the far end of the meadow. Kate looked up at it. "That's nothing but a midden heap, filled with trash."

"That's what the Guardian wants them to believe. He's quite clever, throwing old plumbing and broken crockery at the end where he let them dig their trench."

Kate stopped in her tracks. "Wait a minute. The Guardian—do you mean Sir Michael Bellamy?"

"Yes. He's the Guardian. Miss Culpepper appointed him to the position when she passed our secret to him, and he swore an oath to protect all the People Under the Hill."

"So that's why she wanted him to buy up the acreage!"

Kate realized why the story she'd found had never been finished. *Agatha Culpepper didn't want to give out any hints of the hidden world at Frogsmere—but she left that fragment for me to read, so I would understand.*

She stumbled over a tree root and barked her shin. "How can you see where we're going?"

"I'm a nocturnal amphibian in this world," he told her. "Would you like to hear me sing?"

"No! Not now." In fact, she was having serious doubts of continuing. "Are you sure it's safe? I won't be turned into a frog in some sort of reverse magic?"

"Not unless you do something you shouldn't," he replied. "Ah, here we are." He led her into a dark maw. The way was smooth underfoot and sloped gradually downward. Kate grew claustrophobic. "I can't see!"

"You will in a minute. We're almost there. It's so beautiful, Kate. You'll love it so much you'll never want to leave."

"You did."

The prince sighed. "My father is tired of being king. He says its my turn, and he wants me to marry one of the princesses. I don't like any of them, except Sophie. She's a great girl—can catch a fly on the wing."

"Er, is she a frog, too?"

"Not usually. She knows a lot of magic, like my uncle Alfred, and can stay human-looking Above for hours and hours. Listen, that's her!"

Golunka! Golunka! Gol-gol-lunka!

"Doesn't she have a lovely voice? All the Golunkas do."

Kate felt as if she'd fallen into someone else's dream. "Sophie Golunka? Pretty red-head with big green eyes?"

"That's her. She's a peach."

"Are you going to marry her?"

The prince led Kate beneath low-hanging stalactites. "I don't want to marry anyone yet. But if I do, Sophie . . . yes, I think she'd be the one. She's jolly good fun."

It was so black Kate couldn't see anything but the insides of her eyeballs. "How far is this place? It seems like we're going on forever."

"Oh, we could if you wanted to. It stretches all the way around the globe."

Kate shivered. "I want to go back."

"Don't shout. My head is ringing," he snapped. "I took

quite a tumble when you dumped me out the window. There's a huge knot on my head."

"Please," she begged. "Take me back."

"I sorry," he said, and his voice was edged with steel. "You can't go back. You know our secret now. Only the Guardian can know about us and stay Above. You have to stay Below. You'll be one of the People Under the Hill."

Kate struggled but he pulled her inexorably forward. She felt a draft and realized that they were inside an enormous space. She could feel it stretching out high, high overhead.

Another four or five steps and they turned a corner. The prince fumbled with a key, and a door opened in the middle of the blackness. They came out in a moonlit garden.

Kate gasped in awe. It was just like Miss Culpepper's story. Trees of carved crystal reflected the light from the diamond stars studding the arching sapphire dome above. A giant pearl moon shone down on the castle in the center of the lake. A swan boat glided toward them and stopped.

"Come," the prince said and helped her inside it. *"Swan boat. Take us to the island."*

The boat glided away from shore. The prince made a sign and a silver cup appeared in his hand. "Magic is easy here," he told her. "Even the men can do it." He held out the cup to her. "Drink this. You must be very thirsty."

"Thanks, but I've had enough wine to last me the rest of the night."

And possibly my lifetime, Kate thought.

The prince scowled but vanished the cup. As the swan boat brought them closer to the island, Kate laughed. "I used to wish for a fairy prince to carry me off to his kingdom. I never imagined this in my wildest dreams."

"It is beautiful, isn't it?"

"I hear music."

"Yes. There is a ball tonight."

"Really? I'm glad I'll get a chance to see it."

"Oh, there are balls every night."

"I imagine that gets boring after a while," Kate said.

"No. We love balls."

"What do you do in the daytime?"

He frowned. "There is no day here. This is a midnight kingdom."

"It's always night? Don't you do anything else but go to balls?"

The prince shrugged. "We used to have wars, but that got boring. Nobody ever lost. Every now and then some young prince steals a fair maiden away. Then we all ride over and get her back. But now that we have computers they spend most of their time writing E-mail, or downloading music, or playing games on the Internet."

Kate's brain was boggled. She felt as if she'd entered a madman's dream. "Frogs with computers."

"We're only frogs Above," he said testily. "Here we're all princes and princesses. It may not be what you're used to, but you'll enjoy being a princess once you get used to it."

"I don't want to be a princess. I'm perfectly happy as a human being."

He folded his arms. "You could be a princess if you married me. My mother is human, you know, and she's very happy here. And one day, if my parents choose to go Above to finish out their life span, I shall be king and you'll be my queen."

"What about the Princess Sophie?"

"Ah! Sophie," the prince said, and fell silent.

The swan boat docked at a silver pier. "I want to go back," Kate said firmly.

"You can't. Once a human comes to the kingdom they can never return."

"People will notice I'm gone. They'll come looking for me."

"When my mother came here, they all thought she ran off with a servant. A footman. Only Lady Agatha knew the truth, and she never told."

Kate was thinking fast. "Honoria Culpepper. She didn't run off, she came *here*."

"Yes. She's my mother. Queen Honoria."

"And you say that Agatha Culpepper visited her from time to time?"

"It was by special arrangement. Lady Agatha was the Guardian."

"And Agatha returned home again, so what you told me isn't true. You can't keep me here. There *is* a way to go back." Kate stood up. "Let's get this over with."

The prince rose and stepped up to the pier, then leaned down to help Kate up. As he took her hand, she grasped his wrist with her other one and yanked hard. The surprise overbalanced him and sent the prince tumbling into the drink.

"Swan boat," Kate cried. *"To the shore!"*

For a terrible minute she thought nothing was going to happen. Then the boat moved away from the pier, while the prince splashed and struggled.

"Faster!" she cried. "Hurry!"

The dainty boat sailed across the black lake in a wake that shone like diamonds. But when Kate looked back the prince was swimming like a dolphin and gaining on her with every second.

The swan boat lurched up onto the shore and she staggered out, into Michael's arms.

"Kate! My God, I've been so worried!"

"How did you find me?"

"The young sot left his feathered cap and sword behind when he abducted you. By God, I've had enough of this. I'll seal the entrance up with concrete."

They ran up through the dark tunnel with Michael almost carrying her part of the way. Footsteps sounded behind them.

When they reached the opening, he thrust her through and turned to face his adversary. But it wasn't the prince following them. It was a woman in a gown studded with jewels and a fine gold crown on her fair brow.

"Honoria!" Michael exclaimed. "You cannot come out past the entrance. You know what will happen to you if you do."

The frog queen sighed. "I do. But I must see the stars one more time."

"No!" Another shape hurled itself at the queen. "You must not, your majesty!"

"Dear, dear little Sophie. Don't be concerned. I know just how far it is safe."

Kate looked past the queen and saw familiar faces. One belonged to Miss Golunka, who looked stunning in a gown of green shot with gold, and a crown of diamonds in her hair. The other was Mr. Plunkett, in white tie and tails.

The prince rushed up to Sophie. "That was very brave of you, Sophie. And very foolish." He slipped his arm around her waist. "You're a remarkable creature."

"Yes," she said, with a wink to Kate. "I am."

Then the prince swept Sophie into his arms and kissed her.

The queen stepped forward, blocking Kate's view of the cavern, and stopped just at the very point where the worlds of Above and Below met.

"It's the Summer Solstice," she announced, and smiled at the scintillating points of light framed by the cavern's mouth.

"Good-bye," she said to to the stars. "For now."

She turned to Kate, hovering nearby. "You must forgive my son. He's a gentle man, but this is spring, you know. And given that he's half human, the urge to see your world was too strong. But he's all right now that he's back where he belongs."

A wave of her hand and the air twinkled with a million counterfeit stars.

"And so will you two be."

Kate and Michael found themselves outside the barrow in the fragrant summer night. Neither knew why they were there or how they'd gotten there.

"The last thing I remember," Kate said, "we were making love."

Michael pulled her into his arms. "You know what they say about memory. Go back to what you were doing just before and maybe it will come back to you."

And they did.

Epilogue

. . . and the prince stood waiting at the altar for his bride, his heart filled with love. The music began and the Princess Sophie floated up the aisle, her white veil strewn with pearls and diamonds. He'd always loved her, but he hadn't known it, until she'd endangered her life out of concern for the queen.

She was a true princess in every meaning of the word. When they exchanged their wedding vows before the congregation, there were tears of joy in every eye.

"To think you were here all along and I never noticed you until that fateful night," the prince said to his bride.

"Well," Sophie said, with a smile, "you had other things on your mind. And I have to admit that I was quite busy myself."

"But you always knew I was the one for you."

"Oh, yes. I always knew . . ."

"And so," Kate said, "they lived happily ever after." She leaned down and kissed her twin daughters. "Why, Honoria is already asleep! Good night, Trixie."

"Good night, Mummy." Trixie settled her fair head back on the pillow. "Mummy? Did Sophie and the prince really live happily ever after?"

"Of course. Just like your father and I."

"I'm glad. Princess Sophie was very brave to go Above to guard the prince and see that he returned home safely."

"Yes, she was." Although Kate suspected that part of Sophie's plan was to make sure the prince didn't bring back a human bride.

Michael came into the bedroom. "What a lovely picture the three of you make." He smiled down at his wife and daughters. "And soon to be four. Did you like Mummy's new story, darling?"

The little girl smiled. "Oh, yes. It was a splendid adventure."

Kate turned out the light, and they tiptoed to the door. "Sweet dreams."

Out in the hall Michael tipped her face up for a kiss. "It *was* a splendid adventure, wasn't it?"

"This is an even better one," she told him.

They'd decided to make their permanent home at Frogsmere, and Michael's investments had paid off the estate taxes with enough left over for a comfortable life and their joint charity projects. Kate's writing career was booming, and his consulting firm was a smashing success.

They linked arms and walked downstairs. The drawing room windows of Frogsmere were open to the cool autumn air. With the leaves off the trees they could just make out the lights of King's Meadow Convalescent Center blazing in the distance.

"I wish Agatha Culpepper could have lived to see it," he told her. "She was the one who first put the idea into my head. Sometimes our life seems like a fairy tale."

Kate smiled. "I'm glad it's not."

"Confess. Aren't you ever sorry that I'm not a prince?"

"You are to me."

He took her in his arms and they kissed in the blue light of evening.

Soft sounds drifted through the open window:
Chirr-chirr.
Ritchie-ritchie-ritchie.
Golunka-Golunka.